Him, Her, and Paris

Heather Starnes

DEDICATION

To Gary and Grayson, you taught me how to love and live.

ACKNOWLEDGMENTS

To all of you that I've had the privilege to share my life with, thank you. You made me who I am today and helped me pursue my dreams.

CHAPTER 1

Message sent. The tiny envelope icon on Abby Rodgers' phone folded and zoomed away into cyberspace. Abby's jaw dropped along with her stomach as she looked at her phone in her sister's hand. That email could get her fired from her internship.

Her sister, Sarah, grinned, and handed back the phone. Seconds earlier, the flight attendant had left a cup of coffee on Abby's tray table. Abby wished now that she had some vodka to spike it. It would be the only way to survive this flight, but she'd already refused the alcohol because it would give her the urge to pee the whole flight. She gripped the leather seat as if her anxiety would transfer to the chilled material. "Why did you send that reply?" she asked.

Luck was with Sarah since there was a small aisle between them. Otherwise, Abby would've wrapped her hands around her twin's neck and squeezed the last breath from her.

"You needed a little motivation," Sarah said as she flicked her blond hair from her shoulders. "Accepting the invite without a date would be social suicide. We're going to Paris, and this is one of the most important parties of the year. If you show up alone, go ahead and stamp 'loser'

1

on your forehead." She held her index finger and thumb in an "L" shape over her face.

"But I don't have a hot boyfriend who would fit perfectly in their ad campaign." Abby pointed the phone at Sarah. "Gilda will chew me up and spit me out for dinner." This internship was her last chance to prove herself to her parents. She didn't want to think about what her father threatened to do if this didn't work out. Her college tuition and trust fund depended on her making this job a success. Her pulse quickened as she tried to calm the raging seas of anger that surged inside her.

"Gilda will eat up your ideas. Come up with a boyfriend, and you're all set," Sarah said as she reached up and adjusted the air vent. "Maybe some hot guy will sit next to you."

Abby slumped back against the seat and stared at the raindrops sliding down the small oval window. Eight hours on this plane before she'd arrive at her new home. At least she was in first class, but even that no longer excited her. Coffee aroma engulfed the cabin, calming the nerves and excitement that plagued her stomach. Glancing at her sister, she remembered the hope she had for this trip as an opportunity to start over. This was her chance to repair their relationship, but it seemed Abby was the only one interested in doing so. She twisted to her side and punched the foam pillow at her back, but her eyes remained glued to her supervisor's original email that was still on her phone's display.

> From: Von Deez Fashion House - Gilda Held
> Your presence is requested at this year's Von Deez After Show Party at Paris Fashion Week. Invitation is for one plus guest. Please inform immediate supervisor of your attendance.

Even though she was reading the text for the twentieth time, Abby found it difficult to breathe. She had dreamed of going but never thought she'd be allowed to attend an after party this early in her career. She'd figured they'd assign her administrative duties but, instead, she had an invitation to the most important after party of the year. Not really an invitation, in the world of fashion, it was a summons.

Sarah jerked the phone out of Abby's hand and dangled the silver device in front of her. A frown framed Sarah's face in her typical pouty expression. She threw the phone back at Abby. "I didn't get invited."

Abby set her eyes on her sister. "You could've if you'd applied yourself." Abby and Sarah were on the same level as interns at Von Deez. Abby worked hard to earn her choice of internships, and she received an assistant position with Von Deez's head fashion stylist, while Sarah ended up with an assignment in the accounting department. Sarah had only received the opportunity after some well-placed donations to the college's scholarship fund, courtesy of good old Dad.

Sarah pulled out her fashion magazines and set them on her tray table. "A total waste." Her eyes darted between Abby and the magazines.

"What?" Abby asked as she glanced around the cabin. She wanted to get away, but she knew she was trapped in her seat until after take-off. She'd rather lock herself in the bathroom the whole flight instead of rehashing her sister's constant criticisms.

"You, in fashion. What a joke." She pointed a French manicured finger at Abby's outfit. "Look at you. You could've grabbed a few items from the sample room at Von Deez."

"There are other jobs besides walking down the catwalk." Abby tapped her foot in time with the thoughts in her head. Designing marketing spreads and ad shoots appealed to Abby. The layouts were like puzzles she had to solve to create a standout picture. She loved her job. An industry that didn't care about her or her family was the perfect place to lose herself. She cast a quick peek at her wrinkled pants and faded T-shirt. Her two-seasons-too-late ankle boots completed the ensemble. She cared about her appearance, but she valued comfort over fashion when traveling. Who would judge her wardrobe on the plane besides Sarah?

"You'll have to find someone to bring. Zander's not going to fly over to be a stand-in." Sarah picked up her water bottle and took a sip.

Abby rubbed her neck, but the stress refused to release. "I wouldn't need a stand-in if you hadn't sent that reply to Gilda." She kept thinking of ways to send another message without sounding stupid. She kept telling herself that a date wasn't necessary, but she wasn't convinced. Not only was it important, but her date had better be as glamorous as the models in Sarah's magazines. It was only a date, right? Surely, she could come up with someone willing to escort her. How hard could it be?

Abby stood and picked up her open tote she'd left on the empty seat next to her. Sarah always wanted an aisle seat, like Abby, so they never sat directly beside each other. The flight attendants were almost finished boarding the coach class and the plane would be taking off soon. Hoisting her bag over her head, Abby struggled with its weight until two arms intervened behind her. Like enormous tree limbs, they swooped around her and raised her bag to the overhead compartment.

"I don't want you collapsing before we take off. No need to delay our flight." The muscular arms belonged to a deep voice. The guy grabbed her other bag and placed it in the compartment. Abby's gaze fell on him. Her mouth dropped open as she stared into his shamrock colored eyes. He towered over her, standing at least six feet tall. Mesmerized by his muscles that could not be hidden beneath such flimsy fabric of his T-shirt, Abby guessed that he was an exercise fanatic. She couldn't believe the hot guy scenario that Sarah had mentioned was coming true.

She caught herself holding her breath and exhaled her reply. "Are you in this row? Let me move my stuff out of the way." She reached for her iPad, but it fell to the floor in front of the empty seat.

"No, I have seat 5A," he said, slipping into the row behind her. He flashed a casual smile at her.

Her hopes deflated; she stole a glance at her sister. Sarah's giggling rained throughout the cabin, causing a warm flush to spread over Abby's cheeks as she shrunk in her seat. She was positive the guy was laughing too.

"Too bad," Sarah said and nodded at the empty seat. "I'm sure someone decent will sit next to you ... no need to worry. We're in first class, right?" Even though Sarah's laugh sounded cheerful, her snide expression chilled Abby.

Abby shifted her gaze to the seat on her left. Her discomfort with strangers had heightened this past year, especially due to the recent media attention on their family. Sarah taunted her as punishment; a task usually completed by Abby's other sister, but Sarah kindly stepped in with the insults until they met up with Nicole in Paris. It wasn't like Abby didn't deserve the ridicule. She may have done the same if the situation were reversed. Abby wished her life would revert to the way it was a year ago before the accident. If their brother were still there, Abby might have handled this past year differently, might've pushed back at her sisters.

"Still thinking of taking the leech?" Sarah asked as she selected a pink lip gloss from her cosmetics case. Her complexion resembled a porcelain doll with no imperfections, the look Abby wished she had. Despite being twins, they were complete opposites in looks and personalities.

"No, I doubt Zander could afford the plane ticket and he wouldn't enjoy the Von Deez party," Abby said, frowning.

Sarah wrinkled her nose. "Why do you hang out with him? All he does is come around to eat our food."

"Lay off. He's my best friend."

"As much time as you spend with him, he should be more than a friend."

Abby squeezed her eyes shut. "Do we have to go through this again? He's like a brother."

Sarah's face darkened. "You have a brother." A few seconds passed before she spoke again, after the black cloud dissipated from her eyes. "Zander doesn't hang around you to be brotherly. Good grief, Abs, open your eyes."

Abby rubbed her forehead. Correction-they had a brother. That was the one thing Sarah had yet to accept, and the one thing that kept them apart. He was gone. Jacob, Sarah, and Abby-they used to do everything together. Sarah blamed her for the accident, and Abby couldn't argue a defense. Thinking about that day stole her ability to breathe. Every time she thought about it, all she saw was Jacob's lifeless face staring back at her. The image burned in her memory, and she could never get away, no matter how hard she tried.

Forcing the accident from her mind, Abby searched for a distraction before the memory drove her mind to the crack of insanity. She spotted her iPad on the floor, next to the window seat. Kneeling down, she inched closer to the empty seat. With her head halfway under the chair, she reached for the device, but her fingertips barely touched it.

"Excuse me," a deep voice behind her said. Startled, her head came up and crashed into the tray table above.

"Ow!"

A dull pain commenced at the base of her neck. As she rubbed the back of her head, loose strands of hair escaped from her ponytail and tickled the edge of her nose. Abby caught a glimpse of an amused face. It was him. The hot guy!

CHAPTER 2

*A*bby flipped up her head and saw the hot guy staring at her backside. She felt warmth radiating off her cheeks as she pulled herself off the floor. Great. Her biggest asset was there for him to see.

"4A is my seat after all. Pardon me." His mouth widened into a grin. As the guy slid in front of her, his pants brushed her knee. Abby held her breath at his touch. He bent over the seat to avoid hitting her again and his wavy brown hair tumbled in his face. Abby's heart danced as she tried to shift her gaze from him but she couldn't. The muscles of his upper arms and chest seemed to melt through his burnt red shirt.

"Hi, I'm Jayson." He held out his hand.

She grasped his hand. The heat of his palm warmed her skin. She gazed at his face. A small crease formed on his forehead as he smiled. He had a slight tan, and a splash of blonde streaked through his hair as if he'd been in the sun recently. With his flawless skin and high cheekbones, she wondered if he worked as a model. Possibly a potential model for Von Deez? Abby's insides bubbled at the prospect.

"Hi, I'm Jayson," he repeated, laughing. The roughness of his fingers rubbed at her wrist as his withdrew his hand.

Abby blinked. "Huh? Oh, sorry. I'm Abby. Looks like we're seat buddies." She smiled at him, but she was dying inside. She couldn't have sounded more like an idiot if she'd tried.

"Abs, aren't you going to introduce me? Or are you keeping him for yourself?" Sarah asked as she leaned across the narrow aisle.

Abby cringed at Sarah's nickname for her. She didn't possess perfect abs and didn't want to emphasize that part of her body with a nickname. Reluctantly, she introduced the intruder. "Jayson, this is my sister, Sarah."

"Nice to meet you." Jayson waved in Sarah's direction. "Sisters? I never would have guessed." His eyes moved from Abby to Sarah.

Abby crossed her arms. Typical. She couldn't even pass as Sarah's relative.

Sarah licked her lips and pushed a stray curl behind her ear. "We're twins," she said and Abby flinched, bracing for the comments that would surely come. She heard them every time they met new people.

"Really? But you don't look anything alike," he said.

Abby's posture went rigid. "We're fraternal twins." How could she blame people for questioning them? The only common feature they had were their indigo eyes.

"Rodgers? Are you the Rodgers triplets?" Jayson's eyes narrowed as he glanced at them. "Where's the other one? Don't you always travel together?"

"Not triplets. Just sisters." Abby shifted in her seat, her teeth gritted at the reference the media had created for the three sisters. They'd been on the plane for fifteen minutes and already, he figured out who her family was. Just once, she wished her father wasn't a U.S. senator. They weren't celebrities, but most people in Florida knew the Rodgers name. The fascination with her family's political dynasty and microscopic life pulverized her privacy.

"Wow, I'm traveling with superstars," he said.

With the mocking tone in his voice, Abby's defenses heightened. She sucked in a few breaths. Did he know about the accident? Every media outlet in Florida plastered the story as the main news headline over the last year.

8

Abby took her father's even tone. "We're a byproduct of a well-known politician. I'm sure someone more famous than us is around here somewhere." Abby twisted her hand in a fist, then scanned the luxury cabin as if she truly was searching for her replacement. Her eyes stopped on the emergency exit. It wasn't too late to make an escape.

"Sorry. I didn't mean to sound like a smart aleck." He flexed his fingers and ran them through his hair. "My coach says my mouth gets me into trouble."

Abby regretted her response. His comment was probably innocent but his sarcasm struck her hard. "It's okay." She smiled but it slipped into a cracked line of barely visible lips. "So you're an athlete?"

"I play tennis. I'm going to Europe for some tournaments. First one's in Rome. Then a few more tourneys over the summer."

"A tennis player... I love tennis." Sarah interjected.

Abby's eyes narrowed. Sarah never played sports.

Jayson peered over at Sarah, his lips pursed, not the usual reaction to Sarah's charm. "How often do you play? I'm looking for a hitting partner. I let my latest one go recently," he said as he adjusted his seatbelt.

Abby reluctantly peeked over at Sarah. How would her sister answer the question? Sarah was a true Rodgers and had inherited the family trait-lying.

"I play for fun. Maybe once or twice a month. Abs plays more often. She's practically a professional."

Abby smacked her lips shut before a gasp erupted from her throat. She shrank in her seat and masked her eyes with her hand. She wasn't good at tennis. The few times she'd played, she'd missed more balls than she'd hit. Sarah was probably a better player and she'd never picked up a racket in her life.

"That good? I may need to jet over to Paris and play a few sets with you." Jayson put down his magazine, and rotated his upper body, and faced Abby.

"I...I try to play two or three times a week. I wouldn't say I'm John McEnroe, but I'm not bad. What else keeps you busy besides tennis?" Abby hoped she sounded halfway knowledgeable. McEnroe was a tennis player, wasn't he? She hated lying but refused to let Sarah's fabrication about her athletic abilities embarrass her. Plus, being in the Rodgers family, she'd been taught that a good lie was the truth re-manufactured. It wasn't like the opportunity to prove her tennis abilities would arise.

"Other than tennis, there's not much to me. I'm in college on a sports scholarship, which means I spend most of my time playing tennis. Throw an episode or two of Sports Center in there and I'm your typical male, as you girls would say. How about you?"

Abby cleared her throat, giving her a few more seconds to play with the answer. "I'm studying fashion, third year in college. I'm going to Paris for an internship." Goose bumps ate at her arms as she said the words. Tomorrow, she would be living in Paris and working for one of the world's top fashion designers. It hardly felt real.

"An internship that requires a date for the party," Sarah's voice interrupted. Abby scrunched her lips together to avoid spewing a few insults at her sister. A fight in public would most certainly result in a call from her father. Abby learned it was best to let Sarah and Nicole get their jabs in. She could fight back in private, and she'd certainly let Sarah have it later.

Jayson winked at Abby. "I'm sure she's capable of finding someone to invite."

Her heart fluttered. He'd make the perfect date. "Well, the party's not until July so I have a few months."

"Sounds like you have an exciting year ahead of you. I've spent the last couple of years focusing on tennis and haven't had time for anything else."

"But traveling must be fun," Abby said.

He nodded. "It's cool. Tennis gives me the opportunity to see so many different places. Too bad I don't get to spend much time in any of them." He chuckled, his chest shaking slightly, lassoing Abby's attention. "I have a tennis tournament in Paris this summer. Maybe I'll stay longer and explore."

Abby caught his amused smirk and swore he meant something else. Was he interested in her? She let the possibility slip from her mind. Why would he choose her when Sarah sat across the aisle? Perfect usually gravitated toward perfect—not to her.

"Ladies and gentlemen, we are number one for takeoff. Flight attendants, please be seated." A voice commanded over the intercom.

Abby tightened her seatbelt, as the aircraft roared down the runway and lifted into the air. She glanced over at Jayson. He had reclined back in his chair with his eyes closed. The crease in his forehead had faded. As the plane climbed higher in the sky, Abby sat back and daydreamed about Paris, but Jayson's image kept popping in her head.

Over the next hour, Abby and Jayson talked nonstop. She had a hard time controlling her attraction to him. Not once did he blow her off to talk to Sarah. When her sister did interrupt the conversation, he had a snappy comeback that gave Abby the satisfaction that she had one ally on the plane. She glanced at him. He had his back curled so his arms hid his magazine from Abby's view. Just as she opened her mouth to speak, Abby felt a tap on her shoulder.

"Would you like a beverage?" The middle-aged lady asked as she fiddled with a package of peanuts on the drink cart.

"Water, please," Abby said, her mouth suddenly dry.

The woman poured the drink and placed the cup on the tray table.

"Thanks." Abby looked up at the flight attendant, but the woman had moved her attention to Jayson.

"Sir?"

"Same," Jayson said. He didn't raise his head.

She prepared another drink and reached across Abby to deposit it on Jayson's table. Abby stared at the water droplets beading up on her glass. They slid down the side to form a puddle. She needed to say something. After a few minutes passed, Abby mustered some courage and leaned closer to him. "How's the magazine? Anything worth reading?"

"Nah...the usual stuff on tennis. It's boring, mostly tabloid crap."

"Do you mind if I have a look?" As the last word left her mouth, Jayson jerked up and slapped the pages shut. Abby slid her arm back to avoid his elbow. She hit her cup and tipped it over. A cascade of water raced down her tray and in her lap.

"Oh." She squeezed her legs together on instinct as the liquid seeped through her jeans and ice pellets gathered in her crotch. Abby quickly scooped up the ice as the cool water caused goose bumps on her legs.

Jayson handed her a few napkins. "Crap. I'm sorry."

Abby took the napkins and mopped up the liquid on her tray before pressing them against the fabric of her jeans. "No, my fault."

"I don't think those will get it all. Let me call the stewardess." He pulled out his personal entertainment remote control and pressed the call button.

"No. I'll go to the galley." Abby's cheeks felt feverish as she avoided Jayson's gaze. So far she'd bickered with her sister, snapped at him about her family, and she proved what a klutz she was. Not a great first impression. Abby deposited a few more ice chips in her cup. Unbuckling her seatbelt, she rose from the seat. "I'll be back."

She hurried up the aisle. Luckily, the galley was empty, and she didn't have to endure the embarrassment of drying her clothes in front of anyone.

"Abs?"

Abby looked up in mid-swipe with one of the napkins she'd found on the counter, and saw Sarah staring wide-eyed at her. "Typical, isn't it?" Abby asked as she rubbed at her jeans. Her sister would laugh about this for a while. Abby searched Sarah's face, but it was absent of the catty smirk she usually reserved for situations like this.

"Use this. It'll soak up more." She pushed a washcloth in Abby's hand.

"Thanks but I don't think it'll salvage my attempt to impress Jayson."

Sarah huffed. "You could spill hot coffee on him, and he'd still pay attention to you." She grabbed the cloth and dabbed a few wet spots on Abby's shirt.

Abby straightened her back and stared at the beauty mark on Sarah's temple, identical to her own. The sadness in Sarah seemed to disappear for the moment and the old

12

Sarah was back, the one who would protect Abby from anything and everyone.

"There. It'll be damp for a while but otherwise, good as new." Sarah stuffed the cloth back in her cosmetics case that she'd set on the counter. Tugging at Abby's arm, she started back to the first class cabin, but Abby didn't move. Sarah pivoted around. "Come on."

"No. I want to stay here a little longer." Coldness filled her chest at the thought of facing Jayson.

"Why?" Sarah shoved her arm behind Abby's back, forcing her closer to the doorway.

Abby pulled away. "Whatever he liked about me, it left back there. I'm a complete mess." She motioned to the cabin, knowing she wasn't making any sense.

"Are you serious?"

Abby refused to look at her. She wasn't like Sarah and didn't know the first thing about flirting with guys. Abby felt out of place around Jayson.

Sarah flung her hand to her side. "Fine, but Jayson asked me to check on you. Said something about him spilling his drink on you. That doesn't sound like a guy who hates the sight of you."

Abby twisted her fingers until she could almost see them turn white. It was the first time in months she'd seen concern from her sister. She'd been tempted to tell Sarah to back off with her comments around Jayson but she didn't have the heart to argue with her sister. Abby smiled. "Sounds kind of sweet, doesn't it?" A twinge of excitement soared through her.

Sarah let out a squeal. "Yes, dummy. He's made it obvious the whole flight. I don't think 4A was his assigned seat. I think he moved on purpose." She feathered a few strands of Abby's hair.

Abby fluffed the same hair Sarah just touched. It never occurred to her that he actually moved so he could sit by her. Abby breathed deeply and smoothed out her shirt. "I'm ready." She tossed the doubt from her mind. With new hope that things were okay again between her and Sarah, Abby stood ready to take this opportunity. She straightened her shoulders and walked down the aisle.

Abby quickly slid back in her seat, which was clear of any remnants of the water but avoided Jayson's gaze.

Jayson slipped a water bottle on her tray. "I had them bring you another drink. This one has a top. Spill proof." He tapped the cap.

Abby giggled and the tension in her back escaped. "Thanks. That'll keep me from dumping it all over myself. You want to lend me that magazine now?"

A mischievous grin spread his lips apart. He rolled up the magazine in a tube-like shape and shoved it down beside his armrest. "Like I said, tabloid trash. So Abs, tell me about this nickname."

Abby smiled at his intentional deflection. "Sarah has a habit of shortening everyone's name." He probably guessed she wasn't into sports, but she couldn't figure out what possibly could be going on in tennis that warranted tabloid reporting.

"You don't strike me as an Abs. I think you're an Abigail."

She nodded. "Abigail or Abby, I respond to either." There was a lightness in her limbs, like she was floating. She guessed happiness would do that to a person. It had been a while since she felt this way. Abby glanced over at Jayson. "I bet Sarah will shorten your name before this flight's over. She can't help herself."

"You think so? I may have to take on your bet." He stretched his arms and leaned on the tray table.

"So what are the stakes?" Abby wasn't sure if he meant the bet as a joke, but it didn't hurt to try. She wished she could act like Sarah during these times but she'd have to make do. Obviously her amateur flirting was working so far.

He clicked his teeth and drew in a deep breath. "What would you want?"

"How about if I win, you meet me in Paris one weekend?" Abby studied his face. She might have a shot. He was flirting with her earlier, even Sarah confirmed it. It'd be drinks, nothing serious. Heck, maybe even a date for the after party.

He rubbed his chin with his thumb and dropped his eyes so they met hers. "Alright, it's a bet." He sat back in his seat and held out his hand.

"You haven't told me what you get if you win."

"You caught that, did you? It'll be determined once I win. Are you willing to take the challenge?" His emerald eyes dared her to accept.

She could play his game. His grin told her that he knew she wouldn't decline and she wasn't going to disappoint him. She could always back out later. Even if it was just a game, it was time to play. This was a chance to prove to Sarah that she could find a man. Maybe her feelings were only lust, but it didn't matter. If this worked out, he might be around to escort her to Fashion Week. Abby nodded her acceptance and shook his hand. She was all in.

CHAPTER 3

"Abs...wake up. We're getting ready to land," a feminine voice whispered through the fog in Abby's head. Gradually, Abby opened her eyes and saw Sarah mouthing something at her. Slowly rising in the seat, she rolled her neck from side to side and the sunlight that streamed through the port hole sized window burned her eyes. She squinted to block the light.

"Hey, sleepyhead. I thought you were going to miss the landing," a deep voice said beside her.

Abby recalled Jayson and the flight to Paris. She yawned and stretched out her arms. "I don't remember dozing off." She glanced over and absorbed the sight of his body. With his head and shoulders bent over the tray table, he flexed his arm muscles in an overhead stretch, leaving her to wonder how well-built the rest of his body was. Her eyes traveled down his toned shoulders to the magazine. All she saw was a tennis player hitting a ball on the far page. "You have another flight after this?"

He flipped the page before she had time to focus on the picture again. "Yeah, a short one to Rome. It's been a long trip. I have some practice sessions tomorrow, so I need the rest."

"Ladies and gentlemen, we have begun our approach to Charles De Gaulle International Airport. Flight attendants, please be seated," the pilot's voice announced on the intercom.

"Landing time," Jayson said. He rubbed his hands together as the plane tilted forward in its final decent.

"I've enjoyed talking to you." Abby presented her best smile.

He grinned, exposing a small dimple in his cheek. "My pleasure. I hope you and your sister have a wonderful time in Paris."

Abby's insides melted as she stared at his crooked grin. A flight attendant could hit her in the head, and she wouldn't notice. "I guess you won the bet. Are you going to tell me what you won?"

"The flight's not over yet. Let's see how it plays out." He gave her a quick wink.

Abby's smile faded as she lost hope of getting his phone number, email, anything. The bet was obviously a joke. She bit her lip. Of course it was. She hardly knew him. Nothing would come of this.

As the plane flew lower in the sky, her ears popped and her stomach felt as if it had moved to her mouth. Landings always did that to her, similar to her love life, like the bottom was falling out beneath her. Within minutes, the wheels hit the runway and slowed, sending Abby forward. After a short taxi, the plane arrived at the terminal. When the seatbelt sign went off, Abby stood and stretched her legs. She reached up and opened the compartment above her head.

"No, let me do that," Jayson said.

Picking up her tote, Abby moved out of the way to let him in the aisle. She waved her index finger at the two bags he held in his right hand. "Those are mine." She reached in front of him and tried to take the bags.

"Nah...I'll get them. They're heavy. What did you bring?" He lifted one high above his shoulder to clear the seats. "I could use these as weights in my training sessions."

"Shoes," she said as they made their way up the aisle. All she could think of were the fifteen pairs Sarah had packed in her suitcase.

"Did you clear out your whole closet?"

All Abby could do was laugh. The thought of that many shoes in one bag was hilarious.

They exited the plane and met Sarah at the end of the corridor. Jayson handed the bags to Abby. She readjusted the straps before looking up at him. "Thanks for the help."

His mouth curled up in a grin, reforming the faint wrinkle between his brows. "Well, ladies, I guess this is goodbye. It was nice to meet you."

Sarah took his hand. "My pleasure, Jay."

Abby's eyes widened. Had she heard her right?

A smile grew across Jayson's face. "I guess you won."

"Yes, I did," she said, laughing as if she knew it all along.

"I'm late for my ride." He took a small piece of paper from his pocket and slipped the folded square in Abby's hand. His fingers clung to hers a tad longer than they had with Sarah. Maybe his gesture was her imagination, but Abby hung on to the hope that it was reality. He squeezed her hand. "Email me, and we can take care of our bet." His hand left hers. Smiling, he walked away and disappeared around the corner.

Abby stood in the middle of the hallway, staring at the folded piece of paper.

Sarah clapped her hands. "Absolutely brilliant. I wondered if you got his phone number or something." She jumped around like a teenager going out on her first date. "Well, are you going to read it?"

"Oh yeah...sure," Abby said. She opened the note and stared at his email address. A smile crept up on her face. This changed everything.

"Can I see?" Sarah grabbed the note from Abby's hand. "Hmm...short but definitely an opportunity. I'm sure you'll be talking to him again."

Abby started down the corridor toward customs, hardly able to keep her excitement within her.

Sarah ran up and fell in step with her. "What did Jay mean about a bet?"

Forcing her eyes at the ground, Abby twisted her fingers. "Well, we got on the subject of names. He asked about 'Abs'. I bet him that you would shorten his name by the end of the flight."

Sarah laughed. "I thought he was flirting with me, but he plotted to get me to help with his bet. I can't believe you got that lucky."

Abby bit her lip. "What's so funny? What do you mean, plotting?"

Sarah's giggling persisted, and she raised her hand, stopping Abby. A smile spread across her face, forcing a small hollow in her chin. "He was plotting. We talked while you slept, and he asked me to call him Jay."

Abby's eyes widened. "I can't believe he wanted me to have his email address."

"What's the big deal? It's obvious it's a joke. He may email you, but he's not even staying in Paris. He'll be like every other guy you've been interested in. A failed attempt at love."

Abby's stomach crashed in her body. Sarah's acute talent to smack Abby in the gut with her comments brought reality to Abby. Who was she kidding? Sarah was right. All she had was an email address.

CHAPTER 4

"Sorry, pal. That's her. Abigail Rodgers." Ethan's partner, Nols, slapped him on the shoulder and laughed.

Ethan Gray crumbled the paper in his hand. He glanced around the commons area of the university campus and swore under his breath. Babysitting a lovesick teenager, just what he needed. "How old is she? Sixteen?"

"Be nice, Gray. She's twenty-one. It's routine since Jayson Walters interacted with her on the plane." Nols pulled his sunglasses off his head and wiped the sweat from his brow. "Besides, you need a break from the regular day to day surveillance crap. She's bound to be interesting."

Ethan scowled. Why couldn't he be assigned the blonde chick? Walters usually gravitated toward blondes. Why would he change? He cast a glance over at the mousey girl. Her walnut-colored hair stringing out from her ponytail. She looked every bit American as Mickey Mouse, the wrinkled T-shirt, tattered jeans, and-the obvious sign-those awful furry boots every girl wore, even in the blazing summer heat. They peeked out from the strings hanging off the hem of her pants near her calves. She struggled with her bags and the mound threatened to topple over as she guided her luggage over the cobblestones. "What do we know about her?" Her name sounded familiar, but he couldn't place it.

"She goes by Abby, and she's here for school. All three are sisters. Only two were on the plane, the brunette and the blond. Tom's getting a full work-up on them. It'll be available tonight," Nols said as he fiddled with his phone. He motioned to the stern-faced girl with black hair. "The other one met them at the airport."

"You're sure she's the one he talked to?" Ethan pointed at Abby as she tripped and almost fell headfirst onto the sidewalk. "Jayson Walters wouldn't take an interest in that."

"I confirmed it with Tom. Make contact, file the report, and move on," Nols said. He left Ethan sitting on the bench and walked toward Patrick.

Sighing, Ethan rose to his feet and strolled over to his friends. Because he looked younger than he was, he blended in with the students. Only two years had passed since he graduated and left the university. It was one place he felt at home, so a little part of him was glad to be back.

Patrick whistled. "Check out the blonde. What do you think? Has to be American," he said, his British accent thick as it glided over the words.

"Probably. Look at all that crap." Ethan motioned at the bags with his hand. They laughed as the girls struggled with the luggage. He chuckled even louder when Nols shot him a disgusted look.

"I wish she had shown up last semester. Too bad I'm leaving next month. You're not thinking of having a go at her?" Patrick clicked his teeth, his eyes traveled up the blonde girl's body.

"No, she's all yours." Ethan slapped his friend on the back. She was definitely a knockout. He flipped his attention to Abby. They didn't even look like they should be friends, yet they were sisters. But the dark haired girl and Abby, they were identical images of each other. Stiff-angle in their cheeks and no expression.

Abby had maneuvered her luggage to the top of the hill. She was now helping her sister with her bags. Ethan laughed. Had they ever been overseas before? He was surprised they were allowed to check so many bags on the flight. He had to give them credit. They made it this far.

"No!" Abby yelled.

Ethan's head jerked up in time to see several bags tumbling down the hill. The blonde jumped up and down, pointing to the chaos of luggage. One of the smaller bags rolled down the embankment and came to rest near the alley entrance at Ethan's feet. He shook his head. They were more trouble than the usual shady characters he dealt with.

Patrick had already run to the blonde girl's side and retrieved one of her bags. Just like his friend to swoop in and save a potential shag, but Ethan suspected it would be Patrick that would need saving in the end.

Patrick grinned as the blonde twirled her hair and jutted out her chest. Ethan scowled. Typical Barbie doll. Perfect in every way on the outside but empty on the inside. He picked up the small bag and made his way over to the scene, might as well have some fun with it.

"We arrived today. We're staying for a year," the blonde said as her hand swept a few curls behind her ear. "I'm Sarah." She giggled and tilted her cheek toward Ethan as he approached.

Ethan grimaced at her use of English. She was in France. Couldn't she attempt to speak the language? He leaned forward and kissed her on both cheeks. "Ethan Gray," he said as he retreated behind Nols. He saw the act too many times to count. He needed to stay far away from that one. She'd be dangerous. Patrick could have her.

Sarah waved to her sister, and Abby made her way slowly down the hill, her head lowered. Ethan couldn't see her eyes. Standing beside her, he dwarfed her petite frame. She really was a mouse.

"These wonderful gentlemen are also staying on campus. They only have a few more months, but while they're here, they've offered to show us around the city," Sarah said as she rubbed her hand on Patrick's arm. Ethan shoved his fists in his pockets and stared at the trees behind them.

"That's great," Abby said, her shoulders now relaxed but her frown still remained. Ethan couldn't figure out why a girl just arriving in Paris seemed so sad. She definitely didn't act excited to be there.

"Oh, this is Abs, and that's my other sister, Nicole, over there." Sarah jutted her thumb over her shoulder.

What a name- Abs. He wasn't sure how she warranted the nickname. It reminded him of some obsessed bodybuilder and that image didn't jive with the petite girl that stood beside him. Ethan bit his lip, but failed to suppress his laughter. He stopped when Abby's body stiffened, and she glanced in his direction. Patrick greeted the girls and offered them a kiss on both cheeks. Ethan noticed that Abby's smile couldn't hide her discomfort. As Ethan approached Abby, his eyes fell on her, and he grinned as he kissed her cheeks. Red colored her face, and she dropped her gaze once again. Jayson Walters never would've been involved with her. Innocence wasn't a virtue that attracted Walters, but it did intrigue Ethan.

"They're coming to our rescue and helping us with our luggage," Sarah said. Ethan fought to hold back his disgust. This was one thing he hated about his job - pretending to like people he couldn't stand. Sarah already had Patrick eating out of her hand. They'd be perfect together. Patrick wasn't a one woman man, and the blonde probably didn't keep only one guy around.

Ethan sighed and grabbed two of Abby's bags. "Where to?"

Abby jerked around, staring wide-eyed at him like he'd bit her.

"Bloody hell," he muttered but knew she didn't hear him. Why would she act like he was a disease? Just like his sister's reaction when he'd shown up at his mother's estate unannounced a few years back. A pretentious snob. By the looks of her designer luggage, she had something in common with his mother's family - money.

Abby pointed to the alley. "Building six. It's up the hill."

Ethan trudged along the stone path, slowing his pace so not to leave her behind. He reminded himself again. This was his job. "You're here for a year?"

She nodded. "Yeah, exchange student."

Between the two of them, they managed to gather three more bags. The black haired girl carried one small carry-on and seemed to struggle with that. Ethan shook his head. They acted helpless, but he knew from experience, it was a game to them. Typical rich brats. Ethan forced down his dislike. His job was to befriend Abby no matter how he really felt.

"This is my last semester." He squinted to avoid her gaze. The lies slipped out effortlessly. Deceit was his specialty. "It's a great place to attend school. There's always students on campus. You won't have any problems making friends."

Abby responded with only a nod. He wondered where the shyness came from. From what he saw so far, Abby didn't seem to be the outgoing, curious person that he'd expect to be on this trip. She wouldn't survive a week in Paris. At least she wasn't giving out too much personal information. She definitely had her guard up around him. How could someone so cautious get involved with Walters in a few short hours?

"Here's building six," she said.

Ethan realized he was staring at her eyes, a dark blue sea but clear enough to distinguish specks of gold. They drew him in. He wanted to know more about her, more than he needed for his report. Abby broke his gaze, severing the connection between them and forcing him to focus on the task at hand.

He glanced up at the building. Marble stone towered over them producing a four-story façade. Black stains speckled the stone, showing the effects of rainwater over the years that had run down from the greenish colored drainage spouts. Most of the windows were open, decorated with articles of clothing hung on improvised clotheslines. He motioned for her to get the door. "You got the apartments. The other dorms have shared bathrooms for everyone on the floor."

Her lips turned down in a perfect pout. "Sarah and Nicole would die if they had to share a community bathroom."

He laughed. By the expression on her face, he knew she felt the same way. She probably never had to share anything in her life.

"My room is 215," Abby said as she opened the door for him.

Ethan entered the dimly lit foyer. A round stained glass window near the back of the lobby was the sole source of light. The darkness hid most of the décor and a petite wooden staircase in the back. He could make out a worn couch and side table in the corner. A few magazines draped across the table in a disheveled pile.

"No elevator?" she asked.

Ethan rolled his eyes. Was she related to his sister, Alana? Luckily, with it being dark, she couldn't see him or the annoyance in his eyes. "No, there are stairs over there. Go on up. I'll take this bag up and come back for the other one."

"No, it's okay. I'll take it."

"You sure? It's heavy," he said as he eyed her.

"I can handle it. You go first."

He gritted his teeth but refrained from saying anything else. He was only supposed to make contact, not make sure this girl survived her first night in Paris. That suitcase probably weighed seventy or eighty pounds. There would be no way she could carry it up the stairs, but she seemed determined to try, so he left her there. He lifted the other bag and rested it against his leg as he climbed the stairs. He scaled the two flights with ease and deposited the suitcase at her door.

As he made his way back down the stairwell, he saw her struggling with the bag. She tugged on the suitcase. It cleared the first step, rolled back, and sent her off balance. Ethan stepped down beside her and grabbed the handle. "You didn't get very far, did you?" He smiled as he picked up the bag and twisted his body around on the step. He motioned for her to go ahead. She climbed the steps and paused at the next floor.

"No, it's up one more. This is the first floor." He nodded to the next staircase.

Abby scowled. "So what was the floor downstairs called?"

He laughed. "First time in France?" He didn't have to ask, but she didn't give him much else to talk about.

She nodded.

"They sometimes call it the ground floor or zero," he said.

A giggle escaped her lips and the sound reminded him of an innocent child, one who didn't know about the bad things that happened in the world. He hoped she didn't do anything stupid while she was there. Her type of naiveté was usually a disadvantage in a foreign country. If this girl had that blonde's help, she'd be corrupted soon, if not already. It'd be a shame. She intrigued, then frustrated him all in the first ten minutes of meeting her. He couldn't recall anyone affecting him this way.

When they reached the next floor, he nodded to the left and followed Abby to the last apartment at the end of the hallway. Fiddling with the key, she put it in the lock and turned the knob, but the door didn't budge. Her face flushed, pinking her cheeks and tears watered in her eyes as she pushed on the door several more times. He walked up behind her and set down the bag. Gently pushing her aside, he took the key and turned it two full circles. With the second turn, the lock clicked and the door opened.

She lowered her head and wiped a stray tear from her eye. "Thanks. I don't know why I couldn't figure it out. I must I'm exhausted from the trip."

Instantly feeling something tugging at his insides, he wanted to reach out to her. Her tears weren't an act. Ethan stepped back. He needed to get control of his emotions. He never formed an attachment and certainly not in the first few minutes of meeting his mark. He needed to rein this in soon or he'd be playing her personal protector. She seemed so naive and he didn't want her to fall prey to a big city, but it wasn't his job to babysit her. She was twenty-one, old enough to know better, but from what he saw, possibly too young to care. He was only a few years older than she. He may have been that carefree while he was in school if he hadn't been forced to survive on his own. He shook his head. As an FBI agent, he couldn't afford to be sucked in by every damsel in distress. The case against Walters was the most important thing. Abby was a sideshow. Nothing more. He pushed his feelings deep inside him and motioned for her to go on in. "Don't worry about it. I'll bring your bags."

Stale air hit his face as he entered the room. The curtains covering the window flapped against the wall but the breeze did little to help the stagnant stuffiness. He walked into the lifeless green colored room, his boots squeaking on the checkered linoleum floor. The emptiness of the decor reminded him of the small dorm room his mother provided for him while he was here. All the accommodations were decorated the same there and he felt like he was going back in time. Bare walls glared back at him and screamed for him to get out. Ethan remembered how hurt he felt when his mother left him in that apartment and stated her terms were that he was never to contact her again. He could still see her standing in her freshly pressed suit, her red lips in a shrewd frown, and tapping her fingers on her hips. She provided him a place to live but denied him the love he needed. Even his sister stared at him and didn't say a word. Not even goodbye. He felt the pain creeping to the surface. Why was he dragging up his past, his mother and sister? He hadn't spoken to them in a year, and he enjoyed the peace that came with the exile. It had to be the room. His old room was in this building and it reminded him so much of his past. He forced the memories from his mind. He turned and searched for Abby.

"Abs, where do you want the bags?" His voice cracked and a well-needed snicker escaped his lips before he could control it. That nickname didn't suit her at all.

"Over there is fine." She pointed to the living room.

He set the bags by the desk built into the far wall.

She smiled. "Thanks for the help. I never would've gotten them up here."

"No problem. Hope to see you soon," he said.

Abby clasped her fingers together and glanced around the room. He shrugged at her attempt to avoid eye contact. How could she be nervous around him? He'd done nothing to warrant her edginess. Ethan sighed, not sure what to do. He pulled his hand through his hair. "I guess, I'll see you on campus?"

She grinned. "Yeah, I should be around. Call me Abby next time."

A small flicker flamed in his stomach. Her smile penetrated the well-built wall around his heart. He and innocence didn't mix. He knew what it was. He'd been undercover too long. Too close to criminals. She was something different. That had to be it. He missed normal. He stood there a few minutes. The awkwardness was more than he could take. He never had trouble talking to women before, but she was almost impossible to converse with. It was like trying to pull a confession from a suspect. He wasn't much of a master at conversation, but he could appear to look interested. She seemed to dismiss him before he even arrived, and he hated it. He couldn't figure her out. One minute, she was vulnerable and sweet, the next, she was jittery and cold. It wasn't a direct brush off, but all she had to do was tell him to go. He needed to leave. If he wanted to be treated this way, he'd return to Bingham Manor.

"Set the bags there, by the others," a voice in the hall commanded. Sarah walked in, followed by Patrick. She whisked herself around the room and completed a full inspection.

"Don't you love the décor?" Abby asked.

"Absolutely gross. Where did they find this furniture?" Sarah dropped down in one of the chairs and flung her feet out. "We need to re-decorate. There's not even a couch."

"Look at the bright side, you'll have room for your luggage," Abby said.

Sarah tossed the jacket she'd just taken off at Abby. "Very funny."

Ethan chuckled and smacked Patrick on the back. "Good luck, mate." He shifted around so he could have one last look. This was it for him and Ms. Rodgers. There were no associations between her and Jayson Walters. He wouldn't be seeing her again. Abby had her back facing him. He shook his head and said a mental goodbye to her. The report would be filed tomorrow, and he'd be back investigating his prime suspect.

28

CHAPTER 5

"Yes, sir but I'd be better used in Rome." Ethan paused and held the phone from his ear as Tom yelled back his response. Listening to his supervisor bark out orders, Ethan gritted his teeth. "I know I'm in charge of the Paris operations." Forced to stay in France, he had nothing to do but babysit Abby. Jayson Walters was still in Rome and would be there for a few more weeks. Nols already left on the train to Italy that morning, and Ethan was stuck in Paris. He built the case against Walters and staying here with Abby wouldn't produce any more evidence or get Ethan closer to his promotion to squad leader. He'd worked hard to develop an undercover identity, and now it was useless. Why would a suspected sports gambler hang around a college campus? He'd have to think fast if any of his contacts spotted him there. But he didn't have to worry about that anymore. Tom told him his undercover portion for the Walters case was over.

Despite the report he submitted, the office still wanted him near Abigail Rodgers in case Jayson contacted her again. He tried to convince Tom that the girl probably had no idea how to gamble or that people participated in match fixing, but his boss insisted on the surveillance. Babysitting Abby annoyed him, but Tom refused to hear his side. Tom even suggested having lunch with her.

29

"Yes, sir. I've read the brief." Ethan cleared his throat. "I understand. I'm on campus." He flipped the phone shut and flung it on the table. It landed in a pile of crumbs. Dishes banging in the kitchen behind him amplified in his head and intensified his headache. "This is bloody perfect." He didn't have anything against this girl, but it wasn't his job to look after her. She had nothing to do with this case, but Tom had his reason, Senator Phillip Rodgers. Abby's father was the highest-ranking senator in Washington, so now Ethan's assignment included looking out for Ms. Abigail Rodgers and her sisters. He didn't recognize the Rodgers name until he saw the brief. Ethan had been out of the United States for a few years and didn't witness the senator's rise to the powerful office he held now. So a few seat assignments on the plane resulted in Ethan's new mission- protect Abigail Rodgers.

Ethan scanned the cafeteria. Most of the long tables were full. The chatter of multiple conversations from students getting louder as more people filled the seating area. He had made it a priority not to eat there while in school. The mixed smell of overcooked vegetables and meat always reminded him of the crap they served in the group foster homes. He vowed he wouldn't eat cafeteria food again, but he had to put aside his dislike for a few days to get close to Abby.

Near the hot bar, he spotted Sarah's platinum locks. Not far from her, Abby stood next to the drink refrigerator. She selected a water bottle from the cooler and stepped around a few students to the nearest table. Ethan instantly morphed his face with a carefree smile, something he wasn't used to doing. A smile was rare in the current world he was imbedded in. He almost forgot how.

Ethan waved. "Abby, over here." His movement caught her eye, and her face lit up. An improvement over the look of shock she had yesterday.

Her hair was pulled back in a hairclip, letting her blue eyes dominate her face. He couldn't believe she was in graduate school. She looked like a little girl, but he'd take her any day over her sister.

Abby approached his table. "Hi."

He got up and planted kisses on her cheeks. She blushed. Her reaction sent a smile to his face.

Sarah came up and stood beside her. "Hello." She leaned toward him.

Ethan drew his lips in a thin line. He held back the urge to retreat. Her aggressiveness irritated him, but Ethan gave her two pecks on the cheek, a custom he wished the French would un-adopt. He liked to choose the women he kissed, rather than dictated by a centuries old tradition.

"How was your first night in Paris?" he asked.

"Is Patrick with you?" Sarah cut in as she looked over his shoulder at the table.

"He's in the library's computer lab," Ethan said and diverted his gaze back to Abby.

"What a coincidence, we were going there but couldn't find it." Sarah shifted her lunch tray in her hand and eyed Ethan's table.

"I'll take you after we finish, if you'd like to join me." He went to another table and returned with two chairs. Pulling the first chair out, he motioned for Abby to sit. Ethan scooted the second seat out for Sarah at the head of the table, the farthest seat away from him.

"So Abby, how was your first night here?" Ethan tore off a piece of bread and threw it in his mouth. He shifted his shoulder to block Sarah from the conversation. All she was good for was a carefree shag. He wasn't sure sex with her was worth the pain her personality would inflict. They should rule it a type of torture.

"Uneventful. I went straight to bed," Abby said.

"Time change drags you down." He scanned the cafeteria but didn't see the other sister. To his good fortune, he only had two to contend with today.

"Yeah, I'm not sure I could handle an economics lecture at this moment."

"So you're studying business?" Ethan asked. He couldn't remember what the brief said. He skipped a majority of the report, not feeling the need to do the essential prep work he usually did. They weren't criminals and had no bearing on his current case.

Abby shook her head. "It's a requirement for my fashion program and internship."

"Where's your internship?" Ethan stared at her. Why was she at this school but in fashion? He regretted not finishing the brief.

"Von Deez Fashion House. I start today."

Ethan smiled. It was almost noon. He'd never heard of a mid-day schedule but whatever. "I'm impressed. Von Deez is a couture fashion line. They usually don't have many internship openings." His sister always talked about Von Deez. He almost threw up thinking about it. Fortunately, her endless ramblings benefited him with this conversation. He knew what Abby was talking about.

Abby's eyes widened. "It is. I had to submit several letters of recommendations and a portfolio of my ad layouts."

"Abs had her nose in books all last year. She has no life," Sarah said. Abby flinched but a smile quickly masked her true reaction.

"Her work paid off. Most grad students would kill for that job," he said. He wondered why Abby didn't stand up to her sister. He had the urge to slap Sarah, and he never hit women.

"We're not in grad school. We just completed our junior year," Abby said.

Ethan leaned back in his chair. "Wow, I'm impressed. Usually, internships are reserved for grad students." He'd never heard of an undergraduate selected. There was more to Abigail Rodgers than he thought, or it could be some well-placed money from the Rodgers fortune. He'd gotten that far in the brief.

Abby smiled. "What are you studying?"

"I'm finishing my degree in management. Last semester here." Telling lies meant telling a lot of truths with minor details left out, like he finished his degree three years ago. He didn't know the last time he actually told the truth.

"Oh." Abby frowned as she unwrapped the foil on her sandwich and poked at the bread. Huge slices of cheese and a reddish tinted meat spilled out over the bread. Ethan looked over at Sarah's pizza with an egg in the center of the slice. It looked like a ball of sunshine smothered by mountains of melted cheese. Both girls looked repulsed by the food and he had to laugh. This would be an eye-opening experience for them.

Sarah used her fork to stab at her food, piercing the egg. The yolk spilled out and ran down the cheese. Her nose crinkled.

"Not fond of the food?" Ethan chuckled as he watched Abby study her sandwich. This should be great. She didn't have any idea what she was eating. Rule number one was to always be wary of the meat. She'd learn soon enough.

"It's different." As Abby took a bite, her lips puckered and she spit out the meat. She seized her water and drank half the bottle.

"That bad?" he asked as Abby covered the pieces of meat with a napkin.

"I didn't know it was raw. Everyone else chose it, so I thought it would be safe."

"What did you get? Steak tartare?" Ethan wadded up his sandwich wrapper and started on a salad. He had to agree, the food sucked.

"It did say tartare," she said.

Sarah laughed. "Tartare is raw. Didn't you pay attention in class?"

Abby shrugged. "French class was two semesters ago."

"Well, you got your first taste of France." Ethan slid a few napkins in Abby's direction. "You have plans for your first week here?" He twisted in his seat so he faced Abby. Not that she would blurt out if she planned to meet Walters, but Ethan could easily tell when someone was lying. Abby clearly didn't hide her emotions. She'd be an easy read.

"No, nothing yet. Probably exploring the campus and some sightseeing." She pulled out a pamphlet from her bag and traced her finger over the map. "You know where the computer lab is?"

"It's in the center of campus, in the tall stone building near the main entrance." He tapped on a small square near the middle of the map with his index finger. Ethan noticed Sarah was no longer eating. She had converted her table space into a cosmetics counter. Patrick had found his

33

match in her. They'd probably never had to work for anything and expected everyone to cater to their needs. Patrick had some redeeming qualities, but with Sarah, he wasn't so sure.

"We passed right by it," Abby said as she circled the box on the map.

Ethan wiped his mouth with his napkin. "Are you ready?"

Abby had abandoned her sandwich soon after she'd started eating, so his trip to the cafeteria would be short lived much to his liking. He needed to get outside before he suffocated from the dreary atmosphere. The darkness of the old building was ruining his usually cheery mood. He thought cheery, but his partner would say cheerless.

"Sure, whenever you are." Abby scooted out her chair and picked up her bag.

Sarah was already waiting for them by the door. They exited the cafeteria and emerged back in the glowing sun. Ethan led them down a side path toward the dorms, pointing out the buildings he could remember. He enjoyed being back on campus. He almost forgot the real world outside. His education was the one positive thing his mother provided him. It was one of the only things she provided him. It got him to the position he had today.

Before he knew it, Abby, Sarah and he stood in front of a tall stone building with a clock tower centered on its roof. "There are several study areas inside, a common area, and the computer lab is on the first floor. The library is on the second." He held the door open for them.

They walked down the hallway. Various portraits of men and women decorated the corridor in between white marble sculptures. Ethan steered the girls to the second room on the left. He opened the door and the clicking of keyboards and mice met them. Computers lined the outer wall, creating a large square, and another row formed a small cube in the middle. To the right, a few people worked behind the counter.

"Do you have your computer IDs?" Ethan lowered his voice, almost to the point of being non-existence.

Abby frowned. "I didn't bring it with me."

"I see Patrick." Sarah whipped around them and bounced down the last aisle to Patrick's desk. Ethan breathed a huge sigh. Finally, some privacy. He could have an uninterrupted intelligent conversation with Abby.

Ethan guided Abby down the center aisle and pulled back a chair for her at an open computer. "They have a public ID and password for visitors. You can use that today."

"Thanks." She grinned and pulled the keyboard toward her.

Ethan dropped in the seat beside her, letting his legs flop to each side. "So you haven't seen any of the sights in Paris yet?" He clasped his hands together, and his eyes darted from face to face as he memorized the features of everyone in the room. A habit he had when undercover. Even though the circumstances were different, he couldn't toss aside the ritual.

Abby shook her head. "I'm sure that will change once I get settled." Facing the screen, she clicked on the internet icon. Her eyes shifted between him and the monitor.

Ethan slouched in his chair. Just like the first time he met her, it was like he was invisible. She seemed pleasant in the cafeteria, but her attitude seemed to flip on the way there. He had a job to do, so he forced the conversation. "There are so many things to see around the city. You could fill up the entire time you're here with activities and still not see everything." He shifted in the seat and moved closer to her. "The Eiffel Tower, the Louvre, Arc de Triomphe..."

"Yes, I brought a guidebook." Her gaze drifted to the computer screen.

Ethan stared at her. He felt more than invisible. Her frozen attitude stung him. She was brushing him off, but he wasn't going to make it that easy for her. He was stuck there, so he had to make the best of it. He couldn't leave without piquing her interest. The guys at the office would rib him hard if he struck out with her. He never had trouble picking up women, but Abby seemed to be the exception. He sucked in air and exhaled slowly. "Have you been anywhere in Europe before?"

"Nope, first time."

"It's nice that you're able to spend a year here." He smiled but he felt the effort was wasted on her.

"I'm sure it will be educational." Abby repositioned her head and blocked his view of the screen.

Ethan's smile disappeared. Absolutely nothing. He should've stopped before he humiliated himself. Next, he'd be talking about the weather and other crap. He needed to cut his losses while he still had some pride. Ethan rose from his chair. "I'll let you get to your work." He saw Abby hesitate, biting her lip.

Abby looked up at him. "I'm sorry I'm not very talkative, but I need to turn in my class assignments. They were due last night by midnight. They didn't even give us a break to travel here," she said rapidly like she was trying to find an excuse more than she was interested in him.

Ethan smiled, surprised that she even made the effort. She twisted her fingers so the skin turned a pasty white. He knew it was a lie but he played along. "Sure, I understand. Before I go, I was wondering...if you don't have anything else going on, maybe we can get together later? I would love to show you around the city." He didn't know why he asked, but he'd rather spend time with her instead of observing from a distance. The surveillance part of his job bored him.

Abby pushed her bangs from her eyes and glanced up at him. "Sure. Sounds like fun."

"Great. We'll grab dinner before a tour of the city. Around eight?" If he had to keep track of her, he could get a good meal and charge it to the agency. He studied her mouth and lips. No smile. She'd agreed to dinner with him, even though she didn't want to go. With willpower like that, no wonder Senator Rodgers wanted a bodyguard for her. Ethan suspected she'd agree to about anything to avoid hurting someone.

"I'll see you then," Abby said.

Nodding, he got up. He strolled to the door, clenching his fists, ready to strike out at the first wall he saw. He asked her out on a date. What the heck was he thinking? He wanted to make her pay attention like he forced his mother's family to take notice of him. Tom said to stay in contact, take her to lunch. Not date her. He observed her as she focused on the computer screen. It wasn't exactly what he planned but despite the indifference he felt from her, something attracted him to her. Quirky, naïve, intelligent, all in one, maybe that combination attracted Jayson to her. He could tell she wasn't intentionally trying to be rude but her aloofness baffled him. He could report that he barely persuaded her to accept a date. He laughed. Nope, he didn't want his near disastrous attempt on record.

CHAPTER 6

*A*bby stared at Ethan's back as he disappeared behind the door, and her heart fluttered. Dinner with Ethan excited her and scared her all the same. She never knew how to act when a guy asked her out. She usually froze. Today wasn't any different. He probably thought she was a snob. When she saw him, she couldn't think of anything to say. Why couldn't she act normal when someone like Ethan talked to her? Turning back to the computer, Abby clicked on the internet icon and entered her web mail address. Butterflies tickled her stomach. She'd do better tonight. She'd make more of an effort. Besides, he was nice, and there was no reason for her to clam up. She focused on the screen. Four new messages appeared. Two spams, one from Gilda, and the last one from her father. She clicked on his email.

Dread flooded her as she read the message. Not that she needed a reminder of what would happen if she screwed up while in France. She couldn't afford fights with her sisters or reports getting back that she was out partying. Any incident that her father found out about would jeopardize everything she'd worked for. Abby wondered if her sisters got the same message. Probably not. Since her brother's accident, her parents reserved their conversations with her to strictly email and text messages. She hated feeling like a prisoner to her father's demands, but she needed the trust fund to continue with classes and her internship. She'd already checked on scholarships. None were available due to her family's income. Abby didn't make any money, but she couldn't get help because of what her father made. The red tape was too enormous for Abby to overcome. She didn't blame the system. Why give money away to a student whose family has more than enough to pay for tuition? She'd have to make it work. Abby glanced at the email from Gilda. It was probably a bomb ready to go off. She clicked on it.

Abigail,
Great news that you can make it to Fashion Week and your boyfriend's available for our campaign. You'll be in charge of scheduling the models for Paris Fashion Week. Let me know his name so I can put him on the guest list. Attire is formal. See you @ the Paris office.
Gilda

Biting her lip, she reread the message. She hadn't thought of the consequences when Sarah had replied. Of course Gilda would love the idea of Abby's model boyfriend. Gilda lived for creating campaigns that were unique, and Abby always managed to deliver the distinctiveness that set Von Deez apart. Even though this was the start of her internship in Paris, Abby'd worked for Gilda for six months in New York. Abby sighed. There was no going back. She'd have to find a date and a model for the ad shoot. She possibly could persuade Jayson to come to Paris that weekend. It was worth a shot. He fit the criteria and his participation would save her job. Abby grabbed her wallet. The piece of paper with Jayson's email address stuck out in between two credit cards. Taking in a deep breath, she composed her message.

"I knew you wanted to come here so you could email him. Couldn't you use your phone?" a familiar high pitched voice asked.

Abby twisted in her seat and saw Sarah peering over her shoulder. "It takes too much time to type on the phone." She slumped her shoulders as Sarah pulled up a chair.

"What did you write?" Sarah scanned the email, and a frown crossed her face. "That's it? You should spice it up."

Abby looked at the email. "What's wrong with it? I don't want to sound too eager." Sarah knew how to attract guys. This was Abby's cue to listen. Swallowing her hurt, she smiled. "You want to help?"

"Sure." Sarah slid her chair closer to the monitor. "It's too vague. Be flirty and don't leave it up to him. Guys aren't good at that. Odds are, if you send this email, you'll get a short reply back." She pointed to sentences for Abby to delete. "Ask him about the tournament, maybe where in Rome it is. This is your one chance to talk to him. Don't waste it."

Rearranging the email in her head based on Sarah's advice, Abby began typing. After a few minutes, she sat back satisfied with her revision.

Sarah read over her shoulder. "It's good, but you didn't flirt much. You need to work on that for next time. Ditch the smiley. It's childish." She rolled off the rest of her critique. Abby made a few more corrections, while Sarah flipped through her magazine. Sarah's open bottle of lotion sat on the table. The odor masked as perfume suffocated Abby, but her sister seemed oblivious to it. Shifting in her chair, Sarah glanced at her watch. "You ready to go?"

Hesitating, Abby took a peek at Gilda's email. She couldn't ignore her. "Let me send a couple more, then we can go. What happened to Patrick?"

"We talked for a while and he left for lunch. He invited me, but of course, we already ate." She took her compact out of her bag. "We're going to some club tonight."

"Ethan offered to show me around the city. Maybe we could all go out together," Abby said. Having Sarah there would take away the pressure. Abby could fade into the background. Not that she liked Sarah getting all the attention, but knowing everyone wasn't looking at her allowed Abby some comfort.

"Well, I was thinking more of a date thing with Patrick. You understand, don't you?" Sarah's lips puckered out.

"So you're interested in him?" Abby asked. Nerves ate at her as she thought about an evening alone with Ethan. Should she still go out with Ethan even though she was emailing Jayson? She should be focusing on her internship requirements instead of finding a boyfriend. She needed a model for the ad, and she couldn't see Ethan's lanky frame and baggy clothes impressing Gilda, even if his piercing eyes sent Abby's body in a tailspin. Jayson had the eyes and the body to set Gilda off. But Abby wanted this date with Ethan. It couldn't hurt to go out this one time.

"Patrick's gorgeous, isn't he? Did you see that body? I can't refuse such a hottie." Sarah finished reapplying her lip gloss. "We better get going. I need to get back to get ready. So do you."

"It's only noon. I have plenty of time to get ready, plus we have to go to Von Deez this afternoon for orientation." Abby laughed at the thought of six hours of primping. She doubted the extra time would do her any good. She hit the send icon on her email.

"You need to look perfect for Ethan."

"Who's Ethan?" Nicole, Abby's other sister, said as she marched up to their table. She plopped down and her black hair cascaded down her shoulders.

"He's one of the guys who helped us with the luggage. Brown, curly hair, kind of looks like he never combed it once in his life. We saw him in the cafeteria," Abby said. His vivid ice blue eyes still burned in her thoughts. Abby glanced up at her sister. "Where've you been?" Nicole was already gone when Abby got up that morning. In fact, Abby had hardly seen her since they'd arrived, but disappearing wasn't unusual for Nicole. She'd always been the independent one, while Abby and Sarah stuck close together. More and more since the accident, Sarah was drawn to Nicole, and Abby felt like an outsider.

The relationships between the sisters weren't always that way. Nicole tended to be the outsider. She was born to a surrogate around the time of Sarah and Abby's births. The murky circumstances around their births stirred up a media frenzy and still followed the sisters around twenty years later. They were biological sisters, but the circumstances were complicated. Abby didn't blame Nicole for feeling excluded. Sarah and Abby shared a special bond being twins but since Jacob's death, Nicole was taking Abby's place in Sarah's life. It seemed they could never all be close at the same time, something Abby wished would happen. The isolation hurt her more than she wanted to admit. Abby rubbed her hands together and stared at Nicole. "You do remember the guys that helped us with our luggage, don't you?"

"Oh, right," Nicole said as she twisted her hair into a thick bun.

Abby sighed at the dismissal and gave up on her conversation with Nicole. She tapped her fingers on her watch. "You ready to go, Sarah? We need to get to the orientation by one."

"I'll go with you. I want to stop by the grocery store," Nicole said. "The marché is only a few blocks from here. There's an entrance behind our building. It's much closer than walking to the middle of campus." She led them back toward the apartments and they approached a small gate.

A tiny building was attached to the stone barrier that surrounded the campus. The compartment was only wide enough for a person to stand in comfortably. Abby couldn't believe her eyes when she saw not only a security guard, but a desk inside. The man lifted his head and nodded as they passed. The stone wall separated the busy streets of Paris from the peaceful surroundings of the campus gardens. Cars raced up and down the main boulevard. Small crowds of pedestrians peppered the sidewalks, leaving no room to stand. Abby found it difficult to move with so many people around her.

"It's across the street and down a block. We can cross here." Nicole pointed at the large intersection in front of them. They waited for the light to turn green.

Once across the road, Abby saw a few small boxed structures on the sidewalk and realized they were newsstands. People swarmed around the box, picking out various newspapers and magazines. Nearing the outdoor market, the sisters dodged pedestrians as the crowds thickened. Homemade vendor stands stood on both sides of the walkway built out of concrete block and crates. The girls zigzagged around shoppers that were crammed in the area.

"You can buy anything here. Fruit, vegetables, fish, meat. There's a Chinese vendor a few booths from here. You can get egg rolls and rice." Nicole named a whole list of food items, causing Abby's tongue to salivate even though she'd just eaten.

"We don't need too much. Abs and I have plans for dinner," Sarah said.

"Really?" Nicole's eyebrows lifted. Small creases formed across her forehead, ruining the smooth canvas.

"I'm going out with Patrick, and Abs landed herself a date with Ethan." Sarah picked through the crowd and approached the nearest fruit vendor. Sorting through apples, she lifted each one to her nose.

"Patrick and Ethan? I knew Sarah made fast work of men but you, Abby? What happened to the guy from the plane? Have you already cast him aside?" Nicole's eyes interrogated Abby, causing her to shrink back. Even though Nicole had not been with them on the trip over, she'd managed to find out about Jayson from Sarah.

"It's not a date. Ethan asked me to dinner. He's showing me around the city. You can come if you want." Abby shifted her weight and stepped back, putting a few feet between them. Having Nicole there would be better than going alone. That was saying something about Abby's apprehension about guys since she hardly ever wanted to spend time with Nicole, especially with the way Nicole had treated her since the accident. The more she thought about it, Abby didn't think going alone was a good idea anymore. She hardly knew Ethan, and Nicole was better than no one.

Nicole smiled. "I don't think I'll join you. I'm sure Ethan's invitation was only for you."

"I haven't forgotten about Jayson. I emailed him this morning," Abby added, not sure why she wanted Nicole to know. Her interest in Jayson was for Von Deez, but with the constant taunts from her sisters, Abby was beginning to think Jayson was also the only way to show her sisters that she was capable of finding a suitable man.

"You think he'll email you back?" Nicole's questioning tone implied that she thought otherwise.

"Why wouldn't he? He didn't have to let me win." Abby's voice rose.

"Calm down. I'm only asking a simple question." Nicole held up her hand and stepped out of the aisle as Abby sorted through the bananas. "Let you win? What's that about?" Nicole picked up an orange and handed it to Abby. "This is the best place to get produce and it goes fairly quickly."

Abby grabbed a bag and picked out some bananas to go with the orange. "We had this bet that Sarah would shorten his name by the end of the flight. You know how she does that, right?"

"Yeah, I know." She rolled her eyes and motioned for Abby to continue.

"While I was asleep, he asked her to call him Jay, guaranteeing I'd win the bet."

"Jay? That's so stupid. You sure Sarah wasn't flirting with him?" Her voice lowered to a whisper. Abby stepped forward to hear her last few words. "What did they talk about?"

Abby's brow crinkled as she studied Nicole. "She said they spoke about me mostly."

Nicole smirked. "I'm glad she was able to help you out."

"She helped me write the email to him too," Abby said.

"Oh?" Nicole's eyes narrowed, forming slits. She reached out and took the bag of fruit from Abby. "Don't spend too much time thinking about plane boy. You don't want to disappoint your date. Sarah will be angry if you make her come home early and end her date with Patrick."

Abby caught sight of Sarah. She was a few people ahead of them in the line. She waved as they approached and motioned to the entrance of the outdoor market. "I'll be at the newsstand."

Abby nodded and turned back to Nicole. "Ethan isn't a date. He's a nice guy, and I think he'll be a good friend to have around, but that's it." She didn't want Nicole telling their father she was dating a total stranger her first week in France. Nicole was a direct line back to the family. Her father would know before the end of the day.

"He probably has more than friends on his mind. Guys don't usually ask you to dinner and a night out because they want to be friends." Nicole's eyebrows lifted as if they were telling Abby to open her own eyes.

Abby shrugged. "We just met. Besides, I don't feel like sitting around doing nothing. If I don't go, I'll be waiting all night for Jayson to email me." She wanted to go out and have some fun, but deep down, she needed to figure out this Fashion Week disaster. She was sure her feelings for Ethan would not save her internship and she knew Nicole felt she didn't deserve to go out and have fun.

"You spent eight hours with that jockstrap. How could you be this infatuated with him?" Nicole asked.

Abby placed her items on the checkout counter. "I don't know. He'd be a perfect date for Fashion Week and model for the campaign."

Nicole shook her head. "Sounds more like a fantasy than anything. You'd do better spending your time getting to know Ethan. Your plane boy isn't even here. I doubt emailing each other is going to magically transport him to Paris for Fashion Week."

Abby scrunched her lips together and avoided looking at Nicole. Why did she care who Abby spent her time chasing? Nicole didn't know Ethan or Jayson, so what gave her the right to tell Abby whom she should spend her time with? Ethan wouldn't fit in with all the glamour of Van Deez, and arguing with Nicole was more trouble than it was worth. Abby fiddled with her purse strings. "Do you think Ethan would go to Fashion Week? He doesn't seem the type to mingle with designers, photographers..."

"You aren't the type either but people often surprise you. He may be more suited for that atmosphere than you are. Only way you'll know is to spend time with him."

Abby stared at her then back at the cashier. She dismissed the comment. Ethan didn't fit the image. She needed something spectacular to pull this off, and Jayson was spectacular.

The lady rang up the groceries and pushed them down to the end of the counter to the bagging area. Abby quickly bagged her items and followed Nicole out the door toward the intersection.

Abby searched for the newspaper stand Sarah had mentioned. Near the street, she saw the small square building. With magazines and papers scattered on the shelves, it looked like a jumbled mess. Abby recognized the back of Sarah's curvy athletic figure. The clerk was handing her change.

"Sarah," Abby yelled.

Sarah swirled around clutching a magazine to her chest, her eyes wide. "Hi, girls. You scared me." She shoved the magazine in her bag.

"What did you get?" Abby asked.

"Not much, something on movies. You two ready?"

"Do they have anything good?" Abby wondered if reading French magazines would help her pick up the language. She'd need to get more familiar with the French fashion ads. She started around to the side of the newsstand.

"We don't have time. We need to get to work." Sarah jumped in front of Abby and pushed her toward the crosswalk.

"We have thirty more minutes, and it's only a block away," Abby said, sighing. She gave up trying to get to the booth.

"You don't want to be late." Sarah waved at them. "I'm going to pop in here for a bit." She pointed at a perfumerie. "Call me later, Nic." She formed a phone with her pinkie and thumb and moved her hand to her head.

Abby knew what that meant. Something had happened she didn't want Abby to know about. She probably met some guy at the newsstand and wanted to meet him for dinner. Sarah never wanted Abby to question her tactics. She probably already plotted to dump Patrick. How could Sarah have changed so much?

CHAPTER 7

"Abigail, run these swatches to Jean-Claude." Gilda's shrill voice scratched in the air as she threw the colored fabric squares across the table, already cluttered with buttons, zippers, and cloth remnants.

Abby rolled her eyes at Gilda's back. Abby was only supposed to stay for the intern orientation, but Gilda didn't consider Abby as just another intern. She viewed her as a slave. After working with Gilda in New York, Abby knew a lot of pain was ahead.

"Sure. Jean-Claude is on what floor?" Abby pulled out the map her mentor had given her earlier.

"Across the hall. Remember Jean-Claude, our head designer?" Gilda waved her hand toward the door. "Hurry back. We need to talk about the Fashion Week layouts."

Abby paused at the samples table and closed her eyes. She should confess. It'd be easier than continuing this charade. Abby grabbed the fabric off the side table and darted across the hall.

She tapped on the side of the door, and a short stubby man lifted his marshmallow-shaped head. "Entrez." He motioned for her to enter. His white hair puffed out above his ears, leaving a balding center.

"Here's the fabric," Abby said in French. She bit her lip as she waited for his response. She hoped she'd understand him. The nerves of meeting Von Deez's most famous man almost overtook her. Even Gilda caved to his demands. He was the master of the designs and never had a bad collection according to the press.

Jean-Claude's eyes lifted and stared at her, then at the fabric in her hands.

"Set it over there, and don't wrinkle it." He motioned to a work table full of mismatched swatches and several photo boards stacked on a sewing box. The photos on the panels were of different outfits but resembled a rainbow of muddled colors more than anything. The patterns clashed, but Abby wasn't a designer, only a stylist's intern. She had no idea how he came up with his designs.

Abby carefully laid the fabric on the least disheveled section of the table. He'd probably dump more crap on the swatches and wrinkle them anyway. She made her way to the door.

"You are Gilda's assistant from the United States, non?"

Abby twirled around and faced his questioning eyes. "Yes, but I'm an intern."

He laughed. "No, you're her assistant, so accept it as it is. Means you're my assistant too." He flipped open a few portfolios and spread them out on the desk. "Come over and pick one." He waved her to his side.

Abby moved closer to the desk. Several pictures of models and poses were lined up in a row of five by five prints across each page. She scanned the photos. Some, where the model appeared bored, and others, where the woman practically jumped out of the photograph. Abby drummed her finger along her bottom lip as she disregarded photo after photo, leaving only two.

"I'd choose these." Abby pointed to two near the bottom of the page. The model was leaning against a black pillar. The signature gold Von Deez slip dress from this season popped off her dark skin. Splashes of greenish gold paint dusted her sharp features.

"Her expression is natural, not forced. Her eyes draw you in, then you focus on the dress." Abby's insides were bubbling over. She'd never given her opinion to a designer on layouts before, and she hoped she made sense. She made suggestions to Gilda, but nothing like this.

He studied the picture and nodded. "I like it." He spun the photo around and scribbled a few notes. "Tell Gilda that I approve of you doing the ad project." He turned his attention back to the folders on his desk.

Abby wanted to question his statement but knew from his body language, she'd been dismissed. She exited his studio and stepped across the hall into Gilda's office, just as her boss barked at some employee on the speakerphone. "Don't give me excuses. Give me what I ask for." She threw a pencil at the phone, like she expected it to hit the person at the other end of the line.

"Ms. Held, we discussed this with Alana. She can't commit to being at Paris Fashion Week. She's doing a movie promo on your proposed dates," a feeble voice quivered through the speaker.

"Charley, we contract most of our models out to you. That means you produce results. That means you produce Alana Barash." The fire in Gilda's voice rose the temperature of the room ten degrees. "Let me speak to Paula."

Abby quietly slipped in the room and took a seat at her small desk in the far corner. From her inbox, she snatched the magazine layouts that came in from the ad agency and scanned the proofs for any differences from Gilda's submissions, but she couldn't concentrate with her boss yelling behind her.

"Gilda, daring." A high pitched voice sung through the speakerphone.

"Paula, don't. I want Alana for Paris Fashion Week. Ten minutes for a quick announcement and she can reschedule the shoots when she's available."

"Not possible. She's committed to her movie project in Brazil."

"What happened to I can get you anyone?" Gilda slammed her fist on her desk.

"Alana is not anyone. She's an A list actress and in demand. Everyone wants her."

"Fine. If she's everywhere, I don't need her." Gilda punched the button on the phone, and the line went dead.

"I swear, when I get back to New York, I'm going to fire that agency. They can't get her? What kind of agency are they? Abigail, get over here."

Abby jumped up and moved over to Gilda's desk.

"Tell me about this idea you have. My Alana campaign is dead, so I need something to replace it." Gilda fiddled with her updo and poked a few hair twigs back into the twisted ball at the base of her neck.

Abby forced herself to concentrate. She could produce outrageous pictures with her camera. On the spot, she could tweak an ad layout to make it stand out, but she didn't know what Gilda wanted for her next big idea. Abby stared at the rack of clothing behind Gilda's desk. Von Deez was a couture line, and the designs were always displayed in the chicest boutiques across the world. They had the most desired time slot at Paris Fashion Week. The elite of the elite wore Von Deez. Abby knew first hand. Her mother had an entire wardrobe full of Von Deez City Scape. That's when it hit her, and she could use her sister's lie to add credibility to her idea.

"It's all about attracting the feminine side this year. How about having one model surrounded by some rugged looking guys at a gym? The contrast is brilliant. You don't need a famous name, just regular models. It would be an edgy approach, but Von Deez could break from the classic one theme advertisements." Abby swallowed what little confidence she had. The frown on Gilda's face didn't reassure her.

"How about you use your name to get Alana Barash for that idea. Then it'll work," Gilda said.

Abby scowled at the suggestion. She didn't want to use her name to do anything. She wanted her talent to earn her respect, not her last name. "But it would be bold, a change from Von Deez's usual ads. You don't need Alana to accomplish that. She'd outshine the dress." Abby sucked in a breath. The last sentence didn't come out right. No one ever criticized the designs, and she knew even suggesting something outshining a Von Deez design was taboo.

"Plus, Abby has the perfect athlete. Her boyfriend is a tennis player and he photographs wonderfully." Abby cringed at the familiar soft but strong voice.

Abby jerked around and stared at Nicole's smirking face. Abby gritted her teeth. Why was Nicole there? She didn't even work at Von Deez. "What are you doing here?"

"Who is this?" Gilda demanded, her thin lips in a sharp line.

"I'm Abby's sister. Nicole Rodgers. I work down at the finance firm. Abby has to sign a few papers, so I'm dropping them off."

Abby glanced at her sister. "Couldn't this wait until tonight?"

Nicole sneered and held out the yellow folder.

"Abigail, can you keep your family drama out of the office?" Gilda raked a few papers on her desk and waved her pencil at Abby. "What's this about a tennis player?"

"Abby's boyfriend's a model and a tennis player..."

Abby grabbed the papers from Nicole. "She exaggerates. Nicole, come on." She jerked her sister toward her desk.

Gilda clapped her hands together. "It's perfect. We can introduce your boyfriend as one of the fresh faces for Cityscape. Several male athletes, one female to model the fashion line."

"But wouldn't you want to see her boyfriend first?" Nicole's voice gave a hint of anger at Gilda's easy acceptance of the idea.

"I've seen Abby's photographs. She's got a great eye and picked out the best picture from our painted photos. If she says her boyfriend will work, we'll go with her expertise." Jean-Claude's crackled voice boomed as he stepped past Nicole and in Gilda's office. "I'll authorize this. I feel something different this season. Produce results. Get the proposal and your models lined up by Fashion Week."

Abby stared at him and felt the lump of anxiety building in her throat. This was the opportunity she'd been looking for. Regardless of what they believed, Abby couldn't risk telling them the truth. She had to convince Jayson to be in her ad campaign. Her future depended on this, and she wasn't going to let Nicole destroy what she worked for.

Abby lifted her chin as Nicole scowled and stomped out of the room. "No problem. I'll start right away," Abby said. She may have been oozing confidence on the outside, but she was dying inside. Her chance at success was based on a lie.

CHAPTER 8

"Why in blazes did you did mention my so-called boyfriend?" Abby's voice shook, and she fought to control her anger. She hardly ever yelled, but this warranted a few strong words.

"What?" Nicole flung her messenger bag on the chair in their kitchen and lifted her head like her halo just fell off and tumbled to the ground.

"You know. What you said to Gilda and Jean-Claude." Abby paced around the apartment, while Sarah trailed behind her with her canvas of blush and lipsticks. The feeling of doom pitted in Abby's stomach. Knowing that Nicole was sabotaging her internship set off a fury in her.

"I don't know, so tell me," Sarah whined as she pulled Abby's hair up and twisted it in a knot at the base of her neck.

"Ow! Take it easy." Abby jerked her head to the side, and Sarah's grip loosened. Abby plopped down in a chair near the kitchen table and let Sarah continue her work.

Nicole shrugged and retreated to the bedroom. Rage flowed through Abby, and she burst from the seat after her. Sarah's bobby pins and hair clips scattered on the floor. "Don't walk away. Why mention Jayson? Gilda was happy without him. I can find other models. I didn't need him." Abby's hands flung up in the air, and she almost hit Sarah, who darted in after her.

53

Nicole fell back on the bed and adjusted the pillow under her neck. "This afternoon, you were confident that Jayson would contact you, so I thought he'd be a great model for your ad. He's an athlete. Isn't that the type you wanted in the photo shoot?"

Sarah's eyes popped open. "But...what about..."

"Abby acts like she can persuade Jayson to come to Paris. I thought while he was here, he'd welcome the opportunity to participate in her project." Nicole stared at Sarah.

Abby's eyes moved between them. She jutted her index finger in Sarah's direction. "What were you going to say?"

Sarah's head shot back as she bent down to pick up a few bobby pins. "I thought you were going to focus on Ethan since he was here." She jumped up and seized the brush out of Abby's hand.

"Abby's in love with the jockstrap. I figured she could lure him here with a modeling gig since she alone can't attract him." Nicole smiled. It was one of those I-don't-mean-it smiles. Abby daggered Nicole's back with a glare as she exited the room.

"Whatever. I don't need your kind of help," Abby yelled as she bounced up from the bed. She pulled her plum shirt from her suitcase and draped it over her shoulder. So far, her time getting ready for her dinner with Ethan hadn't bettered her mood. She'd hoped spending some time with Sarah alone would ease the tension. They'd been getting along great until Nicole returned and reminded Abby about this afternoon. Even Sarah hadn't gone this far.

Sarah jerked the shirt off Abby's shoulders. "That's not good enough for a night in Paris. You need something that makes you look hot." She ran over to a pile of clothes near the far end of the room. "How can you work in fashion and have no style?"

Nicole laughed from the other room and only infuriated Abby further. She took a few quick breaths and ignored her sisters. "My style seems to be working fine. I got Jayson's email and a dinner invite from Ethan. Jean-

Claude loved my idea. I think that's pretty good since Nicole doesn't have a date or a new project at work."

Abby glanced in the living room at her sister. Nicole opened her mouth and shut it, leaving Abby satisfied with her retaliation.

Sarah picked a turquoise blouse from the pile and tossed it at Abby. "Please try to dress in a style from this decade. This is perfect. It'll bring out your eyes."

The material was so light that Abby barely felt it in her hand. She had to agree, the jewel tone was a better contrast than her plum shirt. Abby slipped on her pants, sucking in her belly as she buttoned the top button. She eased the sleeveless shirt on over her head, being careful not to mess up Sarah's work on her hair. The only things holding the shirt on were two strings that formed a V around her neck and attached to the fabric near the middle of her chest.

Sarah stood at the door. "Not bad but that bra has to go." She circled around her, flattening the fabric against Abby's lean frame.

"I have to wear a bra," Abby said. The thought of going out without one sent butterflies in her stomach. She didn't know how models were able to strip down to nothing with millions of people around. Abby barely could manage this skimpy top.

"What's wrong with it? I go without all the time but if you're uncomfortable, I have a strapless I'll lend you." She pulled a black bra from her suitcase and tossed it at Abby.

"Thanks." Abby changed into Sarah's strapless version. Cups the size of cantaloupes engulfed Abby's breasts. Sarah's chest was large, but this was ridiculous. Abby huffed. Sarah inherited the breasts while Abby and Nicole grew up chest-less. How could Sarah get all the assets in the family?

Abby tugged and adjusted the bra. It barely stayed on and the extra fabric formed wrinkles that showed through the thin shirt. Abby feared the bra would be around her waist by the end of the evening. She pulled out a roll of two-sided sticky tape from her toiletry bag. Abby expertly taped the bra to her skin like she'd seen the models do at Von Deez. She slid the shirt back over her head and zipped it. The fabric hugged around her stomach. Sighing, she went back to the living room. Sarah sat in the middle of the floor in a huge pile of clothes. Abby relaxed when she saw Nicole was no longer in the room.

"You look fabulous. What do you think?" Sarah asked sucking in her bottom lip.

Abby sidestepped past a pile of clothes and stood in front of the mirror. A gasp escaped her lips. She didn't recognize herself. Rich golden brown ringlets hung on each side of her face. Alluring eyes stared back at her, a deep azure surrounded by a smoky darkness. Shades of burgundy drenched her lips. Abby smiled. "The makeup's wonderful."

"I'm glad you like it. I don't understand why you wear those ridiculous boots all the time."

Abby stared in the mirror. It really was her there. There wasn't any fake hair. There was make-up, but it enhanced the features she already had. Abby beamed. "Maybe if Jayson comes for the after party, you can do this again."

Sarah sighed. "Do you think it's worth it to spend so much time thinking about him? You have a guy right here that wants to take you out. If you focus on Jayson, you'll never give Ethan a chance."

"What about all the excitement earlier?" Abby stared at her. "I need him for Von Deez." This was typical Sarah. Her attention span didn't last long, especially if it didn't directly involve her.

"Don't get me wrong, I encouraged you. You needed to increase your self-esteem. You had the perfect opportunity. Jayson was a practice run but he's not here and Ethan is." She pulled some of Abby's hair and twisted it into a ringlet.

"Let's see how it goes before I decide what to do with Ethan beyond tonight," Abby said. She didn't want to jinx the night by reading too much into the invitation. Ethan might not even be interested in her. Abby wasn't about to assume anything when it came to guys. Abby sighed. If only Ethan was a face of fashion, the decision about Jayson would be so much easier.

A knock broke the silence in the room, sending Abby's heart drumming against her chest.

Sarah jumped up. "I'll get it. You need to make an entrance. Make sure to give Ethan a chance." She put one final hair in place on Abby's head and left the room.

Abby glanced in the mirror one last time and checked her lipstick. Heat radiated through her body. Part was nerves about this dinner with Ethan. The other was the thought of not thinking about her job for one night. She should concentrate on her internship, but the thought of a date made her stomach perform a double flip.

Abby heard Ethan's voice in the hall. "Here goes nothing," she said sucking in a breath. The hair, the makeup and the new outfit. She let Sarah make her over because she wanted this. She couldn't deny it anymore. It was a date. She snatched her purse off the bed and headed for the hallway.

Ethan's eyes widened when she entered the room, and a smile spanned his lips. "You look amazing."

"Thank you. I like your shirt," Abby said as she returned his smile. She regretted her odd reply, but he appeared to accept it graciously.

Dressed in black pants with a long sleeved white button up shirt under a dark gray sweater vest, he looked stately. A hint of commonness showed in his white shirt that he left un-tucked. It peeked out from underneath his vest over his pants. Somehow, he seemed uncomfortable dressed up. Brown waves sprouted from his head in a disheveled pile of curls. She wondered how long he spent trying to make his hair appear messy. But his eyes, the ice blue she'd only seen on the cold waters of Alaska, sent chills down her.

"I brought you flowers. I wanted to give them to you, but Sarah took them already," Ethan said. His smile reversed into a frown.

"Sounds like her. Thank you for the flowers. I'm sure she's putting them in water." Abby knew Sarah probably thought he brought them for her and not Abby.

Ethan bent over and kissed her on both cheeks. "You ready?" He held the door open for her.

Abby nodded. "We're leaving, Sarah. See you later."

Sarah popped her head around the corner. "Bye. Have a good time."

As Abby glided down the hallway at Ethan's side, all she could think about was what she saw in his eyes. It was definitely a date.

CHAPTER 9

"Did you enjoy your dinner?" Ethan asked. Abby stared at him over the candle in the middle of the table. Its flame flickered, cascading waves of amber light and shadows off his face.

"It was great. Everything was wonderful," she said.

They sat outside in the restaurant's deserted courtyard. They and two other couples were the only ones dining. Abby twisted in the chair so she could view the street. The sun rested high in the sky, despite the late hour. Pedestrians rushed by, carrying bags slung over their shoulders, usually with a baguette of bread peeking out of the top. Cars sped by and honking horns interrupted the otherwise peaceful atmosphere. A cool breeze whipped Abby's hair around her head. She loved it. Back home, she never sat in a courtyard eating and observing the world go by. Evenings were spent in the libraries or at one of her father's endless political functions. The change was a blessing.

"Is Paris different from London? Well, besides the language thing." She circled her fork around her plate and scooped up the last piece of her cheesecake.

"It's busy if that's what you mean. It's nonstop, even at night. Big cities are much the same here in Europe. Most have famous monuments and tourist traps. You won't find many true Londoners dining near the tourist attractions, like you won't find many true Parisians eating at the touristy restaurants near the Eiffel Tower." He picked up his glass and sipped his wine.

"What are you going to show me tonight?" Abby asked, barely listening to his answers. Small talk was not her specialty, but she hated silence, so asking questions kept the conversation flowing. It was what she usually did at all of her father's political functions, a bad habit she wished she could break. They'd been there for nearly two hours. Abby's bottom was numb from sitting on the iron bistro seat. She shifted her legs and transferred her weight to her other leg.

Ethan chuckled. His brown curls bounced up and down in time with his laugh. "You're ready to move on. You haven't experienced many Parisian meals, have you? More than two hours is typical for a dinner here."

"Are you serious? I can't believe it takes that long. You could eat and go shopping in that amount of time. One dinner with you and I'm ready for bed." Abby failed to breathe. She shrank in her seat and pulled her arms around her. "Um...that's not what I meant. I mean, it must be exhausting to sit and socialize for that long every night. I didn't mean I wanted you."

He smiled and she could tell he was trying to hold back his laughter. "Now that I know that you don't want me..." He grinned at her and patted her hand. "I thought you'd like to see Notre Dame. It's close. We can grab some ice cream and walk by the river."

She nodded and relaxed her shoulders, grateful he didn't say anything more about her comment. Ethan motioned for the waiter, who promptly came over and brought the check.

"Are you ready?" he asked. Folding his napkin in a symmetrically square, he set it on the table. Abby set hers next to her plate in a jumbled mess. She stole a peek across the table and saw he'd already left money for the bill.

They walked a few blocks, following a side road. The crowd grew as they neared Notre Dame. They passed a few cafes with tourists jammed around the tables. Laughter filled the air as several tour groups blocked the sidewalk, posing for a photo. Weaving around the crowd, Abby followed Ethan into a vast courtyard. He stopped, causing her to nearly run into his back.

"What do you think?" he asked.

Abby followed his gaze. Spotlights lit up the two wide towers shooting up from the foundation. The white stone of the Cathedral that she remembered from pictures was replaced with a golden hue.

"It's beautiful. I've seen photos, but I didn't realize all the detail. The carvings are..." She didn't finish. Abby scanned the three archways carved over the doors. The sheer size of the Cathedral dwarfed the surrounding buildings. She caught a gargoyle staring back at her. A shiver went down her spine at the sight of the eerie creature.

"The small statues right above the portals, that's the Kings' Gallery." Ethan pointed to the middle of the building to a line of carvings above the doors. "The center window there, that's the West Rose Window. We'll come back during the day, so you can tour the inside." He stared up at the towers.

"It's amazing how they were able to build such a magnificent building. We don't have anything like this in the United States," Abby said. "Well, not in Boca Raton anyway."

He laughed. "No, you don't have too many buildings this old. Where is Boca Raton?"

"Florida." It felt great that he had no idea where Boca Raton was or who her family was. She twirled one of her ringlets in between her fingers. "Have you always lived in London?"

Ethan stared at the building a few seconds longer before turning his gaze back on her. "For the last few years, I've spent the school year here and summers in London. I'm here this summer for a job." He shoved his hands in his pockets, causing his shoulders to tense.

"So your family lives in London?"

Ethan didn't answer right away but he shook his head. "I have an uncle in Manchester." He combed his fingers through his hair and turned to face her. "Would you like some ice cream? There's a great cafe down the street."

Abby nodded. She thought she detected some sadness in his answer. Something she could certainly understand, not wanting to talk about life, especially family. Abby and Ethan wandered through the courtyard in front of the Cathedral. Cuddling couples occupied several park benches that seemed to be standing guard on the outer portion of the squared yard. Abby wondered if she'd ever be sitting in the park with him.

"Abby."

Abby blinked. Her cheeks burned when she realized Ethan was trying to get her attention.

"Did you decide on what flavor of ice cream?" he asked.

Could he tell she zoned out the entire time they were strolling across the courtyard? She cleared her throat. "Chocolate is fine with me." She caught a quick glimpse of his face as he leaned over the counter to talk to the store clerk. Abby didn't think he noticed her daydreaming. It hadn't been long, only a few minutes. How could she be thinking about him that way? She didn't need to get involved. She had one objective and that was to develop a great campaign for Von Deez. No distractions and Ethan was definitely a distraction.

Ethan nudged her on the shoulder. "One chocolate ice cream."

Taking the cone, Abby licked the melting ice cream as it dripped off the side. "Thanks."

"Let's sit over there," Ethan said.

Abby followed him to a wrought iron park bench nestled under a group of trees. She plopped down beside Ethan. "I love ice cream."

Ethan smiled as he licked his own melting cone. "I'm glad you're enjoying it," he said after a few minutes.

"So what else is there to do in Paris?" Abby studied the continuous line of tourists who paraded around the park, stopping to snap a few pictures of Notre Dame, then continuing on down the street.

"Depends on where your interests lie. There are hundreds of museums, the Louvre, Musee D'Orsay. As for the nightlife, there are several bars near campus where we hang out. You and your sisters should come."

Abby cringed. The thought of going to a club with Nicole and Sarah nauseated her since it always reminded her of her brother's accident. She forced her reluctance out of her mind. "Sounds like fun. Thanks for showing me around."

"No problem. I was wondering if you'd like to meet me for lunch tomorrow." He moved closer to her, his leg touching hers. The heat of his breath warmed her cheek. Sensing his mouth moving to her lips, Abby lowered her shoulder to evade his advance. Her elbow hit the arm of the bench, sending the cone into her lap. She stared as the chocolate ice cream formed a half frozen half liquid puddle between her legs. It seeped through her pants and goose bumps surfaced on her skin. She froze up, just like the ice cream, when he tried to kiss her. Would the kiss have been that bad? He was trying to kiss her, right? Now, she wasn't sure what his intentions were.

Abby grabbed her napkin and tried to blot the mess. "I can't believe this. I made it all the way through dinner without spilling anything." She searched for more napkins. Ethan handed her all he had. He laughed, but it was friendly laugh. Certainly not one that was making fun of her.

"I didn't know ice cream was a new fashion, but you wear it well. I'll get you some more napkins." He got up and went back to the ice cream parlor.

Heat radiated off of her cheeks. Would he try it again? There was still the goodbye. Part of her was thrilled with the prospect of his kiss, while the other still wanted to recoil and hide. What would it be like to kiss him? She needed to get over this nervousness. He was normal, and that's what she wanted, so why was it so hard?

Ethan returned and handed her some napkins. Abby wiped the ice cream off her pants. She still wasn't sure if kissing him was the best idea but dropping ice cream on her pants was not the ideal diversion. Plus, she wouldn't have any props later, if she chickened out again. She rubbed at the stain but only managed to wipe pieces of the napkin on her pants. Small white specks decorated the stain.

"Would you like some water so the stain won't set?" he asked.

Abby ceased rubbing the spot and snuck a quick look at Ethan. Was this really a guy talking to her? Did he actually know what would make a stain not set? Usually, it was club soda or some weird thing like that. Abby wadded up the napkin in despair. "No, it's only ice cream. Besides, it's on the pants, so it won't be noticed."

"I meant for the chocolate stains on the shirt," he said.

Abby saw the brown specks on the turquoise fabric, scattered around the hem near her waist like little freckles. Abby held her breath. "No. It's silk. It needs to be dry-cleaned. Do you know of a good place near campus?" The longer Abby stared at the stains, the larger they seemed to get. Sarah would kill her.

He sat beside her. "I'll take it with me tonight and drop it off tomorrow on my way to work."

"You're working on a Saturday?" Abby asked. She thought only crazy industries like fashion required people to work weekends.

"Finishing my thesis paper. I get more done there than on campus. It's hard to concentrate with so many people coming and going," he said.

"What's your paper on?"

Ethan grinned. "You want to hear about some boring thesis?"

Abby laughed. "It could be interesting. The topic has to be entertaining for someone to write over two hundred pages on it."

He shook his head. "Nope, it's a boring subject. I won't subject you to the torture." He finished the last bite of his ice cream. "You ready for a stroll along the river?"

Abby yawned. "Do you mind if we headed back to campus? I'm getting tired." Images of him grabbing her hand and putting his arm around her as they strolled in the moonlight entered her head. She feared that a romantic stroll would lead to other things and why rush it? Knowing her, she'd jump in the river if he tried anything.

"Sure. Let's head back." He stood and offered Abby his hand. Smiling, she took it and lifted herself off the bench. A simmering hunger flowed through her from his touch.

The wind picked up as they crossed the bridge over the Rhine River. Abby looked back one last time at the Cathedral. The golden lights flickered as tree limbs swayed in the breeze, playing tricks with the light and casting shadows on the ground. He hadn't let go of her hand.

CHAPTER 10

Bloody hell. That was all that ran through his head since Abby and he left the restaurant. Ethan gritted his teeth and held her hand. She played a good act. Shy like she was innocent, but he knew it was a lie. Someone as reserved as Abby pretended to be wouldn't send emails to a guy she hardly knew, and she wouldn't go out with a stranger like him. He didn't know how much longer he could fake being smitten with her, but he'd have to continue for a while. Once Tom informed Senator Rodgers that Abby had contacted Walters, the Senator insisted an agent be assigned to Abby for the summer. He didn't want his daughters exposed to any threats, especially after the loss of his son. Ethan didn't blame him. The brief detailed the accident. His kids were travelling down the coastal highway on their way back from a party. A storm had recently passed through the area. Abby's car hit standing water and hydroplaned into a tree. There wasn't much the EMTs could do for Jacob Rodgers. Twenty-four, the same age as Ethan, too young to lose your life. The only thing that confused him was that the details leading up to the accident were vague, as if they were deliberately left out. He contributed the omission to the Senator. High ranking government officials were known to strike sensitive material out of regular reports. He'd ask Tom for the full report.

Ethan forced his mind back to Abby. All he could think about was the incoming message in Walter's email account earlier this afternoon. The intentional blow-off at the computer lab was so she could email him. He wondered why she agreed to this date. She'd been quiet the whole night, almost like she wanted to be somewhere else. The more she remained a mystery, the more motivation he had to pursue her against his better judgment. He should leave her alone. If she was determined to be with Walters, then so be it. It wasn't like he had to date her to protect her.

If Abby hadn't been involved with his suspect, he would've dumped her right after lunch yesterday. He was playing second best to Walters, and even if this was a ruse, he didn't like coming in second. But he wouldn't stop. He had orders to keep her safe, and he wouldn't ignore them. It was the detective in him that kept him around but his desire to stay was more than the orders he had to follow. He'd arrived at her apartment, expecting the mousey girl from the other day, but he'd gotten a caramel-haired version of Sarah. He barely kept his eyes and his hands off of her all night.

"How many more stops is it?" Her soft voice interrupted his thoughts. The subway car rumbled along the tracks, squeaking every so often as the car shifted in the turns.

"One more. Cité Universtaire."

"I appreciate the tour. If Sarah and Nicole do one of their disappearing acts, I'll be able to find the metro and get back to the apartment." She let go of his hand and sat down in the seat closest to the door. Her eyes stared at the map on the far wall.

Ethan plopped down beside her. "Paris is a safe city, but I don't recommend riding on the metro alone late at night." He suppressed the urge to jerk her up and shake some sense into her. Her attitude was so nonchalant. She should be more aware of the danger, but he had no idea how to tell her so it didn't sound like a lecture. He was sure she got enough of that from her parents. Plus, he felt it was ironic for him to warn her when he was in fact lying to her.

"I won't make it a habit." She punched him lightly on the shoulder. "If I need help, I'll call you."

The gesture surprised him, and he smiled. "Does that mean you want my number?" He held up his mobile.

Her eyes grew wide, and she shifted in her seat so his leg no longer brushed up against her thigh. "I guess so." She pulled out her phone. "What is it?"

"Let me do it. It's a U.K. number, so it has a special entry." He took her phone and pushed a few buttons to access her phone book. After entering his information, he looked over and saw her studying the map again. Glancing at the screen, he flipped through the contents on her directory. Nothing with Jayson's cell phone number. He could eliminate having to access her phone records. All she had was his email address. Shifting his eyes, he noticed her fiddling with a button on her purse. He quickly focused on her text messages next. Nothing but one from Von Deez. Even though Ethan knew it wasn't related to the case, he opened it. He held his breath as he read, a wave of guilt flowed through him, but it didn't last. Guilt wasn't an admirable trait when deception was a requirement for the job. He scanned the text. She wasn't embellishing her internship and his curiosity heightened again. Who was this girl?

He exited the messages. "Here you go," he said as he set her phone back on the main screen.

She took the phone and dropped it in her purse. "I'll call you if I get my luggage stuck on the stairs again."

He laughed. She had a sense of humor, a nice change from the aloofness that dominated their previous encounters. "Try not to pack so much." The subway slowed, and he motioned for her to move toward the door.

"Most of those bags were Sarah's."

He shook his head. "Nope, not buying it. As an intern for Von Deez, I suspect all those bags belonged to you."

She giggled, and the curls that framed her face fell and covered her eyes. His hand automatically reached out and pushed back her hair. He liked the feeling of her skin against his too much. The soft and delicate smoothness. He pulled back, letting his hand drop to his side and watched her exit the subway.

They continued up the block and through the main entrance on campus. Several guys stood by the large oak near the library. They stopped their conversation and stared at Abby. Ethan couldn't help but glare at them. She wasn't aware of the attention and his anxiety heightened. Surely, she knew the reactions she was getting. He looked over at her and knew instantly that she wasn't acting. She truly was oblivious to the attention. Those guys would've been over there talking to her if he wasn't around. How was he going to protect her? He wrapped his arm around her waist and guided her up the alley to the apartment.

They ascended the stairs and walked down her hallway. He followed behind her and studied the curves of her hips. Ethan swore under his breath. He needed to end this. He couldn't risk compromising the case because he can't keep his feelings in check. He should observe her from a distance. He'd break off the contact after tonight. Play one last act and get out.

"I had a great time tonight," Ethan whispered. His lips closed in on her ear. He wasn't so sure he was playing now. He meant it. If this was the last time he was close to Abby, he wanted to make sure he remembered her.

Abby shied away and opened the door, allowing the hall light to engulf the dark apartment. Laughing, he followed her as she moved across the room with a renewed quickness, an obvious ploy to put distance between them.

His eyes stayed glued to the muscles in her calves, the tan skin peeking out from her capri pants. The flip flopping in his mind aggravated him. He'd always stuck to his decisions, but he was relenting. He needed a good challenge, something to occupy his time until the team got back from Rome. She needed someone to look after her. She had made several bad choices, getting involved with Jayson, inviting that bloke to Paris, and there was her naïve trust in Ethan. She'd asked him into her apartment. Rules were different in Paris. An invitation like this to a French guy was an invitation to bed. He sighed and closed the door behind him.

Abby flicked the light switch and motioned to the room. "I would offer you a seat, but you can see we don't have much furniture. There are chairs by the table or the beds."

Ethan almost choked. This girl was beyond unbelievable. Her innocent comments were sending him into a crazed state of desire. He very much would love to see her bed, with her in it. The heat rose in his body, and he suppressed the surge of desire that ran through him, surprised that it hit him without any warning. After a few deep breaths, he scanned the bare room. Most students didn't have any more furniture than they did. He hadn't when he'd lived on campus.

"I'm going to get out of this shirt," she said. Her voice invaded his thoughts, and he realized he was staring at her. He caught her silhouette exiting the room. He should've said goodbye at the door. He broke every rule he'd set tonight.

He took two long strides across the room and opened the window. The crisp breeze penetrated the stuffy room and cooled him off. He kept telling himself that he was only there on Tom's orders. He had to remember, the case was most important thing. He'd give anything to be in Rome right now. It would eliminate his unexplained desire for Abby. Maybe he was too much *in character*. He was supposed to play it as if he was crazy about her. He was playing the part too well. Ethan scanned the street. Horns blared as cars passed through the intersection outside the barrier wall. Sirens wailed in the distance. Paris was awake tonight. The breeze developed into a steady wind and his arms shuddered.

The floor squeaked behind him. He turned to see Abby standing near the table, in an old T-shirt with two holes near the waist. The over-sized shirt did little to hide her curves. He knew it wasn't her intent, but her attire made her even sexier. He smiled and let his eyes scan her body. "You look comfortable." He moved closer to her.

Her shoulders stiffened as she thrust her arm out and held the soiled blouse. "For the dry cleaners."

He continued his advance, more focused on pursuing this game. He studied her eyes. They were no longer passive— but a bluish fire erupted from them. He affected her more than she wanted to admit. Grinning, he took the shirt and held it by his side. His hand caught her chin. Before he knew it and before he thought better of it, he locked his lips on hers. He felt her relax, and he deepened the kiss. A craving for her crossed into his core. He brushed his hand across her cheek. The warmth scalded his fingers. A few seconds later, he backed away, surprised by the void her lips' departure created within him. He drew in a deep breath. The shock on her face pretty much summed up his feelings too. His mouthed curled up into a sly grin. He wouldn't detail this in his report. Tom would kill him and label this as an unnecessary series of events. He crushed the shirt between his fingers. "Ab..."

"Sarah will be home any minute," she blurted out.

Ethan sensed her defenses resurfacing and he couldn't help toying with her. "She's with Patrick?"

Abby nodded.

"She won't be home anytime soon." He exhaled a deep breath. He needed to stop before he did something stupid. She was an assignment, not a casual date. This was exactly why Tom should've assigned Nols this duty. Ethan liked the job when it dealt with criminals, not when it involved witnesses that may or may not be involved. He released her hand, not even realizing that he was still holding it. "I need to go anyway. It's an early morning for me tomorrow." He headed for the door. "You never did answer my question about lunch."

Abby stood silent, and he felt sure she'd decline the offer. It would be better for both of them if she did. A few seconds later, she smiled. "Sounds great."

"I'll be here around noon."

She nodded and followed him to the door. "Thanks for the dinner and ice cream."

"You're welcome," he said. Leaning in on the door frame, he pulled her to him and kissed her on the cheek. "Good night." He let her fall back from his grasp as he pulled the door shut. He knew Tom didn't mean to keep that close contact. He couldn't help himself. Every time he tried to put distance between them, he got closer. Abigail Rodgers was trouble. More trouble than any criminal he'd ever encountered.

CHAPTER 11

Why hadn't he emailed? Didn't he receive her message? Or is he not going to write back? Abby stared at the computer screen. One new message from her mother. That was the only email today. It had been more than a week and nothing from Jayson. Maybe she should send another email in case he didn't get the first one. It's possible it didn't make it to his inbox. It could be in his junk mail, and he never saw it. Panic rose in her. That had to be it. He never got it. Abby hit the new message button.

"Hey."

Abby swiveled around in her chair. Nicole stood behind her, staring over Abby's shoulder. Abby shoved some papers in her outbox and moved over to Gilda's desk. "What are you doing here? Don't you have a job?"

"I got off earlier. Don't you realize it's almost five? Get any good emails?" Nicole's eyebrows arched up.

Abby frowned. She had no idea how Nicole could traipses around Von Deez like she owned the place and not one person questioned her. Nicole thought the world catered to her and owed her its undivided attention. She'd visit Abby's office regardless if Abby asked her not to come. Abby sighed and stared at the computer screen. "No, nothing. I got one from Mom, but that's it. I don't

understand. It's been several days. He can't be that busy."
She saw her trust fund, her job, everything slipping away.
What would she write in the second email? She didn't want
to say that she thought he didn't get the first one. What if
he did and didn't want to email her back? She'd look
stupid.

Nicole pushed aside some patterns in the seat and sat.
"It probably isn't a real email address. You don't know this
guy. I wouldn't spend any more time worrying about it."

"I wouldn't, but you told Gilda about him. I need him
for the campaign. I thought about sending him another
message." Abby put away the ribbons that Gilda used
earlier to salvage a dress Jean-Claude practically ripped off
a model. As he put it, she didn't wear it well.

Nicole's nose crinkled. "Why? He obviously doesn't
want to talk to you. Find someone else."

"Who are you finding?" a feminine voice asked behind
them.

Abby spun around to see Sarah hovering over them.
Abby frowned. This was turning out to be a great day.
Sarah scooted a chair across the room and sat down. She
dumped her bag on the table. Abby cringed and prayed
Gilda didn't return anytime soon. Her sisters were
determined to get her fired with these daily visits.

"Nothing ," Abby said.

A snort bellowed beside her. "Come on. Abby. Share
your problem with Sarah. She was dying to help you out on
the plane. Surely, she can come up with a plan now,"
Nicole said.

Abby faced the computer. She couldn't actually see
the screen. All she saw was red. She had to keep her hand
on the mouse or she'd have hit Nicole. Wasn't it enough
that Jayson hadn't responded?

Sarah's eyes darted to the computer. "Is this about
Jayson? Did he email you?" She grabbed Abby's arm,
pushing her out of her way.

"No, he didn't. Nicole thinks it was a hoax." Abby
blocked the screen. "You need to go. I have to proof this
look book for Paris Fashion Week." She opened the
collection of model photographs for the fashion show and
flipped through the pages, hoping her sisters took the hint.

"Oh." A frown appeared on Sarah's face. It certainly wasn't the reaction Abby was expecting. She seemed almost disappointed that Abby hadn't heard from Jayson. Sarah's frown was gone as quickly as it had come. "Nicole's right. You should be concentrating on Ethan. I hear he's into you." Sarah retrieved her compact out her bag and touched up her mascara. All she ever did was reach for that mirror. She'd be a great spokeswoman for a cosmetics company, probably an excellent candidate for Von Deez's new mass market skincare line.

"I told you already. We're friends. You may spend your nights with Patrick, but that doesn't mean I have any desire to spend mine with Ethan." Abby stared at the computer screen. Ethan's kiss affected her more than she'd expected. It was unlike anything she'd ever felt, and the intensity scared her. She could still taste his kiss, a combination of heat and coffee. It still made her insides burn with a hunger she couldn't quite place.

"Is that what this is about? My nights with Patrick. You're not my keeper, Abs. I can stay with whomever I want." Sarah snapped her compact shut, shattering the calm in the room.

"Nights with Patrick? Do tell." Nicole leaned closer.

Abby glanced over at Sarah. She didn't know why Sarah's actions bothered her, but they did. She didn't come home the night Abby had gone out with Ethan. She'd stayed with Patrick. She'd known him less than forty-eight hours, and she'd stayed with him. Why? Did she expect anything serious to come out of it? Abby hated that Sarah thought sex was just a tool, but she and Abby never did see eye to eye when it came to guys or relationships anymore. Ever since the accident, Sarah used men like they were disposable. She tossed them aside before the relationship became anything close to serious.

"I'm concerned. You hardly know him," Abby said.

"I know enough. He's gorgeous. You need to loosen up, or you'll never have any fun. If you had sex once in a while, it would ease all of your uptight tension. That night with Ethan didn't do much good. You still act like you have a corn cob up your butt."

Nicole choked on the water she was drinking. "Seriously, Sarah. You can't judge Abby for not having a serious relationship. Most of the time, you're practically done with the foreplay before you leave the bar."

"I'm enjoying myself. I love men. There's nothing wrong with that," Sarah said.

"Yes, you enjoy yourself a lot." Nicole poked Sarah in the hip.

Sarah laughed as she tried to fend off Nicole's jabs. "I do try."

Abby stared at them, obviously in the minority. Abby didn't feel comfortable casually sleeping with guys. She wasn't in it for just sex. Was she different? Were the majority of people in it for sex first, then companionship second? Maybe that's why she hadn't had many serious relationships. Everything was about sex first. The only guy she'd considered her boyfriend was Chad. They'd dated for about nine months until he decided to find his sexual pleasure elsewhere, when he'd gotten tired of waiting for her. Maybe it was time to look at the physical side of things.

"If he hasn't emailed you by now, he's not going to reply." Sarah brought Abby back from her thoughts.

"I'm thinking about sending him another email in case he didn't get the first one." She bit her lower lip.

"Don't do that. You're prolonging what you know is going to happen. Nothing." Sarah picked up her bag. "Patrick and I are going out tonight. A bunch of his friends will be there. You two want to go?"

"Count me in. I need a few drinks," Nicole said.

"I'll pass." Ethan would be there. This was her usual response when she liked a guy. Avoidance. She had no idea how to act, and she didn't want to risk behaving like an idiot.

"You can only get to know people if you actually go out and meet them," Sarah said in her stern motherly voice as she and Nicole headed out the door.

Abby stared at the computer screen thinking about what Sarah had said. Abby met lots of people, but she usually didn't meet too many people in bars and clubs. Sarah and Nicole thrived in that atmosphere, while Abby usually froze. But when did she not freeze up? She shook off her insecurities and brushed Sarah's criticism from her mind. She moved the mouse and clicked the refresh button on her email. One new message popped up on her screen.

"Ms. Rodgers. Come here, please," a stern male voice bellowed across the hall.

Abby squeezed her eyes shut. Had Jean-Claude heard? He'd surely reprimand her for goofing off.

"Oui, Monsieur?" Abby asked as she jumped up and ran across the hall to Jean-Claude's studio. She spotted him on his knees near a mannequin, pressing the hemline of a pant leg. He snatched a pin from his arm band and stuck it in the fabric.

"Take that thread and sew the other leg." He pointed to a huge box full of thread spindles over by the drawing table.

Abby grabbed a needle and black thread and dropped to her knees.

"I hate celebrities. They insist on wearing the latest designs, but they refuse to come in for a fitting." He huffed as he pulled the thread and cut it with scissors. "You realize this outfit will be seen in Hollywood. Everyone will want one."

Abby carefully pushed the needle in the fabric to tack the hem. "Gilda mentioned that every time you dress someone, she has hundreds of requests from magazines for a sample."

Jean-Claude ran his hand across the length of the pants. "Perfect. The seamstress can finalize the hem, and it should be ready." He rose to his feet and went back to the desk. "You're staying late?" His brows shot up with the question.

"I have to finalize the look book layouts for the show."

He laughed. "I figured you'd be out celebrating the weekend with the rest of the staff."

"No, not me." Abby loved the work, but she didn't care for the lifestyle most in the industry lived. Drugs, alcohol, and sex all ran rampant in the industry. The irony that she'd chosen an industry so opposite to her personality often made her laugh. But her job was one way to show off her photography.

"Those girls, are they models you have lined up?"

"No, they're my sisters. They dropped off dinner," she said, almost laughing at the lie. It would be a long time before they dropped off dinner for her.

He nodded. "I see the family beauty. You all should have been models." He eyed her body. Abby shifted her arms and avoided looking in his direction. She heard rumors that Jean-Claude loved to mix business with pleasure. According to Gilda, it was all gossip. She'd never had proof that he messed with his models.

"I'm clumsy so those heels would get me." She eyed some stilettos sitting in the corner.

He chuckled. "Ms. Rodgers, if I were only younger, you'd be a delight."

Confusion reigning over her, she tried to hide her blushing. His comment wasn't degrading, it sounded like admiration. She knew the tendency of French men. It wasn't uncommon for them to comment on beauty, unlike in the United States, where the same comment would land you a sexual harassment charge. She smiled and tilted her head. "Why would I be a delight?" She shocked herself with her directness.

He took a colored pencil and filled in a drawing of a pleated skirt on his line sheet. "I design you a dress for Fashion Week, non? For your campaign. Perhaps you can find that boyfriend soon."

Abby's eyes widened. Two shocking revelations. Jean-Claude was designing a dress for her. Creating a design especially for her was one of the highest compliments that the head designer could give. But what terrified her the most, what did he mean by finding a boyfriend? Did he know?

Chapter 12

*A*bby returned to her desk and dropped in the seat. He knew. No, he couldn't know or he would have taken her off the project. The campaign was a major advertising venture and Jean-Claude seemed pleased with Abby's work so far. It was possible he didn't know. She moved the mouse and woke up the computer. One new email. Abby held her breath as she stared at the screen. Was she imagining it? No. It was there. Jayson had written her back. Abby stared at her inbox. What was she waiting for? Why hadn't she opened it yet? Barely breathing, she clicked on the email.

Abs,

How's Paris treating you? I'm sure now that you're settled, you've been out partying. The tennis tournament has going great. I've won my first two matches, so I'm hanging in there. Speaking of our bet, I'll be in Paris in a few weeks. Would you like to get together for lunch or something? I won't have much time, but let me know if you can make it.

Jay

Abby smiled as she leaned back in the chair. He was coming to Paris. She couldn't believe it. Abby thought he'd email her back, but she didn't think they'd be meeting so soon. He didn't say how long he'd be there, but there might be a chance he could come back for Fashion Week. Sarah and Nicole would die when she told them that he emailed her. Too bad they had already left. Abby glanced up at the clock. It was after six. She'd send him a reply later tonight. She logged off the computer and gathered her bag. Her dream was still alive. She might still be able to produce her 'boyfriend.'

Abby hurried out of the building toward campus. A slight breeze blew, but provided little relief from the blazing sun. The last few days had been torture. The summer heat finally made its way to Paris and hadn't let up. It had been one of the hottest springs on record in the city. Abby pulled her sunglasses out of her bag and put them on to shield her eyes.

She never exercised this much back home. She usually relied on her car to get her anywhere she wanted to go. In Paris, Abby walked most places and used the metro when she went into the center of town. So far, those trips into town to sightsee were few. The two occasions she went into the city were with Ethan, on their date then lunch the next day. On their second meeting, Ethan was more reserved and never once kissed her, much to Abby's disappointment. Those two dates were some of the best times she'd had in Paris so far. As for the rest of her time, it was spent at Von Deez and on campus. Abby wanted this, didn't she? It's what she'd worked for, but she kept wondering if she missing the fun in life.

Abby trudged up the hill to the apartment house, climbed the stairs to the second floor, and walked down the corridor. She stopped when she spotted their apartment door ajar. Sighing, Abby pushed it open and closed it behind her. Sarah never locked the door and left it open most of the day. All the windows were open, and Sarah sat in the floor with her legs crossed. This was a common sight since they still didn't have a couch.

"You want to wear one of these outfits tonight?" Sarah asked as she stared at the clothes.

Abby laid her bag on the kitchen table. "I'm not going." She opened the refrigerator and selected a soda. Abby glanced over at her sister. She wanted to tell someone about Jayson's email. She longed for the advice

Sarah used to give but that no longer happened. She wanted to shout that he emailed her to anyone who'd listen. Abby bit her lip in an attempt to keep her mouth shut.

"You should go. You've only been out with us once since we got here. You're missing so much fun. Do you like this one?" She held up a tiny knit tank top with delicate white lace detail at the bottom. Abby loved the style but knew she'd feel awkward in it.

"I'm not into the bar scene. You know that." Abby paused. "I do like the shirt." She sat next to Sarah and studied a green camisole lying next to her. How did Sarah get away with wearing this stuff? Abby would be constantly trying to cover herself the whole night if she wore something so revealing.

"We could go to a dance club. You like dancing. Patrick would love to see my moves." She twisted her upper body in some weird dance motion. A mischievous smile crossed her lips. "Please, Abs. You have to come. You sit in this apartment every night like a hermit. I know it has to do with Jayson. You're hoping he'll email you. Forget him, and come out with us."

Abby loved having the apartment to herself when her sisters were out. She felt like she could think without interruption. If Sarah only knew that she was avoiding Ethan because she was attracted to him, Sarah would pitch a fit. Abby laughed. "If I go tonight, will you lay off me for at least a month? I don't go out every night like you, and that's not going to change." Her desire to see Ethan was growing by the minute so it wasn't hard to say yes.

Sarah jumped up and pressed her in a hug. She held Abby tight, almost cutting off her circulation. "What do you want to wear? I have this cute purple cami or maybe the blue tank top?"

She threw the shirts at Abby, and they landed in her lap. Abby remembered her date with Ethan. She didn't feel comfortable the whole night in the skimpy top Sarah had picked out for her.

"How about this one? It's perfect." Sarah held up a see-through white T-shirt with a black skull and cross bones on the chest.

"I'm not a skull kind of girl. I'll wear my own clothes." Abby started out of the room, when something hit her shoulder. She looked down at the white T-shirt lying on the floor at her feet. Smiling, Sarah tossed another shirt in Abby's direction. Abby picked them up and went into the bedroom. Throwing the shirts on the bed, she reached down to take off her shoes. Yawning, Abby sat back on the bed and thought of Jayson. No matter what happened, he'd make a great friend.

...The Eiffel Tower at night. The two of them. The breeze blowing through her hair. She felt herself drifting off. Ethan would offer Abby his coat. As he draped it around her shoulders, he'd lift his hand and brush his fingers across her cheek. They'd feel rough against her skin. He'd shake her arm.

"Abby. Sweetie." His powerful hold transformed into a gentle nudge.

"Abs..." Abby opened her eyes and saw Sarah standing over her.

"Abs, you fell asleep. You only have fifteen minutes before we leave."

Abby rubbed her eyes. Lifting her head off the pillow, she thought of the two shirts Sarah had given her. She'd have to wear one of them and borrow Sarah's strapless bra since her black bra was dirty. Abby stood up and stretched her arms. Taking some of her sticky tape off the night stand, she taped the cups to her chest. Just a little insurance to make sure the bra didn't fall off. Abby laughed and shook her head. The things she did to look good. She pulled the black tank top, then the skull shirt over her head and tried to stretch the material out so it didn't cling to her body. The top shirt fell off her shoulder, draping along her upper arm. The black tank peeked out from underneath the T-shirt and rested over her shoulder. Abby felt like she dropped out of a classic eighties movie. Give her a belt to cinch up the waist and some legwarmers, and she'd be good to go back in time. They say everything comes back in style every twenty-five to thirty years. She'd seen something similar in Von Deez's fall line last week.

Sarah appeared behind her and stared at her in the mirror. "You look great, Abs. Hurry up and put on some make-up. We're supposed to meet the guys in thirty minutes." Sarah puckered her bright pink lips as she touched up her lip gloss then left the bathroom.

Abby smeared some foundation on her face and smoothed it out with a sponge. She chose Sarah's navy eye liner and traced a thick line around her eye. Having Sarah as a sister did have its advantages. Her tips did wonders for Abby's makeup application. Abby quickly twisted her hair up and pinned it so small twigs hung down, framing her face.

"You ready?" Sarah popped her head in the doorway. "I don't know why it takes so much effort on my part to get you out." She chuckled as she tossed a bag at Abby.

Catching the purse, Abby picked up her wallet, lip gloss, and keys, stuffing them in the bag as Sarah shoved her out the door. Abby pushed Sarah's hands off her back. "Okay. I'm going. I'm not backing out."

Chapter 13

"Everyone who's anyone goes to Coco Lobo. Abs, your man, Ethan, will be there," Sarah said, smiling as she glided down the sidewalk. Nicole rolled her eyes as Sarah linked arms with Nicole.

Abby laughed. "Great. I was hoping to avoid him." Why couldn't she admit it? She liked him. Why was it so hard for her to go out and have a good time?

"Ethan seems like a great guy. Even if you're not interested in him that doesn't mean he won't make a good friend," Nicole said.

"I'm sure he wants to be more than friends. He made that perfectly clear the other night," Abby said. She was excited about the prospect but didn't want her sisters to know. If they did, they'd turn face and encourage her toward Jayson.

Nicole let out a laugh. "You can control him. He's probably so crazy about you that he wouldn't want to scare you off."

Abby shook her head. Ethan wasn't the issue. The problem was her. She struggled with having fun since the accident. Why did she deserve to have a life when her brother was dead? Even through the guilt, she couldn't stop thinking about Ethan.

"The club looks crowded tonight. The guys better have a table. I don't want to have to stand all night." Sarah's bottom lip puckered out into a small pout as if she were practicing for some performance to get her way. Abby bet she did that with Patrick. He was probably a sucker for her dramatics. When they got to the door, the bouncer eyed Sarah, then ushered them in.

Strobe lights lit up the club. Straight in front of them stood a huge elevated dance floor filled with bodies moving to the beat of a French dance mix. People jammed the bar off to the left as bartenders manufactured drinks like an assembly line. Tables lined the right side of the club. Abby scanned the room noticing how everyone dressed like they stepped off the latest fashion show runway. There wasn't an unattractive person in the room. Most of her co-workers were probably there. Sarah would pick the hottest nightspot in town. Abby thought she saw a few familiar faces near the bar.

"You must be a thief because you stole my heart," a voice with a strong accent whispered behind her.

Abby twirled around, surprised to see a blonde-haired guy standing there. He was dressed in a faded gray T-shirt, khaki shorts that had seen better days, and some old flip flops that were too small for his feet. His big toe fell off the side. He looked like he just came from the beach.

"What's your name? I'm Kane. I think you could be my angel."

Abby laughed. "I'm sure you can find someone else that line will work on. It's not me." His hazel eyes bore into her. He was cute but warning bells went off in her head.

"Come on now. Give a guy a chance. You haven't gotten to know me yet," he said. She had to admit that he intrigued her. Abby smiled at him, trying to hide her interest. How was it she could easily talk to this guy, but she couldn't say two words to Ethan without sounding like a snob?

"Who's your friend, Abs?" Abby heard Sarah say.

Kane's eyes darted away from Abby. "Oh wow. My angel's friends are smokin' hot. My buddies will enjoy this."

Abby giggled. "Sarah, this is Kane. I'm obviously his angel."

Sarah came over and stood beside her. "Oh, Kane is it? Well, Kane, it's nice to meet you. I'm sure you don't mind if I take your angel away, do you?" She clutched Abby's hand and pulled her away.

"I'll be seeing more of you, Angel. I'll be here all night," Kane said with a devilish grin.

Abby saw fire in his eyes. He had trouble written on him and Abby had a feeling Kane would be back before the night was over. She lifted her hand in a shy wave as Sarah jerked her to the left side of the dance floor.

"It seems I'm popular tonight," Abby said as she followed Sarah through a maze of tables and people.

"Good God, Abs. You don't have to talk to every guy that hits on you. There are about a million Kanes in here. You only need to focus on one guy," Sarah shouted over the music. Abby smiled. It wasn't that bad that she was talking to Kane. Wasn't Sarah the one who said she needed to get out and meet people?

The girls snaked through a group of dancers to a booth near the back corner of the club. Abby saw Patrick, Ethan, and a few other guys from campus sitting at the far table. Nicole was already seated next to a guy Abby had seen before but never met. She had a drink in front of her and a cigarette in her hand. Nicole and Sarah only smoked when they went out and that seemed to be the norm for this group. Ethan was the only one at the table not holding a cigarette. He raised his head as Abby approached and grinned. His hair was still a mess with unruly brown curls all over his head. Abby immediately broke into a smile. He was adorable and his boyish grin made him stand out from everyone at the table.

"Hey Abby. We were wondering if you were going to show," Patrick said as he got up from the booth and motioned for Abby to sit in his place. He pulled over two chairs from a nearby table.

Sarah sat in one of the seats and scanned the table. "Where's the waitress? We need some drinks. It's time for Abs to loosen up," she said as Patrick planted a kiss on her cheek.

"I'll go to the bar. What do you want?" Patrick asked.

"Dirty Martini," Sarah said. Patrick glanced over at Abby.

"Maybe some water," Abby said. Sarah glared at her just as Abby felt a sharp stabbing pain in her leg.

"You're going to have a good time. Get her a rum and Coke. They don't serve water here. Are you crazy?" Sarah scowled at Abby as if she did something taboo.

Abby rubbed her shin trying to ease the throbbing from Sarah's kick.

Ethan chuckled. "So how's my Abby been?" He put his arm around her waist and pulled her closer to him.

Abby blushed. "I'm good. How about you?" He must've been at the club for a while. He seemed more relaxed than she'd ever seen him. His slurred speech confirmed her suspicion that he was drunk. Most of the guys at the table probably had been there for a few hours. Beer bottles and empty glasses littered the table. As she surveyed the group, Patrick returned with more drinks and set a large glass in front of her. Abby took a sip. Alcohol burned her throat as she swallowed, and she struggled to hold back a gag. She took large gulps to avoid tasting the drink.

"Not bad. I took the day off and hung out here. Sarah said you didn't like the club scene." Ethan picked up his beer and polished off the remainder of his drink.

"I feel out of place," Abby said. She sipped her drink. The alcohol burned in her throat, and she coughed.

"You work at Von Deez, and you feel out of place here?" He lifted his mug in the air and motioned to Patrick. "Yo, Pat. Go get another round for the table."

Abby remained silent. Why couldn't she relax? It'd been so long since she'd been herself. Sarah was right. She needed to let go and have fun.

Patrick pushed himself up from the table with his hands. "Hey, man. I think this is your round. I'll go get them as long as it's on your tab."

"I'll agree to that. Make sure you refill Sarah and Abby's drinks. They have some catching up to do," he yelled at Patrick, who was already half way to the bar. Abby leaned back in her seat. She barely drank half of her rum and Coke, and they were already ordering more. As she scanned the table, she realized she was in the minority again. Empty glasses sat in front of Sarah and Nicole. They were waiting for the next round to be served.

Ethan shifted in his seat toward Abby. "Start drinking girl. I know that's the only way to get you on the dance floor."

She laughed at the silly grin on his face. Ethan leaned over and pushed her glass closer to her. He was right. That would be the only way to get her out on the dance floor. She swallowed a few more gulps, feeling her body loosening up as the alcohol began to take effect.

After a few more drinks, Abby couldn't recall how long she'd been there but she didn't care. All she cared about was sitting beside Ethan. She hadn't been herself in months and tonight, she felt like herself. She was having a great time with him. Long gone was the nervousness. They'd been talking nonstop and Abby's spirits were floating. It was the first time in a long time, she was happy.

"It's time to hit the dance floor, Abs." Sarah tugged on Abby's hand.

Abby withdrew her arm and hid behind Ethan. "No, I'm happy here. I'm babysitting this glass." Abby clutched her mug. It was actually her third or fourth drink. She lost count a while ago.

Ethan pushed her out of the booth. "Go on. The dance floor is calling you."

"No, I like sitting here," Abby said.

Sarah tugged on her arm. "Nope. You're going out there. None of these guys will dance, so you're my dance partner," Sarah said.

Abby stood and almost tipped over. Her feet and hands tingled every time she moved. Feeling light-headed, she wobbled behind Sarah out onto the dance floor. They pressed through the crowd as a new techno song blasted out of the speakers above their heads. Sarah moved her body in time with the beat and several guys gaped at her. Abby felt awkward standing beside her. Swaying her hips, she tried to mimic Sarah's moves. She closed her eyes and floated with the music. Hearing Sarah laughing beside her, she opened her eyes and saw Patrick dancing with Sarah.

Feeling someone moving with her hips, she smiled knowing Ethan was behind her.

"Hey, Angel. We meet again."

Abby spun around and saw the guy from earlier, rubbing up against her. He took her hand and twirled her around to face him. Disappointment weighed on her. Where was Ethan? Abby looked up into Kane's eyes. What was it with the eyes of all these guys? The intensity was like looking into their souls. Kane and Abby danced the remainder of the song. She put her arms around him. He leaned closer in and kissed her neck. Abby's mind slowly recognized the move and tried to protest, but her lips remained silenced by the alcohol. Something strong pulled her away from Kane's grip. She twisted her body around just as Ethan yanked her toward him. His face had darkened. His icy blue eyes were now heated.

"I believe you need another drink," he said.

Abby nodded, happy he'd finally showed.

"Whoa, Angel. I don't think we're finished." Kane seized her other hand. Abby pulled away before Ethan had a chance to retaliate.

"Maybe later," Abby said as Ethan hauled her off the dance floor. He moved so fast that she tripped over her feet and almost landed on her butt in the middle of the aisle.

"Your loss, Angel," Kane yelled. He danced over to another girl and moved his hands across her hips. Ethan led Abby to the table and motioned for her to slide into the booth. She dropped in the seat and leaned against the wall. Her head swimming, she tried hard to focus, but her eyes grew heavy. Wooziness overtook her and she couldn't concentrate on Ethan's voice. Her head tingled and it was like her thoughts swayed back and forth.

Chapter 14

"You're a bad girl. You reject me then get friendly with the Aussie on the dance floor," Ethan said as he set a glass in front of her. He rubbed his forehead as he studied Abby. He cursed to himself. The thought never occurred to him that she wasn't a drinker. He assumed a few drinks would relax her, and he could ask a few questions regarding Walters without arousing her suspicions. He thought maybe a couple of drinks, but Sarah went beyond that. She had Patrick buy several rounds for everyone and before Abby usually finished hers. He wasn't sure how much she'd had, but he prayed she didn't get sick.

Abby accepted the glass and took a sip. The liquid dripped on her chin and she licked her lips. "When did I reject you? I don't need any more alcohol." Her voice trailed off and she added about four extra syllables to each word.

"It's only water."

She stared inside the glass. "Don't let Sarah catch you with water. You know, since they don't serve it here." Abby positioned her fingers to mimic air quotes.

He laughed. "They don't serve water to Sarah." Abby's nose crinkled, and her mouth opened, but she shut it as if she still pondered his statement. He scooted in beside her on the bench. "I agree. You don't need anything else. You would entice every guy in here."

Abby flung her arm around him. "You saved me from Kane to take advantage of me yourself. How noble of you."

The sweet honey scent of her perfume taunted him and sent his senses into full chaos. He adjusted his arm so it wrapped around her waist. She was within inches of his face. "I'll only do what you want me to do." He couldn't believe he said it. But how else was he supposed to stay close to her? Everything changed when Jayson emailed Abby and offered to meet her in Paris. Tom suspected he might be using her as a distraction for the media, to get them to focus on something other than the match-fixing scandal. He wanted Ethan close to Abby in case she witnessed something and there was also the matter of Abby's father. He wasn't about to let his daughter wonder around Paris without a bodyguard.

Abby leaned her head against the wall, her eyes drifted from him to the dance floor. Ethan scanned the club but didn't see her sisters. Sarah's jacket was gone and he knew Nicole had left with Alex. He shook his head. With family like this, he hated to see her enemies. They left her with that bloke on the dance floor, a stranger she barely knew, a guy that couldn't keep his hands off her. They should have watched out for her, but no one seemed to be looking out for Abby, including herself.

Even though she wasn't dressed up tonight, Ethan still fought the urge to kiss her. Her natural beauty shined through, and she didn't need the fancy get-up to get him riled up. He rubbed her hand. "You want me to take you home? Sarah's gone. She left with Patrick."

"Nicole's here. I'll go back with her."

"She went to another bar with Alex." Her frown confirmed her annoyance and he knew she was considering walking back by herself. He had to stop her. He rotated her shoulders so he could see her face. "I promise to behave. Do you even remember how to get to your apartment?"

She shook her head. "I'm holding you to it. You better be on your best behavior," she said, slurring her words.

Abby slid out of the booth and leaned on Ethan's shoulder as they exited the club.

The cold air sobered him. As they made their way down the street, Abby swayed back and forth.

Ethan pulled her hand and guided her down the dark pathway. "I never realized what a wild girl you are. We definitely have to get you out more often, but we need to keep you away from all the guys." Ethan put his arm around her and felt her shiver. The goose bumps on her arm prickled the palm of his hand. He fought the urge to wrap his arms around her. His mission was to get her home. She was too much of a temptation.

"Yes, I'm a guy magnet. I'm too gorgeous," Abby said to no one in particular.

Ethan wasn't even sure if she was talking to him. He laughed at the sarcasm in her voice. "I'm sure you are."

She fell in step beside him. "I meet guys everywhere. Even on the plane coming over here, I managed to attract a very nice looking tennis player," she said before she clamped her mouth shut with her hand.

He smiled, the perfect opportunity presented itself. "Must be the famous Jayson. Sarah said you were hung up on another guy." Ethan led her down a small path in the park between the canal and campus.

"Sarah told you about Jayson? She can't keep her mouth shut," Abby shouted at a tree that lined the pathway. She wobbled and Ethan pulled on her arm. He slowed down to allow Abby time to catch up.

He rubbed the inside of Abby's hand with his finger. "She told me I need to make an extra effort."

"He's in Rome for a tennis tournament." She relayed the details about the plane ride without any coaxing from him. Abby's voice trailed off and jealousy hit him. She sure did know how to make a man feel worthless. No wonder he couldn't do anything. Jayson had charmed her. She was infatuated with this guy, but she had no idea what he was, a fraud. She knew him only as a tennis player, but Ethan and the rest of the world knew him as Jayson Walters, pro tennis player and one of the best in the world. She didn't have the information on the match-fixing. She didn't have anything but a fantasy to go on.

They continued along the pathway under the umbrella of trees that shielded the moonlight and he could barely make out Abby's silhouette. Ethan ceased his questions. She'd probably forget the conversation by morning. She pulled away from him toward the middle of the sidewalk. Some of her hair had escaped from her hairclip and stuck out wildly. He wondered if she'd have caught his attention if circumstances were different. He was lying to himself when he said no. He'd have noticed her.

Ethan pulled Abby up the stone path to her apartment building and held her arm as she clung onto the handrail.

She fumbled with her key and dropped it on the floor. "You know, the second floor, first floor stuff is a bunch of crap. It should be standard in every country. I should be living on the second floor not the third."

Smiling, he picked up her key and unlocked the door. "I'll be sure to bring it up to the European Parliament." He guided her into the den.

Abby made one circle around the room, then plopped on the floor. "I'm so tired." She flung off her boots. They bounced off the wall and rested in the middle of the paisley rug. As she rubbed the arch of her foot, her eyes darted around the apartment.

Ethan went over to the kitchen. "You want some water?" The tension in his shoulders lessened. She was home now, and he needed to leave.

"Yes."

He came back in the room and sat beside her.

She took the glass from him and drank almost all of it. "Thanks," she said.

He nodded and gazed at her. "I thought you might be thirsty." He was and it wasn't for some water.

Abby scooted closer to him on the floor. Her eyes were a brighter blue, almost glowing. Her lips, an invitation of pink, were flushed from their walk. He shifted further away but, he stopped when he felt her hand on his knee. He needed to leave before this moved past a point of no return, but his body stayed glued beside her.

"Ethan?"

He turned toward her, and she was so close that her hair brushed his skin on his forehead. Her honeyed smell was driving him insane. Putting a hand on her thigh, he took her glass and placed it on the floor next to him. Before he knew it, she pressed her lips against his. The softness tore into him. He caressed her chin with his fingers, letting his lips move to her cheeks. He slid his hand down her arm, feeling the silkiness of her skin. Using his other hand, he fumbled at her waist and pulled the T-shirt over her head, leaving the tank top clinging to her chest. Ethan's body ached as she arched her back so her body pressed against him. Ethan slipped his hand under her tank top, unhooking her bra. He jerked it off.

"Ow!" Abby screamed and pulled her arms up to her breasts.

Ethan saw the tears in her eyes and backed away. "I'm sorry. I didn't mean to be rough."

She raised her hand and frowned as she looked down at her chest. "It wasn't you. It's the price you pay when you have a sister like Sarah who has boobs the size of watermelons." She took a piece of ice out of the cup and placed it on her breast.

Ethan thought the sight of her rubbing ice on her chest would kill him. He knew she was hurt but it was so sexy. He shook his head. "Why are we talking about Sarah's breasts?"

"It's nothing." Abby tried to snatch the bra, but he held it out of her reach.

"No, wait. Why are you putting it back on? I know I couldn't have caused those cuts." He pointed to the ugly pink abrasions now forming on Abby's skin. He stared at the bra and noticed tape on the inside cups.

Abby stared at the floor. "It's a long explanation."

"Explain it to me. I'm dying to hear," he said. He tried to hold back his laughter, but he couldn't imagine what possessed her to put tape in her undergarments.

"I know how it looks, but I had to borrow Sarah's bra, and she's much bigger than me. I used double-sided tape to get it to stay. Models use it all the time. I guess they don't usually get their clothes jerked off."

Ethan chuckled. He was still holding the bra and he pealed the tape out of the cups. "I'm sorry I ripped off your clothes. Didn't know you had them duct-taped on." It was this quirky stuff that made her irresistible and also that she was sitting naked in front of him.

Abby pushed him back as laughter erupted from him. "It's not funny. It's embarrassing."

"No, it's odd but I like odd." He took another piece of ice and placed it on the small pink scratch that had formed on Abby's other breast. She playfully smacked his hand away. He grabbed her and drew her close to him, engulfing her lips in a kiss.

Abby tore at his shirt and tugged it out of his pants. She slid the shirt over his head and threw it on the floor beside them. He saw her eyes widened as she stared at his chest.

He grinned. "You're checking me out." His voice cracked with amusement.

Abby blushed. "I wanted to see what's in front of me. I don't want to miss anything."

He pulled her to him and lowered Abby to floor. He couldn't think about anything else but the pressure building up inside him. Her fingers traced small patterns along his stomach and the feel of her body near his pushed him beyond reason. He was losing himself in her and, for the first time, he didn't care. He wanted her. He kissed her stomach and moved downward. His fingers lingered below her belly button, gently moving back and forth on her skin. He fumbled with the button on her pants. They loosened around her waist as he unzipped them and he let them fall to her ankles.

"Wait, we can't. We have to stop," Abby said between gasps. "I'm sorry."

Ethan rose and moved up to Abby's lips, kissing her as she pushed him away. He laid back on the floor breathless. His quickened heart rate started to slow.

Abby snapped up her tank top and pulled it over her head. Ethan closed his eyes. He was so stupid. What was he thinking? This was wrong. His hand curled into a fist. He opened his eyes and stared at the ceiling. "Couldn't you have stopped about ten minutes ago?" He didn't mean it.

He was thankful she stopped him. He should've been more mature, but he couldn't think straight, not with her around him.

"I... I don't do this sort of thing."

"It's okay. Come here." He reached over and clasped her hand. Pulling her forward, he kissed her on her forehead. His breathing slowed, and he stared at the ceiling for a long time. He was close to crossing the line, close to losing his promotion all because he couldn't keep his pants on. He heard Abby's breathing deepening. She'd fallen asleep with her head on his chest. What was wrong with him? He took advantage of her. She was drunk and obviously not in a mind to consent to sleeping with him.

Ethan gently lifted her and maneuvered his arms from beneath her. After getting his shirt back on, he picked her up and brought her to the bedroom. He laid her on the bed. As he took hold of the covers, his phone vibrated at his hip. He twisted it to see the display, Nols's cell phone.

"Damn." He went back into the living room and closed the door behind him. He flipped the phone open. "Gray here."

"Where are you?" Nols barked.

"In my bed."

"Who's bed? I'm at your apartment and you're not here."

"When did my personal life get to be your business?"

"Since you started dating a certain young woman." There was silence. "Please tell me you're thinking with your brain and not about some ass."

"Sorry to disappoint you, but nothing's going to happen." He forced his voice to be firm. Nols would kill him before Tom had a chance.

"I know you. That girl is your type, and she'll suck you right in."

Ethan's blood boiled. "I know where the boundaries are."

"Make sure you do because if you get involved with her, it can easily be witness tampering. And she's Senator Rodgers' daughter."

"Witness tampering? She doesn't know anything."

"Maybe not now but that could change once Walters shows up. You need to treat her like a witness despite who her parents are. Walters withdrew from the Strasbourg tournament citing tendonitis. He showed no signs of injury in Rome."

"What does Tom think?"

"Don't know. Tom's ready to approach him soon."

"Who's going to lead the interrogation?"

"Tom, with assistance from you, if needed."

Ethan grinned. Finally, some action after weeks of boring surveillance. "So I'll be out of Paris soon?"

"Nope. Tom's going to start the questioning when Jayson shows up for the Paris tournament. You're still on babysitting detail."

Ethan frowned. The tournament was more than a month away. "How long are you back in town?"

"Indefinitely. Tom thought you might need my help. I'm crashing on your couch."

"Fine."

"I'll see you later. The office wants the latest report on Ms. Rodgers tomorrow. You may want to leave out the details about tonight."

Ethan grunted his reply and snapped the phone shut. Nothing got by his partner. Nols knew him too well, and Ethan had no excuses.

He tiptoed in the bedroom. Abby was curled up with her head pressed in the pillow. He pulled the sheet and draped it around her. She grasped his hand, her eyes still closed.

"Stay."

Ethan halted his retreat. She still had his hand clamped in hers.

"I should go," he whispered.

"No, sleep with me..." Her words were soft, but he heard them clearly. The heat rose in him again. He had to remember she was drunk. She didn't realize what she was asking.

"I'm leaving."

"No, stay here...night." She patted the bed.

He sighed. The death grip on his hand intensified. He wouldn't win no matter what choice he made.

Chapter 15

Feeling something thrust up against her spine, Abby tried moving away and closer to the side of the bed, but she was already on the edge. She flipped on her back and pushed the annoying object. Abby opened her eyes. Bright light struck her as it broke past the curtains. Her head pounded, and she shifted her body. She looked over and found Ethan beside her. His bare chest and firm abs peeked out from under the sheet. Was he was naked?

Abby pressed her fingers to her forehead and tried to play last night's events back. What happened after she fell asleep? Her hands felt her own body, discovering she still had on her tank top and pants, but her socks disappeared sometime during the night. She sighed in relief, but her head continued to ache.

Ethan groaned and reached out, placing his arm over her midsection. "Good morning," he said. A sly smile parted his lips. There was a twinkle in his eyes that Abby couldn't mistake.

They didn't... Did they?

She stopped before anything happened. She was sure of it. The last thing she remembered was the two of them on the floor.

Abby pushed his arm off her abdomen. "I didn't think I would wake up and find you still here and in my bed."

"Well, that's not what you said last night. You invited me."

Abby's jaw dropped. "Oh, crap." She sat up in bed. Her stomach lurched up to her throat. "I remember falling asleep. I don't remember an invitation." How could she be so stupid? She was always careful, making sure she never got into situations like this. One stupid night with too much to drink. Stupid! Stupid! Stupid!

Ethan snickered. His lips were pinched together, holding back a smile. He rubbed her arm, and a twinge went through her body.

"You're so cute when you get worked up. I brought you to bed. I figured you'd be more comfortable here instead of on the floor. I couldn't resist when you asked me to stay." Ethan smiled. His hair was more messed up than Abby had ever seen it, but something about the curls tossed around his head seemed appealing.

"I asked you to stay? A gentleman would've saved me the embarrassment of this morning." Abby examined his face for any clue of what had happened, still not convinced she was in the clear.

"You did. I was going to leave, but I'm human. I couldn't refuse after what happened." He smiled as he took Abby's hand and kissed the top of her fingers. It came back to her, their encounter on the living room floor. As a flood of shame hit her, Abby's arms flung out toward Ethan. She heard a crash and glanced down.

Ethan moaned as he laid in the floor tangled in the blanket. "Why did you push me off the bed? Nothing happened. I'm playing with you." He rubbed his ankle as he twisted out of the sheet.

"I'm sorry. Last night wasn't like me. I don't do things like that. It was a mistake and won't happen again," Abby said. Ethan's mouth parted as if he was going to protest when Abby heard the lock click on the outside door. Panic hit her. Jumping out of the bed, she motioned for Ethan to get up. "Shush. Get back in bed."

"I'm flattered. After all the denial, another invitation." Ethan grinned as he crawled back into the bed. His back muscles tightened as he moved across the mattress.

Abby turned away from the temptation. "Keep it up and you may not live to make it out of this bed." She threw the covers over Ethan, quickly rearranging them to disguise the outline of his body. She could hear the muffled laughter through the comforter. She elbowed the mound just as the door opened. Abby heard keys rattle as they were removed from the lock.

"Abs, Nic, you home?"

"Just a sec," she yelled. Jumping off the bed, she ran and cracked the door open. Ethan's head emerged from the pile of covers. "Stay there. Don't move," Abby whispered.

"No problem." He smiled as Abby slid through the small opening and closed the door behind her. Dread crept through her. She'd never be able to explain this. She was twenty-one and felt like a teenager trying to hide her boyfriend from her parents.

"Hey," Abby said as her head began to throb. She was dehydrated and tempted to push Sarah away from the refrigerator to help herself to a drink.

"I guess we don't have any more bottled water?" Sarah closed the refrigerator door. "How was your night?" Sarah popped the top off of a soda can.

"Fine. Ethan brought me home and left." Abby stared past Sarah at the bedroom door. She hoped that was the end of the conversation. She twisted her head and saw that Nicole's door was still shut.

"That's it? Nothing else? You had the perfect guy and the opportunity. That Aussie guy had Ethan so jealous, it couldn't have gotten any greener in that club. He's not going to keep chasing you if you keep blowing him off. You have to throw him a bone once in a while." Sarah set her soda on the table and left the room. Abby held her breath. She exhaled as Sarah bypassed the bedroom door and went on to the bathroom.

"I don't believe this. You have to actually play the game to get..." Her voice trailed off as she closed the door. Abby ran into the hallway stopping in front of the bedroom door. How would she get Ethan out without Sarah seeing him? Sarah would automatically assume something had happened between them if she spotted Ethan in the apartment this morning. Why wouldn't she? Abby would've. The toilet flushed and water ran from the sink. The bathroom door opened, and Sarah's voice continued right where it left off.

"Seriously, Abs. You're a complete mess when it comes to men. Why don't you give Ethan a chance? Is it Jayson? Why are you so hung up on him? A guy who won't return your emails. Because of that stupid Von Deez party?" She stood in the hall, her hands settled on her hips.

"You don't want to lecture me right now," Abby said, her eyes glued to the bedroom door. Her face was hot with anger. "Whether I spend my time with Ethan or with Jayson, it's my choice and no one else's. Besides, you don't know what you're talking about. Jayson emailed me and he's coming to Paris."

Sarah jerked around, her hair whipped around her neck. "Jayson emailed you back?" she asked as she opened the bedroom door.

A scream pierced the air. Abby stopped short of the doorway because Sarah blocked the entrance. Ethan stood beside the bed in nothing but his boxer shorts. Abby's eyes never left his body. His abdominals stiffened to reveal six smaller ripples. Ethan grinned as he grabbed his pants and slid them over his thighs. Abby couldn't breathe as she stared at his crotch as he buttoned the top button on the pants.

"Morning Sarah." Ethan's crooked smile beamed at them.

Sarah's mouth dropped as she stared at Ethan's naked body. Abby held her hand to her chest so her heart wouldn't pound out of her body. He was handsome, standing there in nothing but jeans. It wasn't the body of the lanky guy she'd pictured when they first met.

Sarah spun around, a bewildered look painted on her face. "Why is Ethan standing naked in our bedroom?"

"I figured that would be obvious," Ethan said.

Abby stared at him in disbelief. He needed to shut up. He was only making the situation worse. Her mind was flying with excuses Sarah might believe. Once Nicole found out, she'd tell their father, and he'd send another scathing email discussing her disregard for the family image. It didn't matter that Nicole and Sarah could do the same thing with no consequences.

Sarah stood in the doorway blocking Ethan's exit. "I have a good idea about what happened here. How you were able to do it with Ms. Prim and Proper? Abs, you still surprise me."

"He's going now. Right, Ethan?" Abby asked. The pleading squeak in her voice irked her. She wished he'd disappear. Her feelings aside, his being there wasn't helping her.

"Actually, I was going to ask you to brunch." Ethan bent over to gather the rest of his clothes off the floor. He pulled the shirt over his arms, covering his chest. A bit of disappointment ran through her as his bare skin disappeared under the fabric.

"I don't think so. I have a few errands I need to get finished today," Abby said. The anxiety was worse than before, she had no idea what to say to him after what had happened.

Sarah had already gone back to the den. Abby heard her yelling into the other bedroom. Now Nicole would know, and Abby didn't want to face her. Nicole wouldn't stir for a few more hours since she wasn't a morning person. Abby would have until the afternoon before the interrogation started.

"You can accept my offer, or stay here and get grilled by Sarah about our night together." He smiled obviously pleased with the dilemma he'd created.

Abby sighed. She didn't have much choice since she didn't want to be questioned by her sisters, especially since she was still nursing a nasty hangover. At the same time Abby wanted to be far away from Ethan. Her face felt flushed as she remembered his lips on hers. She refused to look at him. She needed some time for the humiliation to cease. Her stomach growled. It was already past noon, and she hadn't eaten since last night.

"I think you're saying yes." Ethan motioned to her tummy.

"Okay. Give me a minute while I change. Don't say anything to Sarah. She already thinks something is going on." Abby lowered her voice.

"Something is going on," he whispered, but she continued toward the bedroom, ignoring him.

Grabbing some clothes, she moved to the bathroom, leaving him in the bedroom. Abby closed the door and stared in the mirror. Her hair was a tangled ball on top of her head, half hanging out of the ponytail holder. Leftover eye liner was smeared under her eyes, resembling the dark circles of a raccoon. Geez, she looked hideous. How could Ethan be attracted to that? Leftover makeup was not appealing. Abby quickly undressed. She turned on the faucet and washed her face.

Pain seared behind her eyes every time she moved. Brunch sounded better every minute. She craved something greasy to eat and was dying for something to drink. Abby prayed Sarah was not quizzing Ethan about last night. She poked her head in the bedroom and found Ethan sitting on the bed flipping through one of her fashion magazines.

He set the magazine on the nightstand. "You ready?" Standing up, he gave Abby a broad smile. "We can invite Sarah if you want."

She punched him in the arm causing him to laugh even more as they headed toward the door. Sarah sat at the kitchen table with her head lying on a dinner plate.

"We're going out for some food," Abby said. Sarah's only acknowledgement was a slight movement of her shoulders.

Abby let the door close behind them.

"Why were you standing in the middle of the bedroom in your underwear? I told you to stay in the bed," Abby said as they made their way down the hall and out to the courtyard. She hated her sisters knowing anything about her and Ethan. Maybe a few years ago, she'd have told Sarah, but everything was different now.

Scratching his head, he let his hand fall to his waist. "Why not? She's obviously pushing for something to happen between us. Maybe she'll lay off you now. I don't need her help. I know how you feel."

"Oh, yes. It'll be good for your reputation if everyone thought you got me in the sack. You'll get a slap on the back for a job well done from your buddies. Don't think for a minute that last night had any effect on me. It was a mistake." Abby bit her lip and stared at the stones beneath her feet. What a lie. She loved the way he made her feel.

"What's the worst that could happen? She thinks you and I are sleeping together? She'll stop bothering you, and she'll quit hounding me." He flexed his fingers. "I like you, and I know you like me. You can deny it all you want. I already spent one night with you. Want to try for a second?" He caught her eyes with his. "It wouldn't hurt if you threw me a bone once in a while."

Abby's forehead burned. He'd heard their conversation in the hall. "Great. The French make paper thin walls. What else did you hear?"

His mouth curled into a smirk, but he didn't answer. His silence confirmed he'd heard everything including her comments about Jayson. She wasn't sure how she felt about Ethan knowing about Jayson. Jayson was Jayson. She wondered if he was making a play because he was jealous. Her heart and mind were conflicting. Her brain was telling her that Jayson was her ticket to success at Von Deez, but her heart was telling her that Ethan was her ticket to love.

Silence dominated the air between them. Knowing what he wanted combined with her own awkwardness, she wished she could crawl up in a ball and hide under the covers in her bed. Unfortunately, since Ethan had been in her bed, it was no longer a safe haven. She would always remember his naked chest peeking out from beneath the sheets.

Chapter 16

"If we can't talk, then how about a game?" Ethan tilted his head toward the dart board hanging on the pub's center wall. He didn't like it when she was quiet. He wanted her spunky side to come out, the side he saw briefly before she got wasted at the bar. Had he ruined their relationship because of his careless actions? He should've left her apartment without her, but Nols would be waiting on him and Ethan didn't want to face the interrogation. He kept telling himself Abby was the lesser of two evils. He knew his own lack of control was the issue. He'd compromised himself by staying with her, but he hadn't been able to pull himself away.

Abby shook her head, and her hand went up to her forehead. "No, thank you. I'm still nursing a headache." She squinted as the intense light came through the mahogany blinds and cast a brightness in her eyes. The darkness of the pub would've eased her discomfort, but he'd mistakenly picked the table nearest to the window.

"Awe. Come on. It'll be fun. Definitely better than sitting here staring at the wall while we wait for our food."

"Stay away from the darts, and we'll talk," Abby said.

"Tell me, what's so important about this Von Deez party?" Ethan asked. He popped a piece of bread in his mouth, even though he knew his breakfast would be there any minute.

She stared at the table. "It's nothing. Just a project for work. I'm arranging models for the show and organizing the next ad campaign." She'd grabbed a napkin and tore small bits of the paper, forming a pile of scraps.

"It's obviously more than that. You shut down when your sisters mention Von Deez." Ethan didn't have a report that would detail this information, and he wasn't getting anywhere with Abby. She refused to tell him anything about her family.

Abby's head jerked up. "I'd rather not talk about it."

"You want me to get the darts?

She bit her lip and dropped her gaze. He heaved a heavy sigh. She wasn't going to confide in him, and he wasn't going to press her. He knew what it felt like to be guarded. If she knew about his past, how he grew up in the system and started asking questions, he'd refuse to answer too.

Ethan rose from his seat and walked over to the bartender, who was putting away some freshly washed mugs. Taking the darts from the bar, Ethan strolled back to the table. Handing them to Abby, he moved over to the board. "Imagine you're tossing them at Sarah's face. I'm sure you'll do well with that image."

He crossed in front of her to the side of the table. Abby took one of the darts in her right hand and aimed it at the board. The dart flew through the air, wobbling as it hit the wall and fell to the ground. Ethan laughed harder than intended and the sound bellowed through the deserted pub.

Abby held out her hand for him to take the tiny projectiles. "I guess you can do better than that?"

Ethan chuckled. "Concentrate and aim." He picked up Abby's poor attempt off the floor. She was a terrible thrower and in need of some guidance before she killed someone.

Out of the corner of his eye, he caught a glimpse of Abby pulling back her arm, then bringing it forward and releasing the dart. The next thing Ethan knew, a pain in his arm surged to his back. He wasn't sure what happened. His hand automatically grasped his bicep. He glanced down and saw green feathers stuck out between his fingers. "What the bloody..."

"Why were you near the board?" Abby ran over and placed her hand on his shoulder.

"I didn't know you were so angry with me over last night," Ethan said between waves of pain. Perspiration developed on his forehead and he felt a warm wetness between his fingers. For bad aim, she did a great job at targeting him. He'd remember never to cross her. He could feel the blood running down his arm.

"Actually, my eyes were closed."

Ethan never took his hand away from his arm as he sat, slumped on the bar stool. "You had to throw it blind, didn't you?" The initial numbness had worn off, and the stinging intensified.

By this time the bartender, Tony, appeared beside Ethan and pushed Abby out of the way. Grabbing a towel from the closet, he wrapped it around Ethan's arm. "Aye, that's quite a lass you have there, Ethan. Get to the hospital and take care of this. It looks deep-probably needs stitches." The bartender wiped the sweat from his own brow and then jabbed a chubby index finger at Abby's face. "You have a fiery temper, lass. Get it under control or get out."

Abby's mouth dropped. "It was an accident. I didn't mean to hit him," she said to the bartender's back as he brushed past her, not even acknowledging her response.

Ethan examined the half inch gash that jagged along his upper arm. Maybe a few stitches but he was more worried about the puncture hole where the dart did the most damage. "I guess I'll be making a trip to the campus clinic tomorrow." He stood up. The blood had now soaked through the hand towel. He cursed under his breath. Good thing she didn't have a knife. Injured by a dart. This would look great on his file.

Abby followed him back to their table. "Tomorrow? You need to go to the hospital today. You're bleeding. This can't wait."

"I'm not going to the hospital. This is France. There is so much red tape since I'm a foreigner. I would be waiting forever." If he went to the hospital, it would require an official report, then an evaluation for 'fit for duty'. He wasn't going to be pulled off the Walters case due to a minor accident. He picked up his coat and the bill. He struggled to get his wallet out of his back pocket with his good arm while trying to keep the towel wrapped around his wound. Thankfully, she didn't hit his right arm or he'd have to report it. Even though he didn't carry a gun while in France, his supervisors always wanted to know of injuries to their agents' weapon hands.

"Here, let me get it." Abby put her hand in his back pocket and took hold of his wallet. Her palm brushed up against his buttock. Her movement stopped him in midstep. He clamped his lips shut. If she didn't stop doing these things, he'd have her in bed in ten seconds, injured arm and all.

"First, you invite me to spend the night with you, then you punish me with a dart, and now you can't stay away from my butt. I never know what I'm going to get with you." Ethan's hand pressed her palm up against his buttock.

She jerked her hand out of his pocket. "Shut up. Here's your wallet. You need to go to the hospital."

Ethan threw some money on the table. "Tony's overreacting. The cut isn't that deep. It would be ridiculous to go the hospital for a simple flesh wound." Ethan seized Abby's hand and led her out of the pub, nodding at the bartender as they passed the bar. Ethan winced, his teeth clinched together with every step he took. How could one dart cause so much pain?

Ethan quickened his pace. He needed to clean the wound soon. They went down a few side streets in the direction of campus. Residential buildings with hardly any shops on the street level dominated the area. There were a few bakeries, a newsstand here and there.

"Where are we going?" Abby asked.

"My apartment for a little first aid." Dread crept in his head. He certainly didn't want to go to his apartment with her, but he needed to dress the wound, and he needed Abby to do it. The weight on Ethan's arm increased. He glanced over his shoulder. Abby was half walking, half running to keep at this pace. He slowed his stride, and she fell in step beside him.

"Tony could've cleaned that wound. There's no need to drag me to your apartment."

Ethan concentrated on each step he took. "And have you miss all the fun? You threw that dart at me so you're going to help patch me up. I'm not particularly fond of having open wounds tended to in a bar."

"Did you step out in front of that dart to lure me to your apartment?" Her lips pinched down on her tongue, and her eyes watered. He noticed she was staring at his arm. "That's a lot of blood," she said.

He tightened his grip on her. He needed her to stay focused. "Nah. It's not that bad." His voice didn't sound too convincing, but he wasn't sure how she'd react. He did need stitches but could make do without. He'd been through worse.

Ethan pulled her slightly to the right to a small staircase leading up to the door of a gray stone building. The gray was mixed with black specks as if the building had age spots. Plants dangled off balconies overhead. Most students wouldn't live in an upscale area like this. He hoped Abby wasn't too observant. He glanced up at the large wooden doors. His home away from home. He figured Abby would probably ask how he could afford this place on a student's stipend. He couldn't afford it on an agent's salary. It was one thing his mother had given him. A well-furnished apartment in Paris and dual citizenship between the United States and the United Kingdom. Those were her two contributions to his life besides his education. Too bad, a few years ago, he'd have traded those gifts for a relationship with his mother. Now, all he wanted to do was forget he ever met her.

Ethan slipped his key in the lock and twisted the key until he heard a click. He pushed open the door and moved aside, allowing Abby to enter. "It's on the top floor." He motioned to the stairs.

Abby glanced at the large oak stairway. "No elevator here either?"

Ethan laughed. "No. Too bad you injured me or I could carry your lazy butt up the stairs."

Abby's bottom lip puckered, but she stayed silent.

Ethan took two steps at a time, his palm glided over the carved handrail. Small carved lions tapered up the side of the banister. He loved the unique designs the old structure had. Its architecture was one of the reasons he still kept the apartment. The building had a past unlike him. It had history.

Finally reaching the top level, he held Abby's hand and led her down the hallway to the last door. He took his key out of his pocket and inserted it in the lock. The door swung open and sunlight glowed through the tall windows and lit the corridor.

Windows and glass doors took up most of the two far walls and led to a corner balcony. Long cream drapes moved in front of the window, dancing in rhythm to the breeze. Wooden floors decorated with small etched diamond patterns spread throughout the room. An oyster colored comforter engulfed the mattress. Ethan scanned the room. He breathed a deep sigh at the silence. Nols must have left already.

"Nice apartment. It sure beats the student dorms on campus. Any roommates?" Abby asked as her eyes moved with the drapes as they swayed back and forth.

"No roommates. Why? You want to volunteer?" he asked. She frowned and he chuckled. "Have a seat. I'll be back in a minute." He hardly ever stayed in Paris since he spent most of his time in London. Still, it beat hotel rooms. He pulled the first aid kit off the top shelf of the closet.

The apartment was actually bigger than a typical loft. A kitchen was off to the right of the hallway. Stainless steel appliances decorated the room. The counters were shiny black marble refusing to show any dust. He'd make a nice profit if he sold the place, but something kept him from giving it up.

Ethan strolled back down the hallway. "Here we are. Everything we need." He set the box on the dining room table. Abby moved beside him, scowling, but he held his hand up to ward off her protests. "You owe me since you're the reason I'm hurt." Ethan eased his injured arm onto the table and unwrapped the towel. He inspected the dried blood caked over the wound.

Abby didn't move. "I shouldn't do this."

"Get over here and practice your nursing skills."

Taking hold of her seat, Abby scooted it closer to Ethan. She rearranged the items in the box several times before picking up the gauze.

"You'll need to cut off my shirt. I can't lift up my arm," Ethan said. A lie but he couldn't resist. The shirt was ruined anyway.

Abby grabbed the scissors off the table but stared at the shirt for a few seconds before she cut through the fabric near the collar down to his arm. It fell away from his body, settling around his waist. His heart throbbed. He smelled the fresh flowery scent mixed with honey from her hair. The sweetness subdued him, and he fought the urge to kiss her.

"Use the alcohol to clean it," Ethan said and moved the clear bottle and some gloves in front of her. He held back a smile. Her eyes barely blinked as she focused on his arm, but he saw them dart to his chest and back again.

Abby picked up the bottle and twisted the cap. Taking some cotton balls, she poured the alcohol on them. She looked at the wound, not moving the cotton near it, letting her hand linger on the towel.

"Waiting isn't going to make it feel better."

She shook her head. "No, no. I'm not going to attempt this. You already look like you're going to faint at any moment."

He grasped her hand. "I know you don't want to do this, but you have to. It'll get infected if we wait." Harshness radiated through his voice and he regretted it, but she needed the nudge. He wasn't going to go to a clinic and get bogged down in paperwork.

Sighing, she took the alcohol bottle and another cotton pad. His shoulder muscles tensed as she moved the cotton over his arm and covered the gash. She held the pad on his wound letting the alcohol soak. The stinging intensified to a stabbing pain. Ethan held his breath and let his mind wander. After a few minutes, she removed the last pad.

"I think it's clean. You okay?" she asked.

After the pain turned into numbness, he finally moved. He opened his eyes. "You may have to stay with me to make sure I don't take a fever."

Abby sat back. "Oh, stop it."

He grinned as she fought back a smile. "You may want to think about changing your major. You'd make a great nurse, except for one little thing. You have a tendency to be the cause of your patient's injuries." Ethan's head fell back as he chuckled at his own joke.

She pushed him, causing him to grunt. "Funny, aren't you? You might want to be more cautious around me next time," Abby said, giggling as she gathered the soiled gauze and put it in the trash.

"Next time? I'd enjoy a next time," Ethan said. Abby would never be able to hit him again if she tried. Her aim wasn't that good, but it was fun to toy with her.

Abby dumped several items out of the first aid kit. "Tony will kick me out of the pub if I get close to those darts again. What are we going to use to close this cut? I'm not going to sew it up. I draw the line there."

"Super glue." Ethan rose from his chair and went into the kitchen. Opening the refrigerator door, he took a small tube from one of the compartments. He sat down in his chair and dropped the tube on the table.

"How do you know so much about first aid?" Abby asked.

"I...well, I took a few classes in college," Ethan said. He scowled at his mistake. He almost forgot why he was there.

Abby unscrewed the cap on the tube. "Guess it comes in handy. Move closer to me."

Ethan scooted his chair so his leg rested next to her knee barely grazing her pant leg. A brief rush of pulsating heat hit his insides as her touch tickled his skin. Abby removed the gauze from Ethan's bicep. She opened the tube and squeezed some of the gel into the open gash. With her index finger and thumb, she pushed the skin together as the glue bubbled up out of the thin line she formed with the skin. Abby took a spare cloth and wiped off the excess adhesive. "How long does it take to hold?"

"I'd say about five minutes." Ethan preoccupied himself with her sweatshirt. He traced the embroidered design on the sleeve and felt her toned muscles when he pressed ever so often. She inhaled a few deep breaths every time he stopped. She un-wrapped a gauze pad and placed it over the long gash. He grabbed her hand as she started to get up. Whatever it was, he wanted to be close to her. She stared at him. He leaned forward and felt her breath on his mouth. She was beautiful. Her lips invited him, and he took advantage. He swept his tongue over her mouth and leaned back to gage her reaction. Her eyes were closed and her mouth half open. The sweetness in her expression told him everything. She wanted more. He tilted her chin and consumed her mouth. Sensations tore through his body as he deepened the kiss. The connection he felt was as if a sledgehammer had hit him on the head. This was someone he needed to stay away from, but he wanted to consume himself in her. He needed to be lost in her, to forget there was a lonely life back in London waiting on him once this assignment was over. He let his tongue lick her lips then devoured her mouth once more.

Abby broke the kiss and patted his bandages. Her fingers lingered on her lips as she stared at him. "We're finished." She sat back in her chair, breathing deeply.

He smiled. They weren't finished by a long shot. He flexed his arm and stretched it over his head. "Thanks. Promise me, you won't try throwing darts any time soon," Ethan said. Abby snickered and playfully punched him in his good arm. He held up his hand to deflect her attack. "Whoa now. Don't hurt my healthy one. If you do, I'll make you stay and nurse me back to health." He laughed, grateful his aggressiveness didn't scare her off. In fact, she seemed at ease.

"That's corny. You can turn any situation to your advantage, can't you? You'd throw yourself in front of a car if you thought I'd come running to help," Abby said, giggling.

"If it would work, I'd do it right now." Ethan started to get up and head for the door.

"Okay. I get it. Come back here. I don't feel like doing anymore doctoring today." Abby yawned.

"Last night is catching up to you," Ethan said.

"Yeah, I found some weird object in my bed. I had to dispose of it."

"Oh, that hurt." Ethan grasped his chest with his uninjured hand. "After all that happened, I'm a weird object?" This was the Abby he liked. Carefree and not analyzing her words before she said them. He sensed she hardly ever showed her true self.

Abby smiled. "I've got to go." She picked up her bag from the table. "I need to check my email, then do some laundry."

"Use my computer if you want. I can't help with the laundry unfortunately."

Abby peered at him. Her bangs covered her eyes. "You need to rest. I'll go to the lab."

"No. The computer's already up and running." He pointed to the laptop sitting at a small desk in the corner.

He tugged at his shirt near his waist and eased it over his head, gently pulling it over his bandages and discarded it next to the bed. He glanced over his shoulder. Abby stood across the room, her eyes fixed on him. "Keep staring like that and a guy will start to wonder if he needs to invite you over to the bed." Ethan's voice brought Abby out of her daze.

Her face blushed a deep shade of red. "Sorry, I was daydreaming." She twirled around and darted to the computer. She made it too easy to tease her, and he loved it.

"No need to be sorry. Invitation's always open," Ethan said. At this point, he wouldn't deny her if she initiated it.

Ethan lay back on the bed and closed his eyes. He heard the quiet tapping of the keys on the keyboard. The only thing she could do there was check her email. Jealousy seized his throat. After all that happened, she couldn't wait to email Walters again. Maybe the easiest way to take care of Abby was to eliminate the threat. Get Walters out of her life. It would save them all a lot of trouble. Her father would be happy. Ethan could leave, and Abby would be safe. But he wasn't sure he'd be able to leave once his assignment was completed and that thought terrified him.

Ethan's eyes popped open when the door creaked. A few seconds later, he heard it close. He straightened up on the bed, small twinges of pain sliced through his arm as the skin around his wound stretched. He jumped up and hurried to the window. A few seconds later, Abby's silhouette glided down the front stairs and onto the street as if she were floating on air.

"Do I want to know?" A husky voice bellowed from the hallway.

Ethan turned and saw Nols standing by the door. "What are you doing here? Hiding in my apartment?"

Nols laughed. "Had to. You brought the princess back here. You could give a guy a warning before you barge in."

"It's my place. Stay at a hotel if you don't like it."

He waved Ethan off. "Fine. I'm sure Tom will want to know his top dog spent the night with Senator Rodgers' daughter."

Ethan's shoulders tensed. He selected a shirt out of the armoire and jerked it over his head, ignoring the burning in his arm. "Run the trace on my computer and pull up the last cached webpage."

Nols sat at the computer and banged on the keyboard. "Where's you're brain at? Needed a little slap and tickle?"

"She was drunk. What was I supposed to do? Leave her at the bar?" His fists clinched as he recoiled at Nols's harshness. Not one thing he said would convince his partner. He couldn't even convince himself.

Nols stared at him like a father would a son. "No. Taking her home was part of your job. Staying the night crossed the line. You compromised the agency. I'm required to report it. Senator Rodgers is determined when it comes to his daughters. He'll find out."

"I'm following orders and keeping her safe." Ethan ignored the empty threat. Nols had been his partner since their first assignment out of Quantico. "Find the last website please."

"Yeah, the website. What happened to 'she acts like my sister'? Did her father's deep pockets tempt you too much?"

Ethan jerked around and caught himself before he hit Nols. "Don't bring my family into this."

"Who mentioned your family? I was talking about hers. But since you brought it up, you compare every woman you've been with to your family and find something wrong with the relationship so you can justify breaking it off." He rubbed his eyebrow and stared at Ethan. "Why would you get involved with her, especially with the hell storm this could bring?"

"I don't know."

"She's not one of those girls you can cast aside when you decide she's not up to your standards."

"What's that suppose to mean?"

"Nothing. Forget it." He shook his head. "Promise me you'll stop acting like some sex deprived teenager and focus on Walters."

"I would if Tom would send me to Rome instead of forcing me to babysit her."

Nols's head fell back as he laughed. "I can tell you're hating every minute of it." He moved the mouse and scrolled down the page. "Check this out."

Ethan glanced at the screen. Nols had hacked Abby's email and had a message from Walters dated today. "He asked her to meet him at Geo's." He gritted his teeth. Walters invited her to Geo Peretti's café, the front business for the gambling operation.

Nols clicked his teeth. "You think Walters knows about the Senator?"

"Probably. Getting a senator's daughter involved would complicate our investigation. I wouldn't put it past him." Ethan paced around the room. "Did she reply?"

"I guess you're romancing isn't up to her standards. She didn't waste a moment thinking about you. She's agreed to meet him next week."

Ethan's hands curled into tight fists. "Sounds like her. She has no idea how to keep herself out of trouble."

"I think she can handle herself." Nols laughed and motioned to Ethan's bicep. "Did you think I didn't notice? Exactly how did she manage to injure your arm?"

Ethan groaned and pulled his shirt sleeve lower to conceal the white gauze. Obviously Abby didn't feel anything for him. Why would she? He had nothing to offer her.

Chapter 17

Only a few more blocks. Abby glanced at the street signs. None of the roads looked familiar. She'd taken the metro to the center of Paris and cut across in front of Notre Dame, following a few streets that led her away from the tourist areas. Jayson had chosen a secluded restaurant, and she'd already taken a few wrong turns and had to double back. A couple of pedestrians occasionally passed by her, but the sidewalks were mostly deserted.

Abby walked down a block when something hit her face. Another drop struck the skin below her eye. She didn't even think to bring an umbrella. It had been weeks since she'd heard the weather report. She relied on looking out the window since they didn't have a television. Hoping the rain would hold out until she reached the restaurant, Abby picked up her pace as the rain fell more frequently. She crossed the street, and the sky broke open. The rain pelted to the ground, forming large puddles on the sidewalk. Abby ran to the closest awning, waited for a second and sprinted to the next covering. She stopped at the last canopy. Why did she always have such bad luck? Since she'd been in Paris, she'd been caught in several rainstorms. Not having access to a weather forecast caused her a great deal of trouble, especially since she could never remember to check it while she was on the internet.

The outline of the restaurant taunted her through the white sheets of water. She glanced at her watch. 8:25 P.M. Already twenty five minutes late, she had no way to contact Jayson. She left her cell phone on the table at the apartment. He'd probably leave if she didn't show up soon, if he hadn't already. The dark gray sky's fury didn't show signs of letting up. She'd have to take her chances because she couldn't let this ruin her evening. She lifted her clutch bag over her head. It barely covered her head, but she had nothing else to use as a shield. Abby dashed out from the awning. Water rushed over the tops of her toes and in the bottom of her shoes. Her shirt sagged as it absorbed the liquid. As she ran across the street, the rainwater splashed on the bottom of her pants. She reached the other curb and ducked under the canopy of the restaurant. Wringing the water out of her blouse, Abby stared at her clothes. Her sleeves now hung several inches over her hands. She shook her head and water ran down her face. So much for her fabulous entrance.

Rainwater covered most of the tables and chairs on the restaurant terrace. A few glasses remained on the table closest to the door, and the chairs had long been abandoned. Abby peered in the window. Something moved near the back corner. Shivering, Abby zigzagged around the table and chairs toward the entrance as the cold rain soaked her skin. She opened the door. Bells on the knob jingled and announced her arrival. As she entered, two waiters glanced her way.

"Bonjour, mademoiselle," the one closest to her said. His long nose wrinkled up when he caught sight of her.

"Bonjour," Abby said. She shrank back and could only imagine what she looked like.

"Suivez-moi, mademoiselle." The waiter waved his hand, and she followed him down the center walkway.

Small tables formed a row on either side of the aisle. No one else was dining, which wasn't unusual since it wasn't peak hours, but there were typically a few patrons in and out of restaurants throughout the day. Surprisingly, she and the waiters were the only ones there.

The atmosphere was simple and clean. The floor was worn by the traffic over the years. She didn't see any of the usual decorations that were in American restaurants.

The waiter led her down a dark hallway. One small light flickered on and off briefly showing the bareness of the walls. Abby kept an eye on the waiter to avoid running into him. He opened a door near the end of the corridor. Abby stepped in the room and saw a table in the center of the dining area already dressed with wine glasses, plates, and silverware. Jayson grinned as he turned away from the window and walked over to her.

"Excusez-moi," the waiter said as he left the room.

Holding back her breath, Abby stared at Jayson. He was even more handsome than she remembered. Gone were his running pants and T-shirt she remembered from the plane. He replaced them with dark tan pants and a button up solid blue shirt that he left un-tucked. His hair was cut short leaving almost no hair at all. His green eyes sparkled more now that his hair was no longer there to compete. But something inside Abby seemed disappointed. It was different. The excitement she felt on the plane had deflated. She felt the urge to bolt from the room.

Jayson rubbed his head as if he knew she'd noticed his new haircut. "I thought you changed your mind." He stood by the table eyeing her up and down. "The storm caught you."

His cologne, spicy and sensual, put her in a trance, but she was sure the rapid pacing of heart wasn't from her infatuation. She'd made a mistake. She was there for the wrong reasons. She reached up and touched her hair, which was now matted down on her head. She half-laughed, half-coughed to pull herself out of this panic. "Not sure how you guessed that. I don't have one dry piece of clothing on me."

Jayson chuckled and walked over to the side table near the windows and grabbed a few napkins. He stopped in front of her, standing close, almost touching Abby's arm. "We can't have you soaking wet and miserable." He ran the napkin over her forehead. His hand went to the side of her face and gently wiped some water off her cheek. Jayson's fingers lingered at Abby's chin, barely skimming her skin.

She took the towel from his offering hand, but she didn't use it immediately. She stared at him, unable to move. She couldn't fake this. Being here with Jayson wasn't in her heart.

"It's great to see you," he said.

Abby pressed the towel on her clothes and soaked up the excess water. "Sorry I was late. I didn't realize I was going to get stuck out in the rain. We don't have a television so I missed the forecast," Abby said, blubbering with excuses. She kept telling herself, as long as she kept talking, it'd be okay.

Jayson nodded. "No problem. You don't have a television? Must be hard, not being able to know what's happening in the world. I'm surprised you aren't going crazy by now." He pulled a chair back, allowing Abby to sit.

"Sometimes it's a blessing. If you don't know what's going on in the world, you're spared the worry that comes with it. There's too much crap going on now. It's depressing to watch." She enjoyed the time without the media. In Paris, she was able to leave the political circus of her family's life. It was the one thing she liked about spending time with Ethan. He treated her like she was normal. But Jayson knew her family so there was something different in how he seemed to view her. She saw that now.

"I know what you mean," he said as he licked his lips.

Abby stared at her plate. "I didn't think you would be in Paris this soon."

"Yeah, I have a few more weeks off since I lost in Rome."

"I'm sorry to hear you didn't win." Abby bit her lip and examined Jayson's face. Butterflies still hovered through her stomach. He looked more like a model than she remembered. He'd be perfect for Von Deez even if he wasn't perfect for her heart.

"If I have to lose, I might as well spend my extra time with a beautiful woman."

Abby blushed at the compliment and shifted her gaze from him to her plate again. Confirmation. She'd led him this way. She'd have to give him a chance.

"Did you find the restaurant easily?" Jayson asked.

Abby nodded, now afraid to talk. She didn't want to say anything crazy like she did on the plane or send him wrong signals. Not that he wasn't gorgeous or fantastic to talk to. Ethan kept invading her thoughts. She'd never be able to be more than friends with Jayson.

"I love this place. I found it a few years back. I've been coming back ever since," he said.

"It's great. I'm surprised no one's here."

"They only open for lunch and dinner. Geo doesn't run a café anymore. He likes to open twice a day. People should be showing up soon for dinner." Jayson lifted a wine bottle from the bucket by the table and poured some red wine in Abby's glass. He then filled his own. Abby cringed at the thought of drinking wine and compared the taste to swallowing rubbing alcohol. She usually ordered water or a diet soda, which always made the waiters frown in disapproval. Wine was the standard drink in France. Abby couldn't conform to the norm. She didn't have a taste for it but knew she needed to get used to it before the Von Deez party.

Abby studied the room. A vase full of fresh flowers contrasted the plainness of the decor. A baguette peeked out of a metal basket that sat next to the vase. Taking a sip of the wine, she forced back her instinct to spit it out. She quickly swallowed the rest and tried to not taste it as it went down. Abby twisted the cloth napkin in her hand. "So how's the tennis going?" She winced. He said he lost and she asked him again. How stupid could she be?

The door swung open and the waiter entered the room with a tray. He set several plates on the table. Abby had never seen the foods before. They were decorated like works of art. Flowers and herbs adorned the platters and painted an edible picture.

"Escargot?" Jayson asked and pushed one of the plates from the center of the table toward her. Abby's stomach lurched. She couldn't fake liking escargot. She could drink the wine all night, but she wouldn't eat the snails.

She pushed the plate back. "I'll pass."

He laughed. "You sure? You should try them. They're a house specialty." Abby shook her head. Motioning for the waiter, Jayson said, "She doesn't care for an appetizer tonight. Bring us the next course, s'il vous plait."

The waiter nodded, whisking the snails away from the table. Relief washed over her.

"I was sure you'd try them. I've had them once. It was one time too many." He put his hand over his mouth, hiding the smirk.

A wide grin spread over Abby's face. "You were testing me? That's not very nice." The tension flowed out of her shoulders.

"I wanted to see if you had adopted the French culture. I see you need a few more months here before you start embracing the food." Jayson took his glass and gulped the last of his wine. "What have you been doing since you got here? I'm sure you're enjoying the Paris nightlife."

"Yeah. That and some sightseeing. I love to go to the Louvre and wonder through the different art collections. There are so many things to do here. I probably won't be able to do most of them." She thought about Sarah and Nicole's constant partying. She sometimes needed a break. It was a chore living with them. Going to places like the Louvre let her get away. She'd find one of the secluded art rooms that few people visited and would sit there for hours reading or listening to her MP3 player.

Jayson poured her some more wine. Her taste buds were now numb to the flavor. "It sounds like you're having a great time," he said.

"I am. Not many people get to attend school in a foreign country." Abby stopped, not wanting to babble too much about herself. There wasn't much more to tell. Truth was, Ethan was the one that showed her all the sights and told her about the history. She'd been out with him several times the past week. He was becoming her best friend, well more than that. Without him, she'd probably stay at Von Deez preparing layouts or casting models. He forced her to see the good in Paris.

"Tell me about the tournament," Abby said. She needed Ethan out of her head, at least for the night. Jayson had come all the way to Paris. The least she could do is enjoy herself and give him her undivided attention. It might still be possible to be friends and ask Jayson to do the Von Deez campaign.

"I was doing well in Rome. In my last match, I developed some pain in my wrist. Forfeited the second set. The trainer told me to take a few weeks off. This was the perfect time to come to Paris," Jayson said. His eyes danced, almost playing with the light that flickered from the candle on the table.

"You chose Paris. Any particular reason?" Abby asked, but it sounded more flirty than she wanted.

He chuckled. "I needed to pay up on a bet I lost. Thought you could show me these sights you love so much. I've never had a chance to be a tourist. Do you want the job?" Jayson winked. His eyes were hot green flames burning Abby's gaze. Hints of heat flowed through her body causing her to shudder. Three weeks being Jayson's personal tour guide. It could be fun.

"Yes." Her response came out before she knew it. "Is there anything particular you would want to see?"

"Whatever you want to show me." Jayson's voice was husky, almost seductive. Abby's cheeks burned. She could've sworn he was no longer talking about the sights.

The waiter returned, relieving her of a response. He placed several dishes on the table.

"I ordered before you arrived. These are some of Geo's best recipes, and don't worry, there aren't any snails," Jayson said.

Abby smiled and studied the different choices on the table. She decided against asking what they were. They all appeared to be cooked, so the battle was half won with that small detail. In France, she discovered it was better not to know. She took her spoon and dug into the dish. This was her opportunity to secure him for Von Deez. They could be friends, nothing more. Despite her excitement, the pit in her stomach felt heavier. She had the feeling this evening wasn't going to end how she planned.

Chapter 18

"Okay. So you occasionally go to class. How are you supposed to get your assignments completed?" Jayson asked.

"I went to the first class. Every student was there. The next class, it was me and three other students. Even the professor showed up after the class was half over. I've decided to adapt to the French way and go to class occasionally. I'm surprisingly good at it." She tugged at her shirt and tried to stretch the fabric that had now shrunk from the rain. She had most of her assignments completed for the semester, so she felt confident in her decision. "I work at Von Deez during the week, so that takes up any free time I have."

"Sounds like the type of classes I need to take," he said then laughed. He followed Abby, down a dirt path in Jardin du Luxembourg. The evening had progressed through several bottles of wine, dinner, and now a midnight walk. There were several other couples scattered throughout the park. The stars and moon overhead created a bright sky, allowing Abby to see everything around her.

Small pebbles crunched under her feet as she glided across the pathway. Her body felt like air due to the many glasses of wine. The conversation with Jayson was coming easily now, kind of like how she was with Zander back home, like a brother. She pointed to a path trailing off from the octagonal pool. The statue in the pool's center was barely visible across the massive basin. The moonlight reflected off the water, lighting up the Queens' statues that framed the fountain's edge. A few toy sailboats bobbed up and down in the lapping ripples.

Abby grabbed Jayson's hand and pulled him down the path. "Let's go that way. There's a statue you need to see."

The path was lined by tall, square, pruned bushes, creating a hideaway from the main section of the park. Abby and Jayson twisted through several pathways. Abby knew she probably took the wrong way but she tried to remember the way Ethan showed her.

"Where are we going?" Jayson asked.

"Everything worth seeing is hidden on these side gardens," Abby said as they approached an opening between the hedges. They reached the clearing, and she saw the sculpture standing in the middle of a pruned section of bushes. The Statue of Liberty. Ethan showed her the statue on one of their outings. He'd always found different things to see; things Abby had no idea existed. Most people didn't have the opportunities to see these lesser known attractions.

"I didn't realize there was another one." Jayson moved closer to the sculpture, a miniature version of the original, standing about fifteen feet in the air.

"Pretty cool, isn't it? It's almost like a little piece of America here. I know it was a gift from France but it still reminds me of home." Abby strolled over to a metal bench and sat. The rain finally stopped, giving them an opportunity to explore the surrounding area. They had walked several blocks from the restaurant, and her legs ached. But she was having fun, and she wanted it to continue. She missed Jacob, and she knew now why she liked Jayson. He reminded her of her brother. Jayson seemed carefree and fearless, similar to the traits she admired in Jacob.

"I would have never known it was here. I guess most people don't explore beyond the usual tourist areas," Jayson said as he circled the statue. After a few minutes, he came over and sat beside her. "This is what I like. Being able to see this. I'm always going to cities across the world, but I don't know anything about them. This is perfect." He moved his arm over and curled it around Abby's shoulder. She tensed at the touch.

Abby shifted so she couldn't feel the warmth of his skin. "It's like they hid all these glorious sculptures and dare you to find them," she said. She left out that Ethan usually strolled with her, guiding her in the right direction to make her discoveries.

"It's wonderful. I needed this." He drew her closer so his hand rested at the base of her neck, his fingers gently stroking her skin. She stiffened but allowed herself to relax.

"I'm glad I lost that bet," Jayson whispered. Abby felt his chest slowly rising and lowering as he breathed.

"You lost on purpose. Sarah told me."

"I wasn't sure she'd tell you." Jayson rubbed the back of her hand, causing goose bumps to emerge on her arms. "I couldn't resist. You were so cute trying to play it cool."

Abby pushed herself off his chest and punched him lightly in the arm. He grabbed her wrist pulling her to him. Her face was within inches from his, and she stared into his green eyes that seemed almost glowing in the moonlight. His breath hit her cheek as he exhaled. Tingling shot through her hands as she parted her lips and his mouth came over hers. A fuzziness overtook her mind, but it wasn't pleasant. There was no passion behind the kiss.

His hands surrounded the sides of her neck and forced her head to stay within his touch. Brushing his lips slowly around her face, he kissed her cheeks. She shifted her arms, resting them on his biceps. Not that she had felt up that many guys, but his body was rock hard.

"Let's go back to my hotel," he whispered in her ear as he leaned his head back.

"I would love to, but we can't," Abby said. The brief pause allowed her brain to catch up to her body. Physically, yes, she was attracted to him, but she didn't need to feel awkward about another overnight stay because she might not be so lucky this time. Something might happen that she'd regret. A wave of guilt overtook her. She wasn't weak in the knees and didn't have that fire in her stomach like she did with Ethan.

"Stop now? We just started." Jayson's tongue tickled her earlobe. She sat there a few more seconds before sliding down the bench away from him.

"How about we take this slow, okay?" She knew this wasn't her. She wasn't like Sarah in that she could bed any guy.

"Are you sure? It didn't seem that way a few minutes ago." Jayson moved down the bench toward her.

She raked her hand through her matted hair. "You're too persuasive for your own good. It's time to go." Abby jumped up and her shoes skidded across the small pebbles. She threw her arms out to balance herself.

Jayson's mouth turned downward into a frown. "You know how to disappoint, but you're a challenge. I'll win you over soon enough. I'll take you home." He held out his hand and locked his fingers in hers. "This isn't over," he whispered.

Abby shivered as his breath hit her ear. She had no doubt he was telling the truth. They strolled back through the hedge lined pathway that led to the fountain.

"Since we've postponed our other activities, what else do you have to offer for tomorrow?" Jayson asked. Their arms swung between them as he held her hand.

"You mentioned a tour of the city. We can visit the Eiffel Tower, the Louvre, or Sacre Coeur? It's up to you."

"Sounds great, but I have practice during the day. We'll have to visit them in the evening. We can meet at the restaurant. It's a central location. Would that work for you?" Jayson asked.

They walked by the fountain as they exited the park, and out to the main sidewalk. The street lights cast a yellow hue against the trees and parked cars along the edge of the path. Sirens blared in the distance, reminding Abby that she was no longer in the United States. Disappointment flooded her. It seemed bizarre to meet at the restaurant every night but everything seemed strange since she'd arrived in Paris. Nothing was normal. She reasoned that nights were the only time she had free, even though his timing did complicate her plans.

"You're busy every day? I thought I'd bring you by Von Deez."

"My wrist will be better soon, and I'll start training longer hours. Evenings will be the only time I'll have free. What's so special about Von Deez?" Jayson squeezed her hand. The wind blew harder as the night progressed. Another rain shower was likely to hit soon.

She shrugged. "Remember that party I mentioned?"

He nodded, but she was sure he didn't recall the conversation.

"My boss gave me a carte blanche to design the next ad campaign. Models, everything."

"That's wonderful."

She bit her lip. "I thought maybe you'd be my date for the party and possibly a model for the campaign."

He laughed. "You're serious?"

She nodded, feeling tears beginning to puddle in her eyes, a sure sign of her nerves about asking were getting to her.

He ran his hand over the back of his neck. "I'm flattered, but I'm not a model."

"I know, that's the point. I'm looking for athletes. It's better if you've never modeled before."

"I'm not sure I have the time." His lips formed a thin line, and she could tell he wasn't keen on the idea.

"It's only a party and two or three ad shoots. Von Deez pays very well." She shoved her hands in her pockets so they wouldn't shake. Usually mentioning the compensation worked, but she wasn't dealing with a model. She was dealing with an ordinary guy, so he wouldn't know that Von Deez paid top dollar.

"I'll do it if you go out with me again. I want to see the Paris nightlife."

Abby's mouth gaped open. He'd agreed. She couldn't believe it. "Really?"

"Sure. We both get what we want, right?" He grabbed her hand. "So what club you planning on taking me to?"

Abby stared in front of her and let the Von Deez subject drop. "There's several night clubs where my sisters go often. Coco Lobo. It's pretty good. It usually doesn't start getting busy until late," she said.

"Perfect. Let's plan on going there one or two nights."

Abby dreaded taking him to Coco Lobo, but the victory with Von Deez outweighed it all. Everyone would be at the club, including Ethan. She didn't have much choice. There were only two places she knew, Coco Lobo and the Irish Pub. She didn't dare pick any place with her limited knowledge on night clubs. She could ask Sarah, but that would be disastrous since she would show up at any place she suggested to Abby.

They reached the main road close to the campus just as small droplets of water sprinkled to the ground. Abby touched her hair. It was still plastered to her forehead, stiff from the hairspray and rain mix. She had forgotten about her matted hair and ruined makeup until that moment. They walked in silence down the street leading up to the campus entrance. Abby crept along, trying to prolong her time with him but sooner than she liked, the entrance came into view. Smoking a cigarette, a lone guard stood at the gate. He didn't seem to notice them.

"The entrance is up there. Students only on campus, so I guess..." She didn't finish, hoping it would prevent the end of the date from happening. Excitement erupted in her body as she anticipated Jayson's next move. She was more comfortable now, maybe this time it would be different. She stopped a few feet from the entrance, giving them plenty of privacy from the guard. "This is it. Thanks for dinner. I enjoyed it." She twisted her fingers and stared at the ground but even though she tried, she couldn't avoid the urge to take a peek up at his face.

"Me too. You're one of the most entertaining people I've met in Paris," Jayson said, winking at her. "Meet same time tomorrow at the restaurant? The guys will make us a whole different meal."

"Sure." Abby played with her hands. She wondered when the kiss would come.

His head closed in on her face, landing a quick peck on her check. "I'll see you tomorrow night, Abs."

She smiled as he walked off. He turned, threw his hand up in the air, then broke out into a jog across the intersection to the other side of the street. He ran over to a cab parked at the corner. Opening the back door, he disappeared in the backseat. Abby's heart faltered as she watched the car speed away.

She stood stunned, staring at the rapidly fading taillights. After all that happened, she felt slightly cheated. The goodnight kiss. It was supposed to be the last memory of the night. Hers was non-existent. She sighed as she passed through the gate. It was for the best. She shouldn't hope for or force something that didn't exist. He committed to her Von Deez project. That was her ultimate goal.

The guard was still leaning against the wall. "Bonsoir." His voice tore into the stillness around them.

"Bonsoir," she said as he checked her student ID card.

Abby entered the gate and followed the stone pathway to the apartment. She wondered why Jayson didn't kiss her. Everything was going well. Had she scared him off by declining his offer to go back to his hotel? Surely that wasn't it. He didn't seem too disappointed when she suggested that they take it slow. It was strange. After all that happened, the last kiss of the night was a small peck on the cheek.

"Abby."

She turned in the direction of the voice. A silhouette entered into the light beaming down from the street lamp.

"Ethan?"

Chapter 19

*A*nger seized him. Why would Abby go off and meet that bloke then let him escort her back to her apartment? Was she that clueless? He thought she'd given up on Jayson. Ethan and Nols watched them at the park. It was more than he could take and Nols's ribbing about Ethan's inability to attract Abby's attention ate at him.

"What are you doing here?" she asked.

Ethan rubbed his eyes. "Are you okay? You weren't home when Patrick and Sarah got back to your apartment. It's late." His tone came out more authoritative than he would've liked, but her action warranted the scolding. Didn't she read the news? She could've been attacked and no one would've known where to find her.

"I'm fine. I was out with a friend, and we lost track of the time." She fidgeted with her shirt sleeve. He opened his mouth, then closed it again. How could he say this without sounding like a jealous idiot?

"I'm fine. It's not a big deal. I'm here now," she said before he could respond. She smiled at him. "What are you doing here so late?"

"You went out with that guy you met on the plane, didn't you?" he asked. Tom informed her father of the meeting. The Senator asked Tom to do what was necessary to keep Abby away from Jayson. So far, Ethan was doing a pitiful job. Tom was forcing Ethan back into pursuit mode. He had behaved this past week and kept their relationship professional. Tom said it was now time to increase Ethan's interest. Offer Abby a distraction, and Tom wanted Ethan as the distraction. Abby's father bit on the plan.

Nols objected immediately on his partner's behalf, but Tom refused to hear other options. Ethan already had an established relationship. All they needed was to bump it up a notch. Both he and Nols knew that Ethan could provide a distraction, one too realistic for Ethan to handle. He couldn't be around her and not feel something. His desire for her was always present.

Abby jerked her head in his direction. "How did you know that?" She crossed her arms in front of her chest. The harshness in her voice drove him back on his heels.

"Abby, you need to be more careful. You barely know this guy. You were out late with him, and he brought you home. Now he knows where you live. It's not wise to do something like that in a foreign country. You're not familiar with the customs." Ethan's voice became louder, almost shouting at her. There was too much truth in his words. He wanted to shake some sense in her.

"He's American. He has more in common with me than you. You're British. I should be more worried about you." She shifted and the distance between them increased. "I met him at a restaurant. We went to Jardin Luxembourg, and he was a perfect gentleman. I don't feel comfortable talking to you about this." Ethan remained silent. What could he say to convince her? Thinking about the park made him want to hit Walters.

"You still haven't answered my question. How did you know where I was tonight?" she asked.

"I saw you outside the gates with him." He paused, but she didn't respond. "I'm only trying to look out for you. You hardly know him. Anything could've happened tonight. You shouldn't see him anymore." His fists clinched against his sides. Just remembering them kissing sent a wave of furor down his spine. She deserved better than some low life celebrity involved in criminal activities.

Red darkened Abby's cheeks. "It doesn't concern you. I like you. You're a nice guy, but you can't tell me who to go out with. I hardly know you either, and you're not my boyfriend. Besides, you're not exactly a bystander who has nothing to gain." Her voice amplified under the canopy of trees.

Ethan flinched as if she'd slapped him. "That's what you think I'm doing? I don't need to get rid of Jayson. I can get what I want without sabotaging your other relationships." Ethan moved closer to Abby, causing her to back away. The realness of her words hit him. She acted like she didn't care. If that was how it would be, he'd show her exactly how he felt.

He sensed the hardness of the stone wall as he pushed up against her, and her escape route disappeared. The heat of her arms scorched him as he moved his hands over her skin. A warm burn rained through his body as Ethan's fingers slid up and down her chest. For some reason, she didn't protest. He needed her to stop him but so far she was inviting him to do more with the eagerness of her body as she pressed against him. Closing her eyes, she lifted her chin. It was the offer he needed. His mouth settled on her lips. He could almost taste the sweetness of honeysuckle on her tongue, her scent engulfing every part of him.

"I want you," he whispered. He wanted her more than any woman he'd met. He was fooling himself in thinking this was an act. He meant it. He needed to be with her. Something he never desired before consumed him. He never needed anyone. He always stood alone. It was how he survived, but now, his life seemed incomplete unless he had her in it.

Abby opened her eyes. She grabbed his head and pulled him back to her. Her lips touched his once more. Her aggressiveness motivated him, and he slid his hand under her shirt, moving it up her stomach. He cupped her breast with his other hand. She wrapped her arms around him squeezing him tighter as he moved his hand across her chest.

Ethan pulled away. "Not here."

Leaning against the wall, she dropped her head in her hands. "We need to stop."

"I figured you would say that," Ethan said sucking in air. She was right. He couldn't start something while he was lying to her. Right now, he was as bad as Jayson.

She yanked her sleeves down. "What happened the other night was a mistake. Kissing you just now was a mistake. Don't think this will keep me from seeing Jayson. It doesn't change anything."

Ethan sighed. "Didn't think it would. I don't want you to get hurt. I'll make sure that you don't. I promise you that." It wasn't an empty promise.

Abby opened her mouth but before she could speak, Ethan drew her to him devouring her mouth with his. Sweet waves of warmth flowed through him once more. As quickly as he pulled her to him, he pushed her away. His chest heaved as he tried to take in a deep breath. She stood motionless staring at him. He tore his gaze off her. Why did this have to happen now? He didn't need any more complications, and his feelings for her were definitely complications.

He leaned in so his lips grazed her ear. "Don't call it a mistake. You shouldn't lie to yourself." He slid his arm around her, gently pushing her in the direction of the steep hill leading to her building. "Let's get you to your apartment." They walked in silence. It was different with her. She touched his inner being, a place within himself that he never let anyone near. She was the first person to stir emotion in him. He closed himself off a long time ago, not allowing anyone in. He wasn't sure how she managed to break the barrier. He wasn't even sure he ever had a barrier with her.

The campus was quiet. Ethan only heard the wind rustling through the leaves on the trees. When they reached the building, he held the door as she hurried through. As they ascended the stairwell, he had a significant lead since he took two steps to her one, and he waited on her at the top. She fumbled with her purse searching for the key. Ethan leaned against the door as she looked up. He smiled down at her.

He moved closer to her and took her chin in his hand. Abby rose up on her tip toes to reach him, surprising him with her boldness. His lips touched hers, pressing hotly on the delicate skin of her lips. His mouth parted from Abby's, causing an emptiness in him. He didn't want to stop so soon, but if he didn't, he wouldn't be able to control himself.

"Good night," Ethan whispered. A tiny smirk emerged on his face as he backed away, his fingers still clasped in hers. He let go as he fell back out of reach. Turning, he strolled down the hall, giving her a final look. He didn't know when it happened but he knew what happened. Abby Rodgers stole something from him and he was afraid that it was his heart.

Chapter 20

Abby grabbed the door to the pub, and her fingers fumbled with the handle. Please don't let this be a disaster. Her dinner with Jayson went well earlier in the night but apprehension reigned in her head about subjecting Jayson to Nicole and Sarah's scrutiny. She'd finally told her sisters that he was in town, and they insisted she bring him to the pub by campus. It was a reasonable request since she hardly knew anything about him. She'd acted irresponsibly by going out with him and not telling anyone where she was.

Abby glanced at her watch. It was almost ten. Sarah and Nicole should already be there. She pulled the heavy wooden door and focused on the dimly lit room. Several people sat at the bar ordering drinks. She spotted Sarah sitting at a table in the corner. Abby frowned at the sight. She should've anticipated this. Sarah had gone all out tonight. Her flaxen hair was curled in long wavy lengths, spraying out onto her bare shoulders. Her ruby red lips stood out against her creamy white skin. She picked out one of her most revealing outfit, a thin white halter top and skin tight leather pants. A lone tassel enhancer dangled from her long curb link necklace. Sarah drew attention from most of the guys in the room. It would only be a matter of time before Jayson saw her if he hadn't already.

"Hey, Abby."

She turned her head and saw Nicole waving at her from the bar. She smiled at Nicole's appearance as she walked up to them, thankful it didn't outdo her own look.

"Nicole, this is Jayson," Abby said, standing off to the side when she approached.

"I was surprised you contacted my sister," Nicole said. Her smile dissipated when she stared at Jayson. Abby glared at her, praying this meeting wasn't a mistake. Why would her first words be those?

Jayson laughed. "I understand your skepticism. I assure you, I'm a nice guy." He leaned up against the bar and winked at Abby. She felt heat rise through her body. Jayson's smile would make any girl melt.

"Whatever, Jockstrap. That's what every guy says when they meet a girl's family," Nicole said, staring at him. He shifted his feet and lowered his gaze.

Abby giggled as the silence crippled her mood. "He's been wonderful. Let's drop this discussion. Anyone want a drink?"

"That's a great idea. This round's on me." Jayson pulled out his wallet from his back pocket.

"I've ordered already. You can get the next one." Nicole turned to the counter. The bartender returned with a martini and a large mug of beer. "I'll see you two at the table." She pointed to the corner Abby had seen Sarah at earlier. It was now empty. Only Sarah's and Nicole's abandoned jackets remained slung over the chairs.

"We'll be over in a few minutes," Abby said.

Jayson stared at Nicole as she walked away. "She doesn't like me."

Abby laughed. "Don't know what gave you that idea." A weak smile spread across her face. "Nicole doesn't like many people. She's being herself. I'm surprised you didn't get more than that. She's vicious when she wants to be."

"Maybe." Jayson shrugged. "I'll turn up my charm. That should warm her up."

She hit him lightly on the arm. "Save that for me."

He chuckled. "What would you like to drink?" Jayson asked as he raised his hand and caught the attention of the bartender.

"I'll take a Rum and Coke." Abby chose the only drink she remembered except for the Dirty Martini Sarah always ordered. Abby saw Nicole carrying a martini, which usually meant Sarah was on a man hunt.

Jayson ordered the drinks. The bartender sat two glasses in front of him. He handed her a few bills. "Keep the change," he said.

The bartender glanced at the bills and back at him. Her eyes widened and she smiled at Jayson. "Merci."

"Where to?" he asked as he grabbed the mugs.

"Nicole's sitting at a table near the corner."

They maneuvered down the front aisle leading to and from the bar. Abby squeezed between bodies and weaved a path to the table.

"Where's Sarah?" Abby asked as she chose the seat next to the one Sarah previously occupied. It left only one chair beside Abby for Jayson.

"She's over there talking to some of Patrick's friends. You know she doesn't go anywhere without seeing someone she knows," Nicole said. They had only been in Paris for a month, and Sarah already knew half of the students at the university. Abby shook her head. Sarah always made an appearance with all the guys.

"Have you been here long?" Abby asked.

"About an hour. It's been quiet, not much happening. So what have you two been doing?"

"We went to an Italian restaurant. I've been friends with the owner for years," Jayson said.

"Sounds good. I'll have to try it sometime." Nicole sipped her drink. "How's the tennis been going? Abby says you practice almost every day."

"I'm slowly getting back into it. I didn't do so well in my last tournament. I had an early exit."

"You lost?"

Abby gasped at the bluntness of Nicole's words.

Jayson laughed. "Yeah, I lost. I wasn't having my best match. I withdrew because of an injury."

"Hey guys. I'm glad you made it and you brought Jayson." Abby heard Sarah's voice behind her.

The time had arrived. Abby turned and found Sarah standing over her. Abby could no longer see Jayson's face as Sarah's ample bosom blocked her view. What was it about her? Her breasts were falling out of her halter top. She obviously bought it two sizes too small.

"Sarah, you remember Jayson." Abby went through the useless introduction. She wished Sarah would park her bosoms in a seat.

"Of course I do. Who could forget him? How have you been?" Sarah cooed over in his direction. She pulled up a chair from another table and positioned it in between Jayson and Abby. Abby had to scoot back as Sarah moved in beside Jayson.

"I've been pretty good. How about you?" Abby heard Jayson say, barely hearing his voice through Sarah's back. Sarah and Jayson were huddled close together. Abby tapped Sarah on the shoulder. "Sarah, why don't you sit on the other side. I'm almost sitting on top of you."

Sarah stared at her drink and shrugged her shoulders. At first, Abby didn't think she was going to move. "Okay. I'm practically on top of Jayson anyway. I'm sure he doesn't want me falling all over him." Sarah added before she got up from her chair.

Sarah's breast brushed up against Jayson's back as she passed him. Abby's fists tightened as she watched Sarah's hips swish from side to side, amplifying her perfect butt as it passed in front of Jayson's view. Abby glanced at Jayson. He grinned. He was watching her not Sarah.

The one room bar amplified the music as it bounced off the walls. Abby noticed the dullness of the décor for the first time. Lanterns hung on the walls, providing flickering light that jumped off people and cast shadows on various parts of their bodies. The bar was only half full, leaving several empty tables scattered around the room. The chair legs were uneven, resulting in wobbling seats as people sat. The tables were damaged, the wood wearing deep gashes from several decades of use. It gave the pub a rugged feel.

"I like this bar. Do you all come here often?" Jayson asked raising his voice over the music coming from the dance floor.

"We come here a lot. We also go to Coco Lobo, but this is a quiet alternative. It's not far from campus," Abby said knowing she hardly ever went to either place. She stole a quick sip of her drink and washed away the dryness in her throat.

"This Coco Lobo sounds interesting," Jayson said.

"It is. You'll have to come with us one night. It has an awesome dance floor." Sarah blurted out.

"Probably regular customers the bartenders and bouncers know by name?" Jayson asked. His eyes stopped wondering around the table and focused on Abby's face. His gaze seemed to be tearing her clothes off, but Abby knew her mind was imaging it. She shifted her head, trying to hide the redness that burned her cheeks. His fingers grazed her hand as he took hold of it.

"Abby has barely told us anything about you," Sarah said. She produced one of her seductive smiles, one that would ignite a man's insides on fire.

"There's nothing much to say. I'm a regular guy, who happens to play a lot of tennis. Some say I'm good at it. I'm lucky to be able to travel around and play the sport. I've been playing tennis most of my life. Right now, I'm burnt out. I've been trying to relax and concentrate on nothing. Abby's been a great distraction." Jayson smiled at Abby, causing her mouth to curl up into a small grin. Sarah sipped on her martini. Her smile had faded.

"If you're burnt out, why are you spending everyday practicing? Abby says you practice during the day, then hang out with her. Doesn't seem like you're relaxing," Nicole said. Abby shot her a pleading look, but Nicole ignored her. Abby appreciated Nicole's curiosity, but her cross-examination was getting too severe.

"I can say I'm burnt out and I want to relax, but I still need to train. The sport will leave me behind otherwise, and I'm not ready for that." He took a drink of his beer. "In a way, I am relaxing. I don't usually get to hang out like this. I'm always at the hotel, reviewing previous tennis matches or doing some type of preparation for a tournament. At least now, I'm doing something different."

"When's your next tennis tournament?" Abby asked. She hoped her question would lead the conversation to an area that would force Nicole to stop badgering him. He didn't answer immediately, almost as if he didn't want to answer the question at all. His reluctance confused Abby.

"I'm not sure. I withdrew from an upcoming tournament due to my injury, so it may be awhile before I enter another one. It depends on my wrist." Jayson wiggled his wrist back and forth before flexing his hand from side to side.

"You don't look injured." Nicole resumed her grilling.

"Stop hassling him. Injuries aren't always visible." Sarah finally spoke. She smiled seductively at Jayson.

"I have some tendonitis in my wrist. Not enough to cause a serious injury but enough to bother me while playing. I was advised to take it easy and not to aggravate it." Jayson downed the remaining beer. "Anyone need another?" He held up his mug.

"Sure. I'll take the house beer." Nicole slid her glass across the table.

Abby knew Nicole would never pass up a free drink. Jayson glanced over at Abby. She shook her head. She still had half of her drink left.

"I'll take another. Dirty Martini." Sarah purred at him.

"I'll be right back." He jumped up and headed to the bar.

Sarah squalled, letting out a sound imitating a small furry animal. "He's so hot. How can you not jump on that?" Sarah licked her lips, almost salivating.

"I thought you were going to strip him down right here," Abby said peering over at her.

"If you don't, I will. Just letting you know," Sarah said. Abby hoped she was joking, but she suspected Sarah meant it.

"Something seems weird." Nicole bit her lip, sucking it into her mouth.

"What? With Jayson?" Sarah asked.

"He seemed uncomfortable talking about tennis? If something was a big part of your life, wouldn't you want to talk about it?" Nicole asked. Sarah and Abby stared at her.

"How would you respond? You interrogated him like a criminal. I wouldn't have brought him here if I knew you were going to turn into an investigator, and Sarah was going to turn into a sex machine." Abby slumped in her seat. She hoped Jayson would come back. If she were Jayson, she would've bolted for the door.

"No, listen to me for a sec. If he was told to take it easy and not aggravate his wrist, why would he practice as much as he says he does? Seems strange to withdraw from a tournament due to injury, then practice every day while injured." Nicole clicked her teeth as she stared in the direction of the bar.

Abby sat there, silent, and couldn't come up with an answer.

"I wasn't flirting. I was being friendly," Sarah said. She hadn't said a word the last few minutes, and Abby almost forgot she was there. Her comment brought Sarah's behavior to the forefront of Abby's mind. The poutiness of her voice revolted Abby.

"Please, I would hate to see what flirting was if that wasn't it. Knock it off." Abby glared at her. Sarah nodded and Abby relaxed her fists.

A few minutes later, Jayson returned to the table holding a tray full of drinks. "I figured we all needed a few more." He set a full martini glass and one of the shot glasses in front of Sarah, then he placed two glasses in front of Abby.

"Rum and Coke for you." Jayson put a beer and a shot in front of Nicole. He deposited the tray on the table opposite of them and sat beside Abby. "Alright, ladies. Drink up." He grabbed his shot, held it up in the air, and turned it to his lips, swallowing the liquid in one gulp.

"Salut." Sarah took hers and did the same.

Abby stared at her own. Shots did not agree with her. She hardly ever drank them, and she didn't particularly want to drink this one either. She would end up lying by the toilet all night.

"Drink, Abby," Sarah yelled at her.

Abby felt all eyes at the table fall on her. She stared at the small clear glass. The grayish brown liquid had settled at the bottom with a milky foam on top.

"I'd rather not. I'll take the Rum and Coke." Abby pushed the shot glass out of her reach. She wouldn't have a repeat of her night with Ethan. She wanted some control over her emotions later on. She didn't want alcohol making her decisions. If anything happened, it would be because she made the choice. Not that she was romantically interested in Jayson anymore; they were friends, but it didn't hurt to keep a level head.

"Aww, come on. Jayson bought it for you," Sarah whined, pushing the glass back in front of Abby.

"I don't do shots." Abby's voice was firmer than she wanted. Sarah was only pressing her to drink the shot because she knew Abby hated them. "Thanks." She smiled at Jayson and pushed the glass back again.

Jayson laughed. He took the shot and downed it in one swallow. He squeezed Abby's hand and winked at her. Goosebumps sprung out on her arm. His eyes lingered on hers a few seconds. That same fire she'd seen at the park was present now.

"Jayson, are you playing here, in Paris?" Sarah asked.

Jayson's eyes darted away from Abby's. She wanted to kick Sarah for interrupting the moment, but, unfortunately, she was too far away to reach her with her foot.

"I doubt it," Jayson said.

"I figured that's why you were here." Sarah rested her eyes on his.

He stared at her for a moment before answering. "It's a competitive field, and I'm not one hundred percent right now. I don't want to hurt myself worse than I already am." Abby wondered what tournament Sarah was referring to.

Sarah shrugged her shoulders and took a sip of her drink. Jayson stared at her a few seconds before turning toward Abby.

He ran his hand over his buzz cut. "Enough about me, we should talk about you girls."

Sarah stood up. Abby stared at her as Sarah waved her arms causing her shirt to tighten around her gigantic chest. Abby didn't even turn to look at Jayson. She knew where his eyes were. Those breasts were magnets, drawing the attention of every guy in the room. Abby twisted around instead to see who Sarah was waving at and nearly hit the floor after she spotted Sarah's target. Abby immediately recognized the brown curls on the head that was moving toward them.

Chapter 21

Ethan froze when he saw Jayson sitting beside Abby. He should've known Sarah was up to something when she called and invited him to the pub. He couldn't believe Abby was playing this childish game with him. Fury built up in his chest as he thought of Abby using him. After all he'd done to convince her father to let her stay in Paris, he felt stupid that he actually thought she was mature. At least now, he could let Nols know that he found Jayson. They'd lost him a few hours ago, but he should've known that Jayson would be with Abby.

Ethan stared into Abby's eyes. The wild blue kept him mesmerized. Why she would do this, he had no idea. But he knew one thing, Abby had better recalculate her tactics if she thought this crazy trick would work on him. Her little plan would backfire. Just yesterday, he left the interrogation room after a meeting with Jayson and his lawyers. Walters was now officially named a suspect in the investigation. This encounter would work to Ethan's advantage.

Ethan took a slow breath and released it. It would be his pleasure to watch Jayson squirm.

"Hey," Ethan said as he approached the table. Abby glanced in Ethan's direction but didn't acknowledge him at first, almost as if she were surprised by his arrival. She was a great actress. He stuck his hand out in front of Jayson. "I'm Ethan."

Jayson glared at him, his brows drawn together. "Jayson, nice to meet you." He slowly took Ethan's hand and shook it, before quickly drawing it away. Jayson stiffened and he shifted in his seat.

"I'm sorry to interrupt. Saw the girls over here, and I wanted to stop over and say hello. I haven't seen Abby since the other night, so I wanted to make sure she was okay."

"I'm fine," Abby said quickly and didn't look at him, but he saw the red creeping up on her neck. Great, he hit a nerve with her.

"Good, well I'll leave you all to your drinks." He twisted his body in the direction of the bar. He had what he needed, the pleading in her eyes, begging him, like she wanted him away from Jayson. She should make up her mind. Did she want to play this game or not?

"Join us. We have plenty of room," Sarah said. She scooted a chair over to the table. Ethan stared at the seat like it was a death sentence. He wouldn't sit on one side of Abby while that criminal was next to her. He got what he wanted. Jayson had no clue why Ethan was there, and he probably thought it was an intimidation tactic by the FBI. Ethan knew he couldn't risk alienating Jayson too much or his lawyers would file harassment charges against him. As much as he would love to torture Abby at her own game, he couldn't risk the investigation.

"Nah, I'm meeting some friends here," Ethan said. "If you're still here later, I'll stop by. He pushed his way into the crowd and straight toward the bar. "Whiskey," he yelled at the bartender. It was Ethan's night off, so he could afford a few drinks. Someone else was supposed to watch Abby tonight. He needed a break. Ethan snatched the glass out of the bartender's hand before she set it on the bar and brought it to his mouth. "Give me another."

Who was he kidding? He didn't blame Abby for her attraction to Jayson. They were from the same class, privileged kids who never had to work for anything. Even though Abby had no idea Jayson was a famous tennis player, she probably knew they were similar in backgrounds. People like that attracted each other.

"Do I need to call my lawyers?"

Ethan jerked his head around. Jayson's irritated face glared back at him.

"Not unless you plan on giving me some information on Peretti." Ethan seized the new drink and downed it.

"We discussed this yesterday. My lawyer will contact you with my decision."

"Sure, I'll wait for his call. Shouldn't you be hanging out with your girlfriend?"

"Well...I...she's not my girlfriend."

"She's cute. A little feisty sometimes. And my favorite, that cute mole on her temple. Kind of reminds me of that model you used to date. Help me out here. What was her name?"

"Leave Abby alone."

The tone of his voice confirmed Ethan's suspicions. Jayson wanted Abby for something, and he didn't want Ethan interfering. He was sure Jayson didn't just want to date Abby. Ethan turned and drove daggers in Jayson's chest with his eyes. "Now why would I leave her alone? I like her, and we've had fun together the times we went out."

"Don't harass her, Gray. She's a nice girl." Jayson's fists clinched as he said the words.

"Right, so why is she with you?"

Jayson's hand clamped down on the arm of the stool next to Ethan. "I can date anyone I want. I'm not charged with any crime." Jayson jabbed his finger in Ethan's chest. "Leave her out of this." He turned and walked away.

"Sure, I'll do that," Ethan said as he raised his glass in a toast before bringing it to his lips. He let the liquid linger in his throat. The burning masked the pure hatred he had for Walters. He had to hold back all of his rage or he'd have decked the guy when Jayson touched him. That jerk would end up costing Abby her internship and the freedom she had there in Paris. She didn't even know it and Ethan still couldn't tell her. Tom had denied his request to brief her on the investigation. He said the Senator didn't want Abby to worry. Her father couldn't see that she was no longer a child who needed to be isolated. She was a woman who needed to go out on her own and experience life. Ethan twirled the glass around on the table. Maybe he should tell her anyway. He was no longer undercover with the Walters investigation. The only people who didn't know his true identity was Abby and her sisters. She needed to know so she could make better decisions instead of hanging out with this lowlife.

Ethan smelled the sweet honey scent before he saw her. It almost made him forget the game she was playing. He frowned. "I'm surprised to see you. Jayson's not here."

She didn't say anything.

Ethan motioned to the bartender. "Give me another and take care of hers too." He nodded at Abby's mugs. Three drinks in under thirty minutes. Nols would probably have to escort him home after he was done tonight.

Abby scooted the glasses back. "No. That's okay. I'll get mine."

"Tell him what you want. Don't argue," Ethan said flatly.

Abby drew in a deep breath. She ordered her drink. "Thanks. You didn't have to buy my drink." Grabbing a napkin, she pulled small pieces off the corners and rolled them up into small little paper tubes.

"You're welcome." Ethan fell silent. She still couldn't be around him without being nervous. They were back to that again. "Will you quit that? You're always littering the table with those damn paper scraps." Ethan swiped the pile to the floor.

Laying the napkin down, she pushed it across the bar out of her reach. "What are you doing here?"

"Oh, I don't know. I thought I'd drop in on your date." Ethan stared at her.

She lowered her eyes. "I didn't think you'd be here."

"Sarah invited me, but you know that, don't you? I didn't realize we were playing a game. That is what you're doing, isn't it?"

"No. There's no game. I didn't know you'd be here." Abby stopped when Ethan held up his hand in front of her.

"It seems too convenient to have two guys chasing after you and we both happen to show up at the same place. What does Sarah have to gain by asking me here?" Ethan refused to look at her as he stared at the wall. The bartender returned with the drinks and set them on the counter.

"I need to get these back to the table." As she started to pick up the glasses, he put his hand on hers.

"Where is he now?"

"Jayson? He's with Sarah on the dance floor," Abby said.

Ethan's face turned hot. "Don't you see what type of guy he is? Why would a guy dance with your sister while he's here with you?" Ethan squeezed Abby's hand tighter. He knew his eyes were revealing the fury building in him.

She broke the gaze. "I told him he could. All of this is Sarah's fault. She created all of this." Abby barely got the words out before Ethan's head flew back as he laughed.

"You gave him permission. That's great. Let me guess. Saying no would've made you sound jealous? Sarah may have set this up, but Jayson chose to do what he wants. Stand up to your sisters for once in your bloody life. "

"How I handle my sisters is my business."

"Jayson's a player like Sarah's a player. Why do you let them run all over you?"

"No, this isn't Jayson's fault. He didn't suggest the dance. She did. She's the one who wanted you here..."

"He didn't decline either. He's playing with you, Abby." Ethan shot back.

"No one is running all over me. I choose whom I want to be with. Sarah invited you here to distract me, but it didn't work. You don't have that much effect on me."

He shook his head. "Why can't you see that I know what I'm talking about when it comes to this guy? He's bad for you."

"How do you know? Do you know him?"

Ethan jerked his head around and faced her. "You don't have to know someone to know that they aren't good for a person. Trust me on this."

"You're jealous because I'm with someone else tonight. You need to back off." Abby twirled around just as Ethan wrapped his arms around her waist. He leaned against her so her back pressed against his chest. The sweet sugary scent tantalized him. Even though he was furious with her, he couldn't leave her alone.

"You can't deny you feel something for me. I know you care because you wouldn't have come over here. I'm a patient guy. I'll wait, but I won't stand by and let someone hurt you." He kissed the back of her head and released her. She stood there a few seconds before walking toward the table.

Ethan threw the money on the counter for the tab and headed for the door. His orders were to protect Abby Rodgers and he would, even if she hated him for it. This would be the last night Abby saw Jayson Walters.

Chapter 22

*A*bby reached the booth to find Nicole tapping her fingers on the tabletop's wooden planks. "Holy cow, Abs. Did you go to a bar in Italy?" Nicole snatched her drink from Abby's hand.

"Sorry. I ran into Ethan. It took longer than I thought." Abby sat in the chair beside Nicole. Her body still reeled from his touch. She knew he knew it too. Her anger threatened to consume her. How dare he tell her what to do? She was going to explain to him that she and Jayson were friends, that he was helping her with Von Deez. She wanted Ethan to know that there was nothing going on but when he lectured her like her father did, she snapped. She didn't need someone else controlling her life.

"How did that go?" Nicole had already drunk a third of her beer.

"Not well. He told me what I already knew. Sarah invited him. Then he went on to badmouth Jayson for dancing with Sarah." Abby took a sip of her drink and cringed as she remembered the hurt in Ethan's eyes.

"I can't believe you let her get away with that," Nicole yelled across the table, her voice almost drowned out by the music.

"Which part? Sarah inviting Ethan or taking Jayson out on the dance floor?" Abby asked. She brought her glass to her lips and swallowed the remainder of her drink, wishing she had another one.

"Both. You know how she is. You didn't think she'd try something like this?"

"I thought all she'd do was some harmless flirting. I didn't know she was going to perform all-out sabotage." Abby stared at her glass. She figured Nicole would be the one to do something to embarrass her, not Sarah.

"You better figure it out or she'll ruin everything you have going on with both of these guys." Nicole played with her hair and stared at the dance floor. "Ethan may be right about Jayson. He could've danced one song with Sarah, but he's still out there."

Abby looked over at her. "I doubt he could say no to her. She always gets what she wants. I don't know what I'm supposed to do." Abby let out a huge breath. She'd let Sarah walk all over her since their brother's death. It had been almost a year but she still couldn't bring herself to fight with her.

"Make up your mind about who you want. It's obvious you like Ethan. With Jayson, I'm not sure if it's him or the mystery surrounding him that excites you," Nicole said.

Abby stared at the stained glass windows that towered in front of her. They now appeared almost black since the sun had set. Her irritation increased as she thought of Sarah and Ethan. Both wanted to sabotage her relationship with Jayson. She wouldn't allow them to succeed. If Ethan thought she and Jayson were more than friends, she'd give it to him.

"You can't keep seeing both of them." Nicole pointed behind Abby. "Jayson's on his way back here."

Abby's heart skipped a beat as she turned around. "Hey you," Abby said as Jayson approached the table. "You were out there a long time."

Small beads of sweat rolled down Jayson's face. "Yeah. I was finally able to pull myself off the dance floor. Are you having a good time?" Jayson sat and draped his arm around Abby's shoulders.

She smiled. "I'm glad to see you remembered I was here." Abby taunted him with a fake frown.

"Were you feeling left out, Baby?" Jayson squeezed her shoulders.

Abby flinched at the nickname. It always reminded her of a possession, but she let it slip from her mind. "A little," she said.

Jayson pulled her closer and kissed her. "Better now?"

Abby tensed but relaxed when she thought about Ethan's demands. No one would tell her what to do. "Maybe a little more?"

He smiled and kissed her again. "How about now?"

Abby nodded. "You ready to leave?" She grabbed her purse, not waiting for Jayson to answer. She was ready to get as far away as possible from Sarah and Ethan. "Nicole, you have a way back to campus?" Abby asked as she got up from her chair. She finally broke eye contact with Jayson after he nodded. She quickly glanced at her sister.

"Yeah. I need a few more drinks. The night is still young," Nicole said.

"See you later." Abby followed Jayson to the exit. She tried not to glance back at the bar. She didn't want to see Ethan on her way out.

"Where to?" Abby asked. The cool wind hit her face as they exited the door, bringing relief to her sweaty cheeks.

"How about my hotel? We can have a few more drinks and do whatever else we want."

The offer intrigued Abby. Tonight with the girls had been a total failure. Abby knew what a trip to his hotel meant. She was ready. It was time to get naughty. A way to escape the hurt. If everyone thought the worst of her, she might as well dip into the sins of love.

"Sounds good. Lead the way," Abby said as she accepted his extended hand and left her doubts at the bar.

Chapter 23

"This is your hotel?" Abby asked as she examined the plain exterior of the building. She couldn't believe Jayson was staying in this dreary place. He had private dinners arranged for her at Geo's and a chateau as temporary residence where he conducted his tennis practices. This didn't look like a place he'd stay. The deserted street and dark building looked like the hotel should be in the ghetto.

He took Abby's hand and helped her out of the car. "It's the back of the hotel. The front entrance is difficult to get in and out. Cabs usually drop off people here."

They entered through a small door near the center of the building. Hidden in the shadows, Abby never would've seen it. Staring down the hallway, she couldn't tell any difference in the decor. It still looked awful to her. Jayson led her down the corridor to a small room with several elevators. With no decorations on the walls, Abby wondered if they were in a hotel. It was more like the inside of an old apartment building. They entered the elevator and Jayson pressed the button for the top floor. The elevator's elegant décor eased her concern. It was lined in stylish brass fixtures and had a wooden floor with a crisscross pattern. She sighed with relief.

The elevator doors opened, and Jayson and Abby stepped out into another hallway. The furnishings transformed from bland to chic. Dark wood tables stood near the walls with brass lamps centered on top. She had entered a high-end hotel, probably one of the most luxurious hotels in Paris.

"It's this one here." Jayson stopped in front of one of the doors not far from the elevator.

Abby stood beside him gawking at the fancy decorations. Paisley wallpaper in blues and reds decorated the upper half of the walls. Blush burgundy runners covered the wooden floors. Jayson opened the door, and Abby entered. The exquisite décor continued into his suite.

"Wow." Abby walked around the open living room. She slid her fingers across the back of the couch, allowing the fabric to brush her fingers. Hearing the noise of the street below, she moved over to the open windows. She peered out and discovered the Champs-Elysees below. She recognized the Arc de Triomphe not far from her view. It dwarfed everything around. The street filled with people was still busy, even at the late hour. The trees twinkled with bright white lights, falling in line along the road from the Arc de Triomphe to the Ferris wheel in front of the Louvre.

Jayson came up behind Abby and put his hands on her shoulders. "It's stunning at night, isn't it?"

"I can't believe you have a room with a view like this. It must be in high demand," Abby said.

"My coach knows the right people," Jayson said grinning.

He dropped his arms so they fell around her waist. She leaned back against him, resting her head on his chest. She could do this. He liked her. She liked him. Bending down, he caressed her neck with his lips. Abby closed her eyes. The roughness of the stubble on his chin brushed up against the curve of her shoulder.

"Why don't we finish this evening in the bedroom?" Jayson teased Abby's ear with his tongue. He took her by the hand, guiding her to the next room and pushed her to the edge of the bed. Abby sat on the fluffy comforter, sinking into the covers. Jayson dropped down beside her. Wrapping his arms around the bottom of her waist, he pulled her to him. He leaned forward taking her mouth into his. Running his hands up along her neck, he gently pushed her back so she lay on the edge of the bed. Jayson took his hand and pulled her shirt up to her shoulders revealing her pink bra.

"Oh yeah. I like that." Jayson's voice was husky. His eyes grew hot as he moved his hand over her breast. Cradling her hips, he bent down and kissed her stomach. She stared at the ceiling. The passion wasn't there. Sure, her body was responding to him, but it was only physical. She should feel something, but she didn't.

A buzzing sound caught Abby's attention. She tilted her head and spotted the red light blinking on the phone sitting on the nightstand. Feeling Jayson's lips leave her stomach, she rose, and leaned back on her arms. Jayson stared at the phone.

"You getting that?" Abby asked as relief showered her.

He gripped her shoulder and pulled her back down from her sitting position. "No, it'll wait." He buried his head against her neck.

Abby twisted away from him. "It's late so it must be important."

"It'll only take a second." Jayson kissed her on the cheek and jumped up. He hurried over to the nightstand and grabbed the phone.

"Hello?" Stretching the phone cord as far as it would go, he walked across the room to the open window. Abby propped herself higher on her elbows and stared at the artwork on the ceiling for the first time. It reminded her of several paintings she'd seen at various buildings in Paris. Angels and clouds decorated the corners and stared down on her. She relaxed and lost herself in the artwork.

"Abby."

She heard something in his voice. She glanced at him. The lust she'd seen earlier had vanished from his eyes.

Jayson frowned. "We'll have to continue this another time."

Abby pushed herself upright on the bed. Tension in his face deepened the lines on his forehead as he stood with his arms crossed.

"Sure, another time." Abby flopped back down on the bed and sent a silent thank you to the angels floating in the painting above. Maybe they were looking out for her.

Jayson took her hand and pulled her off the bed. "Something's come up I have to take care of."

"I hope everything is okay," Abby said as she picked up her shoes and slipped them on.

"Everything's fine. It's my manager. I have a minor issue that needs to be addressed." He closed his arms around her and drew her into a long kiss. His lips lingered on hers.

"I promise, we'll pick up where we left off. There's so much left for me to explore," he whispered in her ear.

Abby nodded. She wasn't sure there was anything left to explore. She couldn't do this with Jayson again. It didn't feel right.

Jayson picked up the phone. "I'll call the front desk and arrange for a cab to pick you up." Abby's mouth gaped open. He wasn't going to take her home. He already dialed the number on the keypad. Turning around, she searched for her purse, which she spotted lying on the couch in the living room.

Jayson came over to Abby. "The cab will be downstairs in ten minutes." She frowned as he approached. "Abby, I'm sorry. I feel terrible, but I promise to make it up to you." He ran his hand through her hair. Seizing her neck, he pulled her into another kiss. He backed away and took her hand, leading her to the door.

Jayson retrieved a few bills out of his wallet. "Take this for the cab fare."

Abby forced a smile and stared at the money in his hand. "You don't have to."

"Yes, I do," he said as he opened the door. She entered the corridor and turned back to see Jayson leaning on the doorframe. Even though she was relieved, it was strange, the way he was forcing her out.

He pecked her on the lips. "I'll talk to you soon."

Abby reluctantly smiled before heading down the hallway to the elevator. She heard the door close behind her. Not only did her night end early, but she had to walk herself to the cab stand. He didn't even escort her outside.

This wasn't how this night was supposed to end, and she hoped everything was okay between them. She didn't want to lose another friend.

Chapter 24

"You want to do what?" Tom barked. He slammed his hand on the desk, and the container of pens jumped.

Ethan slumped in the leather seat and glanced at his supervisor. Tom's deep wrinkles in his cheeks intensified as he frowned, exposing his irritation.

"I want to be reassigned. Moved away from Abby Rodgers. She's too attached, and the whole plan was to protect her from getting hurt." He hoped Tom didn't suspect the truth, that one of his top agents, the one who never got too close, had fallen for his mark.

"Absolutely not. If I take you off the Rodgers girls, you're off the Walters case too. Senator Rodgers expects his daughter to be safe and away from Walters. If it means she gets attached to you, so be it. It's better than getting involved with a criminal." He shuffled a few papers on the desk. "How's it going? Is Walters leaving her alone? I need the Senator off my back. He's calling every day."

Ethan shook his head. Instead of talking about the latest on the gambling evidence, he was forced to discuss his relationship with Abby. He wished he was back where he was before he'd met her. "We intercepted an email from Abby saying that it was better if they stopped seeing each other. They haven't been together in the last two weeks."

"Your charm must be working again, Gray."

Ethan remained silent. It didn't add up. Abby seemed infatuated with Jayson. Why would she break it off with him? He knew it was nothing he did. He hadn't even been able to put his plan in motion to force Jayson away from her. Abby had avoided him since Walters showed up in Paris. Charm or not, it wasn't Ethan that influenced her decision.

"How about transferring it to the CIA or Secret Service? He's a senator. They are allowed to have agents for protection." Ethan's teeth clamped down on his lips as he saw his boss's neck turn redder.

"You want to hand off the duty to the CIA? You not up to guarding a few girls? It's not like this is the President's family. Really, Secret Service?"

Ethan sucked in a breath. "He is President pro tempore of the Senate and number three in the presidential line of succession. Secret Service would be ideal for his family. They had the protection in the United States."

Tom stopped shuffling papers and glanced at Ethan. "The Senator didn't want Secret Service agents guarding his girls here because they did a glorious job protecting his son, didn't they?"

Ethan lowered his head. He couldn't argue with Tom. The girls were masters at providing Nols with a surveillance challenge and they didn't even know they were being watched. With the Secret Service, they would be notified about the surveillance. Their freedom would be gone.

"Are you finished with your political history lesson? I'm impressed you know the line of succession for the U.S. Presidency but it doesn't help your argument." Tom snapped.

Ethan nodded but refused to look at his supervisor.

"Very well, I'll compromise with you. Stay with her until Jayson Walters leaves for London and I'll assign a few agents to the girls. After that, you can be reassigned to the U.K. and you can pick up the investigation. We need you there anyway. They like that you're a resident. Helps with that uptight territorial police force. They're threatened by us."

"Thanks," Ethan muttered. At least, he'd be back on the case, back where he belonged.

"What about the other sisters? They involved with Walters?" Tom banged on the keyboard, not looking at Ethan.

"Not that we can tell."

Tom went back to his mound of paperwork. "Good. Report back in a few days."

Ethan nodded and headed out the door. Nols jumped up off the couch as Ethan marched by.

"Well, what's the verdict?"

He didn't look at his partner. "Still with Abby until Jayson leaves for London."

"I'm sorry." Nols fell in step with Ethan. "How you going to handle it?"

"I'm fine. It'll be a week. Two at the most." He didn't have to hide it from Nols. The guy picked up on Ethan's bleak mood immediately.

"It'll work out. Do it for two weeks, then let it cool off. Once we finalize the Walters case, you can find her again. If she feels the same way you do, a few months won't kill you."

Ethan stopped in his tracks. "It won't work. I've lied to her for the past few months. She won't forget that. How am I supposed to tell her that I'm not a student. I'm an FBI agent. How do I do that?"

"It's all fair. Look at how she's treated you. It's not been all honesty on her part."

Ethan gritted his teeth. "Yeah, well, I forced her to choose and she chose Walters."

Nols shook his head. "Then why bother? I don't understand how you can still feel this way about her."

"My job is to protect her no matter how she treats me." Ethan stared at the bulletin board on the far wall. Despite her seeing Jayson, he knew Abby cared about him. He could see it in her eyes but it was almost as if she was afraid to open up. He could relate to that. "She's hiding something."

Nols shook his head. "Don't do it."

"Do what?"

159

Nols shrugged. "Since I've known you, you've never cared about anyone, but when you met her, you started caring about more than this job. You'd be a fool to throw this away. Don't look for trouble that's not there."

"I'm not. She doesn't deserve what I'm doing to her. She deserves better. She's a senator's daughter from one of the richest families in Florida."

"First off, she'll get over the lies. You've lied to each other. Look at her family, she's used to it. Second, you've got to let go of your past. So you grew up in foster homes and never knew your parents. You've let that rule your life and now you're judging Abby because she's had a more privileged life? You're an FBI agent with ties to Britain and France. Dual citizenship in the U.S and Britain and the FBI's dream agent. Your life, as bad as it was, produced some major opportunities for you."

"Yeah, I know I'm a regular FBI super-agent."

"You are, so you need to quit hanging onto the past."

"That's not what I'm doing"

"You use it as an excuse to keep everyone away from you. You let Abby in. It may be against policy, but I'll be a fool to report it."

"You should. I've pretty much crapped on my career. This case could blow my promotion."

"Let me worry about Jayson Walters. You gave us most of the evidence. Let Tom and Steve take care of the rest. We don't need much more."

"Sure, hand off the work I did."

"Yes, you have another case."

"Abby Rodgers is not a case."

"When a U.S. Senator requests assistance, it's your job, regardless of your feelings"

"Remember that when you're asked to testify at my disciplinary hearing."

"I will. I won't recall we ever had this conversation."

"Sure."

"You think Walters will leave her alone?"

"Don't know. It doesn't make sense for Abby to dump him."

"Maybe she likes you."

"No, she made it clear last time I saw her. She was free to see whomever she chooses."

"You may have a shot now." He hit Ethan on the back.

"Thanks for that encouragement."

"If Abby continues to see Walters, her father will fly her back to the U.S. He wanted her to stay, but he won't risk losing her."

Ethan nodded. It would mean she'd forgo her internship. Based on her file and what she confided in him, she had worked her first two years in school solely to win that job. It would crush her. He knew she buried herself in the internship since her brother's death. It was her escape like his job was his escape from his reality. To lose it was to lose her sole existence. He could sacrifice a little recognition in order to help Abby save her internship.

Chapter 25

"You can't sit there and not tell us how it's going. You've been out with him several times and not one word from you," Nicole said.

Abby nibbled on a piece of bruschetta the waiter had brought. She'd agreed to afternoon shopping with Sarah and Nicole, but was unsuccessful at deflecting their questions about Jayson.

"There's not much to tell. We spent several evenings together. Since he's training more during the day, that's all the time he has now." Abby shifted in her seat, hoping her voice didn't give her away.

Sarah sat across from her and stopped eating her salad. "Why haven't you brought him to Coco Lobo?" she asked as she examined her well-manicured nails.

"After the incident with Ethan, I figured Coco Lobo isn't an option," Abby said.

The girls nodded, acknowledging Sarah's attempt to lure Ethan to the bar. Abby had successfully avoided Ethan since the encounter. She missed him but didn't want to face the guilt from hurting him. She'd been crushed because Jayson hadn't called since the night at his hotel room. Even if they were just friends, the rejection stung. She'd lost the model she centered her campaign on. She didn't want to face the fact that she may have lost Ethan too.

"It's better this way. I don't think Ethan and Jayson would get along very well," Sarah said, snorting.

"Don't start." Abby cut her off.

"What? Something wrong? Things not so rosy in your love life?" Sarah asked, jumping all over Abby's bleak mood. "You've been acting depressed for days. What's going on?"

"Nothing. Everything's fine. I miss having Ethan around. That's all." Abby knew there was truth in that statement even though Jayson was still on her mind.

"Well, at least you have some feelings for him. I was beginning to wonder if you enjoyed hurting the poor guy," Nicole said.

Abby swung her head around letting her brown hair fall in her eyes. "What do you mean? I'm not hurting him."

Nicole shook her head. "You shouldn't ignore Ethan. I don't think you know how vulnerable you can get when you play with someone like Jayson."

"I think I understand that," Abby muttered and lowered her head, already knowing how the hurt felt. Jayson hadn't returned any of her phone calls. He'd disappeared.

"Good because here's your chance to show it." Nicole turned to Sarah. "Don't we have a hair appointment this afternoon?"

Sarah stared at her, a blank look in her eye. "I don't know."

"You remember. We made it a few weeks ago. You don't mind if we skip lunch, do you?" Nicole asked as she yanked Sarah by the arm and pulled her up out of the chair.

"Oh, yeah. I remember," Sarah said still acting as if she didn't know what Nicole was talking about. Abby watched as they picked up their bags and left. What was going on? Sarah practically kidnapped her to go shopping. Now, they were ditching her for a hair appointment.

"Abby." A deep voice spoke behind her. Goose bumps surfaced on her arms as she recognized the husky British accent. Abby turned to see Ethan. He looked amazing standing there in the afternoon sun, his hair scattered on his head in its usual organized mess. She loved how it looked like he just woke up. Gone was the clean appearance, replaced with a more casual rough look with his day old growth on his chin.

Abby shook her senses back, willing herself not to be attracted to him, but what was the point? If she screwed up her job, she might as well give in to love.

Ethan walked over and took the chair recently vacated by Sarah. His mouth broke into a huge grin. "I'm glad I finally caught up with you. You've been avoiding me." He motioned the waiter over and ordered an entree Abby didn't recognize.

"I've been busy with school. The Fashion Week Party is in a few weeks. I haven't had much time to hang out. How have you been?" Abby felt bad that she'd purposely avoided him. Her guilt escalated with him sitting in front of her along with the Fashion Week Party weighing on her. Gilda asked her again for her date's name and she still had no answer for her since Jayson was no longer available.

Ethan laughed. "That's not true. You've been avoiding me. Believe me, I understand and I'm sorry."

She didn't say anything. What did he have to apologize for? This was all her fault.

"I'm willing to back off, but you'll have to do something for me," he said taking a big gulp of water from the glass the waiter had set down on the table.

Abby saw something daring in his eyes. She'd probably agree just to get him to stop staring at her that way. "What is it?" she asked, already knowing it had to be something that benefited him.

"Stop avoiding me. I'm your friend regardless of what happened."

"Okay." She wished it were more than friends, but she just got him back. She didn't want to jinx it.

"Second, you have to give me a chance. I won't force you to not see Jayson, but I want an equal opportunity. I think I deserve that."

"Why? I haven't been nice to you lately. Why would you want to hang out with me?" Abby asked. After how she acted, she didn't have a clue why he would want to be with her.

"I gave you a few reasons to treat me badly. I figure I need to spend some time with someone who'll call me out when I'm misbehaving." His mouth formed a lopsided grin.

She could see him trying to anticipate her response. Abby almost laughed at him. If he only knew that Jayson was no longer around, he wouldn't be fighting so hard.

"You said you were backing off." Abby prayed it wasn't true, but she couldn't bring herself to tell him. She couldn't afford anymore distractions from the Von Deez campaign, no matter how handsome the distraction was.

"I am. I'm not going to physically try to persuade you but I could coax you with my charm."

Abby blushed and turned her head away. Yup, she was so disguising how she felt. Not even close.

Ethan rubbed his forehead. "I want to spend time with you so I'm willing to take a hands-off relationship if I have to, for now." He winked at her.

If she agreed, she'd be seeing Ethan exclusively by default. At least she wouldn't have to juggle seeing two guys at once. Sarah did it well. For the past week, she was seeing Patrick and some other guy Abby had never met. Abby welcomed her busy schedule. Sarah didn't have enough time to hound her now. Today was the first day in a while that Sarah had lunch with her and Nicole. The only reason Abby agreed to go out was because she had nothing better to do. Abby was tired of doing nothing. Lately, all she did was lie in bed or stare out the window, wondering what she was going to do about the Von Deez Party and her trust fund. She wanted to be free, free to live her life how she wanted. She was starting to believe that Ethan must be the answer.

Abby sat up. "If I accept, here are my rules. There won't be any sleepovers or late night meetings in the campus courtyard. Agreed?" She waited for him to nod. "You need stick to our arrangement about keeping your hands off." She had to get some type of promise from him since she couldn't trust herself. She didn't want to trust herself. She liked him but now wasn't the time. She had to stick to her guns.

"Agreed." Ethan tore into some bread and popped it in his mouth. "So is this the beginning of our second date?" he asked in between bites.

Abby watched his neck muscles flex as he chewed. "Now? I figured we would start this deal next week."

"You doing anything after lunch?"

Abby shook her head.

"Me neither. Seems like the perfect time to begin." He pushed the bread basket toward her. "Eat." He smiled as he dug into another piece and started on the entree the waiter had brought.

Abby looked at her own spaghetti as she tried to digest what had happened. She got suckered into this arrangement. She had to admit it. Ethan was good at getting what he wanted.

Chapter 26

"What are we doing here?" Abby asked, studying the buildings. It looked like every other street in Paris with small shops on the corners and cars littering the sides of the street.

Lunch went well. They talked about school and how Abby was adjusting to Paris. He listened patiently as she explained the details of her internship, giving her advice on the workings of the Paris business world. She was happy to be able to let her guard down and be herself. It was like the times she remembered with him before Jayson came to Paris. She didn't worry about impressing Ethan anymore. She enjoyed being herself around him. As Abby scanned the area, she heard Ethan laughing behind her. She twirled around. "What's so amusing now?"

"You. You've got tunnel vision. You need to take in your surroundings."

"I don't." Abby pouted. She searched the area. What was so special about this neighborhood?

"We're going there."

Placing his hands on her shoulders, Ethan turned her to her right. He pointed up in the air and she saw it. The Eiffel Tower soared over the surrounding buildings. It was only a few blocks away and took over the whole sky. The building in front of her hid most of the lower part, but she could still see the middle and upper portions. "Come here." Abby glanced over at Ethan. He had moved down the street.

As she walked along beside him, more of the tower came into view between two buildings. It was like the alleyway was a frame to enhance the tower's beauty.

"I never imagined it was this big," she said, mesmerized by the fact that one of the most famous structures in the world was so close.

Ethan nudged her. "I can't believe you haven't been here yet."

Abby smiled. "I've been waiting for you to take me."

He stared at her, his eyebrows raised. She knew he was questioning if she was flirting. It was the truth. She had been waiting. It wouldn't have been the same without him.

"Today's the perfect day. It won't be too hot. Did you bring your camera?" he asked as they walked down the street.

Abby patted her bag at her hip. "Of course, I always have it on me."

They merged into the crowd of tourists on the main route, obviously on their way to the same attraction. Abby stared at the huge structure as it loomed overhead. It was perched on its four steel feet, ready to overtake the adjacent buildings, like an animal that lost its way and decided to take refuge in this Paris arrondissement. Surrounded by aging stone buildings and monuments, the tower looked like it arrived a century too early.

Rounding the corner, they passed the TGV train stop and entered the park at the base of the tower. Dozens of school-aged kids darted around the grounds while people lounged on the grass. Further down the pathway, several spectators cheered on the teams from an intense soccer match. Crossing a small path, Abby and Ethan reached the base of the tower and the four feet that housed the ticket booths.

"Two tickets for the top? My treat." Ethan motioned to the nearest leg. They made their way across the area to the long snake-like line. "Do you want to walk up? It's a little over three hundred stairs to climb." He squeezed her arm.

"No, thank you. Doesn't anyone use elevators here?" Abby asked, giggling.

"I guess that's two for the elevator." Ethan approached the counter and purchased their tickets. He returned and handed one to Abby. She looked at the card. They had ten minutes until boarding.

Ethan pointed out the loading station opposite the ticket booth. "Let's head to the elevators. There's not too much to do down here. If we stand around, the street vendors will hound us."

Abby nodded.

Several people mingled in the area. Street vendors mixed in among the tourists, aggressively peddling their goods. Abby and Ethan waited in the crowd for a few minutes before the attendant opened the gate. The pack moved forward and converged at the entrance. Abby's body wedged against Ethan as people squeezed through the mass of bodies toward the doors. She could feel Ethan's firm butt muscles pressed up against her. Oh, crap. She had to get away from him before her no distraction rule went out the window. A mere brush against him sent her in a dizzy spiral of emotion. How could she pretend he didn't affect her? He had to know. Her stomach fluttered as the heat of his body warmed her.

They inched their way to the gate, stopping briefly to hand the tickets to the attendant. Breathing heavily, she whispered prayers of joy when they moved to a more open area.

The operator motioned for them to get on the elevator even though it was already crammed full with people. Abby didn't budge. There was no possible way they would fit in the compartment. Definitely the French way, personal space had a different meaning there. Ethan pushed her forward. Barely grazing her back with his chest, Ethan fell in place behind her. It wasn't too bad. She could handle the small contact.

"Scoot closer to the front. There are more people getting on," Ethan whispered.

"I can't. There's no room." Abby chewed on her lip as she felt Ethan move closer. Now his whole body was sandwiched against her.

"Attention. Les portes fermeront maintenant." A feminine voice on the intercom announced. The elevator car jerked as the doors closed behind them. Ethan adjusted his stance as people moved to the middle of the elevator to avoid the sliding doors. Something pushed against her butt. Very firm, it settled in the small valley above her buttocks. Abby closed her eyes. She felt like she couldn't breathe as Ethan's chest touched her back. His breath hit the hairs on her head, tickling her scalp. Ethan fidgeted behind her and warmth rose through her body. He felt so good.

"Get off at the first stop," Ethan whispered. The heat of his breath only added to her longing. She felt his muscles tense when she squirmed.

"Quit moving." Ethan grabbed her arms and forced her to stand still.

Abby shallowed her breathing. The next few minutes felt like hours. She tried to distract herself by thinking about other things, but she kept coming back to the mass she felt pressed up against her back. At least, he was having just as much trouble controlling himself as she was. With curiosity getting the best of her, she knew she'd never be able to resist Ethan if she couldn't even control her own thoughts for a few minutes.

The elevator slowed to a stop, and the doors opened just when she thought she couldn't take it anymore.

"Sortez, s'il vous plait," the announcer said through the loud speaker.

Abby sighed. Finally, people around her began to depart and Abby moved to the door. As she stepped out onto the platform, the crisp cool wind chilled her as it ripped through her hair.

"Remind me to find an elevator with lots of room next time," Ethan said as he walked up behind her, his eyes darting in both directions in a quick scan of the platform.

"I'm sure you enjoyed that."

Ethan grinned. "That's right. I enjoy torturing myself. I love how you tease me with that delicious body of yours."

"That's not what I was doing," Abby said, alarmed that he thought she was playing him.

"Right. All of that squirming was not for my benefit."

She opened her mouth to respond but knew they could trade barbs all day. Not wanting to add to her own torture, she left it alone. If she made a big deal about it, he'd ensure they'd go back down in a crowded elevator. She couldn't handle it again. She'd need him to satisfy her pent up desires, just not right now.

Abby surveyed the area, searching for a place to stand. People stood at the rails looking out into the skyline. A few empty spots remained. The viewing platform was a perfect place for taking pictures. Several sightseers posed near the center of the railing, while two teenagers crowded around a pay-per-view binoculars stand.

"How about that spot?" Ethan pointed to a small space where a tour group had just vacated. A few people took their place but some room still remained.

She nodded.

Ethan put his hand on her back and guided her to the opening near the railing. That one instance of contact sent goose bumps throughout her body. She increased her pace so he no longer touched her. She knew he'd already guessed her resistance was breaking. A hunger stirred inside her body, and it intensified the more time she spent with him.

Reaching the railing, she gasped at the view. She could see the entire city as the buildings flowed out one after another. The park below was now a cluster of small dots sprinkled across the grassy area, moving every so often.

"What do you think?" Ethan asked.

The breeze picked up as they stood there. Abby regretted her decision to wear her hair down. The wind whipped strands in all directions. She tried to smooth it back in place, but once she lifted her hand, it immediately began flying again. Sighing in defeat, she left it alone and focused on the miniature metropolitan below her.

Ethan pointed off in the distance. "There's Notre Dame."

Abby recognized the two towers rising from the sea of buildings, barely making out the circular window pane. Taking her camera out of her bag, she took pictures of the various landmarks. It was amazing to see all the architecture and styles rising up, forming a mélange of shapes to create the city. "This is so cool. I doubt there's a better view in the city," Abby said as she snapped away with her camera.

"It depends on the view you want. From the top of Sacre Coeur, you have a great view of the Eiffel Tower. You haven't experienced the best part of the tower yet. We still have the second platform to go." He nodded at the elevator.

Abby studied him, amused by his boyish excitement. "You enjoy this so much even though you've been here several times. Why?"

"Every time I come here, I see something new. Try to imagine all those people out there. I'm captivated by what I see. It goes on forever. Time seems to stand still up here while it continues down there." Ethan pointed to the city below.

She looked down and watched the little specks move around in the park and understood what he meant. Life seemed to go on without them. "It's almost like you can forget your life up here." Her cheery mood was rapidly deteriorating. This was the one spot Jacob wanted to visit. Up until this very moment, she hadn't realized why she avoided coming there.

"What could you possibly want to forget?"

Abby blinked back a few tears. "Sarah. Nicole. Von Deez." She wouldn't break down, not in front of Ethan. She had a second chance with him. She wasn't going to scare him away with her dark family secrets. Abby wiped her bangs from her forehead. "Just usual stuff. Nothing I can't handle."

She turned around and faced the inside of the platform. There were several rooms inside, and she spotted the gift shop. Abby loved shopping for souvenirs, and she always required a keepsake from each place she visited.

"You want to go in?" she asked, pointing to the small store.

Ethan nodded. "We better go now while the crowd has died down. People just left on the elevator. Better enjoy it. There will be others to take their place."

Abby cut through a small group of people and headed to the entrance. The windows of the shop displayed every souvenir imaginable. T-shirts, post cards, spoons, and magnets. Every item offered the image of the Eiffel Tower. She strolled through the aisles, scanning the products. Most were cheap trinkets that would probably break not long after she'd gotten them home. Shelves of various tacky mini Eiffel Tower figurines stood near the back of the shop, a perfect memento for her visit. She smiled, knowing most visitors couldn't resist this unsightly knick-knack.

Abby picked one up, examining the plastic and guessed it would turn colors one day. She might have a pink Eiffel Tower in a couple of years and that suited her just fine.

"Did you find anything you like?" Ethan asked as he came up beside her.

She giggled and held the miniature tower in her hand. "It seems so wrong to leave here without a mini Eiffel Tower." Abby twirled the small trinket in her hand.

"You going to get one?" He glanced at the shelves of souvenirs.

Abby shook her head, feeling a bit childish that she wanted such a memento. Her brother started the tradition, but he was gone now. It was time to break the habit. She placed the figurine back on the shelf. "I'll get a few postcards to put in my scrapbook," she said and made her way to the card stand near the middle of the store. "I won't be too long. You want me to meet you somewhere?" She looked over at Ethan. He was still staring at the mini Eiffel Towers. The wind had blown his hair in a wild mess. How could it look messier? She didn't know. It made him more down to earth, the boy next door type. He no longer appeared as uptight as he did the first night that they went out. His broad frame filled out his wrinkled jeans and T-shirt. She could see the strength in his well-toned arms.

"Meet me at the elevator. If we hurry, we can make the next one going up," Ethan said.

"Okay. It'll only take me a few minutes." Abby scanned over to the postcards. She selected four and took them to the cash register. She paid the lady for the cards, took her change, and headed out of the shop, searching for Ethan.

Abby hoped the next elevator ride wouldn't be crowded. Another ride like earlier and her deal with Ethan would be terminated. She'd probably be all over him. Inspecting the mass of people, she searched for Ethan's tall physique. A movement caught her attention, and Ethan's head materialized in the crowd. He waved and pointed to a small gap in the line. She circled around a group of school children and walked up beside him.

He eyed her small bag. "That was quick. I figured we'd have to wait for the next elevator. I know how you are about shopping."

"A less crowded elevator would benefit me more than shopping at the moment."

A mischievous smirk appeared on his face. "True. There aren't many people waiting, so it shouldn't be too bad."

"Remember to control yourself," Abby said, trying to downplay the incident, but it came across more like a dare. His eyes seemed to accept her challenge.

"Since you won't let me relieve your tension, we'll have to behave this time," Ethan whispered.

She turned and punched him in the arm. "I have no tension."

"Sure you don't. Let's get on before we wait too long and get stuffed in there again." Ethan placed his hand on her back, and she entered the elevator, moving to the side of the small doorway. Leaning against the corner, she left some room between her and the wall. Ethan stood beside her, avoiding any physical contact. Everyone finished boarding and the elevator ascended. Abby saw the city skyline through the steel beams as they moved higher and higher. It took a couple of minutes before the elevator stopped. They stepped off into a glass enclosed viewing area. Immediately, Abby felt the tower sway. She froze, trying to steady herself. "You feel that?"

"Yeah. The wind's strong today. You'll get used to it in a few minutes." Ethan placed his hand on her shoulder. "Come over here and see the view."

The city seemed to stretch for miles. Buildings that looked large from the first floor, appeared tiny, almost blending in with the cityscape. The small specks of people in the grassy area were no longer visible. Hues of gray and white splattered across the city. Abby noticed several panoramic pictures on the railing in front of her indicating landmarks. She recognized the Arc de Triomphe on the map. She spotted a small circled roadway and saw the arch in the middle. It was so small from this view, but she remembered how it towered over her when she stood on the Champs-Elysee.

"Let's go outside. You can get some better pictures," Ethan said.

Abby moved to the exit door, dodging people as they hurried to catch the elevator as if the city was going to disappear at any moment. She reached the door and waited for several people to descend the narrow stairway. Abby darted up the stairs before anyone else decided to come down. The wind blustered around the corner of the building, sending her hair in all directions.

"Seems a little dangerous out here," Abby shouted over the gust of wind as it hit her in the face. She forced her eyes open.

"A few more pictures and we'll go back inside." She heard Ethan say. He'd taken over her camera during the time she was fighting her losing battle with her hair.

Abby followed Ethan over to the railing. She stood there a few minutes while he took several photos. Abby turned so she faced the interior of the tower to prevent her hair from smacking her in the nose.

"One last picture, Abby. You can't leave here without a picture of yourself on the Eiffel Tower." Ethan yelled over the pounding wind.

"No. It's okay. My hair's a wreck," Abby said, but her voice seemed soft and she wasn't sure if he heard her.

"You're getting your picture taken. To make you feel better, I'll be in it with you." His head twisted around, searching then spotting something. "Stay right here." Ethan jogged over to a middle aged man standing by the door. After a few minutes explaining the workings of the camera, Ethan walked back to the railing beside Abby.

Reaching over, he pulled her to him and rested his arm around her waist. "Pretend you like me."

"Sure. I can act like I'm happy when I'm in the middle of hurricane force winds," Abby yelled. The old man barked several French words at her, but they were lost in the gust of wind.

"He said to smile. He can't understand why you look so miserable when you're with such a handsome guy." Ethan squeezed her arm. "Quit pouting."

Abby forced a quick smile as the man instructed them to move to the left. He took a few pictures, jabbering away to Ethan. She waited for them to finish their conversation. Her lips were dry and she could hardly keep her eyes open.

"Are you ready to go back in?" Ethan asked, laughing.

Not waiting on him, Abby nodded and headed to the doorway. She forced her way down the stairs, deciding not to pause for anyone coming up. Entering the lower level, an instant rush of warm air greeted her. She brushed her fingers through her hair.

"You missed some strands." Ethan took hold of some of her hair and smoothed it in place. His hand lingered, caressing her cheek. Gazing into his eyes, she felt like she was in one of those sappy romance movies where the guy and girl were on the Eiffel Tower, expressing their true love. Too bad those romance stories never occurred in real life. Somehow, the situation didn't fit with Ethan and her. If anything happened between them and it didn't work out, she'd lose the only true friend she had there. She backed away. No matter how she felt, she didn't want to risk it, did she? Her mind was screaming no while her heart was saying yes.

He let his hand drop to his side. Abby glanced at her watch. She was surprised to see it was eight already. "What do you want to do now?"

"How about dinner at the pub? You should be hungry by the time we get there, since you ride at a snail's pace," Ethan said, mentioning the bikes they had rented earlier in the day.

"Oh, please. I'm much faster than a snail." Abby straightened her T-shirt. Her stomach growled on cue. "Food sounds great."

"Let's go to the elevator." Ethan led the way to the exit sign. As they waited in line, Abby slipped her arm through his. She didn't even think about what she was doing. She'd risk it. At this moment, she didn't care that Jayson hadn't contacted her. She felt the weight lift off her. All she cared about now was being right there in that moment. It was peaceful, without demand. She didn't feel pressured to conform to some image she felt she needed to be for someone. Right there, right now, she was just Abby. She was going with her heart.

The elevator arrived and only a few people exited the car. As the day got later, fewer people made their way to the top of the tower, but more people were ready to leave. The line moved toward the elevator doors and people packed the compact car. Ethan stood behind Abby as they waited to board. Several minutes passed before they squeezed into the elevator. She held her breath as the doors closed. Ethan shifted closer to her. Once again, Abby could feel his body pressed up against her back. She sucked in her bottom lip between her teeth. Why was life a big game of torture?

Chapter 27

Walking alongside his bike, Ethan watched the occasional boat float down the canal. He eyed the water aimlessly as it rippled toward the shore and crashed into the stone wall. Abby and he just left the pub. It was time. If anything was going to happen between them, he had to be honest with her. She needed to know who he was, the real Ethan Gray and that terrified him. He glanced over at her. She was staring at a couple strolling hand in hand across the street.

"You up for another adventure?" he asked. He knew the perfect place and he'd have the privacy he needed.

Abby's brows crinkled. "Couldn't we save it for another day? It's getting late and I should get home."

"It won't take long." Ethan took hold of her bike and picked it up effortlessly. Moving the bike next to a large tree that grew through a hole in the sidewalk, he threaded the chain through the back wheel and locked the two ends together.

A yawn escaped her mouth, and Ethan sighed. This would be tougher than he thought. "Humor me."

She smiled and nodded.

Ethan grabbed her hand and led her across the deserted road. Instead of continuing on the sidewalk, he turned down a small alleyway. On one side was the tall stone building that housed his flat. It looked almost silver as the pale moonlight bounced on the gray stone of its façade. On the left, a tall concrete and iron fence blocked the view. Unkempt bushes in dire need of a severe trim overtook the fence and partially blocked the alley. Ethan parted some of the more dense brush that narrowed the alleyway and held it back, allowing Abby to move through the overgrowth.

"This is it," Ethan whispered, when they stopped in front of the unkempt brush and could go no further.

"Are you serious? There is nothing here but weeds," Abby said. A branch caught her sleeve in its thorny grasp. She fought with the barbed bush and finally freed her shirt.

He laughed. "Have a little faith in me." Abby needed some adventure in her life and this would be the beginning.

Ethan clutched her around the waist.

She struggled in his hold. "You said nothing physical," Abby said, her voice squeaking.

"Relax. The only way in is to climb the wall. You'll need a boost."

Abby dropped her protesting hands from Ethan's arms. He lifted her up, and she grasped some of the limbs. Her first attempt produced a bunch of leaves that tore off effortlessly in her hand. Releasing the foliage, she grabbed a vine and pulled herself up. She threw her leg over the stone fence and straddled the wall.

"Go on over. The ground should be clear." He waited for her to jump down to the other side. Hoisting himself up, his cleared the wall and let his feet thump down on the other side.

A luscious garden hid behind the combination of fence and drab bushes. Neatly trimmed roses, wild flowers, and completely landscaped walkways winding around huge trees stood before them. After he brushed the dirt off his pants, he slid his arm around her shoulder and felt the tension in her back release. A good sign since he promised her nothing physical.

Ethan led her down one of the paths. The trees kept watch over the smaller delicate rose bushes that crept up on either side of the large trunks. The dirt path was littered with petals: red, pink, fuchsia, forming a kaleidoscope of color.

"I don't remember this in any of the tourist books," Abby said.

Ethan took her hand and pulled her down the walkway. "It's not. It's a private garden."

"Private?" Abby stopped, causing her hand to depart from Ethan's. "We broke into to someone's garden?" She stiffened and looked around wildly.

Ethan grinned. He came back to her, recapturing her hand. "What did you think? I forgot my key?" He decided not tell her that it was part of his apartment building grounds.

"We need to leave. I can't get caught doing something illegal. I'll lose my internship."

"Relax. It's late. No one will ever know if we keep quiet." Ethan tugged on her hand, but she refused to move. He turned back to her. "Abby, it'll be okay. Nothing's going to happen."

"Do you make it a habit of breaking into private property? How many unsuspecting women have you brought here?" Abby asked.

He glanced over at her and laughed. "Do I detect some jealousy in that question?"

Abby frowned.

"Just you. Tonight seemed like the perfect time to bring someone with me."

A bench rested near the end of the path. Thick vines intertwined up the side and formed a canopy of lush green leaves blocking out the moonlight. Abby sat on the concrete slab. He saw her tremble.

"Cold?" He wrapped his jacket around her shoulders. His arm lingered, still draped around her. Ethan pulled back, and Abby grabbed his hand, preventing his retreat. He relaxed his arm, and his hand rested in hers. He needed to tell her. She was finally opening up, and he was going to blow her world sky high. She let her head fall on his shoulder.

Abby lightly ran her fingers back and forth on the back of his hand. He shivered at her touch. He let his lips skate across her forehead, barely touching her skin. Her warmth seared his lips, radiating down to his core. He leaned back and stared at her. "Do you ever think, if you were walking in someone else's shoes that maybe somehow, your life would turn out different....the people you meet would treat you differently, your relationships would be different?"

Abby peered up at him. "What do you mean?"

It wasn't coming out right. He wasn't good at this. "I don't know. If I were someone else, had a different name, a different personality. Would it change things between us?" He wasn't remotely what she deserved, but he wanted her more than anything.

Abby sat up sharply. Ethan's hand fell out of her grasp and left the cool air nipping at his skin. "If this is about Jayson-"

"No, no. That's not what I meant." He cringed. The thought that she still cared about Walters ate at him. "You know, if we met at a different time in our lives, a different place. Where do you think we'd be now?" He rubbed the back of his neck. If only he'd met her somewhere else, but he knew it was not how they met but the truth that ached in him. The lies about his job might not be between them, but he'd be in the same place he was now. Lying to her. Lies about himself.

"I don't know. We could be doing the same thing as we are now or we might have crossed paths and gotten no further than a hello." He could see the confusion in her frown.

He took her hand and cradled it in his. "What if we met back in the U.S.? Do you think you'd have gone out with me? I mean, you have your family back there. There'd be no need for a personal tour guide." What he really meant was, would she find him worthy enough for her? He was sure he already had the answer.

She laughed. "What would you be doing in Boca Raton?"

"I don't know, maybe I'd be vacationing." He could tell he wasn't making any sense. The looming doom in his stomach intensified.

She patted him on the arm. "I don't know, maybe. How would I know? Are you planning a trip to the States?"

"I may move there. Different environment." He could if wanted. Transfer to the States. He'd do it to be close to her.

"What about your family in England? I'm sure they'd miss you."

The pit in his stomach returned. The only family he had was his mother and sister. His mother was incapable of missing him. He swallowed the bitterness in his throat. "They'd get over it. I'd come back to visit them."

"Tell me about them. I imagine they're low key, right? Like you? Probably the complete opposite from my high maintenance family," she said as she picked a rose from a bush climbing the trellis and plucked the pedals one at a time.

"Yeah, something like that." He stared off into the garden. His mother was anything but low key. She demanded perfection and discarded mistakes like him. "I don't visit my family often." It felt good to tell someone. Nols was the only other person he'd confided in, even though his FBI profile file was available for anyone to see at the bureau.

"Too busy with school?"

He fought the urge to brush aside his feelings, but he wanted her to know him. At least something about him besides the lies. "No, my family and I don't get along."

"Oh, I can relate to that. Look at mine. Nicole's sole mission in life is to make me miserable."

He laughed. "At least they're around to bicker with. It's me, my sister and mother, and that's been only in the last five years. I had more of a family, if you can call it that, growing up in the children's home." The lump in his throat ached. He didn't realize how much it still hurt, but the pained expression on Abby's face upset him worse. She must've thought he was a freak.

She grabbed his hand and squeezed it. "You grew up without a family?"

The gesture warmed his heart, and he brushed her palm with his fingers. "Yeah, but you deal with what life gives you, right?" He patted her hand. He didn't want her feeling sorry for him.

"I can't imagine. Why if you had a family, would it take all those years?"

He knew what she was asking, and he thought he was prepared to tell her, but how could he tell her that his mother gave him up when he was five days old? He'd known since he broke into the records hall on his twelfth birthday on a mission to find his birth parents, convinced they were looking for him. Too much watching that orphan Annie crap. He should've known Daddy Warbucks wasn't in his future. His own mother didn't want him, so how could someone like Abby want him? He put his arm around her. "They tried to find me, and they eventually did. Everything worked out."

"That's good. I'd hate to think you'd lived all those years alone."

Pain gathered at his chest. He lived in that group home for eighteen years. He worked hard to get where he was, but the scars were still there, lying beneath the surface. He couldn't do it. How could he tell her the guy sitting there wasn't who she thought he was?

Abby raised her head just enough to look up at him. "You sure that's all it is? Seems like there's more to it."

"Nah. I was just talking." He glanced past her and out in the mix of greens and colors of the garden.

She laid her head back on his shoulder, and he watched the moonlight cascade down on the roses, dropping a silvery hue on the petals. The light danced across the garden, playing a concert of colors. He wished he could stay there in that moment forever. At least now, she thought he was a good guy. His past and present were about to catch up to him, and it would destroy his future.

As he pulled her close, he felt the first raindrop. Thick and wet, it pelted him on the side of his head. Another one, then another.

"Not again." Jumping up, Abby threw her bag over her head to shield the increasing rain. "How are we going to get out of here?"

He laughed as he grabbed her hand. "The same way we came in. Want a boost?"

Chapter 28

"You said this was going to be hands-off." Abby's body went rigid as the thunder rumbled.

Ethan chuckled as he led her through the doorway. "There's a storm outside. Did you think I'd stay huddled under that tree when my flat was across the alley?"

She stood by the door, ready to bolt. "We could've made it to the metro stop." She fidgeted with her hands. The grumbling of thunder sounded like it was in her head. She needed to get away before she broke down. She couldn't let Ethan see what a sappy wuss she was.

Ethan ran across the room and shut the windows, closing the loft off to the howling wind and panes of rain as they assaulted the glass. "The rain already soaked the floor. Throw me a towel from the kitchen."

She heard him, but his voice seemed distant like it was floating away from her. Desperately, she clung to it, but she couldn't pull herself out of the fog.

"Abby? What's wrong?"

She tried to answer, but all she could muster was, "Stop. He's gone."

"Who?" Something pulled her and then she was sitting on the couch. "Abby, who's gone?"

The lightening flared bright light through the room, and her brother's face flashed in her mind. Why hadn't she gotten there sooner? Why hadn't she gone with them? She felt the frozen rain on her head mixed with the warmth of his blood as she tried to keep Jacob's wound from bleeding. The stench of gasoline filled the air and Jacob's eyes-the life was absent from his indigo eyes. The same indigo eyes like hers. No matter how hard she tried, she couldn't get him to look at her. If only Sarah had not done it

"What did Sarah do?" Ethan's voice pulled Abby back, and she focused on his hands as they clung to her arms.

She didn't realize she'd spoken, but she could tell by his face that she had relayed every detail that replayed in her head. Abby lowered her eyes. "Nothing. She didn't do anything." Only Nicole knew, and it was better that way. The pain stabbed at her heart. Sarah had suffered enough, and this would only cause her family more pain. They believed Abby was to blame, and there was no reason to drag the memories back.

"Tell me." Ethan squeezed her arm, and she looked into his eyes. What would it be like if someone else knew besides Nicole? Her father, her mother, even Sarah held her responsible. Her sister never remembered what had happened. She saw the doubt in Ethan's eyes and knew she wouldn't be able to convince him to leave it alone.

"Last year, my brother died in a car accident." She stared at the white wall in front of her. It was the first time she'd said the words, and the reality of it hit her.

"I'm sorry." Ethan wrapped his arm around her, but she didn't deserve the gesture. She longed for the safety there, but she didn't deserve the security anymore.

She wiped a tear from her eye. "Jacob, Sarah, and Nicole were out partying that night. I'd refused to go because I didn't want to be stuck as the designated driver." It seemed stupid now. Her petty sulking had resulted in her brother's death. "I went to the library instead. There I was reading while Jacob was dying." The pain didn't stop now. The tears flowed out like a river unleashing a flood.

"Don't you think you're being too hard on yourself? You can't be responsible for your siblings every second."

She sniffled. "That's just it. I should have known. I knew they'd be drinking. I knew they'd drive home. Don't you think I should've stopped that?" Anger and resentment came to the forefront, consuming her.

He caressed her hair. "Maybe, but your brother and sisters are adults. They're responsible for their actions."

"My brother *was* an adult. He's dead now." The silence terrified her, amplifying the thunder as it boomed in her head and transported her back to the mangled car.

"Sarah crashed the car into a tree. Straight into a tree." Abby's voice choked on the tears. Small muffles of air escaped her throat. "I killed him."

"No, you didn't. If anyone is responsible, it's Sarah," he said. He wrapped his arms around her and rocked her back and forth.

"She may have been driving, but I set it all in motion. I should've driven them home. I should've protected him, protected her. I can't help him anymore, but I can help her." Abby straightened her back and wiped below her eyes. A thin line of black from her mascara dirtied her finger.

"What do you mean?" He stared at her, and she almost thought he already knew what she was going to say, but how could he? He didn't know anything about the accident.

"It's been better that everyone thought I was driving. Sarah's been able to move on. The truth would kill her." Sarah had moved on, hadn't she? Maybe not the way Abby had hoped, but she was sure Sarah would become herself again.

Ethan banged his hand on the armrest. "Are you telling me you took responsibility for the accident, and you weren't even there?"

She nodded, and the tears flowed freely. It was a freedom to know she wasn't hiding behind some hushed up investigation her father ordered to be buried. Someone else knew. She wasn't hiding anymore. She could lash out, be angry at Jacob, at Sarah, at herself. She held onto Ethan's shirt for several minutes before she wiped the lingering tears from her eyes. It was enough to get it out. She could move on. She could face the pain.

He rubbed the back of her head. "How can you do this after the way they treat you?"

"It wasn't always that way. Sarah and I used to be close. We're twins. We've got a bond that can't be broken. I'll find a way to get that back," Abby said. She had to believe Sarah would forgive her. Right now, it was like a piece of her was missing, hollow without Sarah.

"But to be treated like crap while you figure it out? Sarah doesn't deserve the sacrifice you've taken," Ethan said, his voice rising. Abby could see the anger in him, and she understood. He couldn't understand why she did it. It wouldn't make any sense to him, but it did to her.

"She does. She used to be different. More alive, less engrossed in herself. Losing Jacob caused her to lash out. You don't know her well." Abby grabbed her coat and pulled it over her shoulders, like she was covering a wound.

"Don't you think losing Jacob and you is causing her to lash out?"

She picked at her shirt and pulled a loose string from the seam. "It's better than her having to deal with knowing she was driving the car." Considering the way Sarah had coped when she believed Abby had caused the accident, there was no way she could handle the truth.

Ethan grabbed Abby's shoulder so she was forced to look him in the eye. "You're trading one hurt for another."

She shook her head. "Sarah's fragile. I can handle the blame."

"Can you? You can't protect her forever."

Abby sat motionless. Yes, she could. If it meant Sarah would be able to eventually accept Jacob's death, she'd lie again. Ethan hadn't seen Sarah that night. She was broken, unable to function. When Nicole called Abby, she knew by the deep hollow in her stomach that Sarah was hurt. It wasn't physical hurt but a mental pain, something far more difficult from which to recover. Abby felt it in her soul. If Sarah blaming Abby made it easier, she had to do it. Nicole had convinced her Sarah would never be able to handle the true events of that night, and Abby agreed. Sarah looked for their parents' approval more than anything. She'd struggled to win their mother's acceptance, all of the girls had, and causing Jacob's death would've been the final blow. Abby craved her parents' approval, too, but she'd learned to survive on the security of her siblings. Ironically, protecting Sarah meant losing the sanctuary she cherished. Without Jacob and Sarah, Abby had nothing.

But her sacrifice would let Sarah live. No, it was the right thing to do. She only needed to figure out how to live with the horror herself.

Chapter 29

"No Way. I'm not getting involved in that," Nols said as he crammed his sub sandwich in his mouth. Lettuce soaked in mayo dumped out on the plate. He discarded the remnants of a tomato in the waste basket by his desk.

"Come on. I don't have time to read the full accident report." Ethan jerked his hand off the desk and ran it through his hair. "Put in the paperwork to get the records released and look it over."

"Are you crazy? You're asking to get Senator Rodgers' son's accident report. I'm not putting my name on the log for the request," Nols said as he grabbed a napkin and raked it across his mouth.

Ethan swallowed the urge to deck his partner. After Abby's confession, Ethan spent the next two days trying to research the accident. Anyone with any brains could see Abby's confession was a lie, but the case had been closed within a few weeks, ruled an accident. It may have been an accident, but everyone was eager to let Abby take the blame. He banged his hand on the counter, drawing the attention of a few staff members across the room. "I'm telling you, Nols. Something's not right. People screw up all the time. Why would Abby go to such lengths to cover for her sister? She doesn't seem the type to lie, but she'll ruin her life with this secret."

Nols rolled his eyes. "Thought you didn't care?"

Clenching his jaw, Ethan pulled his chair beside Nols. "I shouldn't, but I'm beyond that. She keeps saying how messed up Sarah is and how this would kill her. It doesn't make sense."

"They were kids. Young people do stupid stuff all the time. Why would this surprise you?" He flipped through a notebook while stuffing leftover sub crumbs into his mouth.

Ethan stood and paced around the desk. "Because Abby's smart. She might be naïve about a lot of stuff, but this doesn't sound like her."

"Sounds like you know her pretty well. How well?"

"Knock it off." Ethan clinched his fist as he glared at his partner.

"Relax, man. I'm joking. Don't you think you're fussing over her too much? This is your usual, 'I have to fix everyone else's problems' crap." His voice seemed forced, like he didn't want to have the conversation. "I question Tom every time he puts you in a situation like this. It's like you can't help it. You have to rescue everyone."

"Don't use your psycho-babble on me." Ethan jerked a surveillance photo off the printer and went back to his desk. He hated Nols's background in psychology. Every time he turned around, Nols was analyzing him. Ethan pointed his finger at his partner. "This isn't about me."

"Yes, it is, and it's time to discuss it," Nols said in an equally stern voice.

"Is this an official session?" The tightness in Ethan's chest increased as he threw a dirty look at his colleague.

Nols coughed and wiped the crumbs off his mouth. "No, but you need to stop and look at the big picture. You're going to hurt this girl."

Ethan scoffed. "You're the one who said to go for it. Didn't you say Abby would be good for me?"

Nols wadded up his sandwich wrapper and tossed it in the trashcan. "Yeah, that was before you started the same self-destructive patterns. It was before I realized she was another candidate for saving. This is about your need to compensate for your crappy life."

Nols was going to try and convince him that his mother abandoning him was the cause of every decision he made. Ethan thought too much about his family already. He knew he was worthless so there was no going over it again. He crossed his arms. "I'm not going to talk about my mother."

"Didn't think you would, but saving Abby won't win you her love."

"Who said anything about love?"

Nols laughed. "Do you love Abby or do you love the idea of saving her from herself?"

Ethan fumed. "Sod off, man."

Nols grabbed a pencil and scribbled something on his notepad. "That's it. Shut down. If you refuse to talk about yourself, this relationship with Abby will fail. We're finished here."

Being dismissed by Nols plowed rage through Ethan's body. "What do you want me to bloody say?" Ethan yelled at him. Luckily, everyone had left the room. Ethan could yell as loud as he wanted.

Nols sat back, smiling. "Finally, some *bloody* emotion. Can't you cuss without putting *bloody* in front of every word? You Brits crack me up. "

Ethan pushed his chair back so hard, it tipped over. "I'll say it. I'm screwed up. Poor Ethan was left at an orphanage when he was five days old. His mother was more concerned with her career than taking care of a newborn. Then when his uncle took him in, that lasted only six months, when the money ran out. It was a shock to poor Ethan when he was rejected a third time when he finally found his mother. Yes, he grew up without a family and took a job as an undercover agent so he could pretend to be anything he wanted and avoid reality. That pretty sums up your take on me, right?"

"I wasn't going to be that melodramatic. I'm glad you're so accepting of yourself." Nols put his hands behind his neck, letting his elbows hang out like chicken wings.

"You're an asshole; you know that, right?"

"So you keep telling me."

Ethan picked up his mug and downed the bitter coffee. Nols was only trying to support him, but Ethan was beyond help. All he could do was help others. Sure, there'd been other women. He'd helped them; then manipulated them into reciprocating what he felt they owed him. It was an ugly cycle. He received a moment or two of feeling loved then he'd push it away. With Abby, it was different, wasn't it? This time, it wasn't about him. Yes, he had the need to protect her, but that was because he wanted to be with her.

Ethan shoved his hands in his pockets and stared at his partner. "So Doc, tell me the answers to help my screwed up life."

"Leave the accident alone. You can't fix Abby's mistakes. It's called being human."

"You want me to let this go?" Ethan asked, but he knew the answer.

Nols threw some papers in his outbox. "Yes, keep Abby's secret. Don't try to fix her."

"You realize not reporting Abby's confession is against the Bureau's code of ethics." Ethan sat back and watched his partner give him a half-hearted shrug.

"You break the law all the time undercover. If Abby's confession is true, there is no evidence to charge Sarah. They never tested her blood alcohol at the scene. They'd more likely charge Abby with false statements."

Ethan stared at his partner. "You read the file?" Surprised that his partner had already taken the time to make the request.

Nols nodded. "Against my better judgment. Anyone could see the inconsistencies in Abby's statements, but it seems like they wanted to sweep this one out of the way quickly. I doubt the truth will result in anything but legal issues for Abby."

Ethan nodded. "This secret will destroy her."

"It may but it's not your job to save her," Nols said, a twisting smile on his face.

Ethan looked out the window at the gray skies. What little sunlight there was danced sparkles of reds and golds on the wooden tables. As quickly as the light came, it darkened and left the tables drab. His partner was right. He couldn't save Abby to save himself. With the revelation,

Ethan discovered he wanted more from Abby. He wanted her to love him, and he knew that was impossible.

"Who are you saving?"

Ethan jerked his head around and saw Tom leaning against the door frame. "No one," Ethan said and shifted in his seat, but he noticed the all-knowing look in Tom's eye. He probably had the office bugged.

"Didn't think so. How about you return the printed copies of Jacob Rodgers' file back to records before some other agency comes sniffing around." He pointed a file folder at Ethan. "I figured you'd be gearing up for Walters instead of researching cases outside of your jurisdiction."

Ethan remained silent. It did little good to give Tom an excuse. His boss didn't believe in them. Everything was black and white, and if it didn't fall in those categories, you'd better find your way back and quickly. He stood and followed Tom down the hall to the interrogation room.

Ethan rubbed his neck almost to the point of raw. "He here yet?" The case against Walters was almost complete. A couple years' work was about to pay off.

Tom nodded. "And about four lawyers that I'm sure won't let him answer any questions."

Ethan swore. An hour interrogation would turn into five. The lawyers would sit with their pads of paper, scribbling furiously while holding their hands up every few seconds. They'd lean toward each other, mumble, then lean over to the client and whisper the proper response. Usually no more than five or six words, not enough detail to help or hurt but enough to satisfy as an answer.

Ethan rung his hands together. "This is to finalize the deal, right?"

Tom shoved a paper at Ethan. "More or less. His lawyers worked a good agreement."

He grabbed it and scanned the contents. "Can't we charge him with more instead of plea bargaining?"

Tom pulled Ethan to the side of the corridor. "A plea bargain gives me Peretti. I don't like it, but Peretti is a better catch in Washington than a celebrity. Once we're in there, I don't want one word out of you. Got it? I can't have you running on feelings because you and Walters are screwing the same girl."

Ethan jerked back and tried to swallow the bile building in his mouth. He'd never heard Tom sound so cold. Ethan forced his hand to relax and straighten from the fist that automatically cocked. "What are you saying?

"Whatever sideshow you have with Abigail Rodgers, it ends now. Walters is out of her life, so our job is done. Senator Rodgers is satisfied. I want you out by the end of the week. A private guard detail will take over. We're in London by next Friday." He slapped Ethan on the shoulder like he was going over the next play for a soccer match.

Like that, Tom had barked out the marching orders. Ethan slumped slightly against the wall as a heaviness overtook him. His time with Abby was about to end.

Ethan straightened his body as Tom opened the door to the interrogation room. A stifling heat permeated the dark squared room. Ethan grimaced when his eyes met Walters'. The hatred in Jayson's expression was infectious. Ethan kept his face cold and calculated. He hadn't worked on this case for two years to have it wretched from him.

Ethan sat at the right side of the cheap folding table and scooted his chair so he could rest his elbows on the tabletop. He stared at Jayson, who was now whispering to his lawyer. The suit was shaking his head and snapping his fingers to get the attention of his colleague.

"We ready to do this?" The lead U.S. prosecutor walked in and dumped a few files on the table. Dressed in a dark navy suit, he echoed the company man look. Nathan Parsons had been working on this case the same amount of time as Ethan. He had a no-nonsense approach to each case and always covered his bases. Ethan was sure he'd drawn up an iron clad plea bargain that would force Jayson to cooperate but still allow the guy to reap the benefits of his tennis career. That's how it went. The rich and famous could negotiate on their name and wiggle out of any crime. Jayson was no different.

"Nathan, our client is prepared to cooperate as long as his name is not leaked to the media outlets. We also request there be no harassment by any government officials." The beady eyed man stared at Ethan.

Ethan let a sly grin escape. How could he say that was harassment? He'd met with Jayson five times and not once

194

had Ethan laid a hand on him. What did he think this was, a luxury resort?

"Harry, our agents behave professionally at all times," Nathan said and his eyes darted to Tom.

Ethan stole a glance at his boss. The vein was pulsating in Tom's neck.

"When has any of my agents harassed your client?" Tom's usual even voice threatened to break.

The beady eyed man coughed and cleared his throat. "We're not accusing anyone, but there have been suspect occasions where my client felt threatened and pressured."

Tom laughed causing his hair to flip back off his forehead. "If he hadn't done anything wrong to begin with, we wouldn't be discussing this."

The tall lawyer sat straight in his seat and pointed his pen at Tom. "Our client is not admitting to any crime."

"Okay. Okay. Let's get back on track. This banter is going nowhere." Nathan waved his hands like he was trying to gather the troops. "All the paperwork is laid out based on the deal we've discussed. Immunity in exchange for testimony on Peretti." He shoved the first folder toward the entourage of lawyers. The brown suit grabbed the folder and flipped through the pages, nodding like he was approving every word.

He shoved the folder over to the navy suit. "Looks in order, Harry."

Ethan held back a chuckle. He knew the lawyers already had an advanced copy of the agreement. They wouldn't dream of letting their star client sign something they hadn't spent a butt load of billable hours on.

Harry nodded and slid the folder in front of Jayson. Walters looked from one lawyer to the next. He grabbed the pen and scribbled his signature on each page his lawyer pointed at.

After a few minutes, it was done. Two years of Ethan's life now came to fruition. He'd provided enough evidence to hang Walters, but, in the end, the justice department wanted the bigger fish, the brains and money behind the gambling ring. Ethan sat, void of any emotion. It seemed rather anti-climactic. His job in Paris was complete. Walters signed the plea bargain and was away from Abby because of him. He'd accomplished what Abby's father wanted, what Tom wanted, and what he wanted to a degree. He had to face the truth. It was time to let Abby go.

Chapter 30

"I thought I'd find you here."

Ethan glanced up and saw Abby smiling at him. His eyes darted to the door. "Tony let you in?"

She giggled and took the seat just vacated by Nols. "He frisked me for weapons." She winked, and Ethan almost spit out his beer. She wasn't that far off. Tony would search her if he thought she had concealed weapons. He was a stubborn bloke from the other Agency who didn't particularly like playing a bartender.

Ethan grinned and downed the remainder of his drink. Her being there tormented him. She had to be angry that Jayson was no longer around. He'd caused that to a degree, not that she had any idea what he'd done. He certainly didn't think she'd seek him out, especially after she confided in him about the accident. "What brings you here?"

"You." The glimmer in her eye had him intrigued.

"Want another tour of the city?"

"I figured you could help me with a project at work." She slung a large, black bag from her shoulder and dumped it on the chair beside her.

He winced. Nothing good could come of this, but he forced a half-hearted smile anyway. She worked for Von Deez, meaning it had to do with fashion and the ritzy side of life, something he knew he couldn't pull off. "What is it?" She didn't answer. Was it that bad? He patted her arm. "Tell me. I figured you knew by now, I don't bite."

She blushed. He couldn't get over how beautiful she was in an ordinary way. Not over- the-top gorgeous, but everything about her drove him crazy. She shifted in her seat. "I need a favor."

"Ask." He dreaded her response. A favor for her would probably get him fired. He wished she'd say what she needed, so he'd know what damage control he'd have to do later.

She pulled out several notebooks and laid them out on the bar. Sketches of clothes, models, and colors were all he could see. It didn't appear to be anything but a mess of drawings. Yet, she seemed to see some sort of pattern. "I'm doing an ad campaign, and I lost the model I had lined up for the photo shoot."

Horror struck him in the stomach with a wave of nausea. She was asking him to pose for Von Deez? He shook his head immediately. "I'm not modeling for you."

She frowned. "Not even for some test shots? I'd like to get some location pictures today and I need a model." She had a pouty expression he knew probably always resulted in someone giving in to her. This time he'd be that someone.

"Test shots only? This won't be published, right?"

She jumped up, squealing as she hugged him. "I only need some shots with a model at my potential locations. Got any ideas?" She twirled her finger in a tiny curl at the base of her ponytail.

He shrugged. "What's the theme?" He gave up on finishing his conversation with Nols. His partner was long gone by now. He wanted to spend the afternoon with Abby anyway. He only had a few more days before he left for London.

Abby rearranged a few of the sketches so they lay out in a line on the bar. "Sports. I want something that takes the dirt and grime of a sport and blend it with the elegance of the clothes."

Ethan grimaced. He had no clue what she meant. Grit and grime. It was like she was talking about a football game played on a muddy field. "I can't help you on this. You've been to almost every part of Paris. You haven't thought of anything?"

"No. Gilda is still hung up on this actress she wants for the fall line promotion. She thought she'd be perfect for the sports theme. I tried to talk her into using the art of Paris like Monet, but it was a no go."

Ethan stood and threw a few Euros on the table. "Well, you won't find it sitting here." He grabbed her black bag and slung it over his shoulder.

"Where are we going?"

"Don't know, but we might as well search for your perfect location," he said as he followed her out of the bar. Once outside, he drank in the cool air. Truth was, he needed to distance himself from her. Her body sitting so close to him made him crazy.

She looped her arm in his. "I'm not sure it's out there."

"Sure it is." He looked down at her perky smile which seemed to hide any sadness about Jayson's disappearance. The guilt washed over him, but he'd only done what her father had asked. He'd gotten rid of Jayson. Now, Ethan needed to make himself disappear, even if he wanted to spend more time with her. He didn't deserve it.

"You thought of anything yet?"

"Huh?" He stared at her. "No, not yet."

She sighed. "Maybe it's just as well. It wouldn't have been a good campaign anyway."

He laughed. "Giving up? That doesn't sound like you." He threw his hand up. Why hadn't he thought of it before? "How about the football games they play near the Eiffel Tower? It's as good as you'll get to dirty."

"I need a sport without helmets."

Ethan laughed and pulled her into a hug as they walked down the street. "Football here is soccer. No helmets involved."

She glanced up at him, grinning. "Thanks for setting me straight. It could work. You play?"

He nodded. "I do. You want to head to the Eiffel Tower?"

"Sure, maybe you could play a game or two. I need some candid shots."

"Not today." He pointed to his loafers. The idea tempted him. He hadn't played all summer, and the lack of recreation was wearing on him.

She frowned. "I guess the shots of the area will be enough."

He relaxed his shoulders. He still had a chance at not being in her photos. He didn't need his photograph floating around Von Deez, at some off chance, somebody was liable to recognize him.

"Hold on," Abby said. She stopped and pulled her phone out of her pocket. He stood beside her as she clicked on a few buttons. "Crap." She glanced at her watch.

"What?" He peered over her shoulder.

She looked up. "I have to go to Von Deez."

Relief flooded his body. The perfect escape for him. "We can do this later, right?" He waited as she typed a response on her phone.

"How about you come with me? I'll show you around."

He shook his head. He needed to meet with Nols even though he knew Tom would want him to stay. He wanted to stay, but their relationship couldn't last much longer.

Abby took hold of his hand and dragged him down the street. "Come on. I'd love to show you what I do. It's always boring telling Sarah and Nicole." She tugged on him until he quit resisting. "You'll be a newbie, so it'll be exciting."

The uneasiness in his stomach overpowered him. He knew more than she thought. His sister, not to mention his mother, was completely immersed in the Hollywood scene. He stepped back. "I'll pass. Fashion's not my thing."

She laughed and grabbed his arm. "I'm not asking you to go shopping. I want to show you where I work. There are plenty of men at Von Deez. It's not only women."

Ethan stalled his walk. "You actually think I have something in common with these men?" He'd put up with his sister trying to parade him around under the spotlight. He wouldn't let Abby do it too. He searched her face, and the conflict in him eased. He could tell she truly wanted him to see Von Deez, not to use him like his sister had. He tipped his head and forced a grin. "I'll go, but I'm not modeling." He braced himself as she hugged him again. The sweetness in her action took his breath away. He loved that his going to Von Deez made her happy. If he could do these small things, then maybe when his lies blew up, he wouldn't feel so guilty.

The uncertainty ached in his gut. He wasn't part of the glamorous life like his mother and sister. Why did he feel like he wanted to die instead of go to Von Deez?

Abby tugged on his hand. "Gilda wants me there like yesterday."

They made their way on the metro to the outskirts of Paris to the Von Deez office. Ethan looked up at the towering building. He took a deep breath, and let Abby lead him inside. They passed the security desk and headed toward the elevator. Abby punched the button several times. "There are only a few people here today. Most are in London for Fashion week. Jean-Claude loves to know what everyone is doing, even the lesser known designers."

The elevator door opened, and Ethan motioned Abby to get on. "Why aren't you there?"

"Gilda only sent the staff who didn't have immediate Paris deadlines. I have to finalize the photo shoot location plus London isn't as big as Paris's Fashion Week." Abby punched the tenth floor.

Ethan nodded and watched the numbers light up as they passed each floor. As the elevator doors opened, he frowned at the black lobby floor. It glistened like someone spent hours polishing the marble. He followed Abby to the front desk where a young woman with a well-kept updo studied them. She could've fallen right out of a fashion magazine with her couture blouse and multiple silver chains dangling from her neck. "Bonjour," she said as she eyed Ethan. He stared back at her until she finally turned her head.

He didn't belong there. He glanced down at his worn jeans and pullover that he'd picked out that morning. They weren't classy enough for this place. Even the receptionist could tell. Abby leaned up against the desk, chatting with the receptionist, occasionally laughing as the girl typed on her keypad. Unable to stand still, Ethan strolled around the lobby. He gravitated toward the black leather couch, but he didn't immediately sit. A photograph above it caught his attention. The numbness in his throat spread throughout his body. The auburn hair hanging in loose curls, her porcelain skin, ghost white against rich chocolate eyes and rouge lips. This was what she gave him up for. His mother, the former signature model for Von Deez. There he was, standing right in the middle of the life he despised.

"She's beautiful, isn't she?"

Ethan closed his eyes at Abby's voice. "She is." He wasn't lying. His mother was one of the most beautiful women he'd seen in his life.

"Celia Sholes was the face of Von Deez twenty years ago. I think Jean-Claude would kill to still have her around."

Ethan moved away from the picture. "I'm sure she'd agree for the right price. It's all about money to models, right?"

Abby shook her head. "The industry demands younger models now. Celia's what? Mid-forties? Jean-Claude would want her daughter now."

Forty-two, but he knew Abby didn't need to know the specifics. "Cruel industry." He didn't feel sorry for his mother.

"You know, Jean-Claude claims to be the first designer to use an actress to model his clothes. He credits Celia for creating the brand."

The admiration in Abby's voice made Ethan sick. Did anyone know the real Celia Sholes? She wasn't only some famous face plastered on Von Deez's wall. She didn't deserve the respect Abby afforded her. Ethan stepped back and swallowed the bitterness. "Let's start the tour."

Abby clapped her hands. "Sure, right after my fitting."

"What?"

"My fitting. Jean-Claude wants to do the preliminary fitting for my Fashion Week dress." She pushed him toward a pair of double doors. "I'll show you my office, well, Gilda's office. I have a desk by the back wall."

Ethan drug his feet like she was leading him to a firing squad.

"It's the last door on the right. Go in and have a seat." She motioned down the hallway. "I'll be back in a few minutes."

Ethan stepped into the office, careful not to trip on the pile of fabric by the door. The space was anything but glamorous. Papers littered the floor, along with piles of ribbon and mismatched shoes. He wondered how anyone found anything. It looked like a textile factory exploded. Stepping next to a mannequin, he searched for a place to sit, but all the chairs were covered with clothes and magazines.

"Ms. Rodgers. You ready, non?"

Ethan turned and saw a short, balding man pop his head through the doorway. He spotted Ethan and scowled. "Bonjour. Comment puis-je vous aider?" the man asked as he glanced past Ethan.

Ethan pushed himself off the desk he was leaning on. "I'm waiting on Abigail Rodgers," he said in French.

The man frowned. "Come, come. She must still be changing." He motioned Ethan to follow him. They crossed the hall to a large open studio. Ethan tiptoed across the cluttered floor.

"Are you a model? Models wait in the green room." He pointed down the hall.

Ethan stopped mid-step when he noticed the man studying his body. "No, I'm a friend."

The man threw up his hands. "Mon Dieu, she treats this place like a nightclub."

Ethan stiffened. He couldn't believe he'd gotten her in trouble. "I'm waiting for her to finish so I can help with her photo shoot location." He pulled back a huge breath when the man finally nodded.

"Very well. Jean-Claude Phillipe," the man said but didn't bother looking up from his task of sorting through buttons.

"Ethan Gray."

Jean-Claude paused and trained his eyes on Ethan. "Have you been here before?" He took some thread and unraveled it from the spool.

"No."

"You seem familiar to me."

Ethan could feel his stare. He didn't know what to say. He knew what the man was insinuating. Ethan hadn't been photographed with his mother in over six years.

With Alana, it was more recent. Every time she'd come for a visit, he'd been hounded for at least a week before the newer reporters figured out he was only the half-brother, not some new fling. Ethan shook his head firmly.

"Jean-Claude..." the voice said followed by a quick gasp.

Ethan turned his head and nearly fell over. Abby was standing there, wearing only a piece of thin black fabric that barely covered her from her chest to her upper thighs. She draped her arms around her stomach and darted behind a small partition in the room.

"Ethan, I thought you were staying in Gilda's office."

"I..." Ethan couldn't control his mouth. All his brain could concentrate was the image of Abby's slim body draped in the sheer fabric.

"I invited him." Jean-Claude came around the corner and pulled Abby back in the room. "Quit acting so shy. I've seen female bodies before."

Abby pointed to Ethan. "But he..."

Jean-Claude frowned. "I'm sure he has seen them before, but very well. Monsieur Gray, could you sit over here?" He pointed to a chair behind the partition.

Ethan felt his cheeks flaming out of jealousy that Jean-Claude was going to enjoy seeing Abby's very naked body. "What's the difference between you seeing her or me?"

Jean-Claude chuckled. "She obviously doesn't think me a..." He snapped his fingers. "What's the word? Ah, yes. She doesn't think me a sex partner."

Ethan had to laugh. The old man's boldness infuriated him, but he possessed enough poise to carry off the arrogance. He loved how Abby's face reddened, but she didn't miss a beat when she grabbed Jean-Claude's hand. "You ready to do this fitting?" Ethan took his seat behind the partition and stared at the wall. He heard shuffling and grunting, which he knew was Jean-Claude.

"You must stand straight or I can't sew you into this dress," Jean-Claude commanded. Ethan sat and eavesdropped as Abby and the man easily exchanged banter. The man seemed to have a genuine affection for Abby, which increased Ethan's jealously. A few minutes listening to how easily she was with him had Ethan up and pacing the area. Why was it so hard for her to open up to him? Sure, he knew she felt something, but she seemed to be holding back with him. Was it because he knew about the accident?

"Monsieur Gray, you can come back in."

Ethan cautiously stepped around the corner. In fifteen minutes, Jean-Claude had transformed the black cloth into an exquisite dress. He'd pinned extra fabric around Abby's waist and across her chest. Even with the unfinished details, Ethan could tell the end result would be breathtaking.

Jean-Claude circled Abby, his hand on his cheek. "You think royal purple accents or burgundy?"

"Purple." Abby's eyes widened, and Ethan could see she loved this. He wondered if she ever designed anything or if she only concentrated on the photos and ad campaigns.

Jean-Claude walked over to a work table and flipped through several piles of fabric, throwing a few stacks to the floor. He tucked a few swatches under his arm and motioned to Ethan. "Are you escorting Ms. Rodgers to the party?"

Ethan stared blankly at him. Was that what Abby wanted? She'd ask him to a party that he could never go to. Not because he didn't want to, but Tom would never approve it.

"No, he's a friend," Abby said. Ethan sighed. Just a friend. The words were like a bullet in his gut.

Jean-Claude shook his head. "He'd make a great model. Must be the genes from his mother's side."

Ethan jerked his head around and found Jean-Claude studying him intently. Ethan stole a look at Abby, but she was busy pinning a ribbon to her half sewn dress. He turned his attention back to the designer, but he was hunched over a bench, cutting fabric. "You can change now. I have all my measurements."

Abby darted off the raised platform and out the door.

The muscles in Ethan's upper back clenched as he scowled at the man.

"You thought I would not recognize Celia Sholes' son when he walks into my studio?" Jean-Claude asked.

Ethan rubbed his forehead and shifted his eyes to the door. "I don't know what you're talking about." He hoped the old man wouldn't spill his suspicions to Abby. He didn't want her to know what a screw-up he was, that his mother had rejected him. No one understood because his mother now acted like she had a loving doting son when they in fact had no relationship at all. The lie allowed her to play the rouse and she left him alone.

Jean-Claude scribbled something on a paper and pinned it to the purple silk. "I spent twenty years dressing Celia. You look like your mother."

Ethan glanced at the door, hoping Abby wouldn't return anytime soon. He shoved his hands in his pockets and glared at the designer. "It's none of your business."

Jean-Claude grinned. "My dear boy, a man from a Hollywood dynasty family stands in front of me. Your face is new. You do not think I want that for Von Deez?"

Ethan's eyes widened. He wasn't going to get sucked into this business, the same business that took his mother from him. It was bad enough that Abby loved it, but she wasn't consumed with it, not yet. He fidgeted with his phone but could see Jean-Claude looking at him from the corner of his eye.

The old man scowled. "Your participation would excel that girl's career." He nodded toward the door. "Ms. Rodgers is lovely, non?"

Ethan squinted until his eyelids formed small slits as he searched Jean-Claude's face for clues. "She's a remarkable woman."

Jean-Claude nodded. "A great talent with the layouts and camera, but a bit naive when it comes to reality, non?"

Ethan stopped fiddling with his phone case on his belt. "What do you mean?"

Jean-Claude laughed. "I will keep your secret, non?" He pointed his finger at Ethan. "You will tell her soon. Secrets do not stay secret in this industry. Mademoiselle Rodgers will make a name for herself at Von Deez, and she will discover your name soon."

Ethan stared out the window. It wasn't the secret that Jean-Claude knew that worried him. Abby believed in a guy that didn't exist.

Chapter 31

*A*bby's stomach fluttered as she rounded the corner and saw the bar. She was actually getting nervous about seeing him. Standing in front of the pub entrance for a few seconds, she breathed deeply. Abby forced herself to open the door. A cloud of cigarette smoke hit her face and she gagged at the smell. A few inebriated guys stumbled through the threshold, and she waited for them to stagger out.

The last guy turned his head toward Abby. "Oh, wait. We shouldn't leave so soon. Another vixen has arrived."

Reeking of alcohol and sweat, he barely managed to get the words out. Abby wrinkled her nose as the smell lingered around her. She darted into the pub and left the guy at the door. Hearing a few shouts, she ignored them. The guy's attention span couldn't be long. The alcohol would surely make him forget the encounter.

Twisting her purse straps between her fingers, Abby surveyed the crowd. She hated walking into a bar alone. All eyes were focused on her for one brief moment, and she had already been sized up by several guys. She was either dismissed as average or categorized as a potential score.

"You look great tonight," a masculine voice whispered behind her.

Abby's mouth curled up into a sweet smile. She twirled around in Sarah's high heel boots, slipping on the damp floor. Her hair flung into her eyes, temporarily blinding her. Well, so much for sexy. Abby took hold of somebody's arm to balance herself. She heard him grunt at her touch.

"Sorry, Sorry." She told the heavy set gentleman whose forearm she had grabbed.

"Pas de problemes," he muttered, giving her a disgusted expression, proving that it was definitely a problem.

Ethan took her forearm arm and steadied her. "Are you okay?"

Her boots wobbled as she tried to balance on the uneven cobblestones. They were a bad choice for tonight. "I'm fine. A little embarrassed," Abby said, regretting her decision to borrow Sarah's things. She no longer felt sexy, only self-conscious. She looked at Ethan. He was dressed in faded jeans and a gray t-shirt. His lazy smile settled the rolling queasiness in her abdomen. She didn't know what came over her, but she wanted to throw him on the table and jerk his clothes off. Forget her rules. Forget being good.

Ethan laughed as his gaze went down at her boots. "We're sitting over in the corner. Try not to kill yourself getting over there." He led her to a round table near the back of the bar.

Abby spotted her sister sitting by one of Ethan's friends. Nicole's eyes widened as she looked Abby up and down. "I didn't think you would show up," Nicole said. Her mouth dropped open as she took in Abby's new style, but the frown that appeared didn't dampen Abby's mood.

"Another round?" a waitress asked, her British accent stormed the table as she gestured to the empty mugs.

"Yeah. Give us another." Ethan turned to Abby. "What would you like?"

Abby surveyed the table. Her mind went blank.

"You'll like the cider. You have to try it," Nicole said as she patted the chair next to her. Abby followed her hand and sat. "You're dressed like you're out to get a guy," Nicole whispered.

"I figured I'd see what happens. A girl can't have too many guys chasing after her," Abby said. She knew it sounded cliché.

"True. It shouldn't be too hard for you. Wiggle your butt in front of Ethan tonight, and he's yours," Nicole said. Abby smacked her playfully. Nicole laughed and leaned back in her chair as Ethan sat beside Abby. He looked hot tonight. His hair curled over his forehead and covered his ears. It seemed longer, darker, as if he'd just stepped out of the shower. A scent of sandalwood danced off his skin and she drank the sensual scent.

Ethan pulled his chair closer to the table beside Abby's. "Didn't Sarah come with you?" He glanced past her to the door.

"I haven't seen her since she left for the library this afternoon," Abby said.

Ethan's eyebrows rose after her comment. "That seems strange. She usually doesn't miss a night out."

The waitress returned and deposited the drinks on the table. Jealousy rose through Abby. She didn't want to talk about Sarah. Why was Ethan interested in her? He never was before now. Abby grabbed her mug. Beer wasn't her favorite drink, but she took a sip anyway. The lager hit her tongue, causing her mouth to pucker. She wasn't expecting such a sweet then sour taste, a pleasant surprise. It didn't burn, and she loved the apple taste. Abby took another gigantic drink of the golden liquid.

"What is it?" Abby asked, resting the mug on the table. She had already finished half the drink.

"It's good, isn't it? It's an Irish cider. I knew you'd like it. You can quit drinking all this beer and wine you hate," Nicole said.

Abby's face turned scarlet. At least she knew Nicole didn't suggest the drink out of the kindness of her heart. It was all about opportunity to smack Abby down in front of the group.

Ethan nudged her arm. "All this time, you've hated beer and wine and didn't tell us. Good thing we know now."

"Everyone in this country drinks wine like water. I hate ordering soda. It brands me as an American every time," Abby said, her bottom lip puckered out.

"Sarah lays into you too if you don't embrace the culture," Nicole said.

"Exactly." Abby raised her glass toasting Nicole's comment. Nicole's criticism of Sarah was a change, but Abby knew it wouldn't last. Nicole was only interested in Nicole's well-being.

Ethan smiled as he glanced at Abby's almost empty mug. "Don't go anywhere."

She nodded. Nothing would persuade her out of that seat. He rose from the chair and went to the bar. Abby turned her attention to Nicole. "You haven't heard from Sarah tonight?"

"No. She's been spending more and more time with that new guy since Patrick left. She called earlier and said she'd be late." Nicole took a cigarette out of her bag and lit it. "I don't know why I'm smoking. It's Sarah and her stupid embrace the culture crap." She held the cigarette up, examining the end as if it were some type of magic wand. "Abby, I should be more like you."

"Try putting it out." Abby reached over and grabbed for the cigarette. Nicole jerked it away and stuck it in her mouth. She held her breath for several seconds before exhaling. The smoke rose above the table into the air.

"I've committed too many sins to be like you," Nicole said, causing everyone at the table to laugh. Abby sunk lower in the chair. Everyone thought it was a joke, but Abby knew it was more than that. The comment was about the accident. Out of everyone in her family, Abby thought Nicole should've been the one who gave her compassion, but she was actually the worst. It seemed Nicole wanted Abby to suffer. They'd always been competitive, even for their parents' love. Abby thought they were beyond it, but the friction between them was greater than ever.

Abby fluffed her hair. Her new style did little to tarnish her supposed good girl image with this group. She could probably re-virginize everyone in the room if she tried.

"Tell everyone that I'm a saint. It'll help me attract all the bad boys who want to corrupt me," Abby said, knowing she could never get the best of Nicole. Her sister had a comeback for everything.

"Right, keep thinking that." Nicole laughed. "You need to drink that cider because a bad boy is coming to sit beside you."

Abby had to agree with her as she watched Ethan stroll back from the bar. Bringing her mug to her lips, she finished the rest of her cider. The guys cheered her on as she swallowed the remainder of the drink and sat the empty glass on the table.

"Guess you needed this," Ethan said as he returned to the table with a new round of drinks. He glanced at Abby's empty glass then at her. She sucked in a deep breath. He was almost too attractive. She could hardly focus on anything else. She could see his teeth when he grinned, his crooked lower tooth protruding slightly.

His eyebrow lifted slightly when he smiled. "What occasion are you dressed for tonight?"

"Nothing special. I felt like a change. Do you like it?" She leaned over far enough so he could catch a glimpse of her breasts peeking out of the red shirt. Her self-consciousness getting the better of her, she retreated just as fast.

His eyes narrowed, and they didn't move from her chest. "I do, but you're not playing fair."

Abby's heart began to pound. "Why's that?" She would reel him in, and it shouldn't take much more before he'd relent.

"We agreed on a hands-off relationship. You come in here in that outfit. No man would want to keep his hands off you." He grabbed his beer and drank nearly the entire mug.

"Maybe I'm changing the agreement. Are you okay with that?" Abby asked, staring into Ethan's icy eyes.

"Oh, yeah. I'm okay with that. I've always been okay with that." Ethan's hand left the table and traveled down to Abby's knee. She shivered at his touch, even though it was stifling in the pub. She took a tiny sip of her cider. Liquid courage was no longer needed. She knew what she wanted. Heat rose within her as his hand caressed her leg.

"You want a darts rematch?" Abby asked.

Ethan chuckled and withdrew his hand. "No need to threaten me." He leaned in and slung his arm around her shoulder, gently resting his hand along her arm. "Better?"

"Yes." She relaxed in his embrace. It felt great to have Ethan sitting beside her. Abby snuggled up against him as they sat at the table. His chest felt firm and tight as it rose and fell in rhythm with his breathing. Abby lifted her head to see his face. His breathing gradually getting heavier, he stared at her with fevering desire in his eyes. This night would not be over anytime soon. Anymore of this and Abby would be ready to strip him down to his bare skin.

"Quit staring at me that way or I'll have to sit with Nicole," Ethan whispered.

"What have I been doing?" Abby asked.

"You know what I mean. You're practically inviting me to take you home right now. That wasn't part of the deal." Ethan finished off the remainder of his drink.

"I changed the rules, remember?"

"You sure?" Ethan asked as he grabbed her hand.

"Yes."

He reached for his wallet and threw a few bills on the table. "That should cover our tab. Abby and I are getting out of here. You need anything, Nicole?"

Nicole was talking with one of Ethan's friends whom Abby had rarely seen. She was her usual self, interrogating the poor guy. He looked trapped between the wall and Nicole.

Nicole winked at Abby. "I'm fine. Stone will walk me back. It sure took you two long enough."

Not sure how to take Nicole's response, Abby smiled. She yanked her purse out of the chair while Ethan practically hauled her out of the pub. Hobbling behind him in her boots, she tried to keep up with his demanding pace.

"My place?" Ethan asked.

"Sure." She couldn't guarantee that Sarah or Nicole wouldn't barge in at her apartment. This was one time she wanted complete privacy. She didn't understand why she didn't see it before now. He was her type, someone she could hang out with, and tell her problems to. This was what it was supposed to be like. They continued down several cobblestone roads zigzagging their way through Paris to Ethan's apartment. He held her hand, squeezing it ever so often, letting his fingers lightly caress her skin.

They turned the corner and Abby recognized the street where Ethan lived. She followed him up the tall gray stone steps. Taking out his key to open the outer door to the building, he turned around and pulled her to his chest. Leaning down, he held her chin, pulling it toward him. His lips grazed hers, sending shots of fire down her body. His tongue tickled the inside of her mouth.

"I've wanted to do that all night since you stumbled in with those boots on." Ethan leaned in to take advantage of Abby's silence. He crushed her lips against his and sucked on her lower lip.

"I've been waiting for you to do that," Abby mumbled through his kiss.

Ethan pulled away and turned the lock. He pushed the door open, allowing Abby to pass by him. The dark foyer and wooden staircase greeted her. The little carved animals on the banister seemed to be smiling at her, like they sensed her happiness. Ethan and Abby climbed the stairs to the top floor. Seizing Abby's waist, Ethan steered her body to the left and down the hallway to his loft. He fumbled with the key while she wrapped her arms around his waist. With the distraction, he struggled to unlock the door but finally opened it. She entered the living room. Feeling the breeze coming through the windows, Abby barely made out the tall white drapes flapping back and forth in the darkness. She turned and saw Ethan staring back at her.

"You want anything to drink? Water?" Ethan asked.

"I want you."

Ethan came forward and pulled her to him, causing Abby to hit him in his chest. His lips engulfed hers, leaving her breathless. He kissed her then moved to her cheeks, slowly kissing each freckle on her face. "I'm happy you changed the rules," Ethan whispered.

Abby smiled. Moving his hand down to her waist, Ethan gripped her shirt and pulled it over her head, discarding it on the floor. A wave of cool air hit her bare skin, bringing her senses to attention. Tearing off his own shirt, he let it fall to the side, revealing his rippled stomach.

He held out his hand. She accepted it eagerly, allowing him guide her to the bed. Abby dangled her feet off the edge. Ethan sat beside her and put his arm around her, pulling her on the mattress. She lay there staring at the ceiling as he ran his fingers up and down her stomach. This was exactly how she'd imagined it. So perfect. She closed her eyes as goose bumps appeared on her body. His hand slid behind her back, and he unhooked her bra. Abby settled back on the bed, squashing his arm behind her back.

"One-handed?" Abby asked.

Ethan grinned as he twisted his hand out from underneath her. "I'm good with my hands." He winked and removed her bra. A smirk formed from his lips. "No tape this time?"

Lying awkwardly, she moved her arms up to shield her breasts, feeling for anything out of the ordinary. Laughing, she knew it wasn't there, but it didn't hurt to check.

"No. Don't." Ethan held her wrist at her side. "I want to see you." He lowered his head and his lips touched her breast. A moan escaped her mouth. Abby felt as if she were soaring outside of her body. She wanted more. Abby reached out and pulled his head up to meet hers.

"I need you now," she said breathless, never wanting anyone more than she wanted him.

Ethan grinned. "Not yet. I'm not done." He kissed her, moved back down to her chest, and resumed the gentle sucking of her skin. Abby clutched the sheets in her hand, squeezing the thin fabric. Feeling him lift his head up, Abby watched as his hands went down to her pants and unbuttoned the top button. He hesitated and looked at her. She nodded. Ethan unzipped her pants, exposing her white cotton panties. He undid his jeans and let them fall to his feet. He stood in front of her in black boxer shorts.

He moved back over her and rested his hand on her pelvis, as he kissed the area below her belly button.

Slipping his hand underneath her, he took hold of the waist of her pants and pulled them down to her knees. Ethan lifted her knee and removed her pants, leaving only her panties as the final barrier. He leaned over and kissed her lips before moving away. The coldness struck her as the tingling and the memory of his touch faded. She opened her eyes and saw him lying on the bed beside her, looking up at the ceiling.

Abby leaned over and kissed him. "You tired already? Let me get you riled up."

He wrapped his arms around her before retreating and flopping back first on the bed.

Abby lay there, staring at the wall. "What's going on?"

"Nothing. We need to slow down a bit," he said in between deep breaths. He covered his face with his hands.

"Why?" Abby jerked her head up, almost cracking her forehead on Ethan's elbow.

"I don't think this is a good idea."

"It was a good idea a few minutes ago." Abby's voice rose with each word. Her heart felt like it would pound out of her chest. Why would he stop now? This is what she wanted. She thought he wanted it too.

"You're not ready."

"Not ready? I'm more than ready," Abby said. She turned away from him and pulled the sheet over her chest. She was so sure this was the night.

"Abby, Come on. I don't mean it like that. It's obvious how I feel about you. It's not the right time." He wrapped his arm around her waist, but she twisted out of his grasp.

She couldn't believe this was his excuse. "The right time? What about the time before? Was that the right time and I missed it? Were you ready then?" She grabbed her shirt on the nightstand and pulled it over her head. She was not going to lie around naked until he decided he was ready.

"Wait. Something is going on right now," Ethan said.

Abby glanced at his face. She couldn't read it. She couldn't tell what he was thinking. She didn't get it. He insinuated this was what he wanted from her. When she finally came around, he stopped. "What is it? Maybe I can help."

"You can't help me with this. It shouldn't involve you." There was no emotion in his face, and it hurt worse than the physical rejection.

"Doesn't involve me? I'm happy to hear that. At least I know where I stand now." Anger swelled inside her as she ran Ethan's words through her head. She reached over the side of the bed and fumbled around until she gathered the rest of her clothes off the floor.

"What are you doing?"

Abby laughed. "What do you think I'm doing? I'm leaving. It's obvious I'm not getting what I came for."

Ethan's head snapped back as if Abby's words slapped him in the face. Good. It's what he deserved.

He clenched his fists. "It sounds like all you wanted from me was sex."

"You finally get it," Abby said, instantly regretting the words. All she wanted was for him to feel the hurt she felt. Sex wasn't all she wanted. How could things change in a few minutes?

"I thought we had something more than sex going on here tonight." Ethan's mild voice had disappeared, replaced by a cold tone she'd never heard before. A chill flowed through her.

"I thought this could work. This was my mistake," Abby said as she pulled out her phone. She'd get a cab, go home, and forget this humiliation.

"No, it's not. Don't you see? That's the only reason I don't have you on those sheets right now. It's a lot more than sex going on here." Ethan's voice towered over her.

Abby shrank back at the stony tone of his voice. "What do you mean?"

Ethan frowned. "If you don't know, I see no reason to tell you." He got up off the bed and slipped his shirt back on, failing to button it.

Distracted by his well-developed midriff, she couldn't concentrate on the conversation. "I'm lost here. Why are you angry?" How could he be this openly hostile to her?

Ethan laughed. "It's not about sex for me. If it was, I wouldn't be with you right now. I want more. For you, I'm here to satisfy your needs of the moment. I'm filling your time while you wait on your so called perfect guy."

"No, that's not it. Why would you say I'm filling my time?" She bit her lip, forcing the tears to stay submerged.

His eyes bore into her. "If that tennis player were here, would you be with me now?"

"What does Jayson have to do with us?"

"Stop playing games. Sarah told me what happened with you and Jayson. Was it a coincidence you showed up at the bar tonight? You're more like Sarah than you know. At least with her, she doesn't hide behind an innocent face."

Abby jerked around. The pain struck her in the chest. "You're not innocent in this. You knew I was seeing Jayson. It wasn't a secret."

"No, it wasn't. But I didn't use you either."

It was like cold water was dumped on her head. What had she done? He was a nice guy, and she'd treated him like a secondhand store hand-me-down. Abby sank on the bed. He believed her feelings for him were only physical attraction. Why wouldn't he? She hadn't given him much of a chance until now. "Look, I'm not proud of this thing with Jayson, but you knew about him. I wanted him to model in my ad campaign."

"Abby, admit it. I'm pacifying your time until he shows up again."

"No, it isn't like that. I want to spend time with you. You've been my best friend here." She couldn't believe it had always been in front of her.

He scowled. "Best friend? I'm not looking to be your BFF."

Tears sprung to her eyes. How could she make him understand? "I could've been more open about my feelings. I like being with you and I've been denying how I felt. It's more than friendship." She couldn't lose him. Not now.

He sat beside her. "Yeah, well I guess my persuasive charm wasn't all I thought it was if it takes an argument to get you to admit it." A frown grew on his face. "I don't want to be a distraction while you figure out how you feel."

Abby shook her head. "You're not a distraction."

"I don't want you regretting something in the morning," he said.

He put his fingers under her chin and raised her head so she was parallel to his face. She felt the warmth of his lips as he kissed her. "You want to stay the rest of the night?"

Abby leaned over and rested her head on his shoulder. She wanted to be close to him. "Yes." Ethan pushed the covers down and she crawled into the bed. He kissed her on the forehead. "You're not sleeping here?"

"I'll come to bed in a little while." He wrapped the covers around her body. Abby shifted to her side and faced the wall. She knew what she wanted from him and she knew it wasn't for him to be her friend. She only had to figure out how to convince Ethan of her love.

Chapter 32

"You didn't sleep in your bed last night."

Ethan turned around from the open window and watched Abby's heart-shaped face peek out from under the covers. She shifted on her back and scooted her body so she was propped up on the pillow.

Ethan smiled. If she wasn't careful, he'd have those covers off in a second. She looked tempting snuggled under his white duvet cover. He hardly slept knowing she was so close. He should've enjoyed it more, but the truth was pounding to get out. It was Friday. His week was over. Tom expected him in London tomorrow.

"You okay?" She rustled the cover and flopped back against the mattress.

"Oh, yeah. I slept over on the chair." He pointed to the recliner by the bed. "Didn't think I could take lying beside you and not touch you."

Abby motioned for him to sit on the bed. "We can change that."

The fire in her eyes shocked him. The request was genuine and it hurt his heart. He loved Abby even more now, but he couldn't continue this lie. The deceptions he held onto had to end. He backed away from the bed. "Don't tempt me. You need to get to class, and I need to work." He went to the kitchen. He felt like he wasn't trapped in her emotional grasp if he kept his distance. "What do you want for breakfast? I'll run to the bakery."

"Pain au chocolat."

He laughed. "Chocolate. That's not a good food to start the day out with." Ethan grabbed his coat and wallet from the table.

"Why would the French make it if it wasn't good for you?" The mischief in her face brightened his mood.

He threw up his hands, knowing she'd find a reason. "I'll be right back." He returned to the bed, bent over Abby, and kissed her. The kiss was light, but a flood of raw longing flowed through him. Would she stick around after he told her? He doubted it. No one did. His mother abandoned him, then his uncle. Why would Abby stick around? He closed the door behind him and headed down the hallway to the stairs. Why in blazes was he getting breakfast? It wasn't like the truth was going anywhere because he brought her back a croissant. It would be waiting on him, waiting to destroy his life. He jerked open the outer door of his building and the hot humid air of June hit him in the face. He knew he was running. How could he have taken it this far? He'd opened himself up to the hurt he knew would come. Abby couldn't love him, not an unwanted bastard whose mother paid an orphanage to keep him, then tried to bribe him to stay in Europe. If Abby forgave him, she'd never get beyond his personal crap. Ethan swung the door of the bakery open.

"Bonjour, ca va?" the lady behind the counter asked as she beamed at him. The wrinkles intensified as she widened her smile.

"Très bien, et vous?" He walked over to the counter and surveyed the selection, barely hearing the old woman as she began her daily chat. She'd latched on to him the first week he'd stayed in the flat across the street. He'd miss her cheery outlook on life.

"Tell me about the girl you are seeing," she said, straining on each English word. He'd gladly speak to her in French, but she said she loved his accent so he gave up.

He stared at her a second, unable to talk. What happened to the French's need for privacy?

"She special, non?" The lady took out a few pastries and stuck them in the bag, adding extra croissants as she always did.

Was she Nols's mother? The woman could pinpoint anything with her radar perception.

He nodded. "Yes, she is." No use denying it.

"Ah, young love. C'est magnifique." She glanced up at the ceiling, and Ethan was tempted to look up to see if there was a cloud of dreams floating above her. "Ah." She exhaled and clapped her hands together. Coming around the counter, she shooed him out the door. "Go on now. Do not keep love waiting."

Ethan tried to grab his wallet from his pocket. "But I haven't paid you."

"Non, you pay tomorrow." She showed him out the door.

Ethan groaned. He was so sick with love any stranger could see it. Wouldn't that look good? Tom would catch on quick once Ethan was back in London. He gazed up at his flat. It was time to tell the truth. Tom gave him to the end of the week and Ethan had used it all. He had to fill her in before he left. Ethan sprinted up the stairs and stopped as an explosion of light hit his face. He dropped the bag of pastries and extended his arms on instinct, grabbing the first thing he saw.

"Hey, man. Watch the camera."

Ethan took hold of the lanky man and threw him and the camera to the ground.

"You'll pay for that, Gray," the short stocky man with the voice recorder positioned under Abby's mouth rasped at him.

"Get out," Ethan yelled as he elbowed the other guy out of his way.

"Sawyer Houston from the Daily World News," he shouted as Ethan pushed him further down the hall. "What's your relationship to Jayson Walters?"

"What are you talking about?" Abby's voice sounded weak, and Ethan grimaced. He studied Abby's confused face, and his heart sunk.

"Don't play dumb. Jayson Walters, the tennis star. Are you lovers? Betting partners?" Sawyer peppered questions at her. "Sal, get the camera and a few more shots."

Abby stood with her mouth gaped open.

"Are you here with Ethan to discuss the match-fixing investigation on Walters?"

Ethan pushed Sawyer down the hall. "You need to leave."

"Come on, Gray. We want to know who your friend is. Is she part of your investigation?" Sawyer thrust the recorder under Ethan's chin.

Ethan shoved Sawyer back, then slid his arm around Abby and guided her into his flat before slamming the door. He leaned his head against the hard wood frame. Why did that reporter have to show up? He turned around and slung the pastry bag on the side table, not even sure how he picked them back up when he dropped the bag in the hallway.

"You okay?" he asked as he passed her and snatched his phone off the desk. He quickly dialed Nols.

"We've got a problem with that reporter, Sawyer Houston. Go pick him up outside my building." He shut the phone and glanced at Abby. She appeared dazed like she'd been hit with a sledgehammer.

He walked over to her and caught her arms. "Are you okay?" He nudged her and she looked up at him.

"Jayson's famous?" The voice was quiet and didn't sound like Abby.

He nodded but refused to speak. It wouldn't take her long. She might be naïve, but her intelligence would reign this one in. She had most of the information to make the connection between him and Walters.

Her eyes widened as if on cue. "That reporter knew you." She jerked away from him.

"What else did he say before I got here?" Ethan asked, ignoring her comment. He needed to know how far Sawyer got with her before she clammed up. She was still processing what happened; she'd answer.

"Something about match-fixing, an investigation." Her eyes turned to slits as she glared at him. "Your investigation. What did he mean?" She didn't give him time to answer. "He knew you."

Ethan swore. "He's an annoying reporter."

"You know him?" She pressed her lips together. "You know Jayson?"

Ethan chose the one thing that would get him the most anger. It was better if she dealt with the ugly truth. "Jayson Walters, he's ranked number two on the pro tennis tour."

Abby closed her eyes and tears swelled. It tore out his gut to see that protecting her, he'd hurt her anyway. She wiped her eyes. "If you knew who he was, why didn't you tell me?"

"All you have to do is watch Sports Center and there he is. Just because you didn't know is not my problem." The harshness, he knew, stung her. It'd help her get over what he did.

She jerked on his arm. "Not your problem? You lied to me."

"No, not about that." He stared down into her eyes. "Just because you're too naïve to see what a fraud Jayson is, isn't an excuse to be angry with me."

"Explain that." Her hands moved to her hips as she glared at him. He'd never seen her so upset, except when she was describing the accident. He'd finally succeeded in hurting the one person he loved most. It was time to make that hurt permanent.

"Are you that clueless? Do you think everyone has a luxury suite on the Champs-Eylsee, a private château for tennis practice? Come on, not everyone has a rich lifestyle like you." He slammed his fist on his desk. He let his hatred for his mother and his family flow out. He didn't want to hurt her. He hated being so harsh but he had to make her despise him.

Abby jumped back. "You're judging me?" She pointed to the main room of the loft. "What about your extravagant accommodations? Not typical for a college student."

"The rich girl got one right," he sneered. He was at the point of no return. She needed someone to hate and he'd give her someone.

She glanced around the room and back at him. He saw the questions in her eyes. How could he judge her when he lived like he did? Yeah, appearances were deceiving. He may own the flat, but he'd be damned if he took anything else from his mother. The only reason he used it was because it was next to the school and close to Abby. Once this case was over, he'd probably never set foot in there for another five, six years. Lost in his own thought, he glanced up, half expecting her to be gone, but she still stood in front of him. He flung his coat on the armchair as he rounded the corner to the kitchen.

"What investigation are you doing on Jayson?" she asked as she ran after him.

"I can't tell you," he said in a robotic tone, the same attitude he took with any other suspect or witness.

"You can't or you won't?" she screamed at him.

"It doesn't matter." He stopped gathering the plates and stared at the wall behind her, avoiding her eyes.

"You lied about Jayson. That doesn't matter?"

He laughed as the anger boiled in him. "I lied about a lot, but it always comes back to him, doesn't it?"

She marched toward him and pushed him. Surprised by the force, he stumbled back against the refrigerator.

"Who are you?"

He saw her fist curl up, and he braced for the next attack. He'd welcome her hitting him. He deserved it.

He grabbed her arm roughly but not enough to hurt her. "I'm the guy who was ordered to keep you out of trouble. You didn't think your Daddy would let you go to Paris without supervision?"

"Oh...my..." Abby backpedaled and tripped over her shoes but regained her balance. "My dad hired you?"

"You think I'm here by choice?" Every shot he took at her, he felt the pain he inflicted.

Tears welled up in her blue eyes, and Ethan thought he'd never be able to hurt someone the way he was hurting her now. It was better than her waking up one day and realizing what they had was a mistake. She would if they continued their relationship.

"Isn't it enough that I have Nicole reporting my every move?" She bent down and grabbed her shoes. "I can't believe he did this. I've done fine on my own."

He came up behind her. "Sure, like you handled the car wreck."

She twirled around and smacked him on the cheek. "I told you those things as a friend, not for you to hold them over my head." If looks could kill, Ethan's body would've been mutilated and left on the floor to rot.

Ethan rubbed his jaw. "I'm sorry." He didn't mean to take it that far, not about her brother's accident.

"No, you're not." She shoved her feet in her shoes and pulled her sweater over her head. He watched her as she fiddled with her purse strings. She was lost. He wished he could let her go now, but Nols needed more time to apprehend Sawyer. Ethan used the one thing that kept Abby there. Him. "You think this was easy for me?"

Abby glared at him. "You already told me what a burden it was. I don't need any more proof." She stood with her hands on her hips.

"You think I enjoyed watching you hang all over that bastard?" He couldn't think about it without wanting to kill Walters.

"What are you getting at?"

Ethan shrugged, he didn't know. He needed to stall but he wasn't sure what to say. He whipped around her and headed for the kitchen. He took a plate from the cupboard and placed the croissants on them. "You want your breakfast?"

"You're going to eat like nothing happened." The fire in her voice burned his soul. She'd hate him forever.

He shrugged. "A man has to eat."

"You want to do something then start with why. Why this game? My father forced you to watch me, but that didn't mean you had to get involved." She plopped down in the chair next to him and grabbed the pain au chocolat.

He smiled inside. He knew his indifference would force her to stay and fight.

"Part of the job. You want a croissant?" He thrust the pastries across the table.

She stared at it, and he hoped she'd accept it for what it was worth. It wasn't much, but he was sorry he'd hurt her.

"I don't believe you."

He sighed. His skills were rusty. He suspected she knew him better than he'd thought. He wiped his mouth and smeared a slab of butter on his croissant. "Believe what you will. Your father wanted you away from Walters. I did that." He finished off the last bite and wadded up his napkin in his hand.

She picked at the pastry in front of her. "What aren't you telling me?"

He threw his hands up. "What do you want to know?" He'd rather wrap his arms around her and tell her he was sorry, but he couldn't. Not now, not ever again.

"Tell me about the case."

"No."

She jumped up. "I'll go find that reporter."

He sprinted in front of her and blocked the door. "He'll use anything you say against you. Think about all that publicity." He knew she'd received the same lecture from her father. No screw-ups, no encounters with the media. Abby was a prisoner in her father's political world, and Ethan would take advantage of it to keep her away from Walters.

She looked up at him with those golden blue eyes. "I guess you'll have to tell me."

He sucked in his bottom lip. She was playing him. He appreciated that calm exterior when he knew she probably wanted to kill him. He admired her for not buckling under the pressure, a small accomplishment given what he'd done to her. He only wished she'd do the same when her sisters bullied her. He'd offer her the information she could find on the internet. He motioned her back to the table. "Jayson Walters is being investigated for match-fixing and gambling on his tennis matches." He closed himself off from the hurt in her eyes. He rolled off the details like he was reading a report.

Her hand went to her chest. "You've been using me to get information on Jayson."

Ethan grabbed the milk out of the fridge and poured some in two glasses. "No, I'm here to protect you, remember?"

She scowled. "What did you find on Jayson?"

"I can't answer that," he said as he set the glasses on the table and sat in the seat next to her.

"Do you know where he is?"

Anger built inside him and he glared at her. "Why? You want to go see him?"

"No, but..."

"I'm leaving." He waited for her to process what he said.

"I still have questions," she said, jumping up and this time she blocked the door.

"No, I'm leaving Paris." He felt his phone vibrate in his pocket. He took it out and hit a few buttons. Nols's text appeared. Sawyer was in custody.

She moved next to him. "Where are you going?"

He shut the phone before she could see the message. "You already know enough. It's time to go." He moved to the kitchen and washed off his plate.

He could hear her moving around the room. The longer she stayed, the more his will was breaking. He wouldn't last too much longer.

"You can't kick me out. I deserve some answers," Abby said.

"We're done."

She threw her hands up. "Fine. I'll find my answer from Jayson."

He smiled at the threat. "If you know where he is, be my guest." He opened the door.

"No, but I'll email him."

"You haven't talked to him in weeks so don't threaten me." He watched the anger in her eyes turn to rage.

"You spied on me when we weren't together?" She slammed her fists against his chest, but the mental hurt, he knew, went deeper than any physical pain she inflicted on him. He saw the hate in the way her eyes sparked with revulsion.

He drew his lips in a smirk. "I saw everything." His words did what he wanted, but it made him sick to his stomach to see the agony in her eyes.

"How could you do this to me?" She held her arms around her body like she was trying to hold herself together. He wanted to be the one holding her, but he figured she'd knock him dead in the floor if he tried.

He shrugged. "What do you want me to say?"

"Say anything. I want you to deny it. I want you to be the guy from last night, who wanted to be with me," she screamed even though she was directly in front of him. The tears flowed from her eyes and killed his heart.

"You know I can't do that." Those indigo eyes appeared lifeless now, like he sucked out all the hope.

"I get it. It was a job to you. The joke's on me." She turned toward the table and grabbed her purse. He heard her fingers tapping on the tabletop, and he watched the nervous tick in her neck. She stopped and glanced down at her bag. "Would you have told me?"

Ethan stared at the back of her head. It was easier to lie when he didn't have to look into her eyes. "No."

Her body shuttered. She was crying again. He fought the urge to reach out to her as she passed by him. Her flowery scent lingered even though she'd gone. He closed the door. With it, a piece of his heart closed.

Chapter 33

"I need your help!" Abby slammed her bag on the empty chair near the entrance to the computer lab. Nicole jumped in her seat.

"Holy crap, Abby. You scared me. What do you want?" Nicole slouched down in her chair and continued her instant chat session.

"I need a ticket to London on train fifty-four at 4:35 P.M. today." She couldn't believe she was doing this, but she thought back to her argument with Ethan earlier. While she shuffled through her purse, she'd seen Ethan's train ticket on the kitchen counter. With that and a quick stop at the newsstand on her way back to campus, her suspicions were confirmed. Jayson was in London for a tennis tournament. She didn't know when she decided to go to London, but since she knew where Jayson was, there was a possibility that he'd still do the Von Deez shoot. Her chance at love was finished. She might as well get her campaign with Von Deez in order. Her father forced Jayson away. Anger blew through her like a furious wind. What's a little paparazzi? She'd deal with her father. This was about Von Deez, not her. Gilda would love the controversy surrounding Jayson. Every model Gilda picked had a constant presence in the tabloids. She loved to have newsmakers in her campaigns. It was one of the main reasons she was stuck on Alana Barash. Alana was a tabloid's dream with her many relationships and her torrid relationship with her diva mother. She was a poster child for the famous. With Alana, you'd get controversy. Jayson's current problems were right up Gilda's alley.

"Why are you going to London? You know Dad's not going to approve." Nicole looked over her shoulder.

Abby hesitated. She couldn't tell her the truth. Nicole wanted her to fail. She'd tell the family, and Abby didn't want her father sending a whole group of FBI agents to swarm her in London.

"I'm chasing Ethan. It's the beginning of the game. He chased me. I gave in, so now it's my turn to chase." Abby faked a laugh, but her stomach lurched at the thought of him. "You know how it is with guys. Love is never easy." She bit her lip. She should've said it was for Von Deez. She was terrible at coming up with lies. Luckily, Nicole's instant chat distracted her, so she didn't focus on Abby's story.

Nicole's head popped back as she giggled. "You two are hysterical. I've never seen anything like this." She closed down her chat session. "I'll find your train. Do you know the station?" She straightened in her chair and her fingers banged on the keyboard.

"I don't know. I need to be on train fifty-four to London leaving at 4:35 P.M. today." Abby repeated what she'd seen on the Ethan's ticket. She didn't want to ask Nicole, but she was the quickest when it came to understanding the French language, and Abby didn't have time to waste.

"Okay. We'll focus on the train schedule until we find train fifty-four."

Abby searched the screen and recognized a grid of departure times, but the rest of the information was a foreign mixture of French. She needed to attend her French class more often. What had her life become? Reading a train schedule so she could pursue Jayson and convince him to be in her campaign. Her internship was all she had left. She wouldn't lose it.

Her parents would kill her if they knew she was chasing guys around Europe, but she was desperate. Desperate to save her job and her trust fund. Abby studied the computer screen. The schedule was massive, but Nicole breezed through the list. "Here's a train leaving from Gare Nord at 4:35 P.M. This has to be it. I don't see another train fifty-four on the list." Nicole pointed to the next to the last line on the screen.

"I need a ticket," Abby said as she pulled up a seat next to Nicole.

"What type do you want? There are several fares available."

Abby peered over Nicole's shoulder at the screen. She didn't think to look for the class on Ethan's ticket. Wonder if it even mattered? She heard many passengers risked moving between classes, but she didn't think she'd have the nerve.

"I'll take the cheapest one." Abby dug through her bag and found her credit card. "Put it on this." She handed Nicole her card. The cheaper ticket would probably go unnoticed on the bill and, she figured Ethan wouldn't be sitting in the lowest class.

"This fare doesn't have seat assignments. It's first come, first serve. You better get there early, so you can fight for a seat." Nicole hit the enter key, producing a confirmation screen, and printed the page.

"Thanks. Any advice on London?" Abby asked, reading over the confirmation ticket.

"You'll be fine. They speak English there," Nicole said, laughing.

Abby smiled, knowing her sister couldn't resist taking a small jab at Abby's attempts at the French language. No matter how many tutoring classes she took, Abby still managed to assassinate the language.

"You need to hurry and get your stuff together. You don't have much time before the train leaves." Nicole pointed to the door. "Be careful, and don't be like Sarah."

Puzzled, Abby nodded. Did Nicole actually care? "Thanks for the help." She grabbed her bag and ran out of the computer lab. She'd almost forgotten she still had to pack. Heading outside, she took the shortest route to her apartment. She had little concern that Sarah would be there. She rarely saw her in the apartment during the day. Come to think of it, she'd barely seen Sarah in the apartment at night during the last week. Sometimes, Sarah wouldn't show up at the apartment for days, but Nicole said she was fine. The first time it happened, it terrified Abby. She thought something terrible had happened to her, but Sarah showed up a day later as if it wasn't a big deal. Her disappearances occurred more often since Patrick left. Abby cared what happened to her, but she couldn't control Sarah. If she wanted to spend the night at random places, what could Abby do?

Abby reached the apartment and unlocked the door. She entered the dark foyer. Everything looked the same as she'd left it, including her note that was still taped to the door. She didn't think anyone had been home since last night. Clutching her overnight bag, she unzipped it and dumped all the contents on the bed. She selected several shirts and shoes, not bothering to make sure they matched. Abby ran to the bathroom and grabbed her toothbrush, toothpaste, and hairbrush, throwing them along with her makeup into her toiletry case. Hurrying back to the bedroom, she stuffed the remainder of her items in the overnight bag. She squeezed the sides together and zipped it up. Glancing at the clock, she had an hour to make it to the train station. With one last trip around the rooms, she tried to remember if she was forgetting anything. Finally, she lifted the bag from the bed and headed for the door. She scribbled a quick note to Sarah telling her that she went to London. It was more than Sarah would do for her, but she still cared for her sisters. She couldn't let Sarah think she'd abandoned her. As she took hold of the handle, she heard the rattle of the lock. The doorknob twisted and Sarah's head peeked around the corner. Her hair was disheveled like she'd just woken up. Abby guessed she'd just left some stranger's bed.

"Where you going?" Sarah asked as she eyed the bag at Abby's hip.

Abby shifted the suitcase from her hand to her shoulder. "London for Von Deez."

Sarah whistled. "Wow, must be nice. Never thought they'd give you so much responsibility." She selected a bagel from the bread basket. "Guess that's why you weren't at work. I tried calling you."

Abby winced. She'd forgotten that today was Monday. Gilda would be expecting the daily reports on the model schedules and the Fashion Week Show. She'd call her from the train. If Gilda knew she was out trying to snag Jayson Walters as the next face of Von Deez, she'd probably pay for the ticket herself.

"Abby, did you hear what I said?"

"What?" She glanced up and saw Sarah waving her hand in her face.

"I said, do you think it'll be safe? You going alone."

Abby shrugged. "Sure, it's safer than the United States." Sarah seemed genuinely worried, but, of course, she was certain she was imagining Sarah's concern.

"Dad won't like it. He'll fuss when he finds out."

"Yeah, I know." She looked down at her watch. She only had forty minutes to make it to the station. "I have to go." The outer door opened and Nicole stepped in. Abby frowned.

"Hey, thought you'd be gone." Nicole slung her bag on the table and headed to the kitchen.

Abby moved toward the door. "I'm leaving now."

"Did you hear she's going to London for Von Deez?" Sarah asked as she laid a few outfits in front of her. Abby wondered if she was already planning her clothing for tonight and what guy was special enough to gain her attention that evening.

Nicole narrowed her eyes. "I thought she was chasing after Ethan."

Abby's heart quickened. They'd figure it out, but she at least needed to be on the train before Nicole called their father. If Jayson was as famous as that reporter and Ethan claimed, all they'd have to do is look in any major sports site to discover he was in London. She shook her head. "I didn't want to go into details with Sarah. You know how she is when it comes to Ethan. She thinks I need to parade around naked in front of him."

"I do not," Sarah said, pouting. "I think you need to show more interest."

"That's what I'm doing. I'm chasing him to London." Abby laughed and tried to put on a good act. The thought of pursuing Ethan felt like a punch in the gut when she remembered how robotic he treated her. He didn't even care. She'd been foolish to believe his lies. She'd given her heart to Ethan, and he'd smashed it to pieces.

Abby stiffened her back. All that was left to do was salvage what she could of her Von Deez internship. She might not be able to convince Jayson to do the Von Deez spread, but the only thing she was sure of is that she wasn't going to give up without a fight.

"Have fun," Nicole said as she passed her by and into the bedroom.

Sarah followed her. "You think she should go alone? It's dangerous."

"She'll be fine. It's not like she's going into a war zone."

"But what about..."

"Look, I'm twenty-one. I think I can handle a little trip to London." Abby waved and left Sarah staring at her. She whipped open the door and closed it before Sarah could say anything. She took a deep breath. This was it. She was going to London.

Chapter 34

*A*bby pulled her hand back so Gilda's screeching voice didn't permanently damage her ears. After her supervisor stopped screaming, Abby resumed her conversation. "You like the idea?"

"Like it? I love it. You sure Jayson Walters has agreed to do a few photo shoots for the next campaign?" Gilda asked.

Abby could hear banging on the keyboard as she spoke. The department memo on Jayson would probably be out by the time Abby hung up the phone. "Yes, he agreed several weeks ago. I'm going to London to finalize the details." Abby bit her lip on the lie. Was it a lie? He had agreed to do it. Leaving out that she hadn't heard from him in weeks didn't constitute a lie, right?

Gilda detailed a few instructions for Abby, like calling in once a day to give her an update. It went well considering Gilda hated last minute changes or surprises. Abby knew a celebrity like Jayson Walters would be a dream model for Gilda.

Abby nodded at the phone. "I'll call once I meet with Jayson and finalize his schedule." After a quick goodbye, she clicked off the phone and stared at it. This better go well. She'd upped the stakes by promising Jayson Walters. She had to make good on that commitment.

Abby laid her phone on the seat beside her. She took a deep breath and watched the scenery as it whizzed past the train window. Not that she could make anything out, but the blur seemed to add a bit of comfort to her torn up stomach.

"Well, well. We're travelling with Jayson's secret lover."

Abby rubbed her eyes like she'd dozed off, but she knew only a few minutes had passed. When she looked up, she recognized the reporter that was at Ethan's door earlier.

"Sawyer Houston." He held out his hand. Abby hesitated but finally extended her own. He dropped down in the seat in front of her.

"What do you want?" Abby asked.

"A few minutes of your time. I do apologize for this morning. We were rudely interrupted," Sawyer said as he whisked out his voice recorder. "Let's get started with your name."

"How about I ask you some questions first?" Abby shot back at him.

Scowling, Sawyer looked at her, clearly uncomfortable that he'd become the interviewee. "Well, you see. That's not exactly how this works. I ask you the questions, sweetie."

"Don't call me sweetie." Abby pushed a stray hair back behind her ear. "I may answer them later if you answer mine." His fake smile annoyed her. She had the upper hand. He needed her for his story.

"Come on, sweet..." He threw his hand up to his mouth. "Okay. What do you want to ask? I'll go along with this if you agree to answer my questions."

Abby nodded. She wouldn't answer any of his questions when the time came. "Start with Jayson. Tell me about this investigation."

"Guess that means you're not in the same line of work as Ethan. I was sure you were working with him," Sawyer said, raising his hands acting as if the new information shocked him. "Any who...you're asking about an investigation that would take days to cover. You'll have to be more specific." He leaned back and crossed his legs.

Abby gritted her teeth. Sawyer was dodging her questions like a sleazy car salesman. "Why is Ethan investigating Jayson? Who does he work for?" Her questions would give away information to Sawyer like her not knowing about the investigation or Ethan's job. It was all she had to work with at the moment.

"Jayson's being investigated for illegal gambling and match-fixing on his tennis matches. It's a serious allegation in the sporting world." He peered over at her, his eyes narrowed. "As for Ethan, he's a field agent for the FBI. It surprises me that you don't know that. You two seemed very close." His eyebrows shot up as he stared at her.

"FBI? Why would the FBI be in France and use a British national as an agent?" Abby asked, ignoring all of Sawyer's other comments.

"British National? Sweetie, he's been playing you. Ethan is as American as they come."

"American? The accent? It's all fake?"

"Hate to break it to you, but you've been fooled by the best. Ethan's a master."

Abby sat back. More lies. She was an idiot. Why didn't she see this before now? She didn't know Ethan at all. She regained her composure and peppered Sawyer with more questions. "Why is the FBI investigating match-fixing and spending resources on something that seems so petty? Don't they need to protect U. S. citizens from terrorists?" The investigation sounded more than a few bets and a few thrown matches. Why all the surveillance?

"The FBI is tight-lipped on this one. Hardly any information has leaked out. You're my first good lead in months." Sawyer smacked his lips as if he saw her as a juicy piece of meat ready to be grilled.

"It has to be more than what you're saying," Abby said, slouching in her chair. She didn't believe this investigation was only for one player and a few fixed matches. "Tell me more about Jayson."

"I figured you could tell me about him especially since you two seemed like a hot item a few weeks ago." He pushed the recorder closer to her face.

Abby glanced over at him, shocked that Sawyer insinuated something between her and Jayson. "I told you. I'll answer your questions after you finish answering mine. So far, you're a lousy reporter. You've told me nothing about this case, Ethan, or Jayson that I don't already know."

Sawyer leaned in close to Abby. "Here's something that might interest you. Geo's. I believe you know the place. It's not your typical restaurant, but I guess you knew that too. I need to know what you saw while you were there."

She put her hands on her face and stared out the window. Why didn't she see it? Was she so blind she couldn't see something suspicious was going on there? It wasn't normal to meet someone at a restaurant that was never open but always seemed to have the food and the staff necessary to accommodate their meals. Abby thought back to the one day that she passed by Geo's during prime lunch hours. There was not one person dining there. It was completely dark even though Jayson said they were open for lunch on weekends.

"She's finished answering your questions."

Abby shut her eyes, instantly recognizing the voice. She looked up and caught the chill of Ethan's cold eyes. His blood vessels poked out under his skin on his neck and his teeth were clinched. Reaching out, he yanked Abby up by her arm. She felt a dull pain as he squeezed her bicep.

"Wait a minute! You can't manhandle her and escort her away. We're having a conversation," Sawyer said as he jumped out of his seat and stood in the aisle, blocking the entrance to the next car. Several of the other passengers turned in their direction.

"She's finished here. Right?" Ethan turned his eyes on Abby. She nodded, knowing that she didn't have a choice. "Grab your bag. We're leaving."

Abby pulled her suitcase out of the overhead compartment. Ethan leaned over her and lifted the bag out of her hands before it tumbled to the floor. He pushed her to the door, leading to the next car. Abby moved forward to the exit, squeezing by Sawyer, who was swearing at Ethan.

"I can't believe this. You have no right to control what she does," Sawyer yelled.

Abby heard the car door shut behind them, silencing Sawyer's rants. They were near the entryway to the next car.

"Go straight through this car to the first class car," Ethan said.

Abby opened the door and kept her eyes centered on the walkway.

"Take a seat in one of the chairs four rows up on the right," he said.

Abby nodded. Opening the door, she entered the car and moved up the aisle to the window seat. Ethan came right after her and dumped her suitcase in the chair beside her. He sat down in front of Abby and stared at her for a few minutes before he spoke. She shifted her weight from one leg to the other.

"Are you going to explain why you're on this train?" Ethan asked. He settled his hand on the armrest.

"Would you believe I'm going on a weekend sight-seeing trip? I think they call it a mini-break in Europe," Abby said, smiling.

Ethan sat back in his seat. "No, I wouldn't believe it. You led Sawyer here."

"Don't leave your train ticket in plain sight. That reporter seems smart. He didn't need my help. He could've followed you here," Abby said. Was she the reason Sawyer had found his way to the train? She shook her head. Why did she need an excuse? She had every right to be on this train.

"I didn't realize I had a snoop in my apartment," Ethan growled.

Abby looked at him. She'd never seen him as angry as he was now. "Did you think I was going to stay in Paris, especially since you told me so little about what's going on?" She paused, but Ethan continued to stare at her. "I didn't think so. I'm here now, so I'm staying." She twisted her fingers. She hoped he'd say something. The silence was worse than the argument.

"You're returning to Paris on the next train."

"Did you not hear what I said? I'm not going back. You can't make me." She bit her lip. She needed Jayson for Von Deez. This was her one and only chance since Gilda now had a name. Abby had to back her promise.

"There's no discussion. You're not staying."

Abby studied him. He was no longer the same guy Abby knew a few days ago. He was a stranger. If she didn't stay, she'd lose everything. "I know you're an FBI agent, and I can tell everyone. I'll talk to that reporter again. He was very interested in what I had to say." She could tell she had Ethan's attention. "What happened to the accent? Realized you didn't need it anymore?" She wasn't about to leave without a fight.

"I would advise against that. I've been easy going since you discovered this investigation, but if you jeopardize me or it, I'll take you into custody and return you back to the United States. All it'll take is one call to your father," Ethan said, showing no compassion on his face.

Abby shivered. He could actually send her back to the United States. He wasn't threatening her with a return trip to Paris. He'd send her home. He was in control, and she didn't have any say. "How long could I stay in London before you sent me back to the United States?" Abby asked. She hoped he wouldn't follow through with the threat.

Ethan's mouth broke into a smile. "You don't quit. You wouldn't have enough time to do anything. You'd be incarcerated the entire time."

Abby sucked in a huge breath. Time to panic. "You'd incarcerate a U.S. senator's daughter. What would my Dad say? This could get me kicked out of school." As the desperation mounted in her, she wanted to jerk Ethan close to her and force him to let her stay.

Ethan shook his head. "Don't threaten me with your father. I have authorization to do what's necessary to protect you."

Abby slouched in her seat, her eyes wide. He'd never talked to her that way before. Of course, this was the first time she'd dropped her dad's name, hoping that someone would be intimidated. "You don't understand. I have to find Jayson."

"I understand. You can't get enough of that creep. I can't let you stay because you want to explore your love life. Go back to Paris. Remember your internship you've worked hard for," Ethan said.

The hatred in his voice infuriated her. How dare he assume anything. She was ready to give him everything last night, but still, he couldn't see beyond this hatred for Jayson. Abby pursed her lips. "I need Jayson for Von Deez. I'll lose my job if this doesn't work out." Let him hear the truth, but Abby knew he wouldn't listen.

"You realize how dangerous Jayson might be?"

Abby had thought of that, but she figured she'd be in a public place when she met with him. This was strictly business. He'd probably did plenty of endorsements over his tennis career. She cleared her throat and gave him a confident smile. "I promise to be careful. What happened with you has taught me to never trust what I see."

Abby saw a flash of surprise in his eyes, almost like her statement was a revelation for him. He shook his head. "I can't let you do it."

"I'll find a way to get what I want. You can't stop me."

"Want to bet? Go ahead." He motioned her toward the door.

She struggled to hold off the fight that boiled inside her. She had nothing to bargain with but the truth. "If I fail at this, my father's going to take away my trust fund."

She searched his face, but his expression remained empty. In fact, he appeared angry. He leaned back in the chair and crossed his arms across his chest. "Maybe it's time for you to learn that everything is not always given to you. It's earned."

Abby sat back, a heavy pit grew large in her gut. There was no regret in his voice. No apologies. He treated her like a child by telling her to focus on school like her father did. She sat there, watching the scenery fly by as the train sped toward London. The life she'd worked for was going to be swept away.

"Do you want to discuss what's happening between you and me?" Ethan asked.

Abby jerked up her head, eyes wide. He couldn't be serious. There wasn't anything between them but lies. Before Abby answered, she heard a phone ring. Ethan lifted his hand to his coat pocket and pulled out his cell.

"Gray here," Ethan said. Abby leaned closer. Frowning, she sat back after realizing she couldn't hear anything. "I understand." He flipped the phone closed and put it back in his pocket. "You got your wish."

She jerked up in the seat. "What?"

"You're staying in London."

"What changed?" She couldn't believe it was that easy.

"Someone thinks you're working for the FBI. You might be a target now."

Abby's mouth dropped. "What does that mean? Target? Targeted for what?" Gripping the side of the seat, she could feel her whole body shaking.

"They suspect you're an agent. Since you've had extensive contact with Jayson, they have an interest in you." Ethan ran his hand through his hair only causing it to look more chaotic than before.

"I've always been around you. Why are they targeting me now?" Abby's voice rose as her imagination ran several scenarios in her head. She was a student. How could this be happening to her?

"These people are involved in a gambling ring. They're dangerous." Ethan turned his head away. "This is my fault. I let this go too far."

Abby heard the nervousness in his voice. He knew more than he was saying. She rubbed her hands together, trying to make this uneasiness go away. He should've told her how serious this was. She would've never left Paris. "I'll return to Paris as soon as we get to London. I'll just...."

"No, not now. You'll stay in London. I need for you to stay calm and to focus. Since you're linked to this investigation, I need to know where you are and what you're doing. It'll be better if you stay close to me." He took her hands and rubbed her palms. "You'll be fine. I promise."

"How dangerous is this?" Abby whispered, trying to sound brave, but her voice came out like a squeaky mouse.

Ethan smiled and released her hands. "Nothing to be concerned about. It's what you wanted. You wanted to stay in London."

Abby leaned back against the chair. "You're telling my Dad about this, aren't you?" She saw the hesitation in his face. It didn't matter now. In a few days, her father would probably escort her personally back to Florida. Nicole would see to that.

"Let's move to a private compartment. I don't want that reporter to reappear." Ethan rose from his chair and grabbed Abby's bag. He led her to the door. Abby followed the narrow hallway. She searched every face, trying to spy anyone suspicious. Everyone appeared normal. She didn't have the necessary skills to defend herself or spot someone if they were targeting her. She didn't have any idea what she was doing. Ethan's hand pressed on her back and guided her down the pathway. So far, all the compartments were filled with passengers. Abby opened the door to the next car.

"Abby."

She turned and saw Ethan at the entrance of one of the compartments she just passed. She backed up a few feet and entered the tiny room. The seats were similar to the other cars. The room had two bench seats facing each other and a small table attached to the wall that took up most of the space. Abby sat in the seat closest to the window. She watched trees and hills soar by. The train must've been going at least eighty miles per hour. It seemed unreal that yesterday morning she was starting to dream about a relationship with Ethan. Now, she was on a train to London and not entirely sure who the person she was traveling with really was. Her internship was probably gone. Gilda would be searching for a replacement by tomorrow. She'd lost.

"You okay?" Ethan asked. The seat cushion rose when he sat down beside her.

"No. Everything seemed so much simpler a few days ago." Abby couldn't breathe. Her world seemed to be closing in, and she was powerless to stop it.

Ethan grabbed her hand and squeezed it. "That's why it was better that you weren't involved. Is there something I can do to make this easier on you?"

"I want to know; who are you?" she said, turning her head to see Ethan's reaction. Heck, she had nothing else left. Might as well get the truth out of him.

He stared at her. At first glance, she could see the guy whom she hung out with in Paris but then the past day clouded the image.

"I'm the same guy. I haven't changed," he said, almost like he knew that she was thinking.

Abby felt something surge through her core. She fought to control her physical attraction and pulled her hand away. "I'm not sure that's true. You may be the same guy but your motives have changed. Everything about you has changed. You know more about me than I know about you. It's hard to accept that you were spying on me," Abby said as a bitter taste filled her mouth.

"What do you want me to do?"

"Tell me what I want to know. Who are you?" She tried to control her fury, but she couldn't hide the hurt.

He stared at the floor for a minute before looking at Abby. "Okay."

"Before you start, what is your real name?" The question plagued her since she'd found out he was associated with the FBI.

He laughed.

"Don't. It's a legitimate question considering the circumstances," Abby said, irritated that he thought her concern was funny.

"I'm sorry. My real name is Ethan. I didn't mean to laugh, but I do want to clarify I'm not a secret agent with multiple identities."

Abby frowned as he continued to hold back his laughter. He wasn't getting off that easy. "What was I supposed to think? You won't tell me anything. I have to come up with my own assumptions."

"You're right. You deserve answers." Ethan moved closer to her. "I'm a Special Agent for the FBI in the CID division. I specialize in extortion and bribery cases."

"What is CID?" she asked, feeling stupid. Her family was an integral part of the federal government for most of her life. Now, she knew she'd been shielded too much.

"Criminal Investigative Division."

"Why all the secrecy? It's not like this is violent crime and terrorism. Why didn't you tell me?" Abby asked.

"You weren't involved. It's standard procedure. Your father wanted you protected but didn't want all the bodyguards."

"I'm a big girl. I've dealt with things more complicated than this. Why was this different?" Abby tried to put it all together, but it still wasn't making sense. "Telling me about Jayson would've kept me away."

"Senator Rodgers wanted your life in Paris to be normal, especially since it hasn't been long since the accident," Ethan said shrugging his shoulders.

Abby's face reddened. How much more did he know? "You knew about Jacob before I told you? What else is in my file?" Fear took over her anger. She'd confided about not being at the accident. He knew she lied. She wasn't sure what to do. Surely if he told her father, she'd know. Her father wouldn't lie about that secret. He'd confront her. Abby glared at Ethan. He was fidgeting, almost like he didn't want to answer. "How much more do you know?"

"I know enough, okay?"

She sucked in a breath. Her father had probably told him about the last few months in Florida, how Abby had refused to see the counselor, how she never came home from school during the breaks. It wasn't fair. Her father was playing with her life and so was Ethan. Tears threatened to unleash, but Abby wasn't going to give in.

She pushed herself closer to the window and placed her bag between them. "Did you think I'd never find out what you do? You were faking an accent for crying out loud."

Ethan looked at the floor. "I never would've brought up my involvement in this case, but I would've eventually told you about my job. The accent was pretty good, wasn't it?" He avoided her gaze, but she saw a smile crack through on his face.

She scowled at his attempt to soften her anger. "I never would've known. That's great. I feel like an idiot." How was she supposed to get over this? She wanted her friend back, but she was now questioning everything he'd ever said to her. "Your accent needs some work. You should be very careful when you drink."

"I'm kidding about the accent. I've lived in Britain since I was born." He rubbed his eyebrow. "I know I shouldn't be cracking jokes, and saying that it was my job doesn't help. I hope it's something we can work through once this is over."

Abby couldn't believe what she was hearing. What was he saying? She sighed, at least the accent was kind of real. She was beginning to think he was crazy. Abby pushed her hands across her forehead and brushed her hair out of her eyes. "This thing between us. I don't know what the truth is."

Ethan frowned but didn't say anything.

"Why all the secrecy around Jayson? It's like this is a top secret investigation. It doesn't sound as simple as you're making it out to be."

"Jayson Walters is a high profile person. We can't accuse a celebrity of crimes without any proof. That reporter is one of many trying to get leads on this story. The more information that is public, the harder it is for us to make a case against those involved. Walters is cooperating with us."

Abby glanced up when she heard the last words. "What do you mean? I thought you only had him under surveillance. You two know each other?" Her forehead crinkled forming small horizontal lines.

The lights above their heads flickered and shut off leaving them in the dark. The sun no longer came in through the windows. They were in an underground tunnel.

"What happened?" Abby tried to focus her eyes on anything, but all was black.

"Shush," Ethan whispered.

She heard shuffling beside her. Reaching out, she felt the empty seat where he had been sitting.

"I'm going to see what's going on. It's probably a blown fuse. Stay here."

Abby heard the door squeak as it slid open. The hallway was completely black. Even the emergency lighting failed. She heard the doorknob pop and latch back in place. Moving farther away from the door, Abby pressed her side against the window. She hoped Ethan would return soon. Even if she wasn't sure of his motives, she was positive he'd protect her. Abby rocked back and forth in the seat and tried to focus her mind on other things. It seemed like forever since he had left.

"It'll be okay," Abby whispered to herself.

The floor creaked outside in the hallway. Abby jumped to her feet and rushed over to the door. She leaned her head on the panel. She heard a small click as if someone was trying to open the door latch.

"Ethan?" Abby called out.

The clicking on the door stopped. Abby backed away. More than likely, it wasn't Ethan in the hallway. Shivering, she knew whoever was out there could come in at any moment. The creaking started again and Abby heard the latch click on the door as it slid open. Was someone in the room with her? She wasn't sure. Abby took off for the door and hit something solid with her shoulder. The force sent her off balance. Abby regained her footing and moved toward the hallway when she tripped. The top part of her body flung forward and she sailed head first into the corridor. Not able to see, Abby put her hands out to break her fall. Her head cracked against the wall. She saw stars from the blow. Then, all she could see was white eliminating the darkness, but she couldn't make anything out. She tried to pull herself up, but blackness overcame her. This time she knew it wasn't the lights. Her head was swimming as she fought to stay conscious. Her body wasn't responding to her commands. She was fading.

Chapter 35

"Abby? You need to wake up." Ethan swept his hand over her forehead and moved her hair away from the purplish knot now forming right above her eyebrow. He was supposed to protect her. This wasn't a coincidence, was it? His gut told him no. France wasn't a place where violent crime occurred frequently, especially to foreigners. It had to be related to the Walters case. Was this Peretti's work? Whoever it was, they were sending a message. Ethan understood loud and clear.

Ethan rubbed her cheek as Abby's eyes fluttered. "That's it. Wake up, sunshine."

Abby flung her head to the side and brought her hand to her face. "What happened?"

Relief flushed away part of the anger in him when he heard her voice. "You were attacked. Luckily, you were able to make some noise to alert the passengers in the next room." He glided his fingers over her hair. "Did you see anyone?" He didn't have many clues, but the intruder had left something for him. A picture of him and Abby in the garden. The private garden by his apartment. Ethan'd let his love for Abby cloud his judgment, and he'd screwed up. He wouldn't make that mistake again.

Abby shook her head. "It was dark." She looked up at the ceiling. "I tried to run, but I tripped." She closed her eyes, and her body swayed against him. "I didn't realize I was falling until I hit the wall." Grabbing her jacket, she pulled it over her arms. "Why did the lights go off?"

Ethan stared at her. How could he tear her world apart? She was in danger now because of him and Walters. "The conductor said the breaker was blown."

He shifted in the seat and scooted closer to her. This had to do more with him than it did with her. Walters was in London and far away from Abby. The Perettis wouldn't have attacked her if it weren't for his investigation. If he had followed orders, Abby would've been safe but no, he had to pursue her, had to love her. There was one thing he couldn't figure out. Why did they leave her alive? In their business, it was better to get rid of any loose ends. He reached over and gripped her hand. "It was probably a pickpocket. They stole your bag."

Abby struggled to pull herself off his shoulder. "Great. They took my clothes. I'm implicated in a gambling investigation, on my way to London with no clothes, and they stole my favorite pajamas."

Ethan laughed and patted her leg. Only Abby would worry about pajamas. "We'll get you some new ones. I'll pick them out."

"Thanks. I can't wait to see what you'll choose. Are you sure the attacker wasn't part of your gambling ring?" She shifted closer to him and rested her head on his chest.

His heart pounded at the thought of lying to her again. The truth would only scare her, not help her. He kissed her hair. "Let's just say you won't be going anywhere without an FBI escort until we confirm this was a mugging. We'll be in London soon, and we'll get you settled in the hotel." He ran his hand over his front pocket, feeling the picture. "I need to do a few things, so I'll leave you with my partner for a couple of hours."

She stiffened, and her shoulder pressed against his ribs. "I want to stay with you."

Ethan rose from the bench and picked up their belongings. "You'll be fine. Nols is an outstanding agent. I've known him for years." He pushed her purse so it lay beside her. They were fortunate the thief didn't take her passport.

Abby pulled the purse strap over her head so it lay across her body. "I don't want anyone else. I want you." The frailty in her voice stopped him. He knew she only meant that she wanted him to protect her. His heart hoped for more, but he'd wrecked that chance. Abby would never consider dating an FBI agent, especially one that would be stuck as a special agent after screwing up this assignment with her.

He pulled on her elbow and helped her up. "We'll talk about it later." He'd have to brief Tom on what happened, and Abby couldn't be present. He'd wait until she fell asleep before he left her with Nols.

Abby smiled, and he knew he'd satisfied her for now. The train slowed to a crawl as they neared the station. He pointed to the corridor. "Let's head for the door. You need to be checked by one of our medics." He brushed a few strands from her face. Her indigo eyes pierced him and he glanced away. "I'm not sure how serious your head injury is. My medical knowledge isn't as extensive as the other guy's." He'd have her at the hospital as soon as they got off the train.

She frowned as he examined the lump that formed above her left eye. Her skin teased his fingers, and he withdrew his hand. Taking hold of her arm, he guided her out the door. She immediately fell sideways.

Ethan caught her before she hit the wall. "Maybe we should wait a few more minutes." He pulled out his phone and sent a text to Nols informing him to have the medic standing by.

Abby pushed away his arm. "I'm fine. I want out of this room." She shivered and grabbed the side of the door frame. Ethan closed the distance between them and guided her to the hallway where several passengers were already lined up at the exit.

Ethan stood directly behind her, his arm around her waist. "How you doing?"

She nodded. He glanced in her direction every few minutes asking her questions that forced her to respond with words. It felt like an eternity before the train stopped and the doors slid open.

A chilly wind flowed through the corridor. The line began moving, and they soon stepped out onto the paved platform. Gray and dreary, the skies cast a typical day in London. Ethan inhaled a huge breath. London, one of his many homes, but was his favorite. He'd spent his later teen years there, after his uncle dumped him on the street when his mother refused to pay any more money to take care of him. Growing up there, and in the group home, taught him that he had to work for what he wanted. It also taught him he could never have someone like Abby.

The station was cluttered with luggage and people. Several trains were parked in the loading area. Ethan pulled Abby through the crowds as they headed to a smaller line of travelers near the corner of the depot.

"Isn't the line for passport control over there?" Abby motioned to a sign on the other side of the station where a huge crowd gathered at the different windows.

"Yes, but there's one here too. Our car's waiting at the side entrance, so it'll be easier to go through here. Give me your passport."

Abby dug through her purse and produced the passport. Ethan took it and approached the counter. He submitted his own passport plus hers to the official. The border guard examined the documents and nodded as he shoved them back through the small hole in the see-through glass partition. Ethan took the passports and dragged Abby with him through the adjacent door.

"Why didn't he say anything? They always ask why you're entering the country," Abby said, pausing as she glanced back at the guard, who was now inspecting another person's papers. "I thought England would be stricter than France."

"You ask too many questions. Come on. There's our car." Ethan pointed to a black sedan with tinted windows parked by the curb. He reached the car a fraction sooner than Abby and opened the back door. She got in, sat on the tan leather seat before sliding to the opposite side. Ethan followed and closed the door behind him.

"I take it that the trip was satisfactory?" Nols asked.

"We had a small incident. She took a nasty fall on the train and needs medical attention," Ethan said, all business-like. He didn't want Nols spilling any details, not that he had to worry. Nols was a by-the-book agent most of the time.

"I already notified the office," Nols said.

Ethan heard his partner's muffled voice as he spoke into his cell phone. Ethan caught Abby's gaze and patted her leg. "We'll be at the hotel soon. We'll get your checked out."

"Who is Nols?" Abby asked, but she didn't let him answer. Her hand rose to the knot on her head. "I don't need to be examined. I'm fine."

"He's my partner. No arguments about the injury. It will only take a few minutes for someone to check you out."

Abby huffed and stuck out her bottom lip. "Oh sure, force me to get checked out, but you wouldn't go to the hospital when you had a puncture wound."

Nols chuckled. "That was the talk of the office for weeks. Ethan injured by a dart."

"Shut up, Nols." Ethan barked. He rubbed his face with his hand. "Abby, quit arguing. You got smacked on the head and were out for a while."

"Is this person a real doctor?"

"No. It will be one of the agents trained in medical procedures. If you want, I can arrange a hospital visit."

"Aren't you trained in first aid?"

"Yes, I am."

"You can examine me," Abby said and sat back in the seat.

Nols laughed again, and Ethan shot him a dirty scowl. "You're making this way more complicated than it should be." Ethan watched her fold her arms as if she were forming a wall around herself. He sighed. "If I agree, will you be satisfied?"

She nodded.

He pushed his hand in his pocket and dug out a code card. "Here's a key to my hotel room. It's a suite so there is a bedroom for each of us."

Abby took the key and dropped it her purse. The car slowed and entered into a circular driveway. A doorman opened the back door. Ethan climbed out and held out his hand for Abby. He led her through the main entrance of a luxury hotel. The door, trimmed in gold, turned in a circular motion as they entered. Stepping into the main lobby, the chandeliers hung from a high ceiling and gave the appearance of high dollar glamour. Ethan's reflection in the spotless floor peered back at him as the lights twinkled off the shiny marble. He hoped the elegance of the lobby didn't raise her expectations of the room. Ethan led her to the elevator near the foyer, where a winding staircase led to a balcony overhead.

They entered the elevator and the doors closed. Ethan stared at Abby in the golden mirrored door. Small strands of hair sprung from her ponytail. He watched her smooth the hairs back in place. The lump above her left eye had swollen larger over the last hour and pushed her brow down, shadowing her eye. She was gorgeous even now.

The elevator doors chimed and opened. Ethan waited for Abby to exit before he trailed behind her. They walked down the hall to the first hotel room. Ethan opened the door and allowed Abby to enter. He deposited his bag on the desk.

"Gray." Nols motioned him out in the hall. Ethan followed him and closed the door.

"Yeah?"

"Tom called and said for you to contact him immediately."

"That's just wonderful," Ethan said sarcastically as he ran his hand through his hair. "You tell him about the train?"

Nols nodded. "He's not happy about her being in London."

Ethan glanced back at his hotel door. "I'll call him after the medic sees Abby."

"No need." A voice boomed down the hall.

Ethan saw Tom marching down the corridor with several agents behind him like a parade line. Tom put his key card in the door opposite of Ethan's room. "We'll do it now." He pointed to the room.

Ethan followed him inside and shut the door.

"How did Ms. Rodgers get on that train?"

"She bought a ticket, Tom."

"You want to be a smartass right now? How did she know?"

"She's intelligent. She read a few newspapers and discovered where Jayson was."

Tom grabbed a water bottle from the mini bar and twisted the cap. "She's here because you screwed up." He slammed the bottle on the desk and water splashed on the table. "We don't have time to babysit. You were supposed to turn over your duties to the private security team the Senator provided."

Ethan gripped the chair back. "Abby doesn't bark on command. She's like the other members of her family."

"I'm aware of that. The security firm said that one of the other sisters is on her way to London too. Why don't we open the red carpet for these girls?"

"I was only responsible for Abby. Get one of the guys to pick up the other girl."

"Brilliant idea, except I need everyone on the Walters Case." Tom banged his fist on the desk. "Where has your head been?"

"I've done my job. You can't say I haven't." Ethan fought the urge to walk out. He and Tom hardly ever disagreed, but he resented what his boss was implying.

"Why was it so difficult for you to keep your hands off her?"

Ethan raised his head. "Have your tried babysitting a twenty-one-year-old? She's not a child. She's a woman."

Tom stared at him. "You slept with her."

Ethan stared him square in the eye. "No, I didn't." At least he didn't have to lie about that.

Tom raised his hand. "Okay. I shouldn't imply that. We're close to getting Peretti. I don't want to waste my best men on these Rodgers girls." He handed over a file. "The Senator is starting more fires than I can put out. You have to control Abby. I'll send someone else to find the other sister." Tom turned to the computer screen. "You can brief me on the attack later. I talked her father out of coming over here. Told him it was a random mugging. It seemed to satisfy him. If it was Peretti, she'd be dead."

Ethan nodded and left the room. It didn't make him feel any better that his boss thought the same as he. Abby was a target based on the photo left on the train.

Nols was waiting for him in the hallway. "That went well."

Ethan scoffed. "About as well as everything else today." He pinched the top half of his nose and pressed on his eyes. He dropped his other hand to his shirt pocket. "Take this photo and dust it for prints."

Nols glanced at the picture. "Where'd you get that?"

"Someone left it on the train when Abby was attacked."

Nols grabbed the photo. "She'd be dead if it was..."

"I know. That doesn't mean she's not in danger. If you find anything, brief Tom on it. I've got to figure out how to juggle Walters and Abby here in London."

Nols slapped his back. "Walters's match is tomorrow. He's been in contact with Peretti. This case is almost over. We'll take Peretti then guard Walters until he's out of London."

Ethan nodded. "Don't you find it ironic that we're now protecting our prime suspect?"

Nols laughed. "Former suspect. Now witness. We're after the bigger fish."

"I still don't like him," Ethan grumbled.

"I know. He doesn't like you either."

Ethan opened the door to his room and found Abby sitting on the sofa. Its navy and white striped fabric pillows engulfed her body. "You feeling okay?" He walked over and placed a hand on her shoulder.

"I'm fine," Abby said.

He wished she'd look at him. Any emotion was better than this. "Are you hungry? We can order room service."

"I'm starved."

Ethan opened his duffel bag and dumped a few shirts and pants on the dresser. "You can eat once you've been checked out." Ethan scanned the room. Pictures of flowers hung above a small television in the corner. He hated hotels. The bareness reminded him too much of the past. He turned when he heard Abby groan. "You okay?" He knelt down in front of her.

Abby rubbed her eyes. "My answer is the same as the last five times you asked. I'm fine."

He pushed himself up from the floor. At least her temper was still intact. "You ready to eat?" He slid the menu across the coffee table. "The fish and chips are good."

Abby flipped through the menu, and Ethan could tell she wasn't reading the pages. "Sounds good." She let the menu drop on the pillow beside her.

Ethan went over to the phone and called room service. After ordering, he pulled up a chair, so it was in front of Abby. "Samuel's going to check you out."

She put her hand on her forehead. "I don't need to be examined."

Ethan gritted his teeth. "It'll only take ten minutes to examine you, and it'll be done."

"We already discussed it. You can examine me." Her eyes seemed to be pleading with him. His resolve relented as the sadness in her eyes sent stabbing pains straight to his heart. He grabbed her hand. "Samuel is better."

"I trust you."

The words surprised him, and he didn't want to add any more stress to her. He sat in the chair and scooted it closer, so his legs swung out wide and her knees rested in between his. Reaching out, he gently probed the knot on her forehead with his fingers. The heat of her skin calmed the dull ache in his chest. He pressed gently, letting his fingers walk over the wound. It felt okay, but anyone in their right mind would take her to the hospital. She refused to go, so even if he did take her, she'd probably be stubborn enough to decline treatment.

Ethan watched her, his face close to hers. He shouldn't feel this way. His attraction to her burned through him and overtook the hurt in his soul. Leaning forward, he pressed his lips on her forehead. She closed her eyes and took his hand. He wanted to have one more moment. The coolness of her breath hit his cheek. He lifted her mouth to meet his. The touch was delicate. He deepened the kiss. That one moment was what he needed. He needed to know she still cared. Abby sat back, severing the connection between them. The void brought him back to reality. He turned his head away from her. This moment wouldn't change anything.

He let his hands drop to her waist, but he remained close to her, drinking in her scent. He'd never be able to smell honey and honeysuckle without thinking of her. He took a flashlight off the corner table and shined it in her left eye then moved to her right eye. Perfect reaction. More than likely, she was fine.

"Tell me your name," he said.

She laughed.

Ethan scowled. "It's part of the exam. You have to answer the questions."

Abby cleared her throat. "Okay, okay. Abigail Rodgers."

"What's today's date?"

"June 26," Abby said.

"Where are you?"

"London."

"What's my name?" he asked, still staring in her eyes.

"Ethan Gray, but you've lied before..."

Ethan turned away and set the flashlight on the nightstand. "You're fine," he said as he leaned against the seat cushion. They were back to the place they were before, with the lies between them. She was lost to him.

Chapter 36

*A*bby glanced up at the marquee sign. That was it.
Wimbledon Station. She swayed back on her heels as
the subway slowed to a stop. She didn't need
directions to the tournament. All she had to do was follow
the tennis fans.

There were fans of all ages. Small children ran by her,
carrying giant tennis balls. Abby smiled at their
enthusiasm. She'd be excited if she didn't have to look over
her shoulder every few minutes for Ethan or a dozen other
FBI agents she'd seen in the hotel.

She couldn't believe she'd woken up this morning and
Ethan was gone. All he left was a note. He'd left her alone.
She subconsciously rubbed her head, causing it to ache.
She hadn't been alone since she'd been attacked. Now, she
was on her way to the tournament. She probably would've
stayed at the hotel like Ethan's note said, but the news
report detailing Jayson's next match, and the photo of him
and Sarah, weighed in her mind. Abby replayed in her
head what the announcer had said on the newscast. Jayson
was playing today at noon. They also broadcasted a photo
of Jayson and Sarah. It was taken at the pub. Sarah was
hanging on Jayson, and he was kissing her cheek. Anger
penetrated Abby's limbs. How could Sarah do this to her?

Abby fought down the rage. She still needed Jayson
for Von Deez. No matter how much she wanted to confront

Jayson about Sarah, she had to approach it differently. Abby swept her hand through her hair and pulled out the tangles. Her heart hadn't stopped pounding since she'd left the hotel. She'd snuck out of the room after convincing the FBI agent to go the restaurant to pick up her room service. She wasn't going to stay in the hotel all day. Ethan told her the attack on the train was a simple mugging. That conversation sealed her decision to find Jayson. There'd be hell to pay with Ethan, but she figured the hell she'd have to face with Gilda would be far worse if she didn't produce Jayson at the Fashion Week After Party. Regardless if Jayson was the scum of the Earth, she needed him. And she'd make sure he knew he owed her a few photo shoots and an after party appearance.

Abby exited the station and walked a few blocks before reaching a huge plaza. People mingled in small groups, waiting in lines to several venues. Searching for a ticket booth, she saw numerous stations scattered throughout the complex. Abby spotted an official-looking man standing in the sea of people. She darted across the open courtyard.

"Excuse me. Could you tell me where I can get tickets?" Abby asked.

The guy looked at her with a salesman's smile on his face. "Our ticket office is straight ahead, but you'll only be able to pick up pre-purchased tickets. These events are sold out." He turned to the next person in line behind her.

Abby's shoulders slumped as she backed out of the line. Without a ticket, it would be impossible to get in the stadium. She wandered aimlessly around the area. As she started back to the underground station, she noticed a line of people entering the largest stadium. Most were carrying heavy equipment bags. Waiting at the back of the line was the reporter from Ethan's apartment and the train. What was his name? Abby racked her brain trying to recall. Sawyer Houston. This had to be the right arena. Sawyer wouldn't miss Jayson's match. She stepped away from a group of fans and rushed over to the stadium entrance. People streamed by, forcing her to stop several times. She finally cleared the crowds and stepped beside the reporter.

"Mr. Houston. I'm surprised to find you here," Abby said.

The reporter jumped at her voice. "Well, if it isn't the former flame. I'm shocked to see you," Sawyer said, cocking his head to the side.

Winning his trust would prove a challenge so she displayed a campaign smile her father would be proud of. "I was in the area and thought I would catch a few matches."

"Any match in particular?" he asked as he jutted out his shoulder and dropped his bag to the ground.

Abby played along. "I believe it's the same one you're interested in."

"I see." Sawyer stared at her. "What can I do for you? I had hoped to find you again after you disappeared, but I don't think you'd seek me out without a motive."

Abby smiled. "I need a way into the stadium."

"What? You weren't given a ticket by your former lover? Ethan didn't bother to give you one either? Shame. Shame." Sawyer put his hand up to his mouth, mocking surprise. He rifled through his bag and pulled out his voice recorder. "It does add a little more mystery to my story."

"Can you get me in or not?" Abby asked, interrupting Sawyer's personal conversation with himself. Disgusted at having to talk to the sleaze ball, she no longer wanted to hear the surprise in Sawyer's voice as if he didn't know half the things he was talking about.

"What is in it for me?" he asked, his eyelids half-closed like he was falling asleep due to the conversation.

She sighed. She'd bargain with the one thing Sawyer had been trying to find out. "I'll tell you my name. It should be good for your story to be able to identify Jayson's lover." Abby flinched at the words. She felt dirty, to be thought of in that way.

Sawyer jerked his head back and laughed. "Why would I want that? You're old news. In the past." He whipped his hand in the air. "No one cares who you are. They're interested in your replacement. Whoever can identify the mystery woman in this photo will have the scoop." He showed her the photo of Jayson and Sarah. He turned and faced the front of the line, no longer acknowledging Abby's presence.

Abby fought her anger. She tapped him on the shoulder. "I can live with being old news. If you want information about her, I can provide that too."

Sawyer twirled back around in dramatic move causing Abby to back away. "What exactly do you know?" he asked.

"A lot more than anyone else in the media right now. Are you going to help me get into the stadium?" Abby searched Sawyer's face. Why were reporters so hard to read? It was like they were trained as spies.

His beady eyes narrowed. "When do I get my information?"

"After I get in the venue."

Sawyer hesitated. "How do I know you even know anything?"

"What do you have to lose? If I do know something, you've scooped every other reporter here. If I don't, you haven't lost a thing." Abby wondered if her argument would work. Sawyer wasn't as dumb as she thought.

"Fine." He pointed his bony finger at Abby. "I won't be out any less if I help you. Just remember we agreed you'd tell me what you know on this mystery woman."

Abby nodded. "What's your plan to get me inside?"

Sawyer removed a camera from the inner compartment of his bag. "Take this." He handed her the empty camera case. Abby grabbed it and put the strap over her shoulder. She adjusted the bag so it fell above her hip.

"Do you have any sort of identification? They'll ask for it." Sawyer rummaged through his own messenger bag. He pulled out a laminated piece of paper and handed it to Abby. "Here's a press pass. If they ask, tell them you're my photographer."

"I have a passport," Abby said, patting her purse.

Sawyer motioned to the front of the line. "That will work. You're pretty much in now so tell me something about this new girl Jayson is seeing."

Abby hesitated. She didn't want to give away her only leverage before she made it inside, but she didn't want to lead Sawyer on too much longer. She did that on the train and ended up not giving him anything. He'd likely remember that.

"She's my roommate in Paris." Abby volunteered as little as possible.

Sawyer scribbled quickly on his notepad. "Interesting. Was this planned? One of you to seduce him in Paris, then the other one here? Is she employed by the FBI too?"

Abby stood beside him, horrified that he thought she was capable of such a sex plot. She focused her eyes on the ID badge, anything to distract her from Sawyer's outrageous lies. She glanced over at him. "What type of magazine do you work for? I thought you were interested in the gambling investigation."

"World News. We're more of a social magazine. We keep people informed about celebrities and their daily lives. You know, the juicy stuff."

Abby's eyes widened. "You're a tabloid?" It seemed so crazy that she was now in cahoots with the paparazzi.

"I prefer entertainment magazine. We're excellent investigative reporters," Sawyer said, smirking.

Abby shuddered. She held her breath and tried to calm herself. Regardless of his profession, she needed him. She had to regain her composure and not reveal how disgusted she was. Abby needed to be careful or the next thing she knew, she'd end up on his magazine with her picture next to an alien. She nodded. "Okay. I didn't realize your profession. I thought you worked for a national news network or someplace respectable like that." She smiled at him. Well, so much for being careful.

He frowned. "We've gotten a rotten reputation in the past. We're not all bad." Sawyer moved closer to the person in front of him as the line pressed forward.

"Whatever you say," Abby said. She couldn't help but laugh. She didn't believe a word he said, but she'd go with it. "How long have you been reporting on Jayson's love life?" Keep him talking so he couldn't ask her questions.

"About nine months now. He's the hottest story since it was leaked that he may be involved in gambling. Everyone wants to know about him." Sawyer continued on with a few more general details about his reporting. Abby moved up behind him. He continued to talk as the security guard checked his ID and press pass. The guard motioned for Abby to come forward. She held out her documents. The guard studied her before handing them back and allowed her into the venue.

Relief rushed over Abby as she went past security and into the open courtyard of the tennis complex. Gazing around the plaza, she noticed all the decorations, which hung from the lamp posts throughout the park. Huge flags towered overhead. Each one had a picture of a tennis player. Abby didn't know most of them, but her eyes landed on one she definitely recognized. Jayson seemed powerful and determined in his photo. His flag whipped back and forth in the wind, almost intensifying the ripples of his muscles that peeked out from under the shirt. He was like a stranger staring back at her.

"Alright, sweetie. You're in, so give me the information you promised." Sawyer's voice brought Abby's gaze down from Jayson's flag.

She flashed a smile. "Her name is Julie Bowman. She's a student he met in Paris." It came in handy, using her mother's maiden name. At least she wouldn't be throwing her family into the scandal full force. It would take Sawyer awhile to piece it together if he ever did.

"Perfect. Were you surprised to find out she's involved with Jayson? Did you know him before the rendezvous in Paris? Was it a one night stand or were you expecting more from him?" Sawyer asked, thrusting the recorder in Abby's face.

Abby pushed the device away. "No more questions. I gave you her name. I said nothing about answering anything about me. I appreciate your help, but I need to go." She glanced at her wrist, forgetting that her watch was in her stolen bag. She ducked into a crowd of people before Sawyer could ask her anything more.

Sawyer ran after her. "Come on. I need more than that. It'll take me weeks to dig up enough information on just a name. Give me little more?"

She shook her head. "Sorry. That was the deal. Name only."

Waving at Sawyer, she took off in the direction of the main stadium. She didn't slow down or look back. Abby feared he was probably following her every move. Spotting another press entrance, she zigzagged through the crowd of people and inched her way to the front. Several reporters were lined up holding press passes out for security. By the time she reached the entrance, the line had almost disappeared. The guard paid little attention to her as she flashed the press pass.

"Take the left corridor. Go past the locker rooms, and you'll see the main court." He eyed Abby's bag strapped over her shoulder. "Keep all camera equipment out of the aisle. Your press pass must be visible at all times." The guard rolled off the orders, barely opening his mouth. He nodded at Abby and handed her a clear plastic holder for her ID.

"Thanks." She put the pass holder around her neck and entered the dimly lit hallway. Placing her hand on the concrete wall, she felt her way down the corridor as her eyes adjusted to the darkness. Abby's heart began to race. She was actually there. She gripped the camera bag, making sure she looked the part. The corridor opened up to a brightly lit intersection of hallways. People scurried in all directions as they filtered through the entrance. She spotted several double doors labeled locker room straight in front of her. Bright light streamed in from her right. She saw the entrance to the main court.

"Whoa. What new media outlet are you with?" a gruff voice asked. Abby turned and saw a small chubby man with a slightly balding head squinting at her.

"What?"

"What news media?" The old man barked at her.

"Daily World News," Abby answered, grateful she listened to most of her boring conversation with Sawyer.

The man scrolled through the papers on his clipboard. "Here you are. Box sixteen. Go straight through the tunnel. Stay to your right. Box sixteen is about three down on the first row. Stay in your assigned area. Passes visible at all times." The man pushed Abby past him.

She stumbled by and made her way down the tunnel. The sunlight spilled through the opening. Abby strained to see as she shielded her eyes. What happened to the usual gray skies of London? The heat wave had made it there.

At the end of the tunnel, Abby entered the court. Thousands of spectators' seats towered above her, empty and eagerly awaiting fans to fill them. There were several official looking people standing on the court pointing to various areas around the stadium. The vastness of the complex overwhelmed her.

Abby focused her attention on the press boxes on either side of the court. Sure enough, box sixteen was only three boxes down on the first row. She selected the seat to the far left. It allowed some room on her right while also being next to the aisle. She sat the camera case down on the table, opened it, and pretended to shuffle a few items around. Abby unfastened the side pocket and searched inside for a notepad to further confirm her reporter appearance. She pulled out some photos of Jayson playing tennis.

Abby flipped through the pictures. Her hands stopped when she got to one of Jayson kissing Sarah. Abby drew the photo up close to her and saw the outline of the club's stained glass windows behind them in the background. Fury seeped through her. Everything was a lie. It hurt even though she'd seen the pictures earlier on television. She turned to the next one. This one was one of Abby and Ethan outside of campus one night. She serached through more of the photos and discovered many more of her with Jayson and Ethan. Many more of her than of Sarah. How could that be? Was Sawyer not focusing on Sarah now? But his portfolio was mainly of Abby? If anyone saw these, they'd believe Sawyer was doing a story on Abby. She had more pictures than Jayson in the stack. Sarah had only been with Jayson that one night, right?

"Excuse me, sweetie. I believe we're sharing this box."

Abby cringed at the squeaky voice. She glanced up and saw Sawyer beaming at her. She forced a smile as she slid the pictures under the camera bag. "I was afraid I'd lost you in the crowd."

"I'm sure you were concerned about me. I had to find you anyway. I need my camera case back." He held his hand out for Abby to present the bag. "I need some more recent shots of Jayson and I hate to damage my camera."

Abby didn't move, her hands still clamped on the sides of the bag. "I need that camera to pass as a photographer."

Sawyer plopped down in the seat beside Abby. "I'll stay and help you out. Since we're both working for the Daily News, it would look strange for me to leave now, wouldn't it?"

Abby gritted her teeth and didn't respond. She could kick herself for not thinking about the possibility of Sawyer resurfacing. Of course, he'd show up at box sixteen. Abby chewed on her lip, realizing Sawyer was more of a threat to her then she'd previously thought.

Abby quickly put the pictures in her pocket while Sawyer had his back turned. "When does this match begin?"

"About an hour. The players will probably be out to warm up soon. Gives the photographers time to get a few shots. Feel free to practice with the camera," Sawyer said, laughing.

"The players will be out here?" Abby's voice squeaked. The stands were barely full. The press boxes were mostly occupied, but anyone could easily spot her in the sparse crowd.

"Yes, sweetie. What did you think the court was for? A tea party?" He clasped his hands together. "I can't wait to see Jayson's face when he sees you. Fireworks will surely fly when he notices you with me. Old flame versus new flame. Old flame with the reporter. It's going to be a great story." Sawyer continued his needless chatter as Abby franticly searched the court for a better place to blend in with the crowd.

Sawyer seemed too happy she was here and he was confident Jayson would spot her. Everywhere she looked, the press boxes were visible to the court.

Abby glanced down at the bag in front of her. She might be able to disguise herself by holding the camera in front of her face while Jayson was out on the court, warming up. She took out the camera and various lenses, laying them on the table.

Shouting erupted near the corner entrance of the main court. Abby turned and saw most of the media racing to the tunnel. Those on the edge of the circle held their cameras up in the air and snapped pictures as the mass moved inside the court.

Abby saw a few uniformed police officers waving off the reporters as they moved to the tennis court. The reporters dispersed as the group reached the open area beyond the narrow tunnel.

Jayson walked on the court behind the two officers. Carrying two huge bags over his shoulder, Jayson looked magnificent. His muscular calves flexed with each step he took. He was dressed in white shorts that emphasized his tan legs. She tore her eyes off his lower body and moved up to his face. He still sported his shaved head, but his face had more color, obviously from his practices outdoors.

Abby took the camera and raised it in front of her face as Jayson jogged across the court to one of the chairs beside the umpire's stand. He sat and opened one of the bags. Abby pushed the camera close to her face, hoping he wouldn't look in her direction. Abby and Sawyer's press box was straight across from him on the other side of the court and would be directly in his view every time he went back to his seat. Taking out a tennis racket and a few towels, he seemed to be an ordinary tennis player, not someone famous. She found it hard to believe that he was involved in match-fixing. It didn't make sense that a top star would risk it all for money he already earned by winning these tournaments.

Jayson picked up his racket and headed to one side of the court. The other tennis player, Cho, whom Abby recognized from the news report, was already on the court serving. Abby followed Jayson's movements with the camera as he moved back and forth on the court. He returned several of Cho's serves, then lobbed the ball back. Ripping the last return up the line, Jayson held his hand up and jogged back to his chair. He wiped his forehead with a towel, then grabbed the water bottle lying on his bag. Jayson's eyes darted from one section to another and stopped on Abby's box. She stiffened as she peered through the telephoto lens. She could see his emerald eyes almost piercing her through the camera lens. It was as if he knew she was there. His gaze moved on to the next section a few seconds later.

Sawyer huffed. "I'm surprised he hasn't recognized you. I was sure he'd spot you immediately."

Abby turned to face the rear of the box so her back was to the court. "He's probably preoccupied with his upcoming match instead of paying attention to the crowd."

"Scandal is more interesting than tennis matches. I need more juice in this story. What good does it do me to have you here if nothing happens?" Sawyer asked, his bottom lip puckered out.

Abby scowled. "I doubt Jayson cares. He won't remember me."

Sawyer laughed as he sat beside her and fussed with a few of the camera lenses on the table. He held them up to the sky adjusting knobs on the side. "He remembers you. You received a lot more attention than most of his flings. When he sees you, he'll remember," Sawyer said, sending a high pitched squeal into the air. He reminded Abby of a teenage girl who was on the prowl for the popular guy in high school. Sawyer seemed to be having a love affair with Jayson and Abby's relationship at that very moment. He licked his lips. "I think the show is about to begin, sweetie." He jerked the camera from Abby's hands.

Abby sat there, unable to move. It wouldn't take long for Jayson to spot her. Abby looked at Jayson's chair. He was no longer there but had returned to the court and was serving tennis balls to his opponent. She grabbed her bag and tried to move around Sawyer to the exit.

"Where are you going?" Sawyer stepped in front of her and blocked her way to the aisle. "You can't go yet. I need my story." His smile had disappeared, leaving his big lips clinched tightly.

Abby tried to push past him but his thick body didn't budge. "I'm not going to humiliate myself in front of thousands of people so you can get this so-called story."

"What did you expect when you came here? A quiet reunion with your lover? I got you in here. It's now time to repay the favor." Sawyer waved his hands franticly. "Walters! Over here, Walters!"

Abby jerked back to her right trying to get out of the press box. She was trapped. Turning her head back in the direction of the court, Abby saw Jayson staring at her. She saw the surprise in his eyes, then he smiled.

A few uniformed officers rushed to Jayson's side as he continued to stare at her. One whispered in his ear and Jayson's eyes left hers. Abby watched as they ushered him off the court. She recognized Nols as one of the men with Jayson.

"Lady, I need you to slowly turn around." A voice boomed behind her.

Abby froze.

Sawyer was no longer in the press box. She looked over to where he had been. His camera bag, everything was gone.

Abby slowly twisted her body around and faced several police officers that blocked the aisle. The one in front of her took hold of her arm and moved her to the side of the press box.

"What's going on?" Abby asked, barely getting the words out. Her body shook as she felt the handcuffs close around her wrist.

"You're under arrest," the man holding her said as he forced her against the railing and moved her left arm behind her back and cuffed it.

"Arrested? There must be a mistake." Abby's body tightened, and the sound of her heart beating pounded in her head. How could they believe she'd done anything that would warrant arresting her? Was impersonating a reporter a crime? Her sneaking into the stadium?

The officer turned her around so she faced the aisle. "You're being taken into custody. Once we get you processed, someone will explain the charges against you." He turned to the officer beside him. "Take her to the back and wait for the car. We'll transport her to the London police before the FBI can take custody of her."

Abby twisted her head around when she heard them mention the FBI. She caught a glimpse of Ethan moving toward the press box. Catching his eyes in her own, she sensed something wasn't right. He hadn't acknowledged her. His face was blank of emotion causing her to wonder exactly whom she could trust. She opened her mouth but immediately clamped it shut when she caught Ethan's gaze and he shook his head.

"Make sure you get a statement from Walters," the voice barked behind Abby.

Several officers appeared from the crowd and nodded at the man who had handcuffed Abby. They stared at her before walking over to the other side of the tennis court where Jayson was still surrounded by several people.

Abby shivered. Ethan came around to her left side and grabbed her forearm, pulling her to the aisle. She fell in step with him and allowed him to guide her from the press box to the main exit. Several reporters snapped pictures of her as they walked passed. Others yelled at her, trying to get her attention. Abby faced straight ahead, fearing that if she looked in their direction, she'd fall apart. Arrested, there would be no way to hide this from her father.

They continued down the dark corridor for a few minutes. Abby felt the heat off of Ethan's body as it grazed her occasionally.

"Here's a room. I'll keep her in here until the car is out front," Ethan said to the other guy with them.

"I'll come get you." Abby heard him say as Ethan pulled her over to a small door on her right. He opened the door and pushed Abby in. A metal table was in the center of the room with a few chairs over to the side. Abby peered into Ethan's eyes as he stared back at her. He stood so close that their bodies touched.

"Are the handcuffs too tight?"

Those weren't the first words she expected to hear from him.

"Why do I have handcuffs on in the first place?" Abby asked as she moved away and found herself in the opposite corner from him. At least now, he acted like he cared about her welfare.

He ran his fingers around the back of his neck. "It's complicated."

Abby watched as he paced the room. "What happened to trusting you?"

"This is something I can't get you out of. You were supposed to stay at the hotel. You're not supposed to be in London." He stopped pacing and stared at her. "They're arresting you for stalking Jayson."

"Stalking? Me? I haven't tried to make contact with Jayson before today. How could anyone accuse me of stalking him?" Abby wondered what idiot fabricated this fantasy.

"I heard about it right before they took you into custody. Sawyer had something to do with this. He will stop at nothing to get a story," Ethan said as he stood in front of her. His hands clung to her arms.

Abby's defenses softened. The warmth of Ethan's hand emitted a longing in her body. She was reminded of her visit to his apartment a few nights ago. The desire to touch him again ached inside her. Why was her body failing her? She had to pull herself together and focus on this situation. Abby cleared her throat. "What do I do now?" Her mind was swirling with her feelings for Ethan. Those emotions were drowning out the fear of being arrested. All she wanted to do was get these handcuffs off and pull him into a kiss. Was she crazy for feeling this way? After all the lies, her heart refused to listen.

"You need to stop staring at me that way. Someone is bound to notice," he whispered.

Abby exhaled all of her frustration. "Quit looking so sexy, and we wouldn't have this problem."

Ethan snorted. "Only you'd come onto me while you've been arrested. I might not be able to get you out of custody for a while. Don't you get that?"

She turned her head away from him. She couldn't keep doing this. Being angry at him one minute, then lusting after him the next. She needed to get control of herself and focus on the reality. Reality was still there and avoiding the truth would not erase all that had happened. Her job was gone now. Goodbye campaign. Goodbye internship. Goodbye trust fund.

The door swung open wildly, startling Abby. She fell back and hit Ethan in the chest. He grabbed her waist and kept her from falling.

"Abby, what are you doing here?" Jayson asked.

Jayson stood so close that Abby could almost touch his face. "Apparently, I'm being arrested for stalking you. Why are you here?"

"They pulled me off the court and said they had a security breach." He moved his hand and touched her forehead. "What happened to your face?"

Abby rolled her eyes up like she was observing the wound. "I was attacked on the train."

Jayson glared at Ethan. "What is she doing here? She was attacked?"

"She decided to come along," Ethan said, smirking.

"You told me it was too dangerous and to stay away from her, then you bring her here anyway? And she's attacked while she's with you?" Jayson's voice rose as he advanced toward Ethan.

Ethan balled his fists. "It's none of your business."

"None of my business? I've done everything you asked. I'm entitled to some answers," Jayson said, flexing his arms as he held them at his side.

Abby glanced over at Ethan, who backed away from her. "Ethan told you to stay away from me? Is that why you never called me?"

Jayson turned toward her. "I did call you until you made it clear that you weren't interested."

"No, you didn't. I emailed and got no response. I called your hotel in Paris. You had already checked out," Abby said as she stared at Ethan.

Jayson grabbed her forearm, and Abby turned toward him.

"I left early for London. My email was hacked by some reporters so I had to shut it down and get a new one. I sent you a message, but you sent one back saying you didn't want to see me. I called a few times, but I figured Ethan put you up to it," Jayson said.

Abby twirled around and faced Ethan. Her blood raged as she stared at his blank expression. "I never sent Jayson any email telling him I didn't want to see him anymore. Do you know anything about this?"

Ethan threw up his hands. "I'm not in this. I only got involved on your father's orders. Your social life was never a priority for me."

The words stung her. What did he mean, her social life was never a priority? Up until a few days ago, he was an important part of her life. She couldn't believe she'd started to fall for him again. She'd believed all his lies about Jayson being bad, but it turned out that Ethan was worse.

Abby moved toward him, but her handcuffs prevented her from shoving him. "Yesterday, you had another story. What will it be a few hours from now?" She shot back at him.

Ethan stared at her. "I didn't mean it that way. I only mentioned to Jayson that being near him put you in danger. I assumed when he left, he had taken my advice. I never sabotaged your relationship."

The coldness in his words shattered her heart. Abby resisted the urge to clobber him. "I'm supposed to believe you? You've lied from the day I met you." She struggled to hold back tears.

Ethan pointed his finger at Jayson. "And he hasn't? Did you know who he was the whole time you were gallivanting around Paris with him? He kept his identity a secret. Why?"

"I never kept it a secret. She never asked." Jayson interjected.

"Brilliant comeback. I'm sure that will solve everything for her," Ethan said, his hands rolled in fists.

"Stop it. Both of you," Abby screamed. She didn't know either of these guys. Neither one was innocent. She struggled with the handcuffs. She needed to leave. She wanted to get as far away from them as possible. She bit her lip and tried to keep her voice from shaking. "Get these off of me. I need to go." She was going to fall to pieces any minute, and she didn't want to do it in front of them.

"I can't let you go. You were arrested," Ethan said. The softness in his voice hurt worse now than the cold tone from earlier.

Jayson grabbed Abby's bound wrists and tried to undo the cuffs. "Take the handcuffs off of her. You know she's not a stalker."

"I can't. She is in the custody of the British authorities," Ethan said as if it were done.

Jayson glared at Ethan. "I won't be pressing charges, so this is crazy. Can't you see this is not good for her?"

"I can't until she's transferred to the U.S. Embassy. Why don't you talk to the British authorities if you want her released? They arrested her to protect you." Ethan's voice was sharp with disgust as he dismissed Jayson.

"Will you be okay while I sort this out?" Jayson asked.

Abby nodded. She had barely paid attention to their exchange. She didn't want to stay with Ethan alone, but she wanted to get out of the handcuffs. Jayson was probably her only hope.

"Try not to hurt her while I'm gone." Not waiting for a reply, Jayson retreated to the door, leaving a stillness in the room.

Abby refused to look in Ethan's direction. There wasn't much left to say. Everything she'd felt for him was based on lies. She couldn't recover from this. Staring down at the floor, she wondered how long it would take Jayson to get her cleared and free to go. The tension in the room was overwhelming. She could hear Ethan moving closer to her.

"Abby?"

"I don't want to talk to you." She knew it wasn't true. She wanted to know why he chose to lie to her. Every time she was close to trusting him again. Some new deception would surface and slap her in the face.

"I know you don't believe me, but I'm sorry."

Abby detected that familiar tone in his voice, that caring, almost seductive, tone that usually had her in a trance. She wasn't falling for it this time. "Whatever. It's done. Whatever you did or didn't do, it's over. I can't trust you," Abby said. The tears flowed from her eyes.

Ethan fell back against the wall and folded his arms against his chest. Abby caught him scowling as she turned her back to him. She focused on the creak of the door as it opened. Jayson entered the room with one of the officers who'd arrested her in the stadium.

"Well, Miss Rodgers. It seems we have a misunderstanding. Mr. Walters has vouched for your identity and assures us that you're not his stalker." The officer reached down and released Abby's hands from the handcuffs. "You're free to go." As quickly as he entered, the officer retreated, leaving Abby to face Jayson and Ethan.

"So much for an apology for being arrested," Abby muttered under her breath. She heard a small snort from her left and knew Ethan was laughing. She refused to acknowledge him.

Jayson came up beside her. "I'm sorry you got mixed up in this. I hope you'll let me make it up to you."

He was as guilty for lying to her as Ethan, but Ethan's crimes seemed so much more raw to her. Abby smiled. "No harm done. I'm sure we'll find some way for you to make it up to me." She heard Ethan grunt behind her confirming that her words hit their mark. She didn't trust Jayson, but pretending to forgive Jayson was a way to get back at Ethan.

Jayson wrapped his arms around Abby and absorbed her in an embrace that completely hid her body. Tensing as he touched her, she felt like someone different was hugging her, not the same guy who came to Paris. He didn't seem to be the guy who took her to play tennis or for a stroll in the park. He was no longer the cute guy who flirted with her on the plane. He was Jayson Walters. He was famous.

Chapter 37

People rushed across the massive intersection. Time moved on even though she felt like it was standing still. Abby backed away from the window and dropped her weary body in the armchair next to the bed. Most of the past few days' events were behind her. She was no longer mixed up in the match-fixing investigation. The press had died down and the reporters had stopped hounding her. She didn't know the details of what had happened with the match-fixing investigation, but Jayson assured her that it was over. Besides, she didn't want to know the details.

His explanations made sense to Abby. He confessed to kissing Sarah at the bar. He admitted he should've told her, but that kiss was where it started and stopped. Nothing else had happened. Abby believed him. Things were different between them, more like a brother and sister. He made sure she had a place to stay until her passport was returned from the FBI. It finally arrived today along with a note detailing information about her new FBI guard. Abby took it for what it was worth. Her father grilled her over the press about her arrest and Jayson but he was going to let her stay in Europe as long as she had a guard. She accepted she'd never be free from her father's political world. At least she still had her job. Jayson agreed to be part of the Von Deez's ad campaign.

She had accomplished something even though her heart was breaking.

Rubbing her eyes, Abby tried to black out her last image of Ethan. His iced eyes were cold, the love she saw in them was non-existent, as she blasted him for his role in keeping her from Jayson. He never denied it. He stared at her as she continued her tirade and never once gave an excuse or apologized. That was what bothered her most, his failure to give her an explanation. She remembered looking for him to explain, but instead, it was Jayson who rose to the occasion. He apologized for not trying harder to find out why she never answered and was determined to make it up to her. So far, he'd succeeded. He procured her another hotel room when she realized that her only place to stay in London was Ethan's room. His assistant bought her new clothes to replace her stolen garments. The time after her arrest had been better than she'd hoped, but memories of Ethan kept invading her thoughts. She had an empty hole in her heart and didn't think it would ever heal. She hadn't seen him since leaving the tennis center. The FBI agent assigned to her now was some old man. He mostly kept out of sight, so she hardly knew he was there.

Abby sighed as she got up and ran her fingers through her matted hair. It would be time to meet Jayson for dinner soon. He was away most of the day at the tournament and rarely got back to the hotel before nightfall. Abby spent most of her day watching the tennis matches on television. She stayed away from the tennis complex because of the intense media coverage.

Sawyer Houston plastered a picture of Abby in handcuffs on the front page of the Daily World causing a media frenzy that almost refused to die down. Jayson had made several statements to the press denying that he was being stalked, and he wasn't pressing charges against her. That small disaster drew the attention of her father, thus the new guard and a severe tongue lashing. Tomorrow, she'd be returning to Paris to finalize the Von Deez campaign. It was finally happening. She held her breath. It was what she'd worked on. The nerves jumbled and rolled in her stomach. She should be happy, but why did it feel like her world was ending?

Abby grabbed a brush and gently untangled the mess called her hair. She pulled it back in a ponytail. There wasn't much she had to do to get ready. Most of her stuff was stolen on the train, which actually turned out to be an everyday mugging incident instead of being connected to the investigation. Sawyer coordinated everything to create a story to sell to the public. He tried to use some of Abby's belongings to connect her with the stalking. Unfortunately, the police had little evidence to charge Sawyer.

Abby glanced at the clock centered on the wall above the television. It was only four o'clock. Jayson probably wouldn't be back for a couple more hours. She threw on her sweater as she headed for the door. There was no reason for her to stay there. She needed to get out and this would be the perfect opportunity to give Jayson a much needed surprise. The past few days, he'd gone to great lengths to make sure she was okay. She still had doubts but his presence helped her move on. It was time to return the favor. Abby took off down the hallway toward the stairs. Jayson's suite was one floor above. One of his many assistants would be there to let her in.

Abby rounded the corner on Jayson's floor. No one, not even the usual tennis reps or personal assistants, was standing in the hall waiting to enter his room. Abby walked up to the door. It was open slightly, as usual since people were usually in and out during the day. She looked around for someone to greet her. The room was quiet and dark with only the gray overcast sky peeking through the windows. Abby sighed. It figured that no one would be there. She missed having someone to talk to. Staying at the hotel during the days was wearing on her sanity.

She fell back on the couch and grabbed today's paper that was lying on the marble coffee table. She wondered what saucy headline Jayson had today. She never would have believed one guy could attract so much attention. She scanned the first few pages until her eyes stopped on the photo of Jayson and Sarah. Abby felt a surge of jealousy thinking about how Sarah had thrown herself at Jayson and also invited Ethan to the pub to cause havoc in Abby's life. She examined the remainder of the page and barely blinked at the photo of her and Jayson. There was one in the paper almost every day. Laughing at how not long ago, she felt embarrassed to see herself on the front page. It didn't faze her now. She wadded up the paper and threw it at the waste basket.

Abby turned her head as she heard the wood floor creaking under someone's footsteps. She rose from the couch as Jayson entered the room in nothing but a towel. She sucked in her breath as she took in his chiseled body, glistening in fresh drops of water. What little hair he had was wet and flattened against his head.

His eyes widened. "Abby!" His voice masked his shock miserably.

"I didn't realize you would be here. I was going to order room service and surprise you." She eyed him and wanted him to continue to wear his towel all evening. It would be a joy to stare at his well-toned physique all night. They were friends now, but it didn't hurt to have some eye candy running about all night to distract her. She glanced at her watch. "I thought you would still be at the stadium practicing."

His arm moved across her shoulder and steered her toward the couch. "I took off early. My wrist was sore, so I didn't want to overdo it."

"More reason for us to stay in. You need to rest," Abby said, hoping he'd agree to have a low key night. As much as she hated seeing the inside of her room every day, she was tired of having elaborate dinners every night that lasted for hours with all the PR people, coaches, and other tennis players. Jayson's assistants scheduled extravagant gatherings for every night. The dinners reminded her of the political functions she'd had to attend for her father. It was the life she was running from, not one she wanted to relive. She longed to have a normal night hanging out in front of the television.

"It'll only take a few minutes for me to get ready. You've been stuck here all day. You deserve to get out."

She smiled and patted his bare shoulder, then pulled away. "I don't mind." Her faced flushed at the thought of him sitting next to her in nothing but a towel.

"You might not mind, but I need a distraction from all of this."

"Alright." She wasn't sure how these dinners were a distraction, but she knew little about his life.

Jayson stood and brushed a few stray water droplets off of his arm. "Give me a few minutes, and I'll meet you in your room." He backed down the hallway.

"Sure. I'll see you in a few." Abby watched Jayson disappear into the bedroom. She picked up her sweater and wrapped it over her shoulders. Heading to the door, she studied the suite. Jayson spared no expense with accommodations. The room was elaborately decorated with antiques adoring end tables next to the sofa. Gliding her fingers over the soft fabric of the armchair, Abby picked up the navy throw draped over the back. She neatly placed it on the chair, when she noticed a white shirt lying on the cushion. She grabbed the shirt and turned it right side out. Her breathing ceased. It was the same thin cloth fabric, the same skull print on the front. It couldn't be the same shirt.

"Hey, Jayson. You here?"

Abby turned around at the familiar voice to see Sarah standing in the hallway just as Jayson came down the hall. Abby stood there, staring at both of them.

Sarah's eyes grew wide. "Abby."

Abby looked from Sarah to Jayson. Seeing him lower his eyes confirmed her suspicions. She pointed at her sister. "How long has this been going on?" Abby asked the most obvious question, not caring if she got an answer. This was her sister. How could she do this?

"Abby, it's not like that. I didn't start seeing Sarah until after it ended with us. It sort of happened," Jayson said.

Abby inhaled a few breaths. "I'm sure it did. Things like this usually sort of happen. You're going to tell me you didn't mean to do it either. You said it was only a kiss. You failed to mention you were seeing her now." Abby threw the shirt at Sarah. "She's my sister."

"No, I..."

"I don't want to hear it," Abby shouted at him as she headed for the door. She heard Sarah calling her name, but she didn't stop. She ran down the stairs back to her floor. Tears streamed from her eyes as she turned the corner to the entrance of her hallway. Her head screamed and the walls seemed to be closing in on her. She couldn't think. She was naive to believe something like this wouldn't happen. It made sense now. Abby hated Jayson, but she was more angry at Sarah. Why? Sarah had her pick of any guy. Why did she have to have Jayson? Couldn't Sarah tell her the truth instead of sneaking around? Abby grabbed her backpack and stuffed what little belongings she had in it. There was no use staying. It was time to go back to Paris, back to the life she should be living, back to the classes she'd ignored, back to gathering her belongings at Von Deez. Abby continued to pack through the tears.

"Why did you run away before I had a chance to explain?"

Abby turned to see Sarah standing in the doorway. "I don't believe an explanation is necessary. You and Jayson deserve each other." She pushed the clothing down in the bag and zipped it.

Sarah moved over to Abby's bed and sat. "It's not like that. He wasn't good enough for you. Nicole said..."

Abby glared at her in disgust. "I doubt you came down here to explain yourself. Say what you have to say and get out."

"No, Abs. Nicole thought he was bad for you, so I stepped in. I only meant to make sure he didn't hurt you." She stared at the floor. "I met up with Jayson in London and it happened."

"You expect me to believe it started here?" Abby bit back the hatred. She wouldn't believe the lies.

"It's true."

Abby slapped her hands against her hips. "How long have you known who Jayson was?"

Sarah shifted her eyes. "Since the day after we got to Paris. I saw his picture on a magazine at the newsstand."

Abby stared at her. Sarah had known all this time. It explained the shifts in her attitude and the pressure to go out with Ethan. Sarah was plotting the whole time to get Jayson for herself.

Sarah fiddled with the bedspread, twisting it into cone-like shape between her fingers. "I did it for you. You would've gotten hurt."

Abby gasped at the realization that Sarah was responsible for everything she blamed Ethan for. It was all her sisters.

Sarah rummaged through her purse, acting as if this conversation happened every day and took out her make-up compact. Abby couldn't believe she picked this moment to redo her make-up. Why should she be surprised?

Abby pulled the compact from Sarah's hands and slung it across the room. "Did you want him that bad? Why tell me? You have everything you want. You have Jayson. I left there believing he cheated on me."

Tears fell from Sarah's eyes. "Why can't you see I was trying to help you? Ever since the accident, you've tried to destroy our relationship. I'm not going to protect you anymore when it comes to this or our brother's accident."

Abby whirled around. "Protect me? I wasn't even there. I was at the library. You were so drunk you couldn't even sit up in the driver's seat. I took the blame for you. It's the biggest mistake I ever made."

Sarah's mouth fell open. "What?"

Abby pointed her finger at Sarah. "You killed him, not me. You were driving. You hit the tree."

"No." Sarah choked on her tears.

"Truth hurts," Abby said as she threw up her hands.

Sarah grabbed Abby's hand, but Abby jerked free. "I didn't. I know I didn't."

Abby shook her head. "Stay out of my life." Fresh tears stung Abby's eyes as they trickled down her face. Her life was a mess, and she only had herself to blame. Her choices brought her to where she was today. Regardless of what Sarah did, Abby chose to lie about the accident, and she chose to not believe Ethan.

It cost her. She lost the man she loved.

Abby didn't look back as she ran out the door and down the hall to the elevator. She punched the elevator button several times as a couple walked up. The elevator doors opened, and she waited as the couple entered first. She entered the elevator and turned around to face the closing doors. She closed Jayson's chapter in her life. She closed the door on her sister.

Chapter 38

*A*bby stood out on the street, thankful for the fresh air. She sucked it in and tried to stop the tears. Why couldn't she stop crying? He was a guy. She didn't love Jayson. She knew Sarah was capable of this deceit. Her anger was about more than Jayson. It was the escape of the truth, like the weight was gone, and she no longer had the burden on her. She didn't have to lie about the accident anymore.

"Abby! Abby Rodgers!"

Abby heard the screeching voice behind her. She turned and saw Sawyer Houston running toward her, his hands flying wildly around him. Several pedestrians dodged his out-of-control frame as he jogged down the sidewalk.

Abby groaned and didn't try to escape. He'd catch up. It was better to get the conversation over with before he chased her back to Paris.

"Don't you have anyone better to harass?" she yelled at him when he stopped in front of her. His erratic breathing told her that he was far away when he'd spotted her.

"You're still the hottest headline," he said between heavy breaths.

"What do you want?" Abby continued walking to the Underground station.

"Trouble with Jayson?" He kept pace with her as he jumbled around in his messenger bag and pulled out his voice recorder.

"Shouldn't you be hounding Sarah? She's Jayson's girlfriend." The words stung her throat.

"The public wants to know about you. The real Abby Rodgers. They want to know about your obsession with Jayson."

"I'm a normal girl. Tell them that."

"Normal doesn't sell. Scandals, lies, that's what sells," Sawyer said as he matched her stride for stride.

"Talk to Sarah. I'm sure you can get your lies from her." Abby wished the subway station would come into view. She was tired of playing Sawyer's game.

"Oh, I couldn't do that. I have to protect my source."

Abby stopped and turned as Sawyer almost ran into her. "What do you mean source?"

Sawyer's mouth turned up into a wicked smile. "How else would I have gotten the information and pictures?"

"Sarah fed you that information?" Abby's mind reeled. He could have more information on her than she imagined. Details she'd never want made public.

"Wrongo, Chicko! I don't know Sarah. I couldn't do this without your sister's help. I have enough information to leak out stories for months...as long as you and Sarah remain in the spotlight."

"Everything you've reported so far has been false. So much for your source." Abby stared at the sky. Nicole, she should've known.

"I embellish everything."

"You made up the stalking story. You got me arrested. Is there anything else you want to do to me before I leave?" she yelled.

"Lighten up, Abby. The truth never sells. We invent the news. If we didn't, would the truth be worth reading?"

Abby was no longer listening. She had to get away from him, from Jayson, and out of London. She had to leave this fantasy behind. She was going to take her life back from Nicole.

Chapter 39

"Are you going to tell me what happened in London or am I supposed to believe the tabloids?" Nicole asked. She glanced over at Abby who was lying on the bed, her head covered with a towel to block out the light.

Abby mumbled something non-coherent from beneath the towel as Nicole grabbed it and threw it on the floor.

"Why did you do that?" Abby growled as she squinted to shield herself from the offending sunlight.

Nicole sat on Sarah's bed. "You need to stop sulking and get up. What happened in London?"

Abby stared at her. "Stop asking me questions." Twisting her body, she positioned her back to the light. This was the first time she'd seen Nicole since she got back last night. Anger seized her as she watched Nicole act like she didn't know.

"I'll stop asking, but the least you could do is get up and do something. This apartment is filthy. You and Sarah need to pitch in." Nicole stood up and paused a moment, obviously waiting for Abby to respond. When she didn't, Abby heard her head out of the room. "No wonder Jayson and Ethan dumped you."

Abby jumped up. "They dumped me because of you."

Nicole turned around, a fine smirk on her face. "How do you figure that?"

Abby pushed the tabloid paper across the table. "How many lies have you told since you've been in Paris?"

Nicole laughed. "You need to be more specific. I don't have time for your theatrics."

Fury flared through Abby. "The lies to Sawyer Houston. Why?"

Nicole sneered. "Daddy needs to know what a worthless screw-up you are."

Abby held onto the sides of the chair, forcing herself to control her rage. "You get Sarah in on your scheme and mess with my life, and anyone else's that you feel necessary."

"You don't deserve it. Any of it. And I'm going to make sure you don't get it."

"What? My internship? You already destroyed my ad campaign. You know Dad will freeze my trust."

"He should've done it after the accident, but he's got a huge soft spot for you. You can kill his son, and he doesn't blink an eye."

Abby backed up at Nicole's hatred. "You know the truth. We decided to protect Sarah. You thought he should've punished me for something I didn't do?"

"He thinks you did it, and he did nothing. He'd have me shipped off if he'd known I did it."

Abby stared at her. Had she heard her right? "What do you mean you did it?"

Nicole blinked then held her hand up and pushed past Abby. "You're trying to blame me for Jacob's death. Because I forged a few emails to Jayson doesn't mean I'd lie about our brother. You can't blame me for crap you and Sarah did."

Abby's head was swimming. She couldn't think. Was it possible Sarah wasn't responsible? Her hands trembled, and she stuffed them in her pockets.

"Hello! Can we get back to this argument? I can't enjoy screwing you over if you're not paying attention." Nicole waved her hand in front of Abby's face. "Nothing to say? Abs, you're so predictable." Nicole's laugh smacked Abby right in the gut, but she didn't have time to process it. Nicole wasn't finished with her verbal assault. Nicole grabbed one of Sarah's sweaters draped over the bookshelf and flung it to the floor. "It took more effort than I thought. Jayson was hung up on you, and Sarah was convinced you liked him. It took forever to persuade her to go after Jayson, but she's so gullible." Nicole's nose crinkled up as she snickered. "It took a lot of persuasion to get him to believe you didn't want to have anything to do with him. I wasn't counting on you following him to London."

Abby felt like her knees were about to buckle, and she placed her hand on the counter to steady herself. "What do you mean all the persuading?"

"Jayson was determined to talk to you. All the emails he sent to your account. The phone messages. It took a lot of work to get rid of all of that." Nicole cackled as she said the words. "Sarah did great. She finally accomplished the ultimate persuasion. You know, persuasion in bed."

Abby's heart beat like it would thump out of her chest. "Don't you think I'll go to Dad and tell him all of this?"

Nicole raised her hand to her mouth. "He won't believe you since you confessed to the car accident. You've always acted like you were better than me. You and Sarah never treated me like a real sister. It was time to show the family what you really are."

"This is about getting back at me because you feel like Dad loved me more? They treat us all the same, like property. Couldn't you do something like therapy?" Abby wanted to throw Nicole out of the room.

"It wasn't about you. I want what's mine. Besides we're family, you'll forgive me. You always do."

Abby shook her head. "If it's the trust fund you want, you can have it. It's not worth wrecking people's lives over." She picked up her bag and headed to the door.

"Act like you're indifferent. You're where you belong. Alone and on the verge of failure. Have fun at your party," Nicole said. As she passed through the hallway, she swept the table with her hand and mail scattered on the foyer floor.

Abby stared at the ceiling. Everything she'd done the last year had been a mistake because it caused her a lot more than a couple of embarrassing articles in a magazine or a few failing grades. She lost her entire family based on the lies. Abby groaned. The churning in her stomach worsened. She chose her favorite sweatshirt, threw it over her wrinkled T-shirt, and walked into the kitchen.

A small package and several letters laid scattered on the floor. Abby scooped up the mail and laid it on the table. She eyed the package and noticed it was addressed to her. She tore off the brown paper and opened the side. Pulling out white tissue paper, she tossed it on the floor. She took out a gaudy miniature Eiffel Tower keychain. Abby laughed as she ran through the memories in her mind. She was dumb for not realizing how important Ethan was to her. She picked up the keychain and saw a small white piece of paper tucked inside the base. She opened the paper "Always remember. I will."

Tears puddled in her eyes as she stared at the note. Underneath the tissue paper, an envelope was lying in the bottom of the box. Grabbing it, she ripped open the paper and took out a picture of her and Ethan at the Eiffel Tower. Her hair was blowing straight out above her head while Ethan's tousled locks seemed perfect. She remembered how crazy happy she'd been and hadn't even known it at the time. She could tell him how wrong she was. Abby stood and wiped the tears from her eyes. It might not be too late. He did make the gesture. She ran back to the bedroom to get her shoes. He might still be there.

Chapter 40

*A*bby ran across the quiet street near Ethan's apartment. Would he be there? Would he listen to her? She easily maneuvered the normally busy sidewalks and arrived at Ethan's building within minutes. As usual, the exterior door was locked. She rang Ethan's flat and waited. Her insides jumbled up and down. He had to be there. Abby peered through the window and the somber, dark foyer stared back at her. No one was moving inside. She rang the doorbell again. Emotion began to run empty in her. She had nothing left to feel. She'd never see Ethan again.

"Hello, Abigail."

Abby turned in the direction of the somewhat familiar voice. Ethan's partner stood across the road near a few bikes parked against a wrought iron fence.

Abby smiled. She had a small window of hope. If Nols was there, Ethan had to be around too.

"It's great to see you," Abby said as she ran over to him.

"I'm surprised you're here. I thought you were in London." He said it more like a question than a statement.

Abby pulled at her fingers. "Things have changed. I needed to get back to work."

Nols didn't say anything, leaving an awkward silence between them. How should she ask what she really wanted to know?

"He's not here," Nols said. Of course it was obvious she wasn't taking a leisurely stroll. This wasn't a common pedestrian street. She'd only be there to see Ethan.

"I figured as much since no one answered the bell. I'll try back later," Abby said staring at the ground. She didn't know how much Nols knew but guessed he knew enough.

"He's not in Paris."

Abby looked up. "Is he still in London? Jayson said the investigation was finished."

Nols cracked his knuckles. "Jayson tells you what he thinks sounds good. He is all about projecting a good image. He is a public relations master piece."

Abby nodded. It didn't matter. She didn't care about Jayson. "I'm sure I can catch up with Ethan in London."

"He's not in London. He's not on the case anymore." Nols's voice turned cold.

"What do you mean?"

"He was relieved of his duty soon after you were cleared on the stalking charges. A conflict of interest," he said with a hint of annoyance behind his words.

Abby bit her lip. From the short time that she knew he was a FBI agent, she knew Ethan took his job seriously and not finishing a case would devastate him.

"Why would they do that?" Abby asked aloud and didn't intend on Nols hearing.

"He refused to involve you when you stayed with Jayson after the stalking incident. Rejected the orders so they reassigned him." Nols's voice was definitely not as friendly as he was earlier.

Abby shuddered at the disgust in his voice, but she threw aside her discomfort with Nols's obvious dislike for her. "I need to see to him."

Nols shook his head. "It's too late. He's already left for the States."

"Can't you get a message to him?" Abby was not beyond begging for Nols's help.

He scowled at her. "That's not a good idea. Don't you think you've done enough to him?"

"He can make the decision if he wants, but I need to try."

"You almost destroyed his career. He was great at his job before you came along and messed with his head. Let him recover from this damage before you start inflicting more," Nols said, frowning. "He trusted you, and you treated him like his family treated him."

Abby twirled around. "What do you mean?"

"Nothing." He turned toward the street.

She grabbed his arm. "Tell me."

Nols stopped and looked at Abby. "Did he tell you how he grew up? People don't get over things that happen to them. They live with you forever. He opened up to someone for the first time. To you. And when it came down to it, you threw him away."

A coldness sunk in her body as confusion overtook her. "He didn't tell me anything. I hardly know anything about him."

Nols's brows shot up. "Trust me. He told you plenty, but did you listen?"

Abby thought back to their conversations. Ethan talked in generalities, but she wondered if she'd missed the clues Nols was talking about. Abby shrugged. "From what I could tell, he told me lies. He could've trusted me with the truth."

Nols clenched his teeth, and Abby thought he was going to grab her. "What would you have done? The same thing you already did. You left him there to fend for himself, and he took it. He took the blame."

"Blame for what?" Abby felt the anger in her lower chest pushing upward. How dare he take this attitude with her.

"He told your father that it was his fault you got involved with Walters and also took responsibility for Sarah's involvement with him." He wiped his forehead. "After all the crap you pulled, did you think your father would actually let you stay here? All you got was a small lecture by phone call after being with Walters. You thought your Daddy would ask for a new guard and that was it?

Abby lost her breath. Ethan had sacrificed his career for her. "Why did he do that?"

Nols lit a cigarette and propped his foot up on the small barrier wall that surrounded the big oak. "I don't have a clue, but Ethan knew how much your internship meant to you, so he persuaded Tom to talk to your father."

Abby shut down the confusion in her heart. She couldn't be sucked in again. What motive did he have for doing it? She pushed back her bangs and glanced in Nols's direction. "Good, it's the least he could do."

"That's it?"

Abby huffed. "He lied to me, but since you're in the business of lies too, it's no surprise you don't understand." She slowly inhaled to catch her breath. Why the rage? A few minutes ago, she wanted to apologize. She needed Nols. She didn't need to piss him off.

He shoved his hands in his coat pockets. "You don't get it. You lost your pride, maybe you're embarrassed, but he lost a lot more."

"Help me understand what I missed." Abby couldn't decipher what Nols was getting at. She was more confused than ever.

Nols frowned. "You need to discover it on your own." He reached in his pocket and pulled out a business card. "If you need any assistance while you're in Paris, your father has requested you contact me."

Abby took the card and stared at it. Ethan wasn't coming back. It was over. Nols wouldn't help her. With no way to find Ethan, the pain was too much. Abby bit her lip, causing a twinge to shoot through her mouth. The physical discomfort did little to mask what was happening to her on the inside. Even though she'd given every reason why she hated Ethan, she couldn't face the fact that he was gone.

She stood there a minute then turned back to Nols. "I could use your help, but not with Ethan."

He walked over to her. "What is it?"

"I'm sure you know my file. Last year, there was an accident." Abby figured everyone had read her file. A bit of embarrassment blushed her cheeks.

He nodded.

"Could you re-open the case?"

Nols shook his head. "I'm FBI. That would be handled by the local authorities in Florida."

"You told me to listen to Ethan, and he said to let the truth go free."

Nols scowled, but Abby raised her hand to stop his protest. "The truth is still buried in that accident report. You need to find it."

Nols shrugged. "I'm guessing you already know what the truth is?"

"I thought I did, but I think I've been covering up someone else's lie."

He pulled out his phone. "I'll look into it. Your family's not going to be happy with this."

The pit in her stomach ached less, but it didn't completely go away. "They're not happy with the current situation, so it can't get much worse."

"It can always get worse."

Abby watched him leave. For the first time, she noticed the garden gate was open. It looked inviting, like a door of opportunity. She made her choice. She had to live with it now.

Chapter 41

"Abs, I'm so glad you're here. I didn't think you were coming home," Sarah yelled as she jumped up from the bed.

Abby closed the apartment door. She hadn't expected Sarah back so soon, but she shouldn't have been surprised. Finals were tomorrow, so Sarah had to show up. Abby didn't know what to say. She had hatred and forgiveness both whirling within her, but she wasn't sure either one was appropriate.

Sarah seized her arm. "You have to let me explain."

"Nicole told it. I know she talked you into it. It was easy, right? Punish me for everything you thought I'd done?"

Sarah flopped on the bed and glanced up at Abby. "I'm not sure what the truth is anymore. Can we talk about this because nothing's been right since the accident."

Abby held her breath. She'd been waiting to talk to Sarah about the accident for months, but she wasn't sure where to begin. "Go ahead."

Sarah twisted her pinkie back. "That night at the pub, I asked Jayson to back off seeing you, and he refused. I even kissed him, but he wasn't budging when it came to you. Abby, I thought I was doing the right thing. Nicole kept telling me that Jayson being famous was bad, that Dad would go ballistic if you stayed involved with him.

After that, Jayson left, so I thought he'd decided to leave you alone."

"Yeah, he left." Fury burned through Abby at the thought of Nicole's deceit.

"I thought things were going well with Ethan until Nicole told me why you left for London. I knew Jayson was there. You're only impulsive when something crazy happens, so I figured it had to do with him." Sarah took a deep breath. "I didn't want Jayson to interfere with your relationship with Ethan, so I decided to go. You're happy with Ethan, the happiest I've seen you since the accident."

"You decided to sleep with Jayson for my benefit?" Abby had to laugh at the logic. It sounded like Sarah's thinking.

She frowned. "Not exactly. I wasn't going to go that far, but after I talked with Jayson. I liked him."

Abby could see it. Both of them had a carefree, larger than life attitude. They probably had some invisible force drawing them closer without them realizing it.

Abby sat. "Go on."

Sarah paced around the room, her hands moving back and forth. "He told me about the stalking charges and Ethan. I couldn't figure out a way to tell you. I didn't want to hurt you again."

As unbelievable as her story was, Abby wanted to believe her, but how could she? The betrayal was too fresh. Abby bent over and pulled off her shoes. "We don't need to rehash this." She wanted to forget the last few days. She'd be able to forgive Sarah someday, but Nicole was a different story. At least Sarah acted remorseful. Nicole was still reveling in Abby's demise.

"We have to... because of the accident." Sarah touched her on the shoulder. "I need to know."

"Know what?" Abby raised her head so she could see her sister. Sadness engrossed Sarah's eyes.

"Were you driving the car?"

Abby shook her head. "Nicole called me that night and said you wrecked the car. You were passed out at the wheel. I didn't want you to see you hurt again. We were going to have to live with Jacob's death. Why live with anything else?"

"But I was passed out. I couldn't have been driving. Nicole said you came to pick us up." The confusion on Sarah's face clouded the delicate features of her forehead. She raised her hand to her head. "Something's not right."

Abby gripped her arm, forcing Sarah to look at her. "I know. Give me some time to figure it out."

Sarah pried Abby's hand off and picked up her jacket. "We've got to ask Nicole. She knows..."

"Let me handle this."

Sarah stopped and stared at Abby. "You sure?"

Abby nodded. "I'll get the truth."

Sarah bit her lip. "There's one more thing."

Abby sighed, but she didn't want to destroy the small peace that was between them now. "What?"

"What are you going to do about your internship? The model for Fashion Week?"

Abby crunched the thick fabric of Sarah's coat between her fingers. "I don't know. I thought maybe searching for that actress Gilda wanted or another model." Truth was, she had nothing. Not one idea to replace Jayson for her ad campaign. She was screwed.

Sarah paced the room, and Abby was sure she'd walked enough circles to complete a mile. Sarah stopped and hugged one of her pillows to her chest. "You can't give up. We're talking about your inheritance. It's your college fund."

Abby studied Sarah. The concern she had was the closeness Abby had longed for so long. They seemed to understand each other now, but she couldn't bring herself to take that final step. Abby wasn't sure forgiveness was something she could produce at the moment, no matter how much she loved her sister. Abby shrugged. "It's only money, right? Dad always said you can make more. I'll figure out how to get my college tuition."

"You said Gilda loved actresses?" Sarah asked, rubbing her chin.

Abby headed for the door. "Yeah, the more scandal the better. She loved all the paparazzi at the office with this whole Jayson fiasco."

Sarah threw her books on the chair. "Abby, are we good?"

Abby forced a smile. "I haven't kicked you out yet."

"That's better than I could've hoped for." Sarah lay back on the bed. "I want it the way it was, before the accident. We can fix this and your internship too."

"Nothing will be the same, but thanks for trying," Abby said, her eyes filling with tears. "It's time to figure out how to move on." She stared out the window. All the talking and crying had left her throat dry and scratchy. Abby couldn't believe she had any tears left to shed. She had cried so many times at the thought of Ethan and the memories of her brother's death. It would get better. She'd be able to remember the good.

Chapter 42

"Hey, man. I figured you'd be guarding Walters' tennis rackets."

Ethan swung his chair around to face his partner. "Very funny, mate. Samuel has the last shift. Walters will be on a plane to the States tomorrow."

Nols nodded. "You glad to be home?"

Ethan shrugged. London didn't feel like home anymore. Nowhere did, except Paris. It baffled Ethan how he'd disliked Paris before he'd met Abby, but now it was all he thought about.

"I'm sure you're enjoying your freedom. No undercover. No surveillance."

Ethan scowled and flipped through his notebook. Nols's sarcastic humor wasn't going to cut it today. "What freedom? I'm assigned to desk duty. Tom will have me conducting tours for school children at the J. Edgar Hoover building after my disciplinary hearing." He shrunk in his seat. No one ever left a hearing without some type of reprimand. With Senator Rodgers seeking Ethan's blood over his daughters' involvement with Walters, Ethan would be lucky if he still had a job as a tour guide.

Nols sunk down in the chair by his partner. "Why don't you go see her?"

Ethan shook his head. "Nothing will come of it."

Nols twirled a pencil between his fingers. "Abby can make this go away. Her father would call off his dogs if she asked."

"If I did that, he'd make her go back to the States. Let him keep thinking it's my fault." Ethan balled his fist until his fingernails bit into his palm. Abby had enough problems without him loading his issues on her too.

"Abby finally realized that someone ran interference with her father with all that crap in London."

Ethan jerked his head around. "You saw her?"

Nols nodded.

"What in bloody hell? Paris has two million people and you ran into her?" Ethan banged his hands on the desk. How could she get on with her life if he kept throwing reminders at her?

"Back off with the *bloody hell* crap. I don't have time for your personal issues today. I went to check on your flat, like you asked. She was waiting outside. What was I supposed to do?"

"You could've left."

"She wanted to talk to you."

Ethan stared at the printer on his desk. "She was probably taking a walk." His stomach fluttered with guilt so strong he thought he'd pass out. Why was she there?

"Why are you doing this? Anyone can see you two are made for each other."

"Obviously she can't. She chose Jayson." The bitterness on his tongue made it hard to swallow. She didn't hesitate. That bloke had spoken a few words, and she'd believed him. Ethan wondered what had happened when she'd found out that Sarah was with Walters.

Nols laughed. "What did you think she would do? You didn't even speak. You had all the information to destroy Jayson, and you did nothing."

"She should've trusted me."

Nols scowled. "You don't trust her."

"What the..."

"No, you shut up and listen." Nols tapped his finger on the desk. "You said you'd confided in her."

Ethan nodded. "That night in the park."

"No, you didn't. She had no idea what I was talking about."

Ethan jumped up and grabbed Nols, shoving him against the wall. "What did you tell her?"

Nols pushed Ethan's hands away. "Right, you told her?"

Ethan let his arms fall to the side. "I told her a little about the group homes and about finding my family."

Nols shook his head. "You told her nothing."

Ethan sat back down. "I don't want her feeling sorry for me."

"The only one here feeling sorry for you is you. You let Abby make her decision based on half-truths. You haven't told her that you love her, have you?"

"Sod off." Ethan gritted his teeth. Abby couldn't love him, not when he couldn't accept himself.

"Are we going to do this every time you don't like what I say? I love when your British side comes out."

"You two, knock it off," a voice yelled behind them.

Ethan turned to see Tom standing at the doorway.

He flicked his finger at Ethan. "You. Conference room. Now."

Nols slapped Ethan on the shoulder. "Session finished. I'm glad we got all that anger out before the hearing."

Ethan shoved himself back from the desk. He took a deep breath and followed Tom down the hall. He'd never had a disciplinary hearing, so he had no idea what to expect. His brain was telling him to start packing up his desk.

Tom opened the door to the room and flipped on the light. Ethan blinked and stared at the empty chairs.

"Take a seat," Tom said as he walked around the table and pulled out a bottled water from the mini fridge.

Ethan selected a chair opposite his supervisor. "Are we early?"

Tom smiled but it was one of those I'm glad I'm not you smiles. "Just you and me."

"No firing squad?" Ethan couldn't figure out if the new development was good or bad. His boss's mood didn't seem to favor Ethan.

Tom scowled as he opened the folder. "No. The Senator had a change of heart."

"Really?" Ethan sat straight in his chair, waiting for more explanation, but Tom didn't elaborate.

"You're not off the hook." Tom drilled Ethan with a frown. "You blotched up the protection of Ms. Abigail Rodgers, but I'm willing to overlook it since we have Peretti in custody."

The stress in Ethan's gut subsided. "That's it? All I get is a verbal warning?"

"You'll be taking some time off. Three months to be exact."

Ethan jumped up, letting his chair roll across the floor. "You can't do this." His head began to swim with alarm. Three months off the job, he'd go crazy.

"It's the amount of time I enforce if I feel an agent hasn't healed properly from an injury."

Ethan glared at him. "I'm fine."

"Take three months then report to the infirmary at Quantico for an evaluation on your arm." Tom signed a few papers then pushed them across the table to Ethan.

Ethan stared at the order. "You're suspending me for an injury that has already healed."

"No. I'm suspending you for an injury you failed to report. I'd advise you to accept the three months. I can extend it to six."

Ethan clamped his mouth shut. Abby and her darts. "What am I going to do for three months?"

"I don't know. Go to the States. Visit your sister. Don't show up here." Tom motioned to the door. "You're dismissed."

Ethan grabbed the paper and flew out the door.

Nols sprang to his feet as Ethan walked by. "Taking a vacation?"

"Like you didn't know."

"Look at it this way. You'll have a few months to relax. You knew he wouldn't let you out of there without some type of punishment."

Ethan leaned against his desk and closed his eyes. He'd never taken a holiday since he'd started this job.

"What do you plan on doing?"

Ethan shrugged. "Any suggestions?"

"How about Paris? That lady at the bakery misses you. She was telling me about never seeing a man so in love as you."

Ethan wanted to drill his partner in the mouth with his fist. "Right. She said this all while you were paying her for what I owed her?"

Nols shook his head. "I told her you'd be back next week to settle the bill."

Chapter 43

A chill rained up Abby's arms as the droplets hit her skin. Dark skies and gray thunderheads loomed over her. It was time for the storm. A storm named Gilda. Abby smoothed out the tight, silk skirt of the elegant cocktail dress Jean-Claude had made for her. The dress, and her cute Von Deez designer pumps, wouldn't save her internship. Without Jayson as her primary model, Abby's career was doomed. She had no backup plan. Every avenue she'd tried ended with a dead-end.

She inhaled a long breath and took in the fresh scent of the rain. A few months ago, a storm like this would've brought out memories of her brother's accident. Abby thought it was almost calming now. She no longer blamed herself for what had happened. Protecting her sister, she learned, meant telling her the truth. Something she needed to do with Gilda.

She thought of Ethan. He was as close to a boyfriend as she'd ever had. A normal guy, despite the FBI thing. She'd always love him. Who said 'what you think you want is not always what you need?' She had to remember that next time she lost sight of herself. Abby shook off the thoughts. It was time to focus on Von Deez. It wouldn't take Gilda long to fire her, and her father would immediately freeze her trust fund.

Abby raced up the stone stairs and stood under the awning. Staring up at the sky, she had to come to terms with it. Her lie would come full circle tonight.

"Bonsoir, mademoiselle," the doorman said as he took her invitation and opened the door.

"Bonsoir," Abby replied as she stepped into the magnificent foyer of the castle Von Deez rented for this season's fashion week. She dropped her coat and umbrella off at the cloak room and headed for the main ballroom. It was still early, so most of the guests hadn't arrived at the After Party. They were probably still at the trunk show. Abby scanned the elaborately decorated room. In schemes of dark purples and blacks, the room resembled the theme of Von Deez's current collection, along with personal touches of Jean-Claude's designer prints.

"Mademoiselle Rodgers."

Abby turned and saw Jean-Claude sauntering toward her. His stubby body swayed back and forth like he couldn't bend his knees. He bounded over and kissed her on both cheeks.

Abby stepped back and smiled. "Monsieur Philippe, I thought you'd be at the trunk show."

"Non, I prefer the quiet." He motioned to the almost empty ballroom. "But you, my dear, you should be at the show. Gil will not be herself without her right limb."

Abby laughed at his attempt to use American clichés. Although everyone at Von Deez dreaded working with him, Abby found the experience pleasant, even a distraction from Gilda. She slipped her arm through his as he escorted her to the bar. "Are you saying I'm her right-hand man?"

"Too pretty to be a man." He tipped up his champagne glass and swallowed the remaining liquid. "What would you like? A nice red wine?"

"Champagne is fine," Abby said as he approached the female bartender and proceeded to work his charm on her. Abby sighed. It would be difficult disappointing Jean-Claude. He approved her work on the project, and she couldn't complete the assignment. She smiled when he returned and presented a fluted glass filled with the bubbly liquid. She accepted the glass and sipped the sweet champagne. "Merci."

Jean-Claude's mouth opened into what Abby thought was his only expression, a half-smile, half-scowl. He took her hand and led her to the center of the ballroom. "Tell me about your beau, Ethan. That is his name, non?"

Abby choked on her drink and swallowed hard to keep the liquid from coming back up. She was prepared to answer questions about the scandal with Jayson but not Ethan. She'd deflected a lot the last few days at the office, but no one had asked about Ethan before now. "I'm sorry. I..."

Jean-Claude raised his hand. "Non, I shouldn't intrude. I know how dating in this circle can be. Always under the microscope. No privacy."

Abby peered at him, unable to move. Her feelings for Ethan were flooding her body and drowning her. She swallowed the rest of her champagne. "It's fine. There's nothing more between us. It ended a while ago."

Jean-Claude's brow crinkled up. "Oh, I thought..."

"Abigail!" The screeching of Gilda's voice turned Abby on her heels. She glanced over her shoulder at the main entrance and braced for the Gilda guiliteen. The clicking of Gilda's heels on the marble floor was like the countdown to death. She crossed the floor in a few strides with her hands outstretched. "Jean-Claude. It was superb. You outdid yourself again." She gifted him with two kisses.

"Merci, Gil." He bowed in front of her. "The designs were magnifique. Now the promotion begins." He raised his glass in the air.

"I'm anticipating the P.R. now. Two campaigns. Celebrity Chic and Abby's sports theme." Gilda clicked her teeth. "Not that Abby couldn't draw enough publicity by herself with her personal life. We should use her to promote the line." A frown surfaced as she glanced at Abby.

Jean-Claude squeezed Abby's arm and winked. "Oui, maybe Abby's willing to be part of the campaign. Publicity is publicity."

Abby wanted to crawl up into a ball and die. She needed to gather enough courage to blurt out that she had no models for her theme. Jean-Claude loved her plan before he knew about Jayson, maybe that was enough. She cleared her throat. "Speaking of the campaign..."

"Yes, Abigail and I were discussing her boyfriend and the theme. Ethan will be a marvelous addition to the ads," Jean-Claude said as he encircled his arm in Gilda's.

Abby's jaw dropped. "No, I don't think..."Jean-Claude raised his hand to stop Abby.

Gilda grabbed Abby around her waist. "Ethan? Who's Ethan? I thought Jayson Walters was Abby's boyfriend. He is, isn't he? He is here, right?" Gilda looked past Abby, into the crowd in the ballroom. "That's why all those reporters are staked out on our front entrance every morning?"

Warmth rose to Abby's cheeks. Jean-Claude wanted Ethan. Gilda wanted Jayson. She couldn't produce either one of them. "Neither one of them is in the campaign." She yelled it out before someone could interrupt her.

"I can't believe it."

"Look Gilda..." Abby started, but Gilda pushed past her. Abby stood with her face to the wall. She heard the buzz of cameras flashing behind her. Closing her eyes, she turned to confront what she knew was there. The paparazzi probably crashed the party.Instead of flashbulbs exploding in her face, she saw Ethan in a midnight black tux and on his arm was Alana Barash. What was Ethan doing with Alana? Every breath Abby took did little to control the feeling of suffocation in her lungs. She managed to gather some air before Ethan and Alana arrived at her group.

His icy eyes were as she remembered them and all the love in her poured out into her smile. "Hi," she said.

Ethan moved his hand behind her neck and moved her head close to his as he kissed her cheek. "Hello."

"Abby?" Alana pulled Abby in a hug as if she'd known her for ages. "I'm glad to finally meet you after all the phone calls discussing the ad." The action caught Abby off guard and she held her arms at her side.

"Yes, it's nice to finally meet you." Abby drew back as Ethan winked.

Gilda seized Abby's arm and pulled her close. "You've been talking to Alana about the ads?"

Abby felt a pinch at her hip. She shifted as Ethan nodded toward Alana. "Um...yes. You wanted Alana so I thought the surprise would be perfect." She hoped Gilda wouldn't detect the uncertainty in her voice, but her worries went unnoticed with Gilda's preoccupation with Alana.

Gilda wrapped her hand around her mouth then grinned. "This is brilliant. No one suspected we had Alana." She turned to the actress. "Do you care if we announce your participation in our campaign tonight?"

"That's why I came." Alana motioned to Ethan. "You'll be fine here?" She placed a hand on his arm. A twinge rippled through Abby's gut. She was too late. Were they a couple?

Ethan bent down and gave Alana a kiss on her forehead. "I'm sure Abby will entertain me."

Abby's insides plummeted. The affection he showed Alana was more than just friends. It was too close, too personal for it to not be more.

Alana, Gilda, and Jean-Claude headed toward the stage. Abby stared at them, trying to figure out what had happened. A few seconds earlier, she was ready to accept her fate, but had fate intervened? Abby turned to Ethan. "What are you doing here?"

Ethan smiled and linked his arm in hers. "Saving your sorry butt and your trust fund."

Abby cringed. She didn't need saving. Her whole life was built on someone saving her. Her father, her brother, now Ethan. She longed for the security she'd had all her life but realized she was missing what mattered. This one time, she wished it were different. She pulled out of his grasp. "I appreciate what you did, but I should be doing this myself." She wanted him here for her.

He kept hold of her retreating hand. "I didn't have much choice."

"What do you mean?"

A woman behind Abby stumbled and hit her, almost tipping over Abby's drink. "Pardon," the lady said as she shifted in the growing crowd.

Ethan reached over and pulled Abby to the side of the room. Sparks flew through her, and she thought her body wouldn't recover. He motioned to an empty side room. "You want to go over there?"

Abby nodded and let Ethan lead her to the lavishly decorated sitting room. She sat on the velvet couch, leaving room for Ethan. Abby kept her eyes on the coffee table in front of her. "You want to tell me what's going on?"

"What part?"

Abby rolled her eyes at his avoidance tactic. "How about the part with Alana for starters."

He shrugged. "You can thank Sarah."

"Sarah talked to Alana?" Abby sat back and brushed the sweat now beading on her forehead. She had no idea how she could be hot. It was probably fifty degrees with the fans cranking overhead and the cool breeze blowing in from the open windows.

He shook his head. "She talked to me."

"Why, because she wanted information on Jayson?"

"You Rodgers girls can't get enough of Walters, can you?" Ethan's voice turned sour.

Abby winced. "Is Nols still guarding Sarah?" The guard detail stayed well out of sight now. She didn't know who was watching her or her sisters.

He twisted his fingers in his palm. "Yes and no. Sarah broke it off with Jayson so your father hired a private security detail that starts next week."

"That's good. The FBI will no longer have to babysit us and you can focus on the case." A twinge of guilt ran through her at the thought of Jayson and Sarah. Her sister seemed to genuinely like Jayson. Abby felt awkward for possibly causing their break-up. She realized she didn't feel anything but infatuation for Jayson, but her sister's betrayal still rubbed her heart raw.

Ethan frowned and Abby noticed his jaw tighten. "Nope, off that too. I'm on leave."

Dread crept through her. "My father forced you to give up the case. Nols told me."

Ethan scowled. "No, I took some well-deserved vacation days. Needed to figure some stuff out."

"Oh." She wasn't sure it was good news. Although she was relieved her father didn't have him fired, Ethan looked like the vacation was killing him. Darkness framed his eyes, like he hadn't slept in days. Abby watched him fiddle with his cufflinks. The silence acted as a finality between them. She stood. She couldn't take being near him and not being able to be with him.

"Wait, Abby. I..."

"What?"

"I wanted to talk about Sarah."

"What about her?"

He rose from the couch and grabbed her hand. "I hate to see you lose your family over some guy that doesn't matter. You don't have to lose Sarah."

"Sarah lied to me. Nicole manipulated her to hurt me." Tears threaten to ruin the makeup job on Abby's face. She couldn't let him see her this way. She inhaled a breath and waited a few seconds before exhaling. "I let her back in our apartment. Isn't that enough? Forgiveness will have to wait."

Ethan wiped a stray hair from her face. "Don't get upset. Alana was her idea. I won't take credit for it."

Abby wiped the tears from her eyes. "Sarah doesn't even know Alana."

"Your sister did some investigating on me. She should think about joining the FBI."

Abby laughed and some tension fell from her shoulders. "I can see Sarah batting her eyelashes at some unsuspecting suspect."

"Yeah, she found out that my mother was Celia Sholes."

"The Celia Sholes?" He couldn't mean the former model for Von Deez, but his expression told her he wasn't joking.

He nodded.

"Alana's your sister?" Something clicked inside Abby's head before he answered. It made sense, the reluctance to talk about his family.

Abby sucked in a breath. Ethan wasn't a normal guy. He was from a Hollywood dynasty family. He was more like her than he wanted to admit. "Why didn't you tell me?"

He shrugged. "I don't see my family often. I didn't grow up knowing them. They aren't who I am." He shoved his hands in his pockets and moved his body so he was no longer facing her.

"Not who you are? They are you."

He shook his head.

She tugged on his shoulder so he turned around. "You don't like them but they've shaped your perception of me, of my life. You can't say they aren't a part of you." Abby's hands shook at the revelations.

"You don't understand. My mother refused to acknowledge me for the first eighteen years of my life. I grew up in state custody and never knew who my father was. My sister and I never got along until this past year." He clinched his fists. "My family doesn't get to claim any influence over my life." The resentment poured out of him, and Abby sat back. She never realized the pain he'd suffered, but the wounded look on his face confirmed it.

Abby stared at the floor. "I'm sorry." She had no rights to criticize him. She knew nothing of his past, but she wanted to know.

"This isn't how I wanted this to go. I've accepted my family for who they are. Some things are better left alone." He grabbed her hand and rubbed her palm with his fingers.

"But Alana's here. She's your sister."

He smiled. "Yes."

"If you hate your family, why is she here?"

"Sarah said we were both responsible for you not having a model for the show and it was our job to fix it. She mentioned that Gilda wanted a famous name, and you can't get more famous than a Barash or a Sholes, right?" He winked at her as he ran his hand through his hair. "Sarah's a menace to stop when she wants something."

Abby knew Sarah had made a few phone calls, but Ethan did most of it. "What deal did you have to make with Alana?"

He crunched his knuckles. "A promise to come to the United States for a family visit. Alana's determined to have a brother-sister relationship."

"How do you feel about that?"

He shrugged. "It had to happen sometime. I've run from the past and buried myself in my job. I guess it's time to figure out who I am."

"And your mother?"

Darkness shadowed his eyes. "I won't be seeing her. Nothing will change between us."

Abby nodded and left it alone. She had plenty of time to get him to open up to her, at least she hoped so.

Ethan patted her leg. She saw him hesitate and pull his hand away. "I did this for you. You deserve your trust fund and not have Nicole scheming to undermine you. And... I'm sorry."

"For what?"

He gripped the side of the sofa. "What happened with Jayson, not telling you about him. Probably could've saved us a lot of grief."

"Why be sorry? I'm not. For the first time, I'm not in Sarah's shadow. I'm not hiding behind lies to protect myself or her from another lie." Abby realized that she felt free. She was sitting with the one person who knew everything about her, her faults, her secrets, everything, and he'd come back.

They didn't say anything for several minutes.

She watched him cradle her hand, and she flexed her finger so they interlocked with his. "I didn't think I'd see you again. Nols wouldn't tell me where you were. He doesn't like me."

Ethan chuckled. "No, he loves you. He hates me." He took an envelope out of his pocket and handed it to Abby. "I almost forgot. Nols said to give this to you."

Abby sucked in a breath. It was the answer she'd been waiting on. She tore open the envelope and pulled out the paper. It was an official notice from the FBI. She scanned the letter and tears flowed down her face.

"Whoa, what exactly did Nols have in that letter?" He tried to grab the paper, but Abby held it out of his reach.

"It's fine. It's something I needed, something my family needed."

"Do you mind me asking what that is?" He strummed his finger over her cheek.

"The truth. Nicole's finally going to be held responsible for her part in the accident. It's my gift to her." A wave of satisfaction hit Abby.

"Your brother's accident? That'll involve you too."

Abby nodded. "It will. This is my subpoena to testify. I'm liable for my past statements, but it's good. It's time to face responsibility."

Ethan lowered his head. "What about your family? Won't they be angry that the file is public? With this subpoena, the case is no longer sealed."

Abby saw the worry in his eyes, but she couldn't undo this. "It's time to worry less about what the public thinks and more about my family. We need to face the accident."

Ethan pulled her close. "I'm proud of you."

"For what? I probably killed my Dad's political career."

Ethan laughed. "I doubt it. Politicians can work a miracle from a piece of crap. He'll be fine."

Abby wiped the tears from her eyes. "I wanted to thank you for that tacky souvenir you sent me. You realize I take it everywhere." She held up the Eiffel Tower keychain.

Ethan grabbed the keychain and dangled it from his index finger. "Tacky? I would dare say it was thoughtful and moving. Maybe even sweet. But tacky, never."

"It was nice." The heat off her cheeks warmed her face. Why was it so hard for her to say how she felt?

"You ready to talk about us now that we got all the hard stuff out of the way?" Ethan asked.

Abby laughed and knew he was referring to his numerous attempts to get her to open up in London. She regretted shutting down and refusing to talk to him. It was an automatic defensive response. If she refused to acknowledge the pain she held inside, the lies wouldn't hurt so bad. She realized now that the truth never should have stayed buried.

"Is there an 'us'? So much has happened," she said, her voice barely a whisper.

"I was having a good time before Sawyer Houston wrecked it," Ethan grumbled.

Abby frowned at the tabloid reporter's mention. "You should've told me the truth instead of letting me find out from someone else."

"I thought maybe you'd let that slide," Ethan said, grinning at her. "You know, I did bring Alana."

He thought his goofy smile was going to get her to forget this issue, but he was wrong. "Could you at least admit you were wrong? I don't like feeling gullible. I should have known you weren't who you said you were." She sunk lower onto the sofa.

He nudged her slightly. "I did apologize, remember? I'm a very good actor."

She giggled. "Was all of it acting?"

Ethan rubbed his bicep. "Not all of it. I was telling the truth about the darts. I've never been wounded by a dart."

She laughed as he pulled her so her body was flush against his chest. Feeling his lips tease the skin on her cheek, she lifted her head so her eyes were level with his. She saw her future there. Her lips glided over his, leaving her tingling. Ethan wrapped his arms around her and engulfed her in a deep kiss.

She sat back and stared into his eyes. "You're acting needs some work. Starting with the accent. Did you know you lost it when you were drunk..."

"Abby, I told you. I've lived in London for most of my life. The accent's real."

She smiled. "It could use some work, how about you help me with my French and..."

Ethan stopped her with a kiss. It silenced her needless comment as she felt a wave of happiness creep through her. Ethan was here, and her world seemed to be falling back into place.

He pulled back and held her face between his hands. "Do you want to start over, Abigail Rodgers, celebrity stalker?"

Abby laughed. This was how crazy her life had become since she arrived in Paris. "Yes, I believe I do, Agent Gray."

ABOUT THE AUTHOR

Heather Starnes lives with her family in a small Tennessee town along the banks of the Nolichucky River.

When she's not slaving away writing stories on her laptop, she's reading, spending time with her husband, and chasing her four year old daughter around the house.

This is her first new adult contemporary romance novel. Be on the lookout for Sarah's story in the second book in this new series.

Go to www.heatherstarnes.com for more information.

www.ingramcontent.com/pod-product-compliance
Lightning Source LLC
Chambersburg PA
CBHW020231180626
46810CB00006B/2132